MORE PRAISE FOR WILLIAM HEFFERNAN AND *BEULAH HILL*:

"Pulitzer Prize–nominee Heffernan delivers a powerful slice of interracial Americana life and death along with a riveting whodunit."
—*St. Petersburg Times*

"Heffernan is a master of scene setting, characterizations, plot, and dialogue."
—Nelson DeMille

". . . A breathtaking and thought-provoking thriller. Written in simple but effective prose, BEULAH HILL is moving and passionate. It tells a devastating, haunting, and very American story that raises it far above the standard thriller."
—*London Free Press*

"Heffernan promises action and delivers."
—*New York Daily News*

"Heffernan builds the fear chapter by chapter."
—*People*

"William Heffernan's BEULAH HILL is a good novel made better, possibly even great, because it is constructed in the form of a detective story, giving it that added focus that an investigation into a violent death in a small, closed community always provides."
—*Denver Post*

"Nifty stuff, with big hooks from page one."
—*Kirkus*

Also by William Heffernan

BEULAH HILL

by William Heffernan

Akashic Books
New York

©2000, 2003 by Daisychain Productions, Inc.
Published by Akashic Books
Originally published by Simon & Schuster
All rights reserved, including the right of reproduction in whole or in part in any form.
First paperback printing

Cover photograph ©Terry Deroy Gruber/Photonica
ISBN: 1-888451-40-8
Library of Congress Control Number: 2002116772

Printed in Canada

Akashic Books
PO Box 1456
New York, NY 10009
Akashic7@aol.com
www.akashicbooks.com

ACKNOWLEDGMENTS

I would like to thank the many people who helped in the writing of this book. First and foremost my thanks to Michael Korda and Chuck Adams, whose editorial counsel were invaluable. Also my appreciation to James O'Shea Wade, whose early advice, as always, set me on the right course. And, of course, to Gloria Loomis, my agent for the past twenty-two years, whose guidance invariably proves correct—even when I sometimes disagree with it.

I would also like to express my thanks for the generous help I received over the many months of research. Among those who offered valued support were: Olga Hallock, whose knowledge of a Vermont long past is voluminous; Harriet Riggs, who generously shared her own considerable research; Edward Feidner, a curmudgeonly scholar, whose friendship is a treasure; Reverend Robert Martens, who helped greatly in matters biblical; Vermont State Archivist Greg Stanford, who openly discussed the state's less than admirable history of race relations; the staffs of the Rokeby and Alexander Twilight Museums, and, especially, the staff of the University of Vermont Bailey Library Special Collections Department.

For Stacie, the love of my life,
on whom the character of Elizabeth is based.

BEULAH HILL

The Writings of Samuel Bradley, Constable of Jerusalem's Landing, Vermont

SEPTEMBER 30 THROUGH NOVEMBER 22, 1933

It is late September and the first hint of the long cold days that lie ahead fills the air. It is a time when poachers filter out into our Vermont woods after dark, driven by either a need for winter meat, or simple greed, or perhaps nothing more than bloodlust. There they stalk along deer trails searching out prey. It is on cold, clear nights such as this that they hunt, using the light of the moon and stars to illuminate their killing grounds.

Then the moment of the kill passes, and the carcass is lifted to a shoulder and carried to safer ground, away from the prying eyes of the law, there to be slit up its midline, sending steaming entrails into the cold night air.

Such a figure now moves through the dark woods, struggling under a heavy burden. In a small clearing the carcass drops to the ground, coming to rest against the trunk of a large maple. Its midsection has already been butchered, crudely, raggedly, and the entrails spill out with a wet liquid hissing sound. But the animal under the tree on this September night is different; blond hair spills across its forehead, and its face is twisted in unspeakable agony. It is the body of a young man, killed for neither sport, nor need, killed instead for darker, more disturbing reasons.

{ 1 }

I laid down my pen and stared at the page. I was seated at the small desk in my kitchen, which also serves as my official office, going over the list of delinquent taxes, which as town constable it is my sworn duty to collect. In truth, I was trying to find a way not to collect these taxes. This Great Depression we are now enduring has made payment an impossibility for most of our citizens, and I have come to believe that the law must be subverted wherever possible.

I was pondering this dilemma at eight o'clock in the morning when Abel Turner burst in on me awash in sweat, eyes wide with disbelief and terror. Abel is a big man, well over six feet and a good 220 pounds, and terror does not rest easily on his broad, bearded face.

"They kilt Royal," he stammered. "The niggers. They kilt him an' left him in the woods gutted like a goddamn deer."

I stood and shook myself, then walked toward him, still not wanting to believe what he was saying. "Hold on a minute, Abel. Are you talking about Royal Firman?" I asked.

"Tha's right. Tha's right," Abel stammered. "He's up in the woods off Nigger Hill, layin' upside an old maple. His guts are in his god-damn lap." He shook his head; shuddered.

Abel's words sent a chill through me as well, but for a different, more personal reason, and it took me a moment to gather my thoughts.

"What were you doing up there, Abel?" I threw the question at him like a punch to the belly. I knew he lived in another part of town, in an area known as Morgan Hollow, close to his job at the sawmill run by Royal's father. I also knew there was no logging be-ing done in the area he was talking about, so there was no reason for him to be on Nigger Hill.

He stared at me, eyes filled with disbelief. "What the hell diff'ence does it make? I'm tellin' ya that Royal's been kilt, an' the niggers done it."

"I need to know it, Abel." I waited, casually running one finger along my mustache; feeling its slight droop at the corners of my mouth. Then I snapped out at him, "So just tell it." I knew if I didn't get Abel to tell me everything now, I'd get none of it later. Then everything he said would be colored by what he and Royal's father and their friends wanted me to know.

He shifted his weight and refused to meet my eyes. "I was in scoutin' fer deer." He looked up and glared at me. "But I din' take none."

I nodded, but said nothing. Deer season was still several weeks off, and as town constable I am supposed to help the wardens with poachers. But as I said before, this Great Depression we are living through has hit this area hard, and I decided long ago that poach-ing was another law I would try to ignore. There are a bit more than five hundred souls living here in Jerusalem's Landing, some two hundred odd families, and if each of those families needs an extra deer to see them through the winter, so be it.

I stared hard at Abel. Like most people in town, he knew my stand on poaching. It had been a safe answer for him.

"Were you alone in the woods?" I asked.

"What the hell diff'ence . . ."

I raised a hand, cutting him off. "I'm not worried about deer right now, Abel. But if Royal's been killed there's the question of evidence," I explained. "Tracks. Anything left behind. A cigarette butt, the button off a coat. So I'll need to know where you were when you first went in the woods, and every place you went after you were in there. I'll also need to know about anything you left behind, where you might of taken a piss, everything. And I'll need to know the same about anyone who was with you. Otherwise I might confuse tracks and things that you or someone else left behind with those of the killer."

"Hell, ya know who kilt Royal, dammit. There ain't no question 'bout that." Abel's face was red, anger now replacing the terror and disbelief.

"I don't know anything yet, Abel, and neither do you," I said. "Not unless you saw the killing. Did you?"

A tremor seemed to course through his body. "No, dammit. I jus' found him like I said. But I know who done it. And so do you. It was that goddamn nigger, Jehiel Flood. Ain't no question 'bout it."

"So you say, Abel. That's what we're going to go and find out."

I went for my red hunting jacket and my wide-brimmed Stetson, and strapped on the old Colt pistol I had inherited from my father when I had taken over his job. I turned back to Abel. "I want you to take me to where you found the body. But first I want to stop and pick up Doc Hawley and Johnny Taft. If you haven't messed up all the tracks, might be Johnny can lead us straight to whoever did this."

I followed Abel's truck up Nigger Hill, Johnny Taft seated beside me, silent as a stone. Johnny was small and thin and wiry, an Abenaki Indian and the best tracker I'd ever known—better than my father, who'd been known to follow a deer track unerringly for miles, even when the ground was hard and dry as bone.

Behind me, Doc Ben Hawley followed my old Ford, none too happy about being pulled away from his patients. But he's paid an annual stipend to act as medical examiner for the southernmost towns of the county, so he had little choice but to come. In my rearview mirror I could see his lips moving as he drove, still grumbling about the inconvenience, perhaps even the unfairness of it, and certainly the condition of the road, the last being the only legitimate complaint.

Nigger Hill is served by a narrow dirt road, little more than a wagon track, and it is indeed a trial to drive. It runs steadily up along the northern ridge that rises above Addison Hollow. The houses, what few there are, are scattered considerable distances from each other, and much of the land has been abandoned. The hill also has some of the deepest and oldest woods within the county. This is because much of Vermont was clear-cut by the timber barons of the last century and is only now returning to what it once was. Here, however, the land was never logged, save for the fields that were cleared by the Negro farmers, and much of it is covered with ancient oak and maple, stands of beechnut, pine and hemlock and scattered thickets of red sumac.

Now, as we are about to enter October, the hill is awash with color, red and orange already dominant over a background of yellow and fast paling green. It is my favorite time of the year, the time I most like to be in the woods, a time when grouse explode with a fearful thunder of wings that sends already fallen leaves swirling up from the ground in a hurricane of color. There is a splendor about it, and serenity. Yet today, I knew there would be neither.

Johnny Taft grunted, interrupting my thoughts, and I looked to my right and saw we were approaching the handcrafted sign Jehiel Flood had placed at the edge of his farmland. It read "Beulah Hill," his own renaming of the place where he lived, his rejection of the name given it by his fellow townsfolk. Johnny saw me studying the sign and grunted again. He had heard Abel's rantings when we picked him up, and offered this now as some unfathomable comment.

"That supposed to mean you think Abel's right—that Jehiel did this killing?" I asked.

"Don't much care if he did or not," Johnny said. He spoke in a typical Vermont dialect, something most educated Vermonters struggle to be free of. The accent is almost southern in the way words are formed and mangled, the major difference being that they are bitten off sharply, rather than extended in an elaborate drawl. They also are formed at the back of the throat, something that produces a hollow sound that seems, at times, to give off its own echo. Johnny pushed a lock of straight black hair that had fallen across his forehead up under his red-checked hunting cap. "Never much liked Royal," he added, unasked. "Always thought he was a cocky shit an' a goddamn bully. An' old Jehiel's always been nothin' but a pain in the ass. To me this is jus' a trackin' job, an' I sure as hell kin use the money."

I thought about what he had said. Royal Firman was indeed a bully when he sensed vulnerability, and certainly a cocky young man. Or had been. I thought about that, let it sink in; then considered Royal again. He had been a husky, handsome fellow, with wavy blond hair that he had always fussed with, and dark blue eyes that seemed to devour any good-looking woman—married or not—that he happened across. He would be twenty-five now, only two years younger than I, and we had been in school together through much of our youth. But we had never been what you'd call friends. Royal and Abel and three or four others had been part of a small clique since those school days, boys who had grown up together into adulthood, and who—going back to when they were about twelve years old—had developed a reputation as low-level troublemakers. They had never done anything serious; nothing to get the law after them, just mostly mischief that came after some extended bouts with hard cider.

Jehiel Flood, on the other hand, had had countless run-ins with the constable's office. Not criminal matters, mind you, but endless difficulties with the town, the county and the state, and with white public officials of each of those governmental entities. He was not a friendly man, and had once told me that he and his family intended to live their lives according to "The White Man's Law of The Four G's: God, Gates, Guns and Get the Hell Off My Land." To a large extent, during the years I'd observed him, he had succeeded in that goal.

In truth I had known Jehiel since I was a small boy. I had gone to school with his oldest daughter, Elizabeth, who had always been the brightest child in our various classes. Elizabeth and I had been the only town residents of our generation to attend college. We had both received academic scholarships—she to Middlebury, and I to the University of Vermont. I had heard it said—though I had no way of knowing if it was true—that she was only the second Negro woman in Vermont ever to have graduated from a four-year college. Now she lived in her own cabin with her two younger sisters, Maybelle and Ruby, each having moved in with her upon coming of age. Jehiel lived in their family homestead a quarter of a mile distant with his eighteen-year-old son, Prince, who had been named for Jehiel's maternal great-grandfather, the nineteenth-century Negro activist Prince Saunders.

Johnny grunted a third time as we passed the house of old Elisha Bowles, the Negro preacher who ministered to the Free Baptists out of a battered old church on the Main Road. Bowles's house sat between Jehiel's homestead and Elizabeth's cabin, and as I looked out the window I could see him splitting wood in his front dooryard, dressed in the too-small, formal black frockcoat that never seemed to leave his back.

"What's *that* grunt supposed to mean?" I asked Johnny.

"Jus' that ol' Bible thumper. Every time I see him I 'member how he tol' me I was goin' ta hell back when I was ten. Stopped me on the Main Road one day an' axed me if I believed in Jesus, an' when I tol' him my people was Abenaki an' follered the Indian Way, the ol' fool called me a heathen. Said my soul was damned fer eternity. Then the mizzable old bastard started singin' a hymn at me."

"He was just trying to save you, Johnny." I grinned out the windshield.

Johnny grunted yet again. "Shoulda scalped the old nig."

I laughed at the idea. Elisha was as bald as an eagle, had been as long as I'd known him. "Thought you did," I said.

Abel's army surplus Nash flatbed stopped at the side of the road. I passed him and pulled in just ahead, and Doc Hawley came in behind me in his shiny new Hudson Super Six. We were halfway between Reverend Bowles's place and Elizabeth's cabin. I stared at the thick stand of hardwood that dotted the small rise behind which Elizabeth's cabin stood, and the realization of her proximity grabbed at me. I pushed the thought away, then glanced across the road at the battered old shack that belonged to Jeffords Page, the only other resident of Nigger Hill. Jeffords was a bit touched, according to most—a retarded mulatto boy of sixteen, whose parents had died within months of each other the previous year, leaving him to fend for himself. There had been talk about placing him in a county home. Then Jehiel had taken him in tow and hired him as a day laborer, claiming he was a distant relation. Now, like the man he worked for, Jeffords, too, had become isolated and was seldom seen off Nigger Hill.

Abel came around the back of his truck, breaking my reverie, and pointed to some tracks leading into the woods. "Tha's where I went in," he said.

Doc Hawley had come up to where we all now stood. "How goddamn far in is it?" he demanded. Doc was scowling, and his skimpy, reddish beard and angular body made him look almost demonic.

"Two, three hunnered yards. No more," Abel said.

Doc looked down at his shoes. They looked fresh out of the box new.

"You bring boots?" I asked.

"Forgot to," he said. He glared at me, took off his derby and mopped the sweat from his brow with a red handkerchief. "It's no wonder, the way you rushed me out the damned door." His glare returned to his shoes as if they, too, were somehow responsible. "Just got these damned shoes. Come in the mail yesterday from Sears and Roebuck. Those goddamn woods'll scuff 'em all to hell."

"There's an old pair of rubber boots in the trunk of my Ford," I told him. "They'll be a little big, but you're welcome to use them."

Doc snorted derision, but went to the trunk of my Model A and retrieved the boots.

Johnny Taft was crouching by the side of the road where the tracks led into the woods. He looked up at me and raised his eyebrows a notch. "Only one set," he said.

"So we know Abel went in alone here," I said. "After we see the body, and check for tracks there, we'll want to find the place where Royal went in. If his truck's down the road, we should find that spot close by."

What I didn't say was if we didn't find Royal's truck, it might mean he came here with someone else; maybe that he was already dead; his body carried into the woods. I looked at the track Abel had identified as his own. The ground was covered with leaves and was too hard and dry to tell if Abel was carrying anything heavy. There also were no obvious signs of blood. But if Royal had already been dead there might not be much blood at all. I took Johnny aside and asked him to look for the things I was concerned about, then told Abel to lead us to the body, using the same route he had taken earlier, and stopping anywhere he had stopped before.

We moved slowly, taking time to examine crossing trails made by the many deer that populated the area. A good two hundred yards in, we hit a streambed. Johnny checked the track there, looked at me, and shook his head. He had stopped several times on the way in to closely examine leaves for possible blood sign, but in each case it had been spots of red seeping through the autumn orange of the many maples that made up much of this stand of hardwood. It was an hour later, almost ten o'clock, when we reached Royal's body.

Royal was propped up against a tree in a sitting position, and but for the dry, crusted blood that covered his shirt and his open field jacket he could have been resting. His chin was against his chest and a shock of curly, blond hair was splayed across his forehead. I dropped to one knee to better see his face. His eyes were open and glazed like the windows of some abandoned house blindly reflecting the sunlight, but in Royal's case the eyes seemed to be staring in disbelief at his bloodstained chest and the gaping wound in his stomach from which a bundle of gray intestines protruded. I tried to look carefully at the wounds, but they were obscured by leaves stuck in a haphazard pattern across his chest and belly, apparently blown there while the blood was still wet and tacky.

Doc knelt beside the body and began pulling the leaves away.

"Has he been shot, or stabbed, or what?" I asked.

Doc carefully opened Royal's blood-soaked shirt and exposed a row of neat holes across the center of his chest. "Looks to me like a pitchfork did him." He pointed to the wounds. "Got both lungs and the heart," he said. He lowered his hand to the gaping wound in Royal's belly. "I'd say this one was done first, and it ripped him open as he twisted and fell. Then he was finished off with the stab to the chest."

"It happen here, you think?" I asked.

Doc shook his head. "Not near enough blood on the ground. Plenty on his belly, though. I'd say whoever did this let him lay for a bit, lay and suffer from the belly wound before they finished him off."

"Goddamn fuckin' nigs."

It was Abel and I rounded on him. "Keep your damn mouth shut," I snapped. "Doc just told us he wasn't killed here. That means anybody could of brought his body in and left it."

Abel sneered back. "Ya know it was that goddamn nig, Jehiel. Ya better watch yerself, Samuel, or some folks might get the notion that yer protectin' his sorry, nigger ass. An' we'd all sure as hell know why, wouldn't we?"

I took three quick steps, grabbed Abel by the shirtfront and pushed him back against a tree. "One more word, Abel, and I'll slap on the cuffs and lock up your sorry ass. You got that?"

I could feel Abel's body tense. He glared at me, but said nothing. He had me by a good thirty pounds and could probably pound me into the ground. But I wasn't worried. I'd known Abel a long time and I knew he didn't have the backbone to try.

I spun away and went back to the body. "Johnny, I want you to look around first. See if you can find a track other than Abel's coming in here. There has to be one somewhere. After you're sure you have the right track we'll rope off that area. Then we'll search inch by inch for any evidence the killer might have left behind."

There was another stream some thirty yards behind the body, and it took Johnny little more than twenty minutes to find the track that led out of it. When I came to his call he was staring down at a heavy impression, his face as close to a smile as it ever came. "Whoever made this, either he weighed four hundred pounds, or he was carryin' somethin' a mite heavy," he said.

I crouched beside the track.

"One problem, though," Johnny said. "The boot tread. It's the same as the one Royal's wearin'."

I stared at the track and cursed.

We returned to the body and I asked Doc to remove Royal's boots. He looked at me as though I was mad, but did as I asked, then grunted and gave me a sly look. The socks were wet and held traces of crumpled leaves. "So you think whoever lugged him in here wore his boots." He pulled back one boot flap and checked the size. "Hell, it's a size twelve. Just about anybody could of fit into these."

"Looks like somebody was playin' this real smart," Johnny said. "I'll go up and down the stream, see if I can find where the track went in. Maybe that'll tell us somethin'."

"Maybe," I said. "But I think the socks are wet because his boots were pulled off in the stream. I think you're gonna find different boot tracks going in, and that's not gonna tell us much of anything. Not the way this land is hunted."

"I'll check 'long the bank, see if I kin find the place they laid him down," Johnny said. "Maybe there'll be a diff'ent boot track close by."

"Do it," I said, then turned to Doc. "How long has he been dead?"

Doc scratched his scraggly red beard. "Since sometime yesterday. Rigor mortis is almost gone." He pulled a pocket watch from his vest. "I'd guess five or six last evening."

I stared down at the body. "I don't understand why nothing got to him," I said. "These woods are overrun with coyotes and ravens." I shook my head. "It's almost like somebody stayed here with him through the night."

Johnny pointed to impressions in the leaves to one side of the body. "Coulda been two people," he said. He knelt and studied the ground, then picked a bit of white substance mixed among the leaves and held it between his fingers. "Candle wax," he said. "Looks like they sat with 'im a long time."

I moved back to the body and lifted Royal's head. His neck was still stiff from the lingering affects of full rigor, but I forced the head back. I wanted a better look at something I thought I'd seen earlier. I brushed away the lock of hair that hung across his forehead. Three small crosses, the middle one larger than the two at either side, had been painted in the center of his forehead.

"Ba-stid," Abel said. "Candles. Crosses." His shoulders shook as another shudder went through him. "Goddamn nigs is doin' voodoo."

The back of Jehiel Flood's house was tucked up against a copse of hemlock and was barely visible from the section of streambed where Johnny and I were crouched over a new track he had found.

"This is the only track north of where we found the body. I haven't checked south yet. I also ain't found no place where Royal was laid down to get his boots off. 'Course whoever stuck him coulda worn the boots right from the start, then stumbled in the stream and gotten Royal's socks wet." Johnny scratched his narrow, pointy chin. "My guess is we'll haveta find the place where he was kilt before we'll know anythin' for sure."

"You boys know yer trespassin' on my land?"

The words had boomed out at us with the deep rumble of a fast-approaching storm, and when I looked up I saw Jehiel Flood's bulky frame stepping through the copse of hemlock. His face was solemn at first, then broke into a wide grin. "I 'spect you think bein' consta-ble gives you the right to go anywheres you pleases." His coal-black eyes snapped to Johnny. "An' you bein' an Injun, you jus' kinda feel all the woods in the world belongs ta you."

I stood and took a step toward him. I am not a small man—six feet tall and one hundred and ninety pounds—but I instantly felt dwarfed by the man's size. Jehiel is easily six foot four, with 240 pounds of hard-packed muscle. He's fifty-five if he's a day, but except for a slight bulge at his middle there's not much fat to the man. The word *formidable* always crossed my mind whenever we met.

"I'm afraid I'm here on business, Mr. Flood."

He raised his gray-tinged eyebrows under the red hunter's cap that covered what I knew was a full mane of nappy white hair.

"All of a sudden you doan call me by my given name no more, Samuel? Hell, I thought all my taxes was paid up to date." He winked at Johnny, enjoying his fun.

"There's been a killing back south in the woods a bit," I said. "Johnny and I are looking for tracks, trying to figure out where the killer went."

"An' you 'spect ta find 'em here?" All humor fled his face and he glowered at me.

I explained about the streambed, and how I thought the killer had used it to cover his trail. "We're just checking every place north and south of where we found the body," I added.

"Who got kilt?"

"Royal Firman."

Jehiel snorted, but said nothing.

"You don't seem surprised," I said.

"Ain't. 'Bout time somebody kilt that snotnosed fucker."

I turned to Johnny. I didn't want him around to hear more of what Jehiel might say. The man's mouth had already gotten him in enough trouble in the town. "Check on south a bit," I told Johnny. "I'll catch up with you when I finish up here."

When Johnny was out of earshot I walked over to where Jehiel stood. "This is a bad killing," I said.

He snorted. "Ain't never hear'd of a good one."

"What I mean is that Royal was nearly gutted, an' Doc says whoever killed him let him lay awhile and suffer before they finished the job. That's sure to get around and stir folks up. Fact that he was found up here on the hill might stir them up even more."

I never used the name "Nigger Hill" with Jehiel. I'm not certain why, since it was the legal name of the road leading up here. It was just something I had never felt I could do. I never used "Beulah Hill" either—Jehiel's name for the land and the road. Instead, I just referred to it all as "the hill."

Jehiel snorted again. "Shi-it, young Samuel. If they had found that boy thirty miles from here, them nasty-assed white folks woulda found a way to blame us, anyways." He let out a low rumbling laugh. "We those bad people, with that bad Negro blood, that ain't been cured by a good dose of white bleach." His mood changed and he glared at me again. "An' don't you go sendin' people away, like you did with Johnny Taft, jus' 'cause you worried 'bout people hearin' what I say. 'Cause what I say is fuck 'em all. An' there ain't a man or woman in this town that don't already know it."

He was telling the truth. Everyone did know it. Nary a man or woman had failed to hear Jehiel's diatribes against the racism that permeates our town, even though most fail to understand that it truly exists. But that's a long and a difficult story that I am not certain I truly comprehend. Or, if I do, it's not one that I choose to acknowledge.

I do know that free Negroes, men and women who were never slaves, migrated to Vermont early in the last century. Here they worked as servants in white households, or as day laborers on local farms. Then, as the years progressed, they were able to buy their own lands, and in doing so tended to cluster together in areas that were inevitably named "Nigger Hill," or "Nigger Road," or "Nigger Hollow" by the people in the various towns where they lived.

Here, in Jerusalem's Landing, some thirty-four Negro families made their homes on our Nigger Hill between 1810 and 1870. Then that number began to decline, until only seven individuals remained—Jehiel's family of five, and the minister, and dumb Jeffords Page. It was a decline in population that everyone understood, but seldom spoke about. Some of those earlier Negroes moved away to seek better lives. But only a few. The main cause for the decline was "the bleaching."

Being largely an agrarian community, marriage and the raising of children who could help work the farms had always been an essential part of life in Jerusalem's Landing. But this was not easily accomplished. As in most rural Vermont towns, white women of marriageable age were always in short supply, with men normally exceeding the number of potential mates. Many poor, rural women simply abandoned the life to which they were born and moved to larger towns and cities to find work, eventually marrying men from those places. Conversely, women among Negro families, given that they had fewer opportunities, mostly chose to remain.

Thus, what became known as "the bleaching" occurred, a mixing of the races through marriage that continued over several generations, until succeeding progeny of original Negro mothers lost their color and, in the eyes of the state, "became legally white again."

It was a belief and a practice that dated back to Thomas Jefferson. It was also one that Jehiel Flood had fought and railed against all his life.

I lowered my eyes and drew a weary breath. I knew there was no point in discussing any of this with him, or the ways I feared it would all factor in to this killing. Jehiel was now giving me a heavy dose of his backwoods patois. It was a sign I recognized—an end to any hope of reasonable conversation. To my knowledge Jehiel had no formal education beyond grade school. Yet he was highly intelligent and well read, and I had learned early in my youth that his mind was as keen as any I would encounter. But today there would be no intelligent discourse. Today he was hiding behind his country dialect and spouting an argument I had heard before. It was one I knew by heart, a diatribe he used as a shield, intended to end all meaningful intercourse. I surrendered to it. "Tell me about these tracks," I said, nodding back toward the streambed.

"My land. Prob'ly my tracks, or maybe my son, Prince. He likes to go back in them woods to hunt squirrel. We favor us a nice squirrel stew now an' then. Also cut our firewood back in there."

"Prince around now?"

"Nope. Sent him and young Jeffords inta town ta fetch some supplies at the store. They be back shortly, I s'pect." Jehiel tilted his head to one side, as if to study me better. "You gonna talk to all the Negroes up here so's you can decide which one of us kilt that little snotnose, Samuel?"

I felt myself bristle. "Dammit, Jehiel. I'm just trying to do my job here. Now why don't you help instead of playing this fool game with me?"

Jehiel threw back his head and let out a great, rumbling baritone of a laugh that seemed to shake the leaves on the trees. "Doan you get feisty with me, son. Weren't so long ago I caught you stealin' apples in my orchard, an' grabbed you by the scruff of the neck an' put a boot to yer bottom. You ain't so big now I can't do it agin."

I lowered my head and shook it in surrender. "I suspect you could. But I'm not here to fight with you. I need your help, Jehiel. If you'll give it. Please."

Jehiel grinned at me out of that great chocolate-colored face. "Well tha's different, then. What you need, Samuel?"

I took a deep, exasperated breath. "You didn't happen to see Royal Firman up in these woods yesterday, did you?"

"If I had, I woulda run his lily-white ass off'n this here hill." Jehiel's voice had lost its hint of humor; had a bit of a growl to it now.

"Why's that?" I asked.

"'Cause I'da known why he was here."

I let out a breath, and continued the game. "And why would that be?"

"Same reason he ever came slinkin' roun' up here. Same reason all them white boys do. Hopin' they can do one of my daughters the favor of servicin' her with they puny white dicks." He narrowed his eyes at me as he spoke the words.

"Royal been up here lately?" I asked.

Jehiel was still studying me through slits. "Caught him hangin' roun' 'Lizabeth's dooryard couple a months back." Jehiel's face softened and he gave me a big-toothed grin. "Jus' showed him the biz-ness end of my Winchester an' he stepped along nicely."

"And that was the last time you saw him?"

Jehiel shook his head. "Come up here a few weeks back with his daddy. That ol' fool's been after me ta let him log my land, even though I ain't never let nobody put a saw or ax to nothin' I own." He shook his head again. "Fool must think I'm addled. Land's ninety percent maple. Wants me ta give up the trees that gives me the syrup that keeps me goin' year ta year. Also got a nice stand of black walnut he wants. Says he'll split the loggin' profits with me." He gave out with another rumble of laughter. "I wanted them profits, why the hell I wanna share 'em with him? I asks him. Then he starts screamin'—you know how that fool is—tellin' me I'm just some ol' nig don't know what's good fer him."

"And what did you do?" I asked.

Jehiel laughed again. "Showed *him* the bizness end of that Winchester. Then I watched him an' his snotnosed boy move along smart-like."

I thought about asking Jehiel if I could take a look in his barn—at his pitchfork, really—but thought better of it. I'd let it sit for now—come back to it later if I had to.

"I gotta go check on Johnny," I said instead. "I'll be back to talk to Prince and Jeffords. I'd appreciate it if you asked them to stay around a bit."

Jehiel grinned at me, as if saying, maybe he would, maybe he wouldn't. "I'll ask 'em," he said, still grinning. "Jeffords'll probably do as he's told. But that boy Prince is like his daddy. Might decide he'd be better off huntin' up a squirrel or two."

I shook my head and turned to go. Jehiel reached out and took hold of my arm.

"How's your daddy?" he asked.

"Poorly," I said. "But hanging on, best he can."

He nodded. "You tell him I be by. Maybe tomorra. Next day fer sure."

* * *

I caught up with Johnny downstream, halfway between Reverend Bowles's place and Elizabeth's cabin. He was using his buck knife to separate leaves along the bank of the creek.

I liked to watch Johnny in the woods. There was something almost spiritual about the way he treated things, the soft way he moved about. He had once explained that the Abenaki believed you never went into the woods unless you needed to. It was the home of the animals, and you went there with the respect given anyone's home.

"Looks like Royal was laid down here," he said, looking up. "Whoever done it tried ta cover the spot with leaves. Problem is they drug over some leaves from back thataway." He raised his chin to indicate a spot farther back in the woods. "But they's beech leaves, an' there ain't no beech trees near this streambed—only maples."

He carefully flicked away some leaves revealing a cluster beneath. It was splattered with dried blood. He looked up at me. "Could be deer blood," he said. "There's a bit of poachin' up here, I'm told."

I could tell he thought it was something else. "I'll take it to the university and they'll tell me," I said.

I picked up a handful of leaves and placed them in a paper bag I had brought with me. "You see that other set of tracks we're looking for?"

"There's some near where the body was laid down." He stared at me, asking if I wanted him to show me, and letting me know he thought the effort would be useless to anybody but another tracker. "They's in the leaves," he explained. "Just track sign that's hard ta see. Nothin' in any soft dirt that'd give a boot print."

I nodded, looked toward where I knew Elisha Bowles's house was and thought about cutting through the woods and talking to him. Then I looked downstream toward a distant path that led to Elizabeth's cabin. Again, I felt a rush of pleasure and anticipation. I decided I'd go there first.

I turned back to Johnny. "Check around here for anything that might of been left behind. Then check to see if you can find Royal's track coming in the woods. I'll meet up with you in half an hour, or so."

Elizabeth's cabin was in a small clearing about fifty yards from the road. It was large for a rural cabin, built to accommodate rooms for her two sisters; the entire structure made of timbers cut from the land. Next to it stood a small, one-room cottage where Elizabeth mixed up the herbal teas and medicines and salves that she had learned about years ago from an old Abenaki woman—her dispensary, she called it, complete with a small bed she could use when she worked late into the night. I thought of the times I had visited her there, tried to fight off the pleasure those memories gave me—mysterious, self-contained, beautiful Elizabeth. Always so much a part of my life.

I turned back to the main cabin and could see smoke curling from the fieldstone chimney. Moving across the rear dooryard, I glanced toward the small barn that stood behind the house. I would have to go there eventually; look for a pitchfork I hoped I would not find. But that would come later, I told myself. I pushed the thought away and continued toward the cabin door, scattering a handful of chickens that were working the hard dirt for any leftover feed.

The door opened before I could knock and Elizabeth suddenly filled the frame. She was dressed in a loose-fitting house shift, the bodice cut low, revealing smooth, caramel-colored skin. She smiled at me—perfect white teeth behind delicate, sensuous lips. Her light brown eyes seemed to offer both pleasure and wariness, and her dark curly hair hung in soft ringlets along her slender face.

"You look as beautiful as ever," I said, unable to help myself.

She ran one finger along the sleeve of my jacket. "It's good to see you, Samuel. I've missed your visits. And your flattery." Her voice was like the soft, satisfied purr of a cat; the wariness in her eyes seemed to disappear.

She stepped back, opening the way into her home. I followed her with the familiar sense of pleasure and excitement I had always felt with Elizabeth.

The years we had spent in school together had been filled with an inexplicable closeness, a need to be in each other's company. At first I had tried to attribute those feelings to the fact that we had always been the two brightest children in our classes. But I knew it had been more. Those emotions had provoked a sense of protectiveness as well, and on the many occasions when the cruelty of children made her the victim of epithets and slurs I had always found myself striking out in her defense. Later, when we were older and in high school together, I often accompanied her on the long walk up Nigger Hill, then lingered at her home, extending our time together.

Jehiel seemed amused by our friendship in those days, his fatherly concern for Elizabeth extending no farther than to assure himself that we weren't falling prey to any immature sexual mischief. Often—perhaps when he thought my ardor was becoming too strong—he would interrupt our time together by asking for help with certain chores. He and my father were close during those years, often hunting together on Jehiel's land, and I knew my father regarded him with both respect and affection. It was something that easily transferred to my impressionable young mind and made him a powerful figure in my youth. In any event, I always found myself unable to refuse his requests.

You will wonder, of course, if Elizabeth and I eventually became more than close friends. We did. It happened when we were in our teens, the innocent fumbling of two curious children. It occurred over a single summer, sporadic at best, then ended suddenly when we went our separate ways to different universities. We had continued to spend time together during the succeeding summer recesses, but Elizabeth had never allowed our youthful romance to blossom again. It was a rejection that had hurt and confused me. Then one day, we were walking together along a trail in the woods on Nigger Hill, ironically not far from where I would eventually find Royal Firman's body. We had stopped to rest by the stream, and it was there that I told her how I felt; how I had felt for many years. It seemed to both frighten and please her, though she remained reticent about her feelings. We sat there in silence for a long time, then she came to me, slipping her arms about my waist and resting her head gently against my chest. I want to think she was telling me that she loved me, too, but that this was the most she could give. But perhaps not. Perhaps it was only sympathy toward feelings she could not return. Elizabeth had always hidden her emotions well, offering only what she felt safe to show, and only when reasonably certain that rejection would not follow. Standing in her cabin now, I realized, as I often had in the past, that rejection was never possible for me. Not where Elizabeth was concerned.

Instead it was I who had felt rejection. It had happened over the succeeding years, when other young men had also sought to visit her—Royal Firman among them. I had kept watch on her cabin throughout that time and had seen them come and go, and though I never knew to what extent any had succeeded, their mere presence had cut me deeply—to the point that, though I continued to keep watch over her, I had stopped visiting myself. Yet, being back now in her small, isolated home seemed to wipe away those feelings, and I again felt the undeniable pleasure I had always known in her presence.

The main room of the cabin was small and neat and bright just as I remembered it. The interior log walls were still painted white and there were new colorful curtains at the windows. A brightly patterned hooked rug now sat in the center of the room, and there were two new chairs directed toward the hearth of the fieldstone fireplace. Beyond was an open kitchen, separated from the main room by a long, narrow dining table, also new, at which now sat Elizabeth's two sisters, Maybelle and Ruby.

Maybelle was nineteen, eight years younger than Elizabeth and I, and she had been a small child, then a young girl, during the years I regularly visited here, so I did not know her well. The same was true of Ruby, who was twenty. But there all comparisons ended. Where Maybelle was short and plump and normally cheerful, Ruby was tall and angular and given to moodiness and sharp words—very much her father's daughter, Elizabeth had always claimed. Both women also had their father's deep chocolate skin tone, and while certainly handsome, neither possessed the near ethereal beauty I had always associated with their older sister. Now both sisters sat staring at me, eyes wary, faces filled with a barely concealed trepidation that also seemed to carry a hint of hostility.

Elizabeth took my arm and guided me to the table. "Would you like some coffee, Samuel?" she asked.

"Yes I would," I said. "I also have to talk to you—to each of you."

The wariness heightened in the eyes of the two younger sisters, and I thought I detected a hint of it return to Elizabeth as well. But it quickly disappeared from Elizabeth's eyes, or perhaps was willed away.

"It's always a pleasure to talk to you, Samuel," she said.

I sat at the table as Elizabeth placed a cup of coffee before me.

"Did any of you see Royal Firman yesterday?" I asked.

Maybelle and Ruby avoided my eyes and said nothing.

"I saw someone," Elizabeth said, almost as if trying to speak before her sisters could. "It could have been Royal. It was a white man. I'm sure of that. I saw him from my window. He was walking through our woods behind the barn. I assumed it was a hunter."

"Did he have a weapon?" I asked.

"I really couldn't tell," Elizabeth said. "I just assumed he was hunting. Few people—white people, I mean—" she smiled then continued, "come up here for anything else, unless they're here to see my father, or come for one of my remedies." She studied me for a moment, perhaps waiting to see if I believed her. "Has something happened, Samuel?" she asked at length.

"Royal Firman's been killed. Murdered." I held her eyes. "We found his body in the woods between this cabin and Reverend Bowles's place."

Elizabeth took a deep breath. "Murdered." She said the word as if it were incomprehensible.

"He was stabbed; more than once—with a pitchfork. And someone stayed with the body for a time." I let my eyes fall on two candles that sat on the table, but my glance seemed to draw no reaction. I knew I had to be careful about what I said, yet knew immediately that I wanted to tell Elizabeth everything.

"So you sayin' somebody up hereabouts killed him?"

It was Ruby, her words angry, and spoken as sharply as the rigid lines of her face.

"I don't know who killed him," I said. "It appears he was carried to the place we found him. He could have been carried in from the road. Johnny Taft is out there checking for tracks."

"Then why'd you ask if we'd seen him?" Ruby snapped.

"Because that would tell me he was already here when he was killed," I said.

Ruby smirked at me; gave a derisive snort.

"So you do think it was somebody from hereabouts." It was Maybelle this time, and her heavy, pouty lips trembled slightly as she spoke.

"Girl, you are talking like a fool," Elizabeth snapped. Her eyes shot from Maybelle to Ruby. "You both are. Samuel is just doing what he is supposed to do—try and find out where Royal was before this terrible thing happened. So help him, don't argue with him."

"I din see nobody," Maybelle said. "Not Royal or nobody else. Leastwise nobody that doan belong up here."

There was a small bandage on Maybelle's throat. "Did you hurt yourself?" I asked.

She quickly glanced at Elizabeth, then nodded. "I cut myself in the barn. I was movin' a roll of barbwire."

I looked at Ruby. Her eyes were still angry, still glaring with accusation. "I ain't seen Royal Firman since I doan know when," she said. She turned her glare on Elizabeth. "An' I din see no white man neither."

I sipped my coffee, then turned back to Elizabeth. She was shaking her head.

"I'm sorry, Samuel," she said. She looked at each of her sisters in turn and let out a weary breath.

"What time was it you saw this man you thought was hunting?" I asked.

Elizabeth considered the question. "It wasn't long after I had gotten home from school," she said, then seemed to consider the question again.

Elizabeth taught first and second grade at our town school. She had been hired three years after she graduated from Middlebury College with a teaching degree. The position had been vacant for two of those years, and only after it was clear that no white person was interested had the school board offered the post to her. Until then the first- and second-graders had taken classes with the third- and fourth-grade teacher.

"I was changing into my house clothes," Elizabeth said, interrupting my thoughts, "and I looked out my bedroom window and saw a man headed farther back into the woods. But he was too far away to see him clearly."

"But you could tell it was a white man?"

"Yes. I remember thinking it was a stranger. If it had been a Negro I wouldn't have thought that."

"What was he wearing?"

Elizabeth seemed to think again. Her eyes took on a faraway look, then she shook her head. She looked at me. "I don't remember, Samuel. It could have been a hunting jacket. Maybe that's why I assumed it was a hunter, but I can't be certain."

"If you do remember, I'll need you to tell me," I said.

"Of course, Samuel," she said. "Of course I will."

Elizabeth went outside with me, and we stood together on the hard-packed dirt of the dooryard. The chickens wandered around our feet, still pecking away for any overlooked morsels of feed. I glanced toward the small barn off to my right.

"You'll be wanting to look in there, I expect?" Elizabeth said.

The question confused and embarrassed me. It had been exactly what I had been thinking when I had glanced at the barn, but hearing her say it made me feel as though I had accused her of Royal's murder.

"I'll be having to look in everyone's barn," I said.

"I know, Samuel. Come." She led the way across the yard, glancing back over her shoulder and smiling. When we reached the barn she swung back one of the large double doors and stepped inside.

The interior of the barn was divided into thirds. On the left was a penned area for the chickens with a double-tiered row of boxes for their nests and a small exterior opening out into the yard.

At the rear was a single stall for the one milking cow Elizabeth kept, empty now with the animal out to pasture. Next to it was the roll of barbed wire on which Maybelle had cut herself. To the right was an open storage area, and above it a hayloft with a ladder leading up. I glanced up and saw a pitchfork embedded in a bale of hay.

I drew a deep breath, went to the ladder and climbed it. The loft was dark and musty, and I could hear the scratching of a small rodent as it scurried away. I withdrew the pitchfork and held it to the best light, but even in the dim lighting I could tell it was clean— almost new clean.

When I climbed down the ladder I walked around the barn, seeking out any telltale signs of blood. There was a patch of fresh straw a few feet from the ladder, and I returned to it and kicked the newer straw aside to see beneath it. There was nothing there.

I was about to apologize for even looking, when Elizabeth crossed the hard dirt floor and came up to me. She was close now, so very close, and she raised her hand and gently stroked my cheek. Her hand was soft against my face, and it sent a chill through me as memories came rushing back, the softness of her body, the sweetness of her taste.

"Oh, Samuel, I'm so glad you're here," she whispered.

"Yes," I said, unable to help myself. "Yes, so am I."

(2)

Reverend Elisha Bowles was still at work in his front yard, now busy stacking the logs he had split earlier. The man was always busy with something—part of his Protestant work ethic, he claimed. And whatever he took on, which was much, he did it with a maximum amount of bluster and singing and noise. Now, even before I saw him, I could hear his high, rich tenor singing a hymn I had known since childhood—singing it with the same gusto he might impart at one of his services.

Would you be free from the burden of sin?
There's pow'r in the blood, pow'r in the blood.
Would you o'er evil a victory win?
There's wonderful pow'r in the blood.

I stepped out into the reverend's dooryard, and as he saw me he intensified the force of his voice.

There is pow'r, pow'r, wonder working pow'r,
In the blood—of the Lamb;
There is pow'r, pow'r, wonder working pow'r,
In the pre—cious—blood—of—the—Lamb.

When he finished the verse he threw back his head and laughed. "And now look how Jesus, in his great wisdom, has sent me a sinner. Have you come to pray with me, boy? Have you come to repent of your wicked ways?"

Unwillingly my mind flashed to Elizabeth's barn, and the sense of deep depression I had felt when I left her returned. I felt my cheeks begin to redden, but fought it off.

"Reverend, you've known me all my life, and I am far from wicked. I'm also twenty-seven years old, but you are still calling me *boy.*"

He threw back his head again as if speaking to the heavens. "We are all children in the eyes of Sweet Jesus," he intoned.

I looked down and shook my head at the cliché, knowing there would be many more to come.

Elisha Bowles was a short, round man, well into his sixties—some said seventies. There was not a hair on his jet-black head, and as he stood in his dooryard the sun glinted off both his scalp and the bottle-lens spectacles he always wore. He dropped a final log on the woodpile, straightened his back and folded his hands across his protruding belly, which stuck precariously out from his frockcoat and strained the buttons on his shirt. It was a position I had seen him take before, often in church, sometimes not, a position that cried out: I am now ready to confront sin that is everywhere around me.

He cast a withering eye on me. "So you deny your wickedness, do you, boy?"

"I do, Reverend. I strive for goodness in my life," I said.

He eyed me, trying to catch a smile on my lips. I successfully kept it at bay.

He narrowed one eye. "Strange words from a tax collector," he boomed.

I groaned inwardly. "The Apostle Matthew, I believe, was a tax collector," I said.

"Yes, indeed," the reverend said. He raised a finger, his voice booming louder. "But he saw the wickedness of his ways, and forsook that evil to follow the righteous word of our blessed Lord." He narrowed the other eye. "Have you so followed the words of Jesus and forsaken this evil?"

I kept fighting the smile. The reverend was a year behind on his taxes, and tax collection had become one of the many evils in his vast repertoire.

I shook my head. "Elisha, why do you do this to me? I seem to recall words: Render to Caesar the things that are Caesar's—"

He cut me off. "I am truly amazed you can remember your Bible passages," he snapped. "Especially since I have not seen you in church for nigh on to a year." He waved the words away with one plump hand. "But so be it. You are here now. So, I ask you, will you kneel and pray with me and forsake the evil you do?"

"I would, Elisha, but right now I don't have time." I regretted the choice of words as soon as they had left my mouth.

Elisha's eyes widened, then raised up to the heavens. "O Lord," he boomed in a high tenor, "I pray that your ears were not pointed down toward this hill on this sa-ad day. But if they were, ignore the words of denial this sinner has spoken. He is a good child. Wayward in his ways, but still good. Strike not him down for the way he abuses Thee. I pray this with a-ll my heart."

"There's been a killing, Elisha." His eyes were still heavenward when I spoke and he lowered them slowly. They were filled with caution when he looked at me.

"Where?" he asked.

I was surprised by the question—had expected who, rather than where. "Here on the hill," I said. "At least that's where the body was found."

"Buried?" he asked.

I felt a tremor pass through me, and forced it away. "No," I answered.

He considered what I had said, let out a breath, then seemed to take hold of himself. "Who was killed?" he finally asked.

"Royal Firman." I watched his mood darken.

"Do you want me to come and pray over him?" he asked.

I couldn't help thinking about the candle wax beside the body, the three crosses marked on Royal's forehead, and wondering if, perhaps, Elisha hadn't already done so. "We need to keep people away from the scene," I said.

Elisha nodded as he looked past me toward the woods. "You worried they'll be trouble, I expect."

I stared at him, looking for a hint of something in his eyes. "It was a bad thing . . . the way it was done . . . how the body was left." I paused, continued to search his face. "Folks will be riled, Elisha. And looking to place blame."

He nodded his head slowly, pensively. "Yes," he said. "The boy was white. Not bleached white. Real white. An' he was found here . . ." He let the sentence die.

He chewed his lower lip, and I thought he seemed frightened by the idea. But there was nothing suspicious or unnatural about that. The Negroes in the town were few and isolated and vulnerable, and while tolerance had always existed among the white population, I had learned early on that it was a very thin brand of sufferance.

"I have to look around your place," I said. "I'll be looking around everyone's."

Elisha nodded, resigned about what was to come.

"And I was hoping you'd consider speaking about this at Sunday's service. If you might urge people to be patient. Urge them to spread that message. Give me some time to sort this out."

Elisha seemed to consider this, to weigh its merits and its possible dangers. The Free Will Baptist Church was the lone church in Jerusalem's Landing. There were other churches in neighboring towns, but the two closest were some seven and ten miles distant, respectively, so most of the townspeople—those who were churchgoers, save the few Catholics—attended Elisha's service. It was one of the curious contradictions of the town: the willingness to accept, to even embrace a Negro as a preacher juxtaposed with an underlying intolerance that most of the townspeople did not even recognize.

Elisha looked at me with sad, weary eyes. "I will try, Samuel," he said. "But I can't promise I will be heard. These are hard times."

He was right, of course. This Great Depression we were enduring had changed much in our lives. It was a time when resentment and hatreds, normally repressed, boiled up to the surface.

"I understand, Elisha," I said. "But please try."

I found nothing in Elisha's barn or outbuildings, although I must admit my search was cursory at best. An outside observer might think I was providing time so evidence might be hidden, but that was not the case. The evidence, when and if it was needed, would be found. Of that I was certain.

My mind was clouded with that thought as I headed back to Royal's body. I was nearly there when Doc Hawley came stumbling toward me through the woods. He was out of breath, panting like a spaniel. His derby hat was missing, and his lower lip was swollen and bloody. He half fell, half sat on a fallen tree limb and stared up at me.

"They took the body," he said. "When I tried to stop them I got smacked upside the head."

"Who?" I demanded. Jehiel and Prince and Jeffords rushed to mind, and I felt a sudden sense of panic.

"Royal's daddy," Doc huffed. "He came crashing through the woods like a wild man. I gather that Abel sent word to him up at the sawmill, before he came to get you. Anyways, the damned fool was there before I knew what was happening. I tried to talk to him, but he just stood there staring at his son, his eyes all crazy. Then he starts shouting at Abel, tells him he has to help him get his boy home." He paused, fighting for breath. "I tried to stop him, Samuel. I did everything I could. I told him it was a crime scene; that the body couldn't be moved, and that when it could it had to go back to my office first. I even stepped between him and the body, and before I knew what was happening I was flat on my ass. Preserved Firman punched me, Samuel. The damn fool punched me right in the mouth."

I felt my panic grow. "Which way did they head?" I snapped.

"Back toward the road," he said. "Straight on back from here."

I had already turned as he spoke and began weaving through the trees and around deadfalls, running as best I could through the thick clusters of new growth. When I reached the road, Preserved and Abel had just placed Royal's body in the bed of Abel's truck.

Preserved turned as I came out of the woods, his face wracked with inconsolable grief. Then his features changed, became twisted, and he stabbed a finger at me, his eyes glowing in his narrow, pinched face. "You stay away, you nigger-lovin' bastard," he shouted. "I'm takin' my boy home, then I'm comin' back ta take care of them black-assed sumbitches that kilt him."

I slowed my pace; carefully checked to see if Preserved was armed. He was an angry, mean-spirited man, even under normal circumstances, one of those small, wiry types who would use anything at hand in an argument or fight. Now he was enraged beyond any hope of reason and unquestionably dangerous. He was in his late forties, but looked ten years older from long winters working in the woods, and he took two limping steps toward me on the bad leg he had gotten years back when a log had rolled off a truckbed at his sawmill.

I raised one hand, palm out, silently ordering him to stop. My other hand went instinctively to the pistol on my hip. Preserved stopped and glared at me.

"You gonna shoot me, nigger lover?" His face was twisted with hate, a hatred he had held for me every since I was a child. There was a large scar on his left cheek, still visible under a three-day growth of gray-flecked stubble, and it twitched violently all the way to his eye.

My hand moved away from the pistol, but not far enough to matter. "I'm sorry for your loss, Preserved," I said. "But I can't let you take Royal's body until Doc finishes his examination. It's the law, pure and simple, and there's nothing I can do about it." I looked at Abel. He was standing behind Preserved, uncertain what to do next.

"You toss me the keys to your truck, Abel," I said. "We'll drive the body to Doc's office. You can pick up the truck later." Then to Preserved: "When Doc's finished you can take your boy for burial."

Abel kept glancing between Preserved and me, trying to decide what he should do. Preserved snarled over his shoulder. "Drive that truck ta my house, jus' like I said, you dumb-assed fucker."

When he turned back, my pistol was in my hand. "You take one step toward that truck, Abel, and I'll blow a new hole in that dumb ass."

Behind the pair I saw Johnny Taft come around a bend in the road. Unseen by the others he moved to my car and removed the .30-30 he knew I kept under the front seat.

"We've had enough trouble," I said. "Let me do my job, here." My pistol was still pointed in their general direction, but it was pure bluff. I had no intention of using it. I only hoped Preserved and Abel didn't know it, too.

Preserved sneered at me. "The only thing yer gonna do is protect yer goddamn nig friends. Everybody knows what you are, Samuel. Same as yer daddy. Same as yer whole goddamn family. But ya ain't gonna get away with it this time." He turned back toward Abel, prepared to give him another order, but stopped when he saw Johnny twenty feet away holding the .30-30.

I called out to him. "Johnny, anybody tries to get in that truck, you blow their damned kneecap off."

Preserved watched Johnny nod, then turned his glare back on me. I could see that some of the fire had gone out of his eyes. He knew that Johnny Taft could, and probably would do just what I had asked.

Preserved shifted his weight, pawed at the ground like some frustrated animal, then snarled at me through gritted teeth. "Ya think ya won this, don't ya, Samuel? Well I'm gonna get me a real cop up here. Somebody from the sheriff's office, not some piss-assed nigger lover the likes of you. Then we'll see what happens. We'll see . . ."

His words stopped midsentence, and the wild hatred that was there before returned to his eyes. He was looking past me now, and I turned and saw the objects of his renewed rage.

Jehiel, trailed by his son, Prince, and young Jeffords Page, had just come out of the woods behind me. Jehiel had his Winchester cradled in the crook of one arm. He ignored Preserved.

"Heard the ruckus, young Samuel, an' thought you might be needin' some help."

Jehiel stood there big as a house, Prince and Jeffords, though fully grown, looking like small boys behind him.

Preserved began shouting before I could respond. "Yer gonna pay for this, ya murderin' bastard. And there ain't no way this sumbitch constable of yers is gonna keep me from gettin' you an' ever other goddamn nigger on this hill."

Jehiel's eyes moved slowly—almost too slowly—from me to Preserved. The patois he affected when playing with people fled his voice. "There's nobody living on this hill killed your boy, Preserved. We're all sorry for your loss. Don't like to see anybody's boy killed. But I'll tell you this, and you better hear it good. You come up on this hill looking to hurt anybody here, and I'll send that mean-assed, lily-white soul of yours straight to hell."

A crash of branches drew both men's attention. Doc Hawley staggered out of the woods and skidded to a halt, his recovered derby held tightly in his hands. His eyes flashed to the drawn guns and his face suddenly paled under his red beard. "Jesus. Oh, Jesus," he said. "Let's not have any shooting here. God, please. No shooting." His words seemed to break the tension between Jehiel and Preserved.

"There's not going to be any shooting," I said. Taking advantage of the sudden lull, I lowered my pistol and took a step toward Doc. "You get in your car, Doc. Johnny will follow you back to your office in Abel's truck. And he's going to stay there with that .30-30 until I get there. I won't be long." I turned to Preserved as I continued to talk to Doc. "And I won't be going anywhere until you finish your examination." I let the words sink in, then softened them. "Then, when you're finished, we're going to release Royal's body to Preserved."

I stared hard at Preserved, letting him know there would be no further argument. "We'll send word up to your house when Doc's finished. You can bring Abel with you then and get your boy. But I don't want to see either one of you near Doc's office until I send word. If you show up before that, I'm going to arrest you. And that is something I do not want to do."

Doc and Johnny left with Royal's body, followed a few minutes later by Preserved and Abel. It all happened with a minimum of difficulty, save Preserved's continued threats to bring in someone from the county sheriff's office. I listened without comment, knowing it was a meaningless admonition. I was legally obliged to notify the sheriff whenever a serious crime occurred within the town, and planned to do so when I reached Doc's office.

I walked up to Jehiel. It was just the four of us now, four men standing on a lonely country road, surrounded by the peaceful beauty of autumn, the soothing stillness of the woods. I glanced toward the now well-beaten path that led to the place we had found Royal's body, and it all seemed suddenly incomprehensible. Perhaps instinctively, I looked back toward the thick line of trees and small rise that hid Elizabeth's cabin and found myself wondering what she was doing at that moment. Was she in her small cottage—her "dispensary"—mixing up one of her herbal remedies? Busying her mind and body to obliterate the horrors of the day? She was good at that, always had been. It was one of her tricks of survival. And Elizabeth, if nothing else, was a survivor.

Jehiel was grinning when I turned back to him, almost as if he had enjoyed the confrontation. Or, perhaps, he was just reading my thoughts. "Looks like you got your hands full, Samuel," he said.

"Looks like," I answered. "I appreciated your help."

He let out a rumbling laugh, and brought the patois back. "Woulda been more help if I coulda shot that miserable sumbitch."

The words were meant to tweak my nerves, but I ignored them, knowing it was just Jehiel's way. I moved past him so I could face his son, Prince. He was tall and slender, and at eighteen showed no sign of inheriting either his father's bulk or innate intelligence. He was simply a quiet, peaceable boy—someone the locals might describe as "a boy who liked to keep to home"—who worked hard beside his father and spent his free time hunting the woods, or fishing the trout stream that cut through Addison Hollow. I had known him all his life, and had never heard him utter a mean-spirited word against anyone.

"Prince, I need to ask you and Jeffords some questions about all this," I began.

Prince nodded and swallowed, sending his prominent Adam's apple bobbing along his throat. He glanced quickly at his father, then turned his soft, brown eyes back to me. "Don't know much, Samuel. Other than what Daddy tol' me."

"Did you see Royal Firman up here on the hill anytime yesterday?" I asked.

He shook his head. "Ain't seen him fer maybe a week. Maybe more. Not since Daddy run him an' his daddy off."

"That would be when they were up here talking about logging your land?"

He glanced at his father again, as if seeking permission to speak about that day.

"It's all right, boy," Jehiel said. "You tell Samuel what he needs to know."

Prince shifted his weight, more to control his nervous energy than his nerves, I thought. "Tha's the last time I 'member," he said. "Royal's daddy was real mean. Said he'd make us pay. Royal, he just stood there an' grinned at us. But it was a mean grin, like he was sayin' the same thing." Prince's voice was so soft, almost fearfully so, I could barely hear the words.

"You didn't see Royal later? Maybe yesterday in the woods over by Elizabeth's cabin?" I asked. "Or just somebody that might of been him?"

His deep chocolate skin seemed to darken, almost imperceptibly, almost as if the question embarrassed him. He shook his head. "Ain't seen him but that one time," he said.

Jeffords Page was standing behind him, as though using Prince's slender body as a shield. I moved a step to one side so I could face him. Jeffords stared back at me with dull, frightened eyes. He was sixteen, a cinnamon-skinned mulatto boy with the mind of a five-year-old and the body of a fully grown man. He was short and stocky—bull-like, really—and possessed of a physical strength few men ever achieve. His parents—a white father and Negro mother—had died of influenza within months of each other the previous year. He had seemed lost and frightened then, and even when Jehiel had taken the boy on as a hired hand, the fear had never truly fled his eyes.

I also had known Jeffords most of his life, though not as well as Prince. Jeffords, even when his parents were alive, had always seemed to lurk on the periphery, to watch people at a distance, and he was a difficult child to know and to reach with words. He had seemed to like me well enough in the early years, but later had grown skittish around me, and I had often wondered if the badge I then wore somehow frightened him.

But it was Elizabeth who truly captured his affection. He loved her—worshiped, even, was not too extreme a word—and he could often be found working, unasked, around her cabin, chopping firewood, milking her single dairy cow, or making any repairs he thought were needed. Jehiel often said that whenever he went hunting up the boy, he walked straight past the small shack Jeffords lived in, and went on across the road to Elizabeth's cabin.

"How about you, Jeffords?" I asked. "Did you see Royal Firman hereabouts?"

Jeffords stared back at me. He had a way of looking at you that made you feel he was really looking at something else, something no one else could see. He nodded his head up and down, then contradicted the gesture when he spoke. "Ain't seen nobody. Nobody, nobody. Jus' 'Lizabeth, jus' the reverend, jus' the scary man."

"What the hell you talkin' about, boy?" Jehiel interrupted. "What scary man you mean?"

I held up my hand, hoping to silence Jehiel. "What scary man, Jeffords? Did you see someone who scared you?"

"Scary man's the devil," Jeffords said. His voice had become a singsong now. "Tha's what the reverend says. Scary man's the devil. Gots the devil right inside him."

"Lord almighty," Jehiel groaned. "Boy's talkining about the bogeyman. Was scared all to hell about the bogeyman when his mommy and daddy died, and he was all of a sudden alone. That damn fool Elisha told him there was no such thing. Only the devil. That the devil was what he had ta be scared of. Boy ain't never figured out the difference. Ain't talked about it for six months, or more. I thought he finally forgot it. Now here it is, all back again."

I stepped a bit closer to Jeffords, placed a hand on his rock-solid arm. "Is that what you're talking about, Jeffords?"

He kept nodding, which meant nothing. "Scary man sits outside my house. Sometimes, sits outside 'Lizabeth's house. Sits an' watches. When I gets growed, an' gets to be a preacher, I's gonna chase him off. Chase that devil off, jus' like the reverend does."

"He wants to be a minister now, you know," Jehiel said. "Decided that about six months back. I think he likes them hymns Elisha's always singing. Hell, he might as well do it. Folks probably couldn't tell the difference between him an' Elisha anyways. They's both crazy as bedbugs."

I stared at Jeffords. His words had cut at me, and I wondered if there was something more, something he couldn't quite say. Maybe something I didn't want him to say. He was still nodding his head up and down, as if answering my very thought. But even if he did know something, even if he could answer every question about Royal Firman's death, who would believe him?

I turned, prepared to head back to my car. Prince reached out and took my arm. "You think they's gonna be trouble up here on Beulah Hill, Samuel?" he asked, using the name his father had given their land.

"Don't you fret that, boy," Jehiel snapped. "Any trouble that comes, we handle it."

I looked up at Jehiel. "Are you worried Preserved might be back?" I asked.

Jehiel snorted. "Not less he can get five or six of his woodchuck buddies to come long with him, I ain't."

I nodded, knowing he was probably right. "I'll drive by a few times tonight, just in case," I said.

{ 3 }

Her voice came back to me like a song.

"Tell me that you'll protect me, Samuel. Tell me that you'll always love me."

Elizabeth and I had been teenagers when she had first spoken those words. We were together on the coarse blanket she had taken from her home, her smooth, silky skin even softer in contrast. A canopy of forest trees had covered us, as I felt her fingers trace the contours of my chest, then stray lower, following the light line of hair that ran to my navel. Then she had turned and brought her lips against mine, and I had felt the heat of her passion as she pressed harder against me, tasted that heat on her tongue, smelled it on the sweet, hot scent of her breath. Later, hours later it seemed, when our passion had been exhausted, she had drawn back and stared at me, and I had seen that there were tears in her eyes. "Tell me that you'll protect me, Samuel," she had said. "Tell me that you'll always love me." It had been the first time she had spoken the words, and I had drawn her to me and brought my face to hers and whispered in her ear, "I always will, Elizabeth. Always . . ."

I stood under the large pine staring at the small cottage. The cold night air cut against my face as I watched her figure seated now behind the brightly lit window. Elizabeth had spoken those same words to me that afternoon in her barn, and now they returned, along with everything we had said, just as they had kept coming back to me throughout the day.

"Oh, Samuel, I'm so glad you're here," she said.

"Yes," I answered. "Yes, so am I."

I had struggled to keep my voice soft and even. There were questions I had to ask; answers I needed to have. "Tell me about the times Royal came here," I said.

Elizabeth was silent for almost a minute.

"Tell me," I repeated.

"Don't ask me those things, Samuel. It's not important. It never was important."

"But he came here," I said. "More than once."

Again, silence.

"That's true, isn't it?"

"You know it's true." Her voice was soft, the words spoken gently, but each one came at me slowly, distinctly, with the force of a slap. "I'm not a hermit, Samuel. People visit me." She was quiet again, then continued. "Some I'm happy to see . . . like I am now." She let the sentence die, or perhaps it was killed off by my reply.

"Were you happy to see him?" I allowed the question to sit in renewed silence, afraid of the answer that might come. When she finally spoke her eyes were cast on the dirt floor of the barn, and the sound of her voice made me think she was weeping.

"I am not an evil woman, Samuel. I am not a good woman, either. I'm just a woman." She paused again. "Does that make sense to you? Does that answer your question?"

Now the silence was mine. "I don't know," I finally said. "But I do know that I need to understand what happened between you. I need to know what it all meant to you. Royal is dead. Murdered. To understand what really happened I have to know all of it."

After what seemed a long time she spoke again.

"Nothing I can tell you about Royal will help you, Samuel." Her next words were soft and soothing, meant to be. "I need you to love me, Samuel. I've always needed you to love me. Ever since we were children. And, more than anything, I want you to love me now."

I stepped closer, ran my hand softly along her cheek, felt the smooth, soft flesh against my fingers. But there were no words, nothing that I could say. And then she spoke the words that still fill my mind.

"You once told me that you'd always protect me, Samuel. Will you still? Will you still protect me?" The question floated in the air, seemed to fill every portion of the barn, seemed to swirl about us.

"Yes," I said. "I'll always protect you."

I stood quietly under the tree, staring at her lighted window, still thinking back to that previous afternoon. I had waited then for some further response, my need like a knife in my heart. Elizabeth and I had not been alone together for what seemed an eternity, and this was not how I wanted it to be. I had stopped visiting at her home several years ago, when I had realized that other men were visiting her as well. It was something I had always secretly feared, and then suddenly it was upon me. My response had been to run and hide—but to hide only from her.

During that time we were apart I drove by her cabin repeatedly, often leaving my car far down the road and moving silently through the woods until I could see the flickering light of the kerosene lantern that illuminated the windows of her small "dispensary." If someone was with her I would wait and watch, but always from a distance, never wanting to be too close, to see too much.

And Elizabeth knew. I am sure of that, although she never spoke a word about it.

I stood in silence now, remembering it, remembering all our times, both together and apart, her familiar scent still filling every portion of me, the all-too-familiar shadow now behind her window soothing me despite myself. I had been inside that room countless times, sitting silently as I watched her sketch pictures of the herbs and plants she used for her remedies, sometimes allowing her to sketch me as well, serving as her always-willing model. She had kept those sketches of me, tucked them away among her drawings of the plants she used. The only picture I had ever taken away with me was a self-portrait she had done. It was a drawing of exquisite beauty, a drawing that still hung on the wall opposite my bed— Elizabeth, the last face I see each night; the first vision to meet my eyes each morning.

A new sense of anguish surged through me. I wondered if there were now sketches of Royal Firman hidden away as well, and I suddenly knew that I would return and search for them. I would do it when Elizabeth was at school, and whatever I found I would destroy. The planned deception sent a chill through me, filled me with both a sense of urgency and despair.

There was something about this she had not told me; something, for reasons of her own, she could not trust me to know. That feeling had no basis in fact; was nothing more than a deep gnawing doubt inside my gut. The worst possibility rushed to mind and I pushed it away. If she had killed Royal, or if someone close to her had killed him, I had to find a way to hide it, to obscure it. Yet the white population of Jerusalem's Landing would demand an answer. They would insist on knowing why one of their own was butchered on these last few grudging acres of Negro soil.

"Will you still protect me, Samuel?" The words seemed to fly at me like a curse.

Yes, I told myself. Yes. At least I will try.

It was four in the morning when I ended my vigil outside Elizabeth's cottage and made my way down the narrow, dark path that led to the road. The light inside the cottage had gone out hours earlier, but I had remained beneath the tree, watching the darkened window, past and present visions of Elizabeth spilling through my mind.

Now the darkness overwhelmed me, as I moved back toward the road, and I stretched out my arms, feeling my way along this path I had traveled so many times for so many years, lost now, certain I was veering too far to the left or right. My heart leaped against my chest at the sound of a startled snort, and I stopped and listened as a frightened deer crashed through the trees, fleeing the monster with outstretched arms.

I started off again, still feeling my way. Then the road came into view, a dim clearing in the trees, and I turned into it toward the place I had left my car. Again, I came to a sudden halt, as the shadow of another car appeared. It was parked behind mine, and as I moved toward it again the headlights went on, freezing me in their beam. The door suddenly swung open, and my hand instinctively went to my pistol as a dark form emerged and an image of Preserved Firman rushed to my mind.

"Don't shoot, Samuel." The words were followed by a low, hearty chuckle. "I promised the little woman I'd get myself home in one piece."

I recognized the voice of Frenchy LeMay, and watched in silence as his portly body lumbered toward me. When he turned to face me in the light, I saw he was not in uniform, dressed instead in a solid red hunting coat like my own with his deputy sheriff's star pinned to the breast. A matching hat sat atop his very round head, and though partly hidden in shadow I could see his well-lined face was creased into a wide smile.

"Been waitin' fer ya, Samuel," he said. "Actually, I been huntin' ya down mosta the night. When I found yer car a few hours back I figured ya was deep inta some interrogatin', or somethin'." His smile broadened, but there was a hard edge to his words, and I was sure I would see it in his eyes if the light were better. "That what ya were doin', Samuel?" he asked.

I felt my stomach tighten. "Something like that, Frenchy." I readied a quick lie that had some basis of truth. "There was some concern about Preserved Firman. He made some threats this afternoon. I wanted to make sure he didn't come back and try anything foolish. I've been keeping out of sight; checking the houses along the road."

"Didn't figure he'd see yer car, eh?" Frenchy was grinning again.

"I didn't figure he'd come straight in," I said. "I figured if he came

at all, he'd come from lower down and circle in through the woods."
I gave him as hard a stare as I could in the poor light. "Just trying
to play it safe."

Frenchy let out another low chuckle. "Always a good idea,
Samuel. Leastways, that's what my wife tells me." He paused and
scratched his head, as if remembering something. "But ya ain't married, are ya, Samuel?" He went on before I could answer, obviously
not needing or expecting one. "I always thought ya'd hitch up with
that gal ya was always with. What was her name? Let's see. Elizabeth, weren't it? Yeah, that was it." He paused again. "Well, hell,
tha's her place back there, ain't it? The one you was comin' out
from? Sure it is."

"I guess I'm just not the marrying kind," I said.

Another chuckle. "Well, ya better be careful, boy. That's just what
I always told the missus, back a hunnered years ago when we was
keepin' company. An' I sure as hell thought I meant it."

He took my arm and started walking me back toward the cars.
"Talked to Preserved earlier tonight. He sure does have some terrible things ta say about you. Says yer flat out set on protectin' these
folks up here, even after they went and murdered his boy."

"I'm not too popular with Preserved these days," I said. "Never
have been, really."

"Why's that?" Frenchy asked.

"You'll have to ask him." Frenchy knew the reason as well as I,
but it was not something either of us would speak about. At least
not yet.

When we reached the cars Frenchy stopped and began scratching at his head again. "I'll tell ya, Samuel, from what I've hear'd so
far, ya sure went and left us with one messed-up crime scene."

I started to explain the circumstances, but he held up his hand.
"I know, I know. Doc Hawley tol' me all about it. Sounds like ya had
yerself a goddamn circus out here. But it sure as hell is gonna make
things a lot harder now."

"Did you see the body?" I asked.

"Yeah, I saw it. In fact, I got to Doc's place jus' when Preserved got there to pick it up." He paused and gave me a long look. "I tol' him he couldn't have it. Man 'bout threw a fit right there in Doc's office."

"You don't think I should have released the body, then," I said.

"Hell no, Samuel." He reached out and gave my arm a squeeze, as though forgiving me my sins. "I'm afraid we're gonna need that body just a bit longer. I already ordered an ambulance ta take it up ta the hospital in Burlington."

"I'm not sure I understand," I said. "Doc finished his examination, didn't he?"

Frenchy nodded. "Sure did. An' I'm sure it was a damn good 'un. But I want a full autopsy on that boy. I wanna know what he ate, and when; whether he had hisself a woman, or not; what, if anythin', he's got under his fingernails, the whole damned thing." He wagged a finger at me. "We got the cause of death, not much doubt about that, but some of that other stuff might give us a better idea of just when and where that death happened. An' that's somethin' we need ta know."

I grimaced, indicating that I realized he was right. "I'm sorry, Frenchy. I never thought of those things. And I should have."

"Don't worry 'bout it, son. This is yer first murder investigation, I reckon." He raised his eyebrows, turning the statement into a question.

"First, and hopefully the last," I said.

"Well, I done more'n I kin remember over the las' twenty-five years. Kinda like a specialty with me." He grinned at me again, but I couldn't be sure about the honesty of his smile, or if his words were intended as a warning. I needed to see his eyes more clearly to know for certain.

"Anyways," Frenchy went on, "you and me, we're gonna need that body just a bit longer. It's still got a few things it kin tell us." He was keeping his voice soft and even, trying not to sound like he was giving orders, which of course he was. "First off, we gotta go out an' do a little pitchfork collectin', Samuel. See if we kin find one with tines that match up to the holes in that boy's chest."

I told him I had checked the pitchforks in the neighboring houses, but had found no traces of blood on any of them.

"Shit, Samuel, these folks out here may be country, but they ain't fools. A good wet rag an' a little elbow grease'd hide any blood ya could see with the eye." He gave me another knowing smile, and I found his smiles were suddenly beginning to annoy me. Frenchy spread the fingers of one hand and jabbed them toward my chest, as he continued his lecture. "But if we find us a pitchfork that matches the holes in that boy, we'll get us a good microscopic check at the university. Then we'll know fer sure."

"You seem convinced already that Royal was killed up here on the hill," I said.

Frenchy raised his eyebrows. "You got some doubts about that?"

I told him about someone wearing Royal's boots, and using the streambed to mask his trail. "Johnny Taft found Royal's truck about a quarter of a mile down the road, right where the stream turns and crosses it."

"So ya think somebody mighta carried him in all that way, huh?" Frenchy was pulling on his lower lip with his thumb and index finger, thinking that idea through.

"I don't know what I think." I shook my head, trying to emphasize my confusion. "It just seems it would be damned stupid for the folks who live here to kill a white man, then just leave his body out in the open like that on their own land. Especially with bird hunters prowling every stand of wood they can find."

"An' poachin' the odd deer, too," Frenchy added as an afterthought. He thought about that some more. "Yeah, I see yer point." He scratched his head again. "What about this boy, Abel Turner, who found the body? Odd how he found his friend that way."

I shook my head. "I don't think Abel would have the guts to kill anyone."

Frenchy laughed. "Funny ya put it that way. I talked to Abel, too. He was with Preserved at Doc's office." Another small laugh that died almost immediately. "Seems he don't think much of you either.

Tol' me if it wasn't one of the nigs that killed Royal, it coulda been you that done it."

I felt myself stiffen, and wondered it Frenchy had noticed. "He say why?"

Frenchy shook his head. "Didn't seem ta wanna talk around the dead boy's daddy." He tapped his head with one finger. "But I made myself a little note. Gonna talk ta him again, when Preserved ain't around."

I stared hard at Frenchy for several seconds. "That make me a suspect in your book, Frenchy?"

He gave me a hard slap on the shoulder. "Hell no, Samuel. Leastways no more'n anybody else. The only person I know fer sure didn't do it is me." He gave me an exaggerated wink. "But I'm the kinda cop who likes ta let folks talk. An' ya know what? I found that when folks starts makin' accusations agin other folks, they sometimes gets carried away, an' end up shinin' a light right back on theyselves. So I'm jus' gonna give that boy a chance to talk hisself out."

I didn't believe a word Frenchy was saying, but there was nothing I could do to stop him. "What do you need from me right now?" I asked.

"Well, first off, I don't want you to think I'm just rollin' in here an' takin' this investigation away from you. I'm here ta help, even though I expect I got the right to supersede you in this." He waved a dismissive hand. "But that's all bullshit, anyways. So, right now, what I'd like is to drink some coffee back at yer place 'til the sun's up a bit. Then I'd like to get that Johnny Taft outta bed an' have him take us through the crime scene as best he kin. Then maybe we'll talk to some folks an' look at some pitchforks. How's that sound to ya?"

He watched me nod agreement. At that moment I didn't want to speak. I was trying to hide all the terrors that were racing through me, and I was afraid what my voice might betray.

"'Course ya might be too tired," Frenchy added quickly. "Ya get *any* sleep las' night?" Before I could answer he raced on. "I could jus' go out with Johnny Taft alone, if ya need yer rest."

It was the last thing I wanted. "I'll be fine," I said, struggling with each word. "And I'd like to go with you. Sort of make up for all the mistakes I made today."

Frenchy clapped me on the back. "Well that's good, then. Let's go get us some coffee."

Dawn was sending its faint pink glow through my kitchen windows. Frenchy had just gone out to his car. He was headed out to pick up Johnny Taft, then would swing back to get me, before we all headed on up to Nigger Hill.

I needed the time to look in on my father, who I had already heard moving about his bedroom at the rear of the house. My father had suffered a stroke five years ago, and though ambulatory, still had difficulty dressing and getting his own meals with but one fully functioning arm.

I gathered the coffee cups Frenchy and I had used and put them in the sink, then poured a fresh cup the way my father liked it, and moved to the rear of the house as quietly as I could, just in case he had fallen back asleep. I eased the door open and stepped inside. A single bedside lamp lighted the room, and I could see my father's eyes staring back at me. He was seated in the wingback chair we had moved in from the parlor when his illness had restricted his ability to move about the house. He was somewhat better now, and did go from room to room when necessary. Still, most of his time was spent in this room he had shared with my mother until her death, and the walls were filled with family photographs, some dating back four generations, all of it seeming to provide him with some unacknowledged sense of comfort.

I put the coffee on the table next to the chair, then knelt in front of him and began buttoning the shirt and trousers he had already pulled about his body. He was frail now at sixty, the stroke having drained his body of the bulk and strength I had known since childhood. The left side of his face drooped badly, the muscles no longer able to respond, and it turned each expression, be it smile or frown, into little more than a grimace.

"How are you feeling this morning?" I asked. I reached up and combed my fingers through his now-white hair, straightening its nocturnal dishevelment as best I could.

"I hear'd somebody in the kitchen." His words had become badly slurred after the stroke, but over the years I had learned to understand him with only occasional difficulty.

"It was Frenchy LeMay," I said. "We've had a killing."

"Tell me 'bout it."

Before infirmity had taken his body, my father, Arriah Bradley, had served as the town's constable for most of his adult life. Then the job, though unwanted, had fallen to me. But this unexpected event had served a purpose, allowing me to remain in Jerusalem's Landing to care for him.

I told him what had happened, leaving out very little, and watched his eyes darken with concern as the tale progressed. My father has a large head, with a broad nose and heavy lips, a poker face some have called it, but to me his eyes have always revealed what little emotion he would allow the world to see. We look nothing alike. I always favored my mother. Yet we do possess the same propensity to keep our feelings secret.

"They gonna blame the folks on the hill," he said, when I had finished.

I nodded. "That's already started. Preserved Firman is shooting off his mouth about Jehiel being the one killed his son."

My father snorted. "Preserved won't be yer problem. He's a fool, an' a outright sumbitch racist. An' ever'body knows it. It won't be hard ta see what he's up ta." He turned his head and stared at me with his one good eye. "It's t'other folks gonna give ya trouble, Samuel." He shook his head. "Ya best let Frenchy handle this. He's a good man. I worked with him many a time."

I took the coffee cup from the table and placed it in his hand, holding it until I was sure it was steady. "I can't do that," I said.

He stared at me a long time, and I thought I could see regret in his eyes. "I know ya don't wanna. But it be best if ya do." He turned his head to the photographs that lined the wall next to his bed, his eyes settling on the ancient sepia picture of my great-grandmother, Isabel Stewart. Her soft countenance stared out into the room, her broad, Negro features prominent against a starched white collar and wide-brimmed hat.

My father drew a long breath. "Folks ain't gonna forget that yer bleached, Samuel. Not now. Not when they 'spect that them that lives on the hill done this killin'." He reached out and took my arm. "Yer great-grandma's birth certificate said she was a Negro. My daddy's said he was a Negro. And mine says I'm colored." He shook his head vehemently. "But not yers, Samuel. Yers says you is white, 'cause that's the rule. You is third generation, an' according to the rule after three generations the mixed blood is gone, an' the children is white agin." His good eye hardened. "But not ta the folks here. Ta them you is a bleached nigger, an' always will be."

"I can't help what they think, Daddy."

My father let go of my arm, closed his eyes and took another deep breath. He took time to sip his coffee, then lowered the cup to his lap. "Then all I can tell ya is ta be careful, Samuel. Don't ya be trustin' nobody. Nobody a'tall."

(4)

Frenchy pulled the car to the side of the road next to the sign that marked the edge of Jehiel Flood's farmland. He stretched his neck, made a show of reading the sign, then let out a small chuckle.

"Beulah Hill, huh? I take it Mr. Flood ain't partial to the name Nigger Hill."

Johnny Taft snorted from the rear seat. "Jehiel Flood ain't partial to much of nothin'. Leastways nothin' I ever hear'd of."

Frenchy bent forward squinting at the sign. "What's that writ underneath?" he asked.

I leaned out the passenger window and read the small script meticulously printed beneath the name. *"Thy land shall be called Beulah; for the Lord delighteth in Thee. Isaiah, 62:4."* I fought off a smile. "I suspect Elisha Bowles added that. Jehiel's not much for quoting scripture."

Frenchy slapped the steering wheel with his palm. "I like it. With the scripture, or without." He nodded his head sharply, as if confirming his approval. "I like the man's grit. It ain't very neighborly. But it sure is a right clever way to tell a whole town to go to hell."

"Jehiel's never been shy about doing that," I said.

"Oh, I know it," Frenchy said. "I met up with old Jehiel back when yer daddy was constable. Seems somebody had shot a dog that was runnin' deer up on this here hill, an' the owner—feller lived down Addison Holler—claimed it was Jehiel Flood done it. Also claimed yer daddy wouldn't take no action agin' him, 'cause yer daddy was a nig, too, which is how it got to be sheriff's bizness."

"So what happened?" I asked, ignoring the accusation against my father. It was not the first time I had heard such a thing.

"Nothin'. Leastways not about the dog bein' shot. Your daddy an' me went up to Jehiel's farm an' tol' him what the feller said." Frenchy shook his head and grinned. "Well, he jus' laughed at us, Jehiel did. Then he tol' yer daddy he didn't need his friends bringin' no white sheriffs up to his house. An' then he looked me in the eye an' tol' me to get my lily-white ass off'n his land."

"So what'd you do?" Johnny asked.

Frenchy glanced back at Johnny and wiggled his bushy eyebrows. "I got my lily-white ass off'n the man's land." He nodded toward me and let out a short, barking laugh. "An' now look where Samuel, here, done brung me."

We drove in to Jehiel's dooryard, and our arrival sent Jeffords Page scurrying away from the woodpile he'd been working and straight for the barn like a scared rabbit. No sooner were we out of the car then Jehiel and his boy, Prince, came out of the barn, Winchesters in hand.

"Don't think yer gonna need them rifles," Frenchy called, a big grin spread across his face. "We jus' here to ask a couple a questions, an' poke roun' yer land a bit iff'n you'll let us."

Jehiel leaned his Winchester against the barn and walked over. "Maybe you'll do some pokin' an' maybe you won't," he said, his patois firmly in place. He looked Frenchy up and down. "Didn't I throw you off'n my land a few years back?" he asked.

"Ya surely did," Frenchy said. "But I'm hopin' ya won't do it agin.

What brings me here this time is a bit more worrisome than a shot-up dog."

Jehiel nodded. "Sorry 'bout the rifles," he said. "Jeffords jus' came runnin', sayin' all nervous like, how some white men drove up. We bein' a mite careful of white men right about now."

"From what I hear, that makes good sense," Frenchy said. "But Samuel an' me, we're just up here lookin' to find us a couple of things."

Frenchy was wearing a big smile, trying to butter Jehiel up, get him ready for the notion that we'd like to take a look at any pitchforks in his barn. I could tell Jehiel knew what was happening. There was an amused glint in his eye, one he might give some drummer who happened by with a load of snake oil or lightning rods.

He gave Frenchy his own toothy grin. "Well now, why don't you tell me what you're tryin' to find. Might be I kin save you some time."

Jehiel's patois was thick, syrupy. Frenchy nodded. He knew the man had his number, that there'd be no outfoxing this fox. He threw me a glance, as if to say he'd done his best.

Frenchy placed his hands on his hips and turned serious. "Well, sir, we're lookin' fer two things right now. First we're lookin' fer pitchforks, so's we kin measure the distance between the tines. We come up with one that matches the wounds on young Royal Firman's chest, we're gonna want ta take it in and have it examined at the university. Next—"

"Seems to me you'd be needin' a warrant, or some kinda court paper," Jehiel said. "Also seems likely any judge you might be askin' fer one jus' might want some answers b'fore he gives it. Answers like, what makes you think yer gonna find the pitchfork done kilt that boy up cheer on Beulah Hill? Aside from the fact that colored folks lives here, that is."

Frenchy shook his head. "Color's got nothin' ta do with it, Mr. Flood." He was forced to wait as Jehiel's barking laughter interrupted him again. "Leastways not to us," he added.

"I'm real glad to hear it." Jehiel glanced at me and shook his head. It was as if he was asking if I, too, thought he was stupid enough to believe that.

"If you say we need a warrant, we'll get one," I said. "Same goes for Elizabeth's place, and Jefford's and Reverend Elisha's." I paused, toeing the ground with my boot. "Right now, though, I got myself a problem. I got Preserved Firman and Abel Turner going around town saying somebody up on the hill killed Royal. And if we have to get a warrant to look for the murder weapon, well, folks might start believing that somebody up here used the time to make sure that pitchfork never was found." Jehiel started to snort, and I raised my hand against it. "But if I can go back and say that all the folks up here just said, 'Go ahead and look,' well, then, it might be—"

"It might be they'll jus' say we done hid that pitchfork already," Jehiel snapped.

I nodded. "I suppose that's possible, too."

Jehiel let out another snort. "Go look fer yer damned pitchfork. You kin look in my barn; you kin go look under my damned bed iff'n ya want. Same goes fer Jeffords's cabin. An' you kin tell 'Lizabeth I said she should let you look there, too."

"We're obliged," Frenchy said.

Jehiel grunted in reply. "I'll have Prince light ya up a lantern so's you kin look in the dark corners, too. We ain't got no 'lectricity on Beulah Hill. They's had it in town fer five years now. Telephones, too. But they ain't managed to get none of it to no colored folks." He sneered at Frenchy, as if the absence of electricity and telephones proved something.

"Seems like I read someplace that only sixteen percent of the farms all across the state got 'lectricity," Frenchy said.

Jehiel glared at him. He wasn't buying any of it. "You said you was up cheer lookin' fer two things. You tol' me what the first one is. What's the second?"

"Royal Firman's hat," Frenchy said. "Man don't go out without a hat. Leastways not any that I knows. An' they sure as hell don't go in the woods without one."

I felt a sudden sense of shock. I hadn't noticed the absence of a hat. I glanced at Johnny Taft, asking with my eyes if he'd come across one while searching the woods for tracks. Johnny shook his head.

"Sounds right reasonable," Jehiel said. "'Course it don't prove nothin'. 'Cept maybe that somebody took that hat and put it some-place, jus' to make it look like that boy was kilt in a certain place."

"That's always a possibility. Yes, indeed," Frenchy said. "But I'll take some convincin' on that. You see, I think somebody forgot that hat when they kilt Royal Firman. I do believe, we find that boy's hat, we found us the place where he was kilt."

Jeffords Page began dancing from one foot to the other. Then he began shaking his head back and forth. "No, sir. No, sir. I ain't gots no hat. No, no, no, no. I ain't. I ain't."

I took a step toward him and reached out for his arm, hoping to calm him. But he turned and raced out behind the barn and into the woods.

We found pitchforks at every house except the cabin where Jeffords Page lived. But, then, there was no reason to find one there, since Jeffords kept no livestock, or hay to feed them. None of the pitch-forks we did find matched the wounds on Royal's body. Frenchy theorized that the murder weapon had been an old pitchfork, one where the tines were spaced farther apart. He noted that the one we found in Elizabeth's barn appeared to be new. He said he planned to return and talk to her about it after she got home from teaching school. He invited me to come along. We also failed to find Royal's hat, nor did we again see Jeffords Page.

Frenchy seemed unconcerned that Jeffords had run away. Nor was he concerned that talk of Royal's hat had seemed to spook him.

"The boy's addled," he had said. "Mighta thought we was talkin' about some old hat of his, or God knows what. Boy just could put two an' two together an' come up with five, then figgered that would make us think he done the killin'. Never can tell with folks that's simple. When we find him, maybe we'll find out what it was all about." He had shrugged. "An' maybe we'll never find out."

I stopped at Shepard's Country Store and U.S. Post Office to get my father a pack of Lucky Strike cigarettes. The store is one of two in town. It sits next to Doc Hawley's office, and is only five doors down from my own home.

I had left Frenchy at Abigail Pierce's boarding house, where he had taken a room, with plans to meet up with him at four in the afternoon. During the intervening hours, Frenchy would drive back into Burlington to attend Royal's autopsy, and I intended to get some sleep to make up for my previous late night.

"You look tired, Samuel," Hannah Shepard said from behind the counter, as if reading my thoughts.

Hannah, though only nineteen, was in charge of the store. Her mother, Victorious, ran the post office in the back, and her father, Simeon, operated a barbershop in an adjoining building. Thus was Shepard's Store the true heart of the town, its pulse, as Doc Hawley was known to say.

Hannah was smiling as she handed me the cigarettes. "You know your father shouldn't smoke those," she said. "Doc says it's probably what caused his stroke in the first place."

"What brand does Doc smoke?" I asked.

Hannah laughed. "Old Gold," she said. "A little over two packs a day."

Hannah's eyes were dancing with mischief. She wasn't a beautiful young woman, but her eyes and her smile made her seem so. At least to me. I had only come to notice her in the past year or two, after she graduated from high school and started to work in the store full-time. Hannah is small and slender, with light brown hair that is usually tied back in a bun, and it makes her face more severe than her nature warrants. But her eyes soften it, light brown and filled with expectation, and her smile, which she favored me with now, lights up everything around her.

Perhaps it seems odd I should be so taken with a mere smile.

But, despite the photographs found in most auto repair shops and garages, country women seldom have even, white, flashing teeth. They are often buxom as depicted. Sometimes even alluring in their way. But more often than not, their teeth are crooked, or broken, or gone missing in spots. Dental care in the hills and mountains and farmlands is not easily obtained.

"It's terrible about Royal Firman," Hannah said. She wasn't smiling now, and her eyes had stopped dancing. She lowered her voice close to a whisper, even though I was the only customer. "I never much liked him. I always thought he was sorta mean-spirited." She bit her lip. "Oh, God, I shouldn't say that. The poor man not even in his grave yet. Why do you think they done it?"

"Who?" I asked.

"The folks up there on . . . on . . . well, you know."

Hannah never used the name Nigger Hill with me, though I had never asked her not to.

"We don't know who did it," I said. Out of the corner of my eye, I could see Hannah's mother, Victorious, listening intently from her place behind the post office window at the rear of the store. "All we know, right now, is that Royal was carried to the place we found him after he was already dead."

Victorious came forward. "I've got yer mail here, Samuel," she said. She extended her hand, offering up three envelopes. Normally, Victorious would let me get my own mail from the wall of lockboxes in the back of the store. In fact, I could not recall her ever bringing it to me. I took the envelopes and glanced at each one. They were all bills.

I looked up and waited for what would come next, knowing what she was after. Victorious was a small, wiry sort of woman, who lacked her daughter's gentle eyes and transforming smile. Perhaps she had them once, only to have them killed off by time and trouble. Or, perhaps, she had never had them at all.

"Ya look exhausted, Samuel." Echoes of her daughter's words. "This terrible killing musta kept ya up all night."

I nodded, gave her a small smile, and waited for more.

"I must say, I'm surprised there ain't been an arrest yet. Abel Turner was in this mornin' an' made it sound pretty much cut and dry."

"I guess we're lucky then that Abel isn't running the investigation."

"What's that supposed ta mean?" Her voice had become sharp now, borderline critical. "That boy was killed up on Nigger Hill, wasn't he?"

As with her daughter, I had never asked Victorious not to use that name with me. But if I had it would not have made any difference. To most folks in town, it was the name of the road, period. Regretfully, I often used it myself.

I gave Victorious a noncommittal shrug. "It doesn't mean anything in particular," I said. "We know that Abel found the body. And we know where he found it up on the hill. We also know from the physical evidence that Royal was carried to that place after he was dead. What we don't know yet is where he was killed, and Abel tells us he wasn't with him when it happened. Leastways that's what he says." I dropped in the last out of pure meanness, and to give Victorious—and everyone she would tell—something to chew on. My effort succeeded. Victorious looked at me wide-eyed, her mouth formed into a small, shocked circle. I feigned not to notice, looking instead at Hannah as I continued.

"So, no matter what Abel thinks, until we find out where this killing happened, we're still a way from knowing who the killer might be."

"But how ever will you find that out? It coulda been anywheres." Hannah seemed genuinely mystified by the investigative process.

"Deputy LeMay is hoping the autopsy will point us toward the place it happened." I dropped in Frenchy's name to give my assertions authority.

"But what can that tell you?" Hannah asked. "I thought it only told you *why* someone died." She, too, was now wide-eyed.

"Actually, it'll tell us quite a bit more," I explained. "It will tell when he last ate. What he ate. What was under his fingernails. How much blood was lost at the scene of the killing. Maybe even whether the person who killed him was right-handed or left-handed. What was on his clothing and shoes. Or if there were any hairs or cloth fibers left on his body by the person who carried him into the woods. If he was . . . with someone before he died—"

"You mean if he had sex with someone?" Hannah asked, stopping me.

"Hannah!" Victorious snapped out her daughter's name, then caught hold of herself. "All this talk about killin'. It's more'n we need." She shook her head, then brushed back a gray strand of hair that had fallen across her forehead. "Besides, you've got inventory ta do, ta see what stock needs replaced."

Hannah fought off a smile, then excused herself and hurried off. Victorious glared at me.

"I'm sorry, Victorious." I tried to give truth to the lie with a look of pained regret. "I'm just so tired I wasn't thinking about what I was saying," I added.

"She's a young girl, Samuel. Too young fer such talk." Her piercing blue eyes were still hard on me, and the lines around her mouth seemed to have deepened. Victorious was only a few years past forty, but she was a severe woman, and looked ten or fifteen years older.

I knew exactly what she meant. I also knew it wasn't just my words that concerned her. "I best be going," I said. "I want to look in on my father."

"How is Arriah?" she asked.

"Poorly," I said.

"I'm sorry ta hear it."

I nodded my thanks. Perhaps she was.

My father was asleep when I arrived home. Since his stroke he slept through most afternoons, said he was practicing for all the time he'd spend in his grave.

I left the pack of Lucky Strikes on his nightstand, then went upstairs to my own room at the other end of the house, stripped off my clothes and was asleep as soon as I lay down. I didn't awaken until I felt her body slip into bed next to me.

Hannah ran her fingers across my chest and stomach, then began to stroke me until I grew hard.

"I like to feel you get big in my hand," she whispered.

Her breath smelled sweet and fresh. I started to turn toward her, but she was unwilling to wait, and she pushed me back and climbed on top of me. Hannah had undone her hair, and it lay loosely about her shoulders. The low, pleasure-filled moan that came from her now seemed almost feral, and she closed her eyes and rolled her head back, sending her hair flying behind her. Then her head came forward again, as she hunched her body over mine, her hair falling between us like a veil.

"Oh, God, I've wanted this ever since you walked in the store today." Her body stiffened momentarily, and she began to thrust her hips forward and back. "Oh, God. God. God. Oh, Samuel, please. Please. Give me all of you, Samuel. Every last bit. Please, Samuel, please."

We lay beside each other, Hannah's head cradled in the notch of my shoulder, her breath soft and steady, almost like the purr of a cat. I felt dreamy and drowsy and ready to sleep again, and I fought against it. If Hannah and I fell asleep in my bed there would be hell to pay.

"Where does your mother think you are?" I asked. I pictured Victorious Shepard's severe face and rigid body.

"I had ta deliver groceries to old Lucy Cornett. I'll just tell her I stayed to gossip a spell. Old Lucy won't remember whether I did or not."

"What if she comes looking for you?"

I felt Hannah wiggle against me, pleased by her own mischief. "I guess I made it so she couldn't," she said. She let out a small laugh. "I did what I do sometimes. I waited 'til Daddy had somebody in his barber chair, and somebody else waitin' before I left. When I do that Momma can't check up on where I'm at. She can't leave the store and post office with nobody watchin' them."

"If your mother knew you were here . . ."

"Oh, I know. She'd be madder'n a bee trapped under a bucket. But she still wouldn't let herself think I was doin' anything. She'd just tell herself I was thinking about bein' with you, and then she'd give me another one of her lectures about how I'll end up havin' jiggaboo babies if I'm not careful." Hannah raised herself on one elbow and looked down at me. "You think that's true, Samuel? You think that if somebody's got some Negro blood in them—even though they's as white as you, and that blood is way, way back—you think they can still make babies that're black or brown?"

I stroked her arm. The question was pure innocence; the product of an unrecognized prejudice learned since childhood. I smiled to myself. There was no risk of jiggaboo babies, or of any other kind. I had spilled my seed outside her, as I always did, as I did with any woman I was with. All of it in deference to my sexual hero—Onan, son of Judah, struck dead by God in Genesis 38, when he refused to ejaculate into the womb of his brother's widow.

"I don't know about babies," I said. I smiled up at her. "I do know there are a lot of foolish stories attached to Negroes. When I was at the university, there was this time a Negro student had to pull his pants down at a fraternity party, just to show everybody he didn't have a tail."

I took her hand and placed it against my stomach, where the skin was lightest on my body, though still a half shade darker than her own very fair complexion. "You know Jehiel Flood's son pretty well, right? You and Prince were in school together."

Hannah nodded. "He's a real quiet boy. I don't know him real well."

"But you know him to be a dark-skinned Negro."

She nodded again.

"Do you think he's different from me?"

"Well, sure he's different."

"You think if I was that color, it would make me different?"

Hannah blinked several times. "I don't know, Samuel. I just never think about you bein' dark like that."

* * *

Elizabeth's cabin and her adjoining cottage were empty as I expected. Elizabeth was still at school, and Ruby and Maybelle were off tending to their house-cleaning jobs. I entered the cottage and went to the cabinet where Elizabeth stored her pictures. There were dozens upon dozens. The majority were drawings of the plants she used for her preparations, with careful notes written along the sides, explaining what they could be mixed with, and in what proportions, and the benefits that would result.

In the back of the cabinet I found the pictures I was looking for— Elizabeth's drawings of people. There were pictures of her entire family: Ruby and Maybelle, her brother, Prince, even several of Jeffords Page. I stopped at an astonishing drawing of Jehiel. The picture showed only his head and shoulders, yet it seemed to capture every nuance of the man, all his size and strength and ferocity, as well as the gentleness I had always seen hidden deep within his eyes. It pleased me that Elizabeth had seen it there as well. Sometimes children fail to see a parent's gentler side, or the parent keeps it too well concealed from them. Here, it was neither ignored nor hidden.

I flipped through several more drawings before I stopped again. There before me was a drawing of myself, full length, naked to the waist, my shirt dangling from one hand. It was a picture of how I had looked years ago, perhaps in my late teens, my body lean and wiry, my face thin, my eyes filled with far more innocence then they have known in years.

I glanced at the bottom right corner, where Elizabeth always signed and dated her drawings. Her name was there, along with the date: August 1932. It had been rendered little more than a year ago, yet it showed me as I had been at least a decade earlier. Perhaps the year before we had left for college. The time when we were lovers over that very short summer so long ago. I sat and stared, unable to put the drawing down for several minutes.

There were no pictures of Royal Firman. I checked other places in the cottage to be sure, but there was nothing to be found. I thought briefly about searching the main cabin, specifically Elizabeth's room, but that was an intrusion I was loath to make. Instead, I carefully returned everything to its place, hoping to fully mask my visit, then went out to get another more thorough look at Elizabeth's barn.

I first saw the moving figure out of the corner of my eye, but it wasn't until I turned to look more closely that I realized it was Jeffords Page. He was hunched over and scuttling back toward the stream along which Johnny Taft had searched for tracks.

I set out after him, moving as quietly as I could. I had no way of knowing if he had seen me entering or leaving Elizabeth's cabin, but I wanted to know so I could set my story if he spoke of it later. I also wanted to know why Jeffords was running as if the devil himself were in pursuit; what it was Frenchy had said that had so disturbed him.

When he crossed the stream he glanced back, and I knew for certain that he was aware of me. I was also reasonably sure he had been watching me for some time before he attempted to flee through the woods. Now there was no choice. I had to run him to ground and get him to tell me what he knew, everything he knew, even if I had to frighten the words out of him.

Jeffords was much younger than I, but fortunately he was built like a small ox and not very agile. On the other side of the stream the woods became thicker and harder to navigate, and it was there that I easily made up the distance between us. He was only ten yards ahead when we reached a small, natural clearing, and I put on a burst of speed and came up behind him. He was leaning forward as he ran, thrusting himself ahead to try to increase his own pace. I hit him with both hands squarely in the back, and he tumbled forward like a dislodged boulder and rolled to a stop in some fast-browning ferns.

I stood over him, breathing heavily, afraid he would rise and put up a fight. Jeffords is possessed of uncanny strength, something given him, no doubt, to make up for his feeble mind, and I did not want to fight with him. I pointed a finger at his face and let my other hand come to rest on the butt of my revolver. I had no intention of using it. I just wanted to intimidate the boy.

"You lay there and don't you move 'til I tell you," I snapped.

"Jeffords din' do nothin'. Din' do nothin'." He spoke about himself, as he sometimes did, as if the person he knew as Jeffords Page was another being altogether, someone outside his body. But he also did as I said and remained still, his eyes wide, going from my gun to my face and back again.

I kept my finger leveled at him, but let my other hand move off the pistol. "How long were you watching me back at Elizabeth's house?" He shook his head, and I moved my other hand closer to the gun. "Don't you lie to me," I snapped.

"Jus' fer a li'l bit. Tha's all." Jeffords's eyes were darting again, and his voice was shaky. "Seen ya go in ta da med'cine house, so's Jeffords wents up ta da window an' watch ya. Tha's all. Ya jus' sittin' there when he's lookin' in. Then ya gots up, and Jeffords runs off." He shook his head vigorously, then nodded, then shook his head again, all of it to no purpose. "Tha's all. Honest. Jeffords din' do nothin' bad. Din' see nothin' bad. Honest, suh. Nothin' bad a'tall."

I let my eyes rest hard on him. "It's a secret that I went inside the medicine house," I said. "It's part of a surprise for Elizabeth. And it would be bad to spoil that surprise for her. You think Jeffords can keep a secret and not say anything?"

"Don' wanna do nothin' bad ta 'Lizabeth. No, suh. Jeffords don' say nothin'. I promises."

"Not to anybody at all. I don't want you to say anything to anybody. You understand that?"

"Yes, suh. Jeffords understans good. Won' tell nobody, lessen ya sez so."

I squatted in front of him, bringing my face closer to his. I stared him square in the eyes, watching for any lie. "That's good, Jeffords. I know you want to do what's right, and what's best for Elizabeth.

Now there's something else you can do that'll help me. And it'll help Elizabeth, too. You gotta tell me why you ran away from Deputy LeMay and me this morning. What it was he said that scared you."

Jeffords pressed his arms against his sides as if trying to keep something inside his coat tight against his body. His hands began to twitch nervously and his eyes darted everywhere except my face.

"What is it, Jeffords?" I watched his arms press tighter against his sides until he appeared to be hugging himself. "Deputy LeMay was talking about pitchforks he wanted to look at, and about a hat he thought Royal Firman might have been wearing. And that's about when Jeffords ran off. Is that what scared you, Jeffords? Talk about pitchforks and that dead boy's hat?"

Jeffords began shaking his head. His mouth moved for several seconds before words actually formed. "Jeffords don't know nothin' 'bout dat stuff. No, suh, nothin' a'tall."

"But I think maybe you do." I raised my chin toward his arms clutched against his sides. "You got something inside that coat maybe I should see?"

Jeffords's eyes widened and his jaw clenched. He shook his head.

"Why don't you open up that coat for me?"

Jeffords scuttled back on the seat of his pants, then began to shift his weight as if preparing to rise quickly. I moved forward and grabbed his wrist.

"I want you to sit like I told you, Jeffords. We gotta talk this out. Just you and me. And I promise you, no harm's gonna come to you if you talk to me. You believe that?"

Jeffords nodded his head rapidly, but his eyes were fearful and filled with doubt.

"Did you hurt Royal Firman, Jeffords?"

He kept nodding his head, but I knew it meant nothing. "Jeffords doan hurt nobody," he said. "Jeffords prays fer people, jus' like the rev'rend tells him."

"Did you pray for Royal?"

"Yes, suh. I prays for him early this mornin'."

I drew a long breath, then tried again. "Did you pray for him the

night he died?" I could see confusion cloud the boy's eyes. Part of
his simplemindedness involved a complete absence of any sense of
time. Individual days meant nothing to Jeffords. One day simply
blended with the next, and an event that had occurred a week or a
month ago would be as real and immediate to him as something
that had happened that day.

"Did the Reverend Bowles ask you to pray for Royal after he
died?" I asked.

Jeffords smiled, as if suddenly pleased with himself, or perhaps
pleased he knew the answer to my question. "Rev'rend always asks
Jeffords ta pray fer folks," he said. "An' Jeffords does it. Jeffords always does jus' like the rev'rend says."

"Do you use candles when you pray?" I asked.

Jeffords nodded vigorously. "Oh, yes, suh. Jeffords always uses
'em when it dark outside. Ain't gots no 'lec-ticity up here on Beulah
Hill. White folks don' give no 'lec-ticity ta colored peoples, no suh."

Strains of Jehiel's preaching coming through the boy's mouth. I
just nodded agreement. I wanted to ask the boy if he had drawn
crosses on Royal's forehead; if he had sat up with Royal's body with
candles burning beside him. Most of all I wanted to ask if there had
been someone with him when all this happened. But I knew it was
useless. What Jeffords would say—perhaps all he could say—would
be a jumble of facts that could not be trusted as truth. And if I
pressed him, it would only make him run again.

"Jeffords, show me what's inside your coat," I said instead. He
pressed his arms tighter against his side, and I reached out and
stroked his arm. "It's all right," I said. "Nothing bad is going to
happen."

Slowly, reluctantly, the boy opened his coat. Stuffed in an interior
pocket I could make out the front half of a brown workman's cap—
the same kind I had seen Royal Firman wear. Royal had always
worn his rakishly cocked to one side of his head.

"Where'd you find that cap?" I kept my voice soft, nonthreatening.

The boy's eyes darted toward an area of woods that lay behind
Elizabeth's barn.

"What were you planning to do with it?"

Jeffords's eyes darted back and forth, avoiding mine.

"Tell me, Jeffords," I said.

He closed his coat and squeezed his arms tight against his body. "Gonna bury it," he said.

The words hit at me, and a half dozen questions I knew I should ask rushed to mind. Had he already buried the pitchfork? Was he planning to bury the cap in the same place? Had someone come to him after the killing and asked for his help, or had he been there when Royal Firman was killed? Had he gone to that person when he learned that Frenchy was also searching for Royal's hat? Had that someone told him to hide this evidence, too? And if so, most important, who was that someone? Just as quickly I realized I didn't want the answers. Not now. Not yet. I could find out those answers later if need be. I now knew whom to ask.

I handed Jeffords the cap.

"You go do what you have to do," I told him, then watched as Jeffords scrambled to his feet and hurried away to a deeper part of the woods.

(5)

"Deputy LeMay said ta tell ya he'll be down in a few minutes. He's jus' washin' up a bit." Abigail Pierce spoke the words as she struggled mightily to get herself down the stairs, one arm rigid on the banister to support her bulk.

She was a large woman, well over two hundred pounds on a five-foot-four-inch frame. When she reached the first-floor hall, where I sat waiting in a side chair, she stopped and placed one hand over her heart, as if the descent had somehow winded her and she needed to catch her breath.

"Lord almighty, these stairs'll be the death of me. You mark those words, Samuel. You just mark 'em down in yer book right now. Someday they'll be sendin' fer ya to come see how I up an' died right on these here stairs."

Abigail Pierce began fanning herself with one hand, as I fought down a smile. Abigail's rooming house, as it was more commonly known to locals, bore the grander name of the Jerusalem Hotel, and rightly boasted the best dinner table this side of Burlington. It was why Frenchy was staying here—on county money—rather than bunking in with me, and the real reason I would be called in one day to view Miss Pierce's body.

Abigail drew a long breath, signaling she had recovered from her ordeal, and took two waddling steps toward me, as she tugged at the sides of her blue flowered housedress, readjusting its position on her outsized hips.

"Now Samuel, I want to know somethin'," she began. "An' I want the truth about it."

"And what is that, ma'am?" I asked. Abigail was into her sixties, with a full head of gray hair sitting atop her round head. It had been gray like that as long as I could remember, well back to when I was a small boy, and even when I became an adult, and later a town official, I had never been able to accept her suggestion that I call her by her first name.

Abigail folded her hands over her large stomach and stared down at me with piercing blue eyes that looked like intelligent gooseberries. "I want to know when you are gonna arrest one of them colored men up on Nigger Hill, fer killin' that nice young Firman boy."

I studied my shoes for a moment, before looking back at her. One of my strongest memories of Abigail was back from when I was in my teens. She had come to my father to complain about Royal Firman, claiming he had deliberately spooked her horse, making it run off with her buggy, then had called her a "fat, old hag" when she had come after him with a switch.

"Any arrest that's made is really up to Deputy LeMay," I said. "And right now I don't think he figures we've got enough evidence to arrest anyone."

"Well, Preserved Firman is goin' around sayin' that you is stoppin' any arrest from bein' made. An' that boy, Abel Turner, who found the body, is sayin' the same thing."

"And do they say why I would be doing such a thing?" I asked. I knew the answer well enough. I just wanted to force her to say it.

"Well, they's sayin' . . ." She grew suddenly flustered as the words she would be forced to speak formed in her mind. A clever businesswoman, a fact supported by the money that allegedly filled her mattress, Abigail was no fool, even though she often acted like one. She stuttered momentarily. "Well . . . well . . . well, Samuel, you know what they's sayin' the reason is. It ain't like you never hear'd it before."

I nodded. "Yes, ma'am. That is true. But it seems to me that just saying it doesn't make it so."

Abigail seemed jarred by the statement. She stared at me for a moment, then let out a huff of air. "Well, I suppose that's one way to look at it," she snapped, then spun on her heel and headed back down the hall. "Gotta go check on my dinner," she said as I watched her move away. "Deputy LeMay will be down in a minute like I said."

"You shouldn't of hit that boy, Samuel."

I glared at Elizabeth. "He called my great-grandma a nigger slave, didn't he? Said his kin owned her way back, didn't he?" She looked down at the ground and remained silent. "Well, it's a lie," I snapped.

Elizabeth didn't speak all the way up Nigger Hill. She carried her books pressed against her chest, and her eyes remained away from mine. When we turned into her dooryard she glanced quickly at me and whispered: "I'm sorry he hurt your feelings, Samuel."

Jehiel came across the yard, massive and strong and towering over me like some great brown mountain. "Why you wearin' that long face, Samuel?" he called as he drew closer. "You look like you jus' lost the best huntin' dog you ever had."

I refused to answer, and just stared straight ahead. Jehiel turned to Elizabeth and raised his eyebrows.

"A boy said something bad about Samuel's great-grandma, and he had to fight him."

Elizabeth had phrased her words in the most positive way possible, and I felt instant gratitude. I gave her a long thankful look as Jehiel took my arm and led me to a stump he used to split firewood. Then he sat so we were eye to eye.

"You know I know'd your great-grandma real well. And she was a

fine lady who wouldn't want her kin goin' around fightin' with folks. Now, who's this boy you had to fight, 'cause he said somethin' bad about her?" he asked.

I studied the toes of my shoes. "Royal Firman," I said.

Jehiel put his finger under my chin and raised my eyes to his. "Seems ta me that boy is about seven years old, maybe in the second grade?" He waited while I nodded my head. "And you is nine, just like 'Lizabeth, am I right?"

"Yessir."

Jehiel held my eye. "Don't seem like much of a fair fight, Samuel."

I drew a deep breath to push away the tears I felt welling up in my eyes. "He said my great-granny was a nigger slave, and that his kinfolk owned her, and that's a damned lie."

My voice was almost hysterical, and Jehiel placed his hand on my back and began to rub gently. "Well, that boy sure deserved a lickin', no question about that. I hope you whomped him right upside the head."

"I did." I drew a deep breath. "I made his nose bleed all over his shirt."

Jehiel pulled me toward him and squeezed my shoulders between his two huge hands. "That's good. 'Cause nobody got the right to say nothin' bad about Isabel Stewart. She was a fine woman, and a lady all her life."

I smiled and began nodding my head rapidly. "And they taught us in school that Vermont never was no slave state, that we had the underground railroad, and all kinds of good folks helpin' the slaves that run away."

Jehiel looked off toward the road and began rubbing my back again. "That is true, Samuel. Your teacher told you true when she said it." He paused a long minute, then again took my shoulders between his hands. "But there was slaves here, Samuel."

I stared at him, and he smiled regretfully at the disblief he saw in my face. "Oh, you couldn't trade slaves here, that's true enough," he said. "They didn't allow nobody to buy an' sell people like they did in the South. But if you already owned slaves, and then moved here, well, you was allowed ta keep 'em. The gov'ment said they was propity, just like any other propity. Like a goddamn mule. Far as the gov'ment was concerned, them people, they was the same thing."

Bitterness had crept into Jehiel's voice, and I could not be certain if it was bitterness over the fact that things had been that way, or that he was now forced to tell me that they had.

"They did have a law here that said all slaves had ta be set free when they was growed. For women it happened when they was sixteen, and for men, when they was eighteen."

I stared at Jehiel for a long time before I could speak again. "And what about my great-granny?" I finally asked.

The muscles along Jehiel's jaw danced wildly. When he turned to me his voice was the softest I'd ever heard it. "Your great-grandma Isabel was sixteen when she was set free by Amos Firman, the man who'd owned her since she was just a youngin'. That very same day your great-grandaddy, Elias Bradley, went and asked her to marry him. And on that day Isabel Stewart started a new life as a free woman."

"Why . . . why didn't anybody . . . tell me?"

Jehiel let his hands fall from my shoulders. "Sometimes they's things folks ain't partial to talk about. Even when they should."

I stared at Jehiel for a long time. My legs felt leaden, and my stomach was shaking so violently that for a moment I feared I might be sick. Then my body suddenly seemed to float free, as if it was telling me to run from that place, run as fast and as far as I could, and I turned and raced into the woods, my eyes so clouded by tears that all before me was hidden by a great mist.

I don't know how far I ran before I fell to the ground sobbing, or how long I remained there before Elizabeth was at my side. I felt her arms around me, and her cheek pressed against my shoulder, and when I looked at her I could see her own tears coursing down her cheeks.

My chest heaved as I spoke. The words were ragged and broken by sobs, barely distinguishable even to my own ears. "I . . . don't wanna . . . be colored. I don't . . . I don't. I'm white . . . white as snow . . . Look at me, Elizabeth . . . I'm as white . . . as a boy can be."

* * *

"You get yerself any sleep this afternoon, son?"

I looked up at Frenchy as he lumbered down the stairs. "I did, indeed. Not nearly what I would have liked. But enough to keep me going."

Frenchy gave me a look of mock severity. "Still beats all hell out of a formaldehyde-stinkin' morgue, I'm thinkin'. But I'm glad yer a touch rested. Now we kin be gettin' ourselves back to work. I believe that schoolteacher you're smittin with jus' might be home by now, an' I sure do wanna talk to her."

I drove my Model A up on the hill once again, bouncing along wagon ruts that would only worsen by next spring. Then the runoff of melting snow would turn the road into a mire that would grab wheels in a steel-like grip and make travel impossible to all but a rider on horseback. But not today. Today there was only a bone-jarring bounce on an otherwise perfect, clear autumn day. I studied it now. It was a beauty I had failed to notice earlier. There was a cloudless sky so blue it seemed to jump out at you, and the air was crisp and clean, the hillside rich in ever-deepening autumn colors.

"I do believe we might have early snow this year," Frenchy said, spoiling my reverie. "Seems to me the leaves have turned a bit early, an' the air's got a bit of a bite to 'er."

"It's the way we like our autumns here," I said. "You're just used to Burlington. The elevation's higher in Jerusalem's Landing, so the leaves turn a bit sooner, and we get a touch more snap in the air come October."

Frenchy let out a barking laugh. "You tryin' ta tell me I'm a city boy, son?" He let out a snort. "Hell, I've stepped in more cowshit than you've smelt."

I threw him a sideways look. "You've shoveled more, that's known to be a fact for sure."

Frenchy was still chuckling to himself as we drove by Jehiel's sign. He jabbed a finger at it. "Love that sign," he said. "Beulah Hill. That colored man's got boulders for balls. He does, indeed."

I had been waiting for Frenchy to fill me in on Royal's autopsy, but as yet had not heard a word about it.

"I hope you're gonna talk to me about that postmortem you were at," I finally said as we passed Elijah's homestead.

"Was you interested in that?" Frenchy said, all innocence. "You shoulda said somethin'." He turned in his seat so he was facing me. "Pretty much cut an' dried. Just like Doc Hawley thought. Pitchfork to the chest did him a mortal blow. The one to the belly came first, so he did lay there and suffer before the killer put him outta his misery. Right-handed, the killer was," he added. He turned his head away from me and studied the passing woods as if the answer to some question might lie there. Then he continued. "Nothin' much under his fingernails, 'ceptin' dirt. But you'd expect that with a boy worked in the woods. He hadn't ate nothin' since breakfast, an' that was just a fair amount of porridge. Poor man's food fer a poor man's time, I guess you'd say."

I pulled the car into Elizabeth's dooryard and brought it to a stop.

"Oh, yeah," Frenchy said, as we climbed out of the car. "There was one other thing. Autopsy showed the boy had hisself some sex just before he cashed in. Real close to the time, in fact. Doc who did the autopsy said there weren't a damned sperm left in his whole body."

Elizabeth greeted us with a wide smile that seemed to radiate out from the cabin like a sunburst.

"Why Deputy LeMay, it's been so long since I've seen you," Elizabeth began. "I think I must have been a girl, still living at home when you last stopped by."

"I believe yer right," Frenchy said. "I was just talkin' about this mornin' with your daddy. Just ain't that much crime up in these parts. Leastways not enough that yer constable, here, needs the sheriff's office to come an' help. But that means I don't get to see you folks much as I'd like. 'Specially beautiful young women like yerself."

Elizabeth offered a faint, girlish smile to the compliment. I stood watching them both, each an actor in a private play. Elizabeth, as I well knew, was good at playing a role. It was a talent she had nurtured even as a child. But Frenchy was a master. He reminded me of the tale about the fox and a crow, a fable my mother often read to me. "Oh, what a beautiful singing voice you have," said the fox, licking his lips, as he waited for the cluster of grapes to fall from the crow's beak.

Still, Elizabeth was not so easily fooled. "So you're here about the killing," she said, then lowered her eyes to add a touch of sadness to her words.

Frenchy nodded. "I'm afraid the killin' is what we got to talk about."

Elizabeth let out a long breath that seemed to imply a great sadness, then led us into her cabin. Her gramophone was playing a Delta Blues record, featuring Gene Austin's "How Come You Do Me Like You Do." She raised the needle so the sound didn't interfere with our talk.

We sat at the dining table as she got us coffee from the wood cookstove that stood nearby. When she seated herself across from us, Frenchy gave her a broad smile.

"I hear'd in town that Royal Firman used to come up here fer the potions you're known to make fer folks."

My head snapped around at Frenchy's words. Like the details of the autopsy, this bit of information was something else he had held back on.

Elizabeth returned his smile in full innocence. Her eyelids fluttered. "He came here mostly for his father, I believe."

Now it was Frenchy's turn to show surprise. "Preserved sent to you fer potions?"

Elizabeth smiled again. "Not openly. I think that would have been difficult for Preserved—to come to a Negro for help." She took time to sip her coffee, then continued. "Royal always said the medicine was for him. But the potions were for problems of the joints and muscles, and I always doubted a young man like Royal would be so afflicted."

Frenchy had set his hat on the table beside him. Now he pushed it away with his elbow to make room for the pad he had withdrawn from a pocket. He jotted down some notes with a stub of a pencil.

"Where'd ya learn this medicine-makin' talent?" he asked.

"I was taught by Mary Running Deer. She was an Abenaki woman who lived on the hill during the winters. In the summers she migrated to her tribe's hunting and fishing grounds in Quebec. One year she went away and never returned. We assumed she had died.

Frenchy scratched his head with the pencil stub. "I seem to remember her," he said. "Wasn't there talk 'bout yer daddy bein' sweet on her?"

Elizabeth looked at me and laughed. "There was, indeed. Fact is, Samuel and I used to follow him when he would go calling on her. It was years after my mother had passed on, and then one day we saw him headed down the road with some wildflowers he had picked. He caught sight of us sneaking along behind him, and took after us with a stick." She laughed again, enjoying the memory. "Almost caught Samuel when he tripped and fell. After that we followed him every time. But we did it from the woods instead of the road."

Frenchy nodded, patient with her memories. "Folks in town say yer known fer makin' love potions, an' maybe even some that kin be used against an enemy."

Elizabeth gave him another broad, beaming smile that seemed to light the room. "Mary Running Deer did teach me a love potion, but I always suspected it would work only if the person using it expected it to work, and the person it was used on knew it was being employed. Somewhat more of a psychological potion in that respect." She cocked her head to one side, almost like a bird studying a bug it might like to eat. "As far as the other potion you mentioned, the people you spoke with have it a bit backwards. Actually, it's a bundle of herbs worn about the neck in a small pouch. It's supposed to ward off evil wished on you by another."

Elizabeth paused a moment as we both continued to watch her, each of us somehow knowing there was more to come. Then she reached inside her bodice and withdrew a small, deerhide pouch, held about her neck by a slender, dark cord. She raised it delicately between her thumb and index finger, then mischievously extended it toward Frenchy and shook it.

"Oh, you don't need ta scare off no evil from these here quarters," Frenchy said. He gave her a wink. "I'm just stumblin' along, lookin' fer a few answers. Once't I got 'em I'll know what needs to be done."

"I'm happy to help you, Deputy."

He reached across the table and patted her hand. "I know you are," he said. "And please call me Frenchy. Makes me uncomfortable ta hear that 'Deputy' alla time."

The beginning of a coy smile played at the corners of Elizabeth's mouth. "Seems I remember you had a different name." She glanced up at the ceiling as if trying to recall, as Frenchy groaned in response.

"Oh, I do wish you wouldn't remember that. It was Samuel's daddy, that miserable ol' Arriah Bradley hisself, who spread that news to ever'body. Said he did it in defense of his own terrible name, but I think it was outta pure meanness."

"Now I recall," Elizabeth said. "It's Othniel LeMay, isn't that so? And it's a beautiful name."

Frenchy groaned again, then shook his head to add to the effect. He turned to me. "You sure have some cruel folks in Jerusalem's Landing, son. Even the beautiful women seem to rise up when a stranger pays a call." He gave Elizabeth another wink, then patted her hand again, but beneath it all he was suddenly all business. It was like a signal that the acts—both his and Elizabeth's—were about to draw to a close.

"Now why don't you tell old Frenchy what you saw the day before they found Royal Firman's body," he began.

I listened as Elizabeth repeated what she had told me when we first spoke of it—about the white man she had seen off in the woods, the man she had assumed was a hunter just passing through.

"But this man coulda been Royal Firman, is that right?" Frenchy asked.

"It could have," Elizabeth said. "But I really can't be certain."

"Would you say you an' Royal were close—sort of like friends— him comin' up here fer medicines an' such?"

I stiffened at Frenchy's question, thought I heard something sly hidden in the words.

"I wouldn't say we were friends," Elizabeth began. She paused as if wanting to choose the right phrasing. "I would say we were friendly when we had dealings." She gave a small shake of her head. "Royal was not a terribly likable young man. He could be somewhat coarse, and he also made it clear that he thought quite highly of himself. Or, perhaps, he just thought much less of others. Especially women and Negroes and those other people he considered his inferiors."

Frenchy made a note of this with his stubby pencil, then began tapping it on the table. "Samuel told me that yer sisters didn't even see what you saw," he said. "By the way, where are yer sisters? I was hopin' to talk with 'em."

"I suspect they were held up on their jobs. They clean for a family or two. Though not so many now that this Great Depression is upon us. I believe today was their day at Doc Hawley's. He is one of the few folks can still afford outside cleaning work. But you're correct. They did not even see what I saw."

"Do you know if they were friendly with Royal Firman?" Frenchy asked.

"You'll have to ask them, of course. I don't believe we ever discussed their feelings toward him. I do know they were always respectful when he was here, just as they are to any visitor."

Frenchy put his notebook away and gathered up his hat. "Oh, one more thing," he said, as he rose from his chair. "Did you ever make any special potions for Royal Firman himself?"

Elizabeth gave him a long steady look. "Why yes, Deputy, I in fact did."

"An' what was it?"

She reached inside her bodice again and withdrew the deerhide pouch. "It was one of these," she said. "He told me he wore it all the time. To protect himself against the evil that might be done to him."

Frenchy grunted. "Don't seem that Royal was wearin' nothin' like that when he was found."

"I see." Elizabeth nodded slowly, almost imperceptibly, like someone deep in thought. "Perhaps he should have been," she said at length.

"You think she's tellin' us true?" Frenchy asked, as my Model A bounced across the wagon ruts on our way back to town.

"I've never known Elizabeth to lie," I said. "Leastways not to me."

Frenchy seemed to consider that over the next few minutes. "Sure do wish her sisters were about. But I'll catch up to 'em before long."

I continued down the hill, concentrating on the ruts that threatened to throw me off into the woods. "I'm not sure what they'll be able to tell you," I said.

"Well, we gotta talk to 'em anyways." He adjusted the brim on the Stetson he had traded for the hunting cap he had worn the night before, taking time to straighten, then bend it just the way he wanted. "You 'member I told you how that boy had hisself some sex right before he was killed?"

I could feel a chill begin to creep up through my body. "I remember." I chanced a glance at him, and found that Frenchy was staring straight back, eyes hard as coal.

"Well, seems like he maybe left his pants on when he done it, 'cause there was some hairs caught up in the buttons on his fly." He paused for what seemed a full minute before he continued. "And accordin' to the doc who done the autopsy, they wasn't no pubic hairs. They was hairs from somebody's head. You gettin' my meanin', here, Samuel?"

"I understand what you're saying."

Frenchy brought his hands together in a soft slap. "One other thing you should know, Samuel. Accordin' to the doc, them head hairs come off'n a Negro."

{ 6 }

Her breasts were wet and glistening in the dappled sunlight that filtered through the trees. I lay on the ground, sweating in the July heat, still in the same place where only minutes earlier she had hunched over me, her mouth doing that which I had never experienced before, providing me with pleasure that both frightened and thrilled me. Where she had learned this, or heard of it, or read of it, I did not know, nor had I the courage then to ask her. She said nothing before she began, and had only paused to ask that I let her know when my release was imminent. Later, when I did so, she had held me against her breasts so that my seed spilled onto her in huge, erupting gouts. And I see her still, kneeling there as she studies it, plays a finger through it, then looks down on me and smiles.

"Do you love me, Samuel?" she asks.

"Yes, I love you."

"Will you always love me?"

"Yes. Always. Always. Always . . ."

* * *

"You must know who he was with, dammit. There aren't that many Negro women close by." I stared at her, my eyes, my entire body demanding an answer.

"Why do you ask me these things?" Elizabeth shook her head. "Do you expect me to be responsible for every Negro woman I know? I can't do that, Samuel. I can only take responsibility for myself."

I stared at her for almost a minute before responding. She stared back, unflinchingly.

"Do you remember that summer together the year before we each went to college?"

"Of course I remember it."

I drew a long breath. "There were things you did then, things you knew, passionate things. And I never understood how you had learned of them . . ."

She held up a hand, stopping my words. Her light brown eyes seemed to darken and bathe me in deep unrelenting anger; a faint hint of red blossomed on her pale brown cheeks. "It was my jungle heritage," she hissed. "Did you not ever think of that?"

"Stop it, Elizabeth."

"No, you stop it, Samuel. I will not be questioned like this. If you want to know if I slept with Royal Firman before he died, just ask me." She was breathing heavily, the bodice of her dress rising and falling.

"I don't want to know, but it's my job, dammit. And Frenchy LeMay will want to know."

She turned toward the window, beyond which the faint pink glow of sunrise was just beginning to show itself among the trees. Her back was to me. We were in the dispensary, surrounded by the overwhelming smell of her drying herbs and flowers, the room, itself, so small she could not get far from me. "Let Frenchy LeMay ask me then," she said in a softer voice.

"And what will you say?" I could feel a tremble in my own voice, the bitter taste of the words as I spoke them.

She shook her head, whether in weariness or sadness I cannot say. Then she turned back to me, her eyes lowered. "I did not sleep with Royal. Not then, not ever." She raised her eyes to my face. They were filled with defiance. "That is what I will tell him, Samuel."

I stared at her, not really sure what she was telling me, shamed by my unwillingness to simply accept the words as they were spoken. "He'll also want to speak with Maybelle and Ruby," I said.

"When he does my sisters will have to answer him. Not I."

Jehiel gave me a wide smile when I entered his cabin, his eyes drawn to the bundle of newspapers under my arm. For several years now I had saved the daily newspapers my father and I read and dropped them off at Jehiel's house once each week. Since there were no newspaper deliveries to outlying homes, and with the hill lacking the electricity that allowed those of us in town to listen to the news each night on our radios, this was Jehiel's way to "catch up on the white man's world," as he put it.

Morning coffee brewed on the cookstove, and Jehiel poured each of us a cup before he took the papers to his favorite chair by the hearth. He picked up the first issue and immediately grinned at me like some great, happy, chocolate-colored bear.

"Listen to this, Samuel. Woman in Burlington is plannin' a march to stop the repeal of Prohibition." Jehiel's teeth flashed with merriment. "Hot damn, I sure do like that woman's sense of timin'. Roosevelt pushed that there Twenty-first Amen'ment through Congress nigh on to nine months ago, an now we's only needin' one more state to ratify it an' put an end to that stupid law, an' this here fool white woman wants to march agin' it now." He let out a soft chuckle. "I should invite her up to these woods and let her see where I made all my corn liquor fer the las' twelve years." He gave me a wide-eyed look. "'Course you din't hear me say that, Constable."

I offered up my own smile. "Illegal liquor was never my job. That still belongs to the state highway patrol. It's why they were created."

Jehiel snorted. "Them an' those federal revenuers. An' neither one could never catch nobody." He let out a cackle. "You 'member when the gov'mint in Washington gave the state all that money to fight the bootleggers, and the state up an' creates that there highway patrol and bought them all motorcycles to ride on." His laugh grew to a low rumble. "Motorcycles, mind you. In a state tha's got snow on the roads six months of the year." He shook his head, sipped his coffee, and went back to his newspapers.

I very much wanted to talk to Jehiel. If for no other reason than to warn him about Frenchy chasing down the theory that Royal Firman had sex with a Negro just before he died. I say *theory*, because that is what I wanted it to be. Yet I knew that no matter what I said to Jehiel, or how I said it, the response would be a simmering rage. I also knew that should it come from someone else, there might also be violence.

"Look at this here, now," Jehiel said, waving the newspaper at me. "Seems like this Hitler fella, over in Germany, is offerin' cash to pure Germans who will marry up with each other, an' even more cash for each li'l Aryan baby they produces." He shook his head. "Sumbitch, Samuel. You think that if we had us a Negro president, he'd give us colored men a dollar fer marryin' up with some good-lookin' colored gal, then pay us some more iff'n we got her pregnant with some nice li'l colored baby?" He threw back his head in thunderous laughter. "What's them English call that? Carryin' coals to Newcastle?" He slapped the newspaper down on his knee. "This here Hitler, he's not only a racist sumbitch, he's also a goddamn fool. Either that, or he's gots hisself a couple million damned Germans who thinks them puny white dicks ain't good fer nothin' else 'cept pissin'."

He went back to the newspaper and within a minute was off on a new tangent. "Now, here's a good 'un, Samuel. Says here that the CCP, that there Civilian Conservation Corps, is gonna hire itself more'n three million men in the next eight years. An' it says those boys are gonna plant more'n two billion trees, build us some small dams, help out in wildlife restoration, an' tackle some erosion problems across this here country." He shook his head. "Now ain't that nice. We got more'n fifteen million folks outta work, and them that's workin' is gettin' forty percent less than they got four years ago. We got a million farmers on relief—which ain't surprisin' since farm prices are down sixty-three percent, an' a farmer got to pay the price of nine bushels of wheat to buy himself a goddamn pair a new shoes. We got ourselves one thousand mortgage foreclosures each an' every day, an' now good ol' 'You ain't got nothin' to fear, but fear itself,' Franklin Delano Roosevelt, he's gonna plant us some shade trees an' take care of some furry li'l rabbits." He raised a lecturing finger. "Samuel, I just decided somethin', right here and now. I ain't gonna vote no more. Not ever again. I ain't gonna do nothin' that might encourage them stupid sumbitches." A big grin spread across Jehiel's face.

"Frenchy thinks Royal Firman had sex with a Negro woman just before he died." I let the words drop like a white-hot poker. Then I watched the big grin slowly disappear from Jehiel's face. It seemed to happen in increments, until fiery eyes and a straight, angry line of bared teeth replaced the smile.

"He sayin' it was one of my gals?"

"No, sir, he is not. But he is wondering if it might have been."

Jehiel nodded, as if he'd expect nothing less of a white man. Then one eye narrowed on me. "You thinkin' it was one of my gals, Samuel?"

"No, sir, that's not what I'm sayin'."

"What are you sayin', Samuel?"

Jehiel sat before me like a piece of great, brown stone—features as rigid as carved granite. I struggled to get the words right in my mind, then began. "The doctor who did the autopsy—a doctor from the university—found hairs caught up in the buttons of Royal's fly." I did not have the courage to tell him they were hairs from someone's head. I drew a long breath. "That, and the fact that his sperm sac was empty, makes the doctor think that sex took place just before Royal died, and because the hairs were from a Negro, that the sex was probably with a colored woman."

"Lessen Royal Firman liked to have himself a boy now and then," Jehiel snapped.

I lowered my eyes to the floor. "I think Royal's reputation would make that unlikely." Jehiel only snorted in reply, so I continued. "I just wanted you to know all this, so if word gets around town, you're ready for it."

Jehiel hadn't seemed to hear. He was staring off toward the window. "Musta been that gal over to Addison," he said.

"What gal is that?" I asked.

"Colored gal, name of Jenny. Don't know her last name. Works over to Joshua Cory's farm off'n Highway 22. Hear tell she'll take on any buck comes by her place with fifty cents in his jeans." Jehiel's large hand had closed into a fist and was absently striking his thigh. His eyes were still turned away from me, keeping me from reading him well. "Folks say that girl spreads her legs apart so much, they's gonna bury her in a Y-shaped coffin."

I nodded, momentarily uncertain how I should reply. "I'll tell Frenchy," I said at last. "Seems like we can check and see if Royal was with her."

Jehiel continued to stare at the window. "You do that, Samuel. You gonna find it was that gal, or somebody jus' like her."

"There's one other thing I need to talk to you about."

Jehiel's eyes finally came back to mine.

"It's about Jeffords," I said. "I believe he's been finding things, and he's been hiding them away."

"What kinda things?" Jehiel asked.

"Like Royal's hat. I think he found it and buried it someplace."

"An' you want me to get him to dig it up and give it in?"

"No, that's not what I want. Far as I'm concerned it can stay where it is."

Jehiel stared at me, comprehension slowly coming to his eyes. He nodded, but did not otherwise comment.

"What I'm worried about is that he'll find something else that's missing, and that he'll keep it on his person this time."

"Like what? What kinda thing you worrin' he'll find?"

"An Indian pouch that's worn around the neck. We think Royal might of been wearing one—some kind of Abenaki charm that was supposed to ward off evil. But it never turned up on his body when we found him, and I'm afraid it might of fallen off when he got carried into the woods, and then got picked up, maybe by Jeffords. I'm afraid he might be taken by it, and decide to keep it. Maybe even think he can hide it just by wearing it, or by keeping it in his pocket."

"What's this here pouch look like?" Jehiel asked.

"It's just like the one Elizabeth wears."

Jehiel stared at me for several seconds, then slowly began to shake his head. "What the hell you talkin' about, Samuel. 'Lizabeth don't wear nothin' like that."

"But I've seen it. In fact she made the pouch that Royal wore."

"That may be true. That gal makes up all kinda stuff fer folks. But she don't ever wear nunna it herself. Claims she's too educated fer that stuff."

"But—"

"I don't care what you think you seen, boy. 'Lizabeth's my daughter, an' I see her most ever day, and I ain't never seen her wearin' no mumbo jumbo Indian pouch."

Frenchy and my father were at the kitchen table when I returned home at eight that morning. There was a coffee pot between them, along with two half full cups and an ashtray with enough ground-out butts to indicate they'd been sitting there a spell.

"Ya sure out early this mornin'," Frenchy said as I hung my coat and hat and gunbelt on a hook by the door.

"Delinquent taxes," I said. "The bane of this job. Especially with this damned Depression." I caught my father's good eye staring at me, all too aware of the lie I was serving up.

"Ol' FDR'll fix us up," my father said, his voice heavily slurred from his stroke. "Soon's he finds a way ta put all them damned bankers in jail."

Frenchy snorted. "You sound like the same kinda goddamn Bolshevik that we got sittin' in the White House."

My father gave Frenchy a lopsided grimace of a grin. Frenchy was a diehard Republican, whose job depended on the biennial re-election of the Republican sheriff, which was about as safe a bet as you could get in Vermont.

"Sit between us, Samuel," my father said. "Otherwise there's liable ta be some gunplay."

"Well, I better sit, then. You told me Frenchy was the best shot with a pistol you ever saw, and I can't afford to lose myself a daddy."

Frenchy cocked his head so he could look around me as I sat and get a clear look at my father. "That true, Arriah? That you was braggin' on me?"

"That was a'fore I knew yer politics," my father said.

Frenchy let out a barking laugh. "Lord, there sure is a nest'a Democrats in this here town. Thanks be it's a small town, or I'd be outta work fer sure."

"You sure to be outta work, you keep chasin' after wonna the few fool Republicans we got in this here town. Not that I wouldn't like seein' a Republican in jail, mind you."

"Who's that Republican I'm chasin'?" Frenchy asked.

"Jehiel Flood," my father said.

"He's a Republican?" Frenchy sounded incredulous.

"Party of Lincoln. Says he still votes for the party that freed his people from the white man's tyranny."

"Jee-sus. Sounds more like a Bolshevik to me. But if ya say he's a Republican, then I say the man's innocent. Can't afford ta lock up no Republicans. They can't vote when they's in jail."

I gave Frenchy a steady look. "Is that where your thinking is? That Jehiel Flood is our killer?"

Frenchy offered me half a shrug. "The early sniffin' aroun' surely points that way."

"How do you figure?"

"Well, I guess I'm leanin' pretty heavy on what the doc said about the dead boy havin' sex with a colored gal." Frenchy paused to scratch the tip of his nose. "Jehiel admits he run that boy off a coupla times, when he found him hangin' aroun' his daughters." Another half shrug. "Maybe this time he caught him doin' more'n hangin' aroun'."

I felt a chill move through me, a pure, cold anger. I looked down at my hands folded before me to hide any hint of it in my eyes. "Could be," I said. "Could also be a colored farm gal over in Addison by the name of Jenny."

Frenchy sat up straight and turned to me. "Whoa now, what's all this about? Who's this Jenny gal yer talkin' about?"

"Just a rumor I came across," I said. "Seems like quite a few of the local sports head on over to Addison when nature gives them the call."

"An' this Jenny gal is there to give 'em an answer?"

"That's what I'm hearing. Thought we might ride over and have a talk with her. You happen to have a photograph of Royal that we might show her?"

"Got one right in my room over Miz Pierce's place. It's from the autopsy, so it's a touch grim, but it'll haveta do. I'll get it an' we can head on out to see this gal."

My father reached out and laid a hand on my arm. When I turned to him there was a touch of a smile in his good eye. "You mind runnin' over ta Shepard's Store to git me some cigarettes a'fore ya go?"

"Happy to, Daddy."

He gave my arm a light squeeze.

Frenchy seemed to miss the exchange. "I'll go get my pitcher an' meet up with you back here, then," he said.

It began to rain as I left my house to walk the short distance to Shepard's Store. Jerusalem's Landing sits in the foothills of the Green Mountains, and the arrival of an unexpected storm is not uncommon. This can be a danger in winter, especially for those out hunting in the deep woods. Sudden snow squalls can quickly cover a man's boot tracks, and a hunter who has not made use of a compass before entering the woods can have difficulty finding his way out.

My father had taught me a trick to counter that danger, one that had been passed on to him by an old Indian hunter. It was simple enough. Find a stream and follow its downward course. Streams join rivers, and eventually, because of the intrusion of "civilization," one or the other will cross a road. I kicked a stone lying in my path and watched it skitter off to the side, and I thought of all my father had taught me, feeling briefly saddened by the wonderment of what it would be like when he was no longer with me.

The rain intensified and I pulled the brim of my hat down to keep it off my face. As I did I saw Elisha Bowles's old touring car pull up in front of Shepard's Store, and the brief flash of a skirt as a woman hurried inside, a shawl held over her head against the rain. I felt a sudden nervous rush at the sight, knowing it would be Elizabeth, stopping at the store on her way to the school, which lay just a short piece farther down the road. On inclement days, when Elizabeth could not walk, as she preferred, Elisha was known to drive her as he began his daily rounds of doing God's work.

I increased my pace and hurried into the store, throwing only the briefest of waves at Elisha, who was still seated behind the wheel of his oversized car. Inside, I took off my hat and thumped it against my leg to rid it of excess water. Elizabeth, standing at the counter, turned to the sound. Behind the counter, Hannah glanced up as well. Hannah smiled brightly. Elizabeth did not.

"Hello, Samuel," Elizabeth said. "You look close to drowning."

"Very close," I said.

Without a word Hannah bent, then hurried around the counter with a bit of cloth in her hand. "Here, let's mop that water away," she said as she reached me.

She raised the cloth to my face and began to wipe away the water, releasing it to my own hand when I reached for it. Past Hannah's shoulder I could see Elizabeth watching us, but instead of the amusement I expected, I saw a clear note of irritation in her eyes. Beyond Elizabeth, Victorious suddenly left her place behind the post office window and began a march toward the front of the store.

"Your mother's coming," I whispered behind the cloth.

Hannah quickly moved back to her counter. A safe enough distance to escape the risk of jiggaboo babies, I told myself.

"Well, well. We's got us a whole store fulla niggers, now don't we?"

I turned into the glaring eyes of Preserved Firman. The three-day growth of gray-flecked beard that he had worn when I last saw him had now grown to five, but I could still see the angry scar that twitched along his left cheek. Abel Turner hovered beside him, dwarfing the small, wiry lumberman, his normally dull eyes glittering with the pleasure he derived from Preserved's racial slur.

They had entered the store behind me, unnoticed. My mind had been too intent on Elizabeth, then on Hannah's ministrations, and I realized now it was a carelessness I could not afford given Preserved's still-simmering rage. I felt a chill run down my spine, and my right hand instinctively brushed against my side to reassure myself I had remembered to strap on my father's old Colt before I left my house. The movement caught Preserved's eye and produced an evil smile.

I glared back at him and put a hard edge in my voice to challenge his racial epithet. "I promise you, that kind of talk is gonna cause trouble, Preserved."

Abel took two steps to the side, guaranteeing I could not draw down on both of them at once.

"You awful alone ta be talkin' so hard, Samuel." Preserved gave me another mirthless grin that was pure hate. "Or maybe ya expect this nigger bitch ta help ya."

From the corner of my eye I could see Elizabeth stiffen under his words. "Enough," I growled. "No more of it."

Victorious had reached us now, although she had positioned herself at a safe distance. "Now you leave Preserved be, Samuel. The man is grieving his son."

I heard Elizabeth's sharp intake of breath, then felt her spin away, turning her back on all of us.

"Don't ya turn yer back ta me, ya nigger bitch." Preserved's hand struck out with snakelike speed, and before I could move he had grabbed Elizabeth's arm and spun her around so violently that she staggered and fell, the side of her head striking the counter.

My own hand lashed out, and I hit Preserved with every ounce of strength I had. He fell back into a long row of shelves and sent cans and boxes flying. He no sooner hit the floor than his hand yanked a buck knife from a sheath on his belt. I drew my pistol and leveled it at his face, as the three distinctive clicks of a second pistol being cocked came from my right. My body turned to ice at the sound, then a voice brought warmth back to my veins.

"You go ahead an' shoot that sumbitch, Samuel. 'Cause if this'n moves another inch I'm gonna send his brains all over Miz Shepard's canned goods."

I glanced quickly to my right and saw Frenchy, revolver in hand, the barrel jammed up under Abel's nose. A second buck knife that had been intended for my back dropped from Abel's fingers and clattered on the floor.

"Oh, Lord. Oh, Lord." It was Victorious, huffing with fear, her face as white as chalk.

I glanced at Elizabeth. There was a trickle of blood coming from her hairline. I took her arm and helped her to her feet as my eyes went back to Preserved.

"You best put that knife down, before I kill you where you lie," I hissed.

I felt Elizabeth's hand on my arm as I watched Preserved's knife drop to the floor.

"Don't hurt him, Samuel," she said, her voice little more than a whisper. "He's a stupid man. But stupidity isn't a good enough reason to die."

Preserved's entire body strained against the gravity that held him to the floor. "Ya got my boy kilt!" he screamed at Elizabeth. "I know he was up there givin' ya a poke, jus' like ya always wanted him to. An' I know yer daddy come an' caught him, an' gutted that poor, sweet boy. I know that's the true of it, ya black-assed, nigger whore. An' if the law don't do nothin' about it, I'm gonna kill alla ya. Every las' black-assed nigger livin' on that hill."

I leaned down into him, until my face was only three feet away. "One more word, and I'll smash this pistol across your face," I hissed.

Preserved's hand started toward the knife he had dropped, and I cocked my pistol, each click echoing in my ears like a tiny clap of thunder. "Do it," I hissed again, "and I'll kill your sorry ass."

"No, Samuel. Please." It was Elizabeth again.

Preserved's hand moved away from the knife.

"You want to press charges for assault?" I asked over my shoulder.

"No. Please, no," Elizabeth said. "The man has suffered enough. Please just send him away."

"Well!" It was Victorious, huffing again at the injustice she perceived.

"Hannah, can you spare that cloth for the cut on Elizabeth's head?" I glanced at Hannah and saw her nod and reach under the counter. I turned and stared down at Preserved. "You get out of here. Now. This lady just saved you some trouble you deserved. And you leave that knife where it is."

Preserved glared at me, then at Elizabeth, but said nothing more. He pulled himself up and limped toward the door, dragging his bad leg more than usual. He jerked his head at Abel, telling him that he should follow.

Frenchy lowered his revolver, but placed a hand on Abel's broad, burly chest. "You got some talkin' to do with me, son. So you better be at Miz Pierce's hotel no later than six o'clock tonight. An' don't you make me go huntin' ya up. You hear me?"

"Yes, sir," Abel said. Then he scurried after Preserved.

Frenchy turned and nodded to Victorious. "Sorry 'bout the mess, Miz Shepard," he said. He looked away from Victorious Shepard's reddening face and turned a concerned smile on Elizabeth. She was pressing the cloth Hannah had given her to the wound on her head. "I believe we better get you next door to see Doc Hawley, young lady. Let him put a proper bandage on that."

Elizabeth nodded, then turned to Hannah. "Thank you, Hannah," she said. "I'll return your cloth after I've washed it."

"Don't you bother," Hannah said. "It's just an old piece of cloth. I got plenty more."

I gathered together Elizabeth's purchases, as Frenchy led her out the door, then bought a pack of cigarettes for my father. I was struck by that for a moment—whether my father's need of a new pack of Lucky Strikes had almost got me killed, or if his addiction for tobacco had saved Elizabeth from more serious harm.

As I put the cigarettes in my pocket I could feel the eyes of Victorious Shepard burning holes in my back. I ignored her, smiled at Hannah, and walked through the door.

"Well, look at this here," Frenchy said. He glanced from Doc to Elizabeth to me, grinning at each of us. "Lessen you wanna count that Baptist seminary ol' Elisha gone to, here I am in the same room with the only three college graduates in Jerusalem's Landing. An' in the past couple of days all three of ya managed to tangle with the same backwoods polecat." He nodded toward Doc's still-swollen lip, then at Elizabeth's head, then grinned again at me. "Maybe old Preserved jus' don't take kindly to educated folk," he said.

"The man's a menace," Doc said, his face reddening over his earlier humiliation at Preserved's hands.

"Well, if you folks keep lettin' him thump on people, an' not lock his sorry self up, you kin expect more of the same."

"I am grateful to you, Deputy," Elizabeth said.

"Now I told you about that deputy business," Frenchy said.

Elizabeth smiled coyly. "You're right, you did. I am grateful to you, Othneil."

Frenchy let out a groan. "That's not what I meant."

"How did you happen by when you did?" I asked.

"Didn't happen by. I was just crossin' the road from Miz Pierce's place, goin' back to your daddy's house, when I saw you headed fer the store. Then I saw Preserved and that Turner boy go on in behind ya, an' I figured I better get myself down there, quick."

"I'm grateful you did," I said. "I'm not sure where Abel's knife would of ended up if you hadn't come along so smartly." I heard Elizabeth shudder behind me.

Frenchy glanced at her and nodded, then turned his gaze back to me. "Makes a person wonder about that boy," he said. "Maybe you ain't the first person he set out to cut lately." Frenchy nodded again, more to himself this time than to anyone else. "Might be we'll have to take us a serious look at that." He stroked his chin for a moment. "One other thing, Samuel. That old Colt of yer daddy's that you carry around." He let his eyes fall to the revolver in my gunbelt. "That's a single-action pistol if I recollect rightly."

"Yes it is," I said, knowing what was coming.

"Well, me, I prefers a double-action." He patted the pistol holstered on his hip. "Don't have to cock it ta make it ready to fire." He smiled. "Lessen you want the effect of that there noise, like I did back in Miz Shepard's store." He wagged a finger at me. "But that ol' single-action yer carryin', she sure does need to be cocked a'fore she fires. So if you kin take a touch of friendly advice, I suggest that next time yer a mind to fill yer hand, you pull that hammer back as soon as you clear yer holster. That way a fool with a knife won't have a chance to cut you a'fore you send him straight ta hell."

Frenchy and I headed down Highway 22 in my Model A. We had stopped at a small store in Addison Village and had gotten directions to Joshua Cory's farm. The landscape was flat here, close in to Lake Champlain as it was, with the mountains we had come from rising in the distance behind us, and the Adirondacks looming ahead on the New York side. It was here that the river that cut through Jerusalem's Landing emptied into the lake, the same body of water that Samuel de Champlain had used centuries before to explore the land he had named Vermont for its lush green mountains. Now that same lake carried other ships all the way south to New York City and north to Montreal. So it was here that the barges that hauled lumber cut from our shores ended up each week, to be readied for that journey north or south. And with those journeys came what little prosperity we in Jerusalem's Landing enjoyed during these hard times.

What we found at the Cory farm was far from prosperous. It was a dairy farm, down to what looked to be about fifty cows, although the barn clearly had been built to hold four times that number. It

was a story repeated many times across our state, as farmers struggled through this time of economic hardship. Milk and butter selling in stores for ten cents a quart and twenty-eight cents a pound,
respectively, prices far too high for families living on reduced wages,
or no wages at all. Farmers then given no choice but to cut back
their herds to a level they could afford to feed, until those herds
were barely enough to scrape by on.

I pulled my car off to one side, and we approached the rear door
of the farmhouse. When we were thirty feet away the door opened,
revealing a thick-waisted, middle-aged woman, holding a twelve-
gauge shotgun leveled at our legs.

"You police boys come any closer ya ain't gonna walk back ta
that car," she said.

We stopped and showed her the palms of our hands.

"Yer sure right 'bout us bein' police officers, ma'am," Frenchy
called out. "But we ain't here doin' no work fer no bank."

The woman eyed him, then snorted. She lowered the shotgun so
it was pointed at our ankles instead of our knees. "You doan better
be lyin', mister. 'Cause I'll tell ya true. Ya hand me or mine any court
papers a'fore ya leave this here farm, an' yer backside is gonna carry
the weighta my birdshot a'fore ya reaches that car."

"I believe you, ma'am. I surely do," Frenchy called back. "You
Miz Cory?"

"That's who I be. Lucretia Cory. Lucy ta them's I call friends."

"Is your husband, Joshua, about, ma'am?"

She inclined her head toward some fields that lay behind the
barn. "He's out bringin' in the lasta the feed corn."

Frenchy took off his Stetson and scratched his head. "We's here
'bout a killin', happened over Jerusalem's Landing way. We jus' wanna
talk to a gal's supposed to work here, 'cause we think she mighta
knowed the fella got hisself killed."

The woman let out another snort, then swung her shotgun up,
and rested its butt on the ground. "Ya must be talkin' 'bout Jenny,"
she called. She wiped a wisp of graying hair from her forehead. "If
it was somethin' wearin' pants, Jenny prob'ly knowed it."

Frenchy nodded. "Tha's what we hear'd, ma'am. So if you give us permission, we'd sure like to talk to her. Or if you think we oughtta speak to yer husband first, that's okay, too."

"Ya come on up here an' let me get a look at ya," she said.

When we got to easy talking distance, the battered, beaten look of the woman came across more clearly. She wasn't that old, maybe in her early forties, perhaps even less. But time and trouble and farm life had taken their toll. She reminded me of an expression my father had been known to use. She looked like she'd been rode hard and put up wet.

"Jenny's not a bad gal," the woman said. "She jus' likes ta rut with the bucks a bit more than any gal should. An' she ain't knowed ta be too particular 'bout who they is."

"She work here long?" Frenchy asked.

"Since she be twelve. She be eighteen now, almost nineteen." The woman primped at her hair a bit, as if reminding herself, or us, or life in general, that she'd once been that young herself. Then she seemed to catch what she was doing, and dismissed the foolishness. She cocked her head to one side and studied Frenchy, then me. "I guess ya look good enough fer trustin'." She raised her chin. "Ya be findin' Jenny in the barn, muckin' out after the cows. But ya 'member what I said. She be a good gal. An' I ain't gonna have no mistreatin' a her, jus' 'cause she be colored. So ya be easy on her, ya hear?"

We each touched a finger to the brim of our hats. "We will be, ma'am," I said. "I give you my word on it."

Jenny was bent over a mix of straw and muck. She jabbed a pitch-fork into the pile, then swung the prize deftly to her left and dropped it in an old board wheelbarrow with a twist of her wrist. Frenchy glanced at me and raised his eyebrows in a silent commentary on her dexterity.

"Girl knows her way aroun' a pitchfork," he said.

"Aren't many folks hereabouts who don't," I replied.

A smile flickered across his lips, then he looked back at the young woman, who had turned toward the sound of our voices.

"What you genni'men want?" There was a look on her face that seemed to move between curious and coy. But it was clear that two strangers in her barn didn't cause any worry.

"We're here lookin' fer you, darlin'," Frenchy said.

Jenny's look became all coy, now. "Well, I's doin' my farm chores now. But if ya comes back later . . ."

Frenchy raised a hand, stopping her. "It's not that, darlin'. I'm a deputy sheriff, an' this here handsome young man is the constable from over in Jerusalem's Landing. We jus' need to talk to you a spell."

Jenny was not a pretty woman. She was thick throughout the body, as many farm women are, and there was a slight hunch to her shoulders brought on by too much heavy labor. Her face was bit plump, her skin a light chocolate color that had been roughened by exposure to the weather, her eyes a very pale, very pretty brown. I could not see her hair, which was tied back under a kerchief, but the bits that showed through indicated it was a tightly curled brown, similar to the hair taken from Royal Firman's body. In short, there was nothing especially appealing about Jenny, except her sexual willingness and the large, round breasts that were evident beneath the heavy shirt she wore. I suspected these two things were the main attractants for the local sports.

Jenny caught me looking at her chest and smiled. "Ya sure ya a constable?" she asked. Her eyes seemed to offer a great deal more that remained unspoken.

The statement annoyed me, the coy sexuality even more so, and my first inclination was to lash out at her. I held back, trying to understand my reaction. It was simple enough. My only intimate exposure to Negro women was with Elizabeth and her sisters, and it hurt me to find this young girl so openly playing the whore. Frenchy saved me by pushing ahead.

"Jenny, we're tryin' to find out if you mighta known a fella named Royal Firman, from over Jerusalem's Landing way."

"Could be," she said. "I know a fella wit da name Royal. Ain't sure 'bout his las' name." She began to giggle. "Dis boy, he says dat his name is Royal 'cause . . ." She paused, glanced down at her crotch and giggled again. "He says it's 'cause his thang is king."

Frenchy inclined his head to acknowledge her attempted humor, then asked, "Jenny, if I showed you a pitcher, you think you could tell me if it's the fella yer talkin' about?"

"I try," Jenny said.

Frenchy showed her the photograph. It was a head-and-shoulder shot taken just before the autopsy.

"This fella, he sure doan look too good. He looks daid."

"I'm afraid he is," Frenchy said. "Is he the fella ya knew?"

"Tha's surely look like him. Yessuh, 'ceptin' bein' daid an' all."

"But that's the man you knew as Royal?" I asked.

"Yessuh, I do believe it is."

"An' when was the last time ya saw him?" Frenchy asked.

Jenny cocked her head to one side and thought a moment. "Couple days ago, I reckon."

"Can you say exactly what day?" I asked.

"No suh. I doan believe I kin. 'Ceptin' it warrant on Sunday. Sunday's my day off, so's I's always 'member'n dat day real good. Dat boy, Royal, he done come by one day just after chores. I 'members dat, 'cause I was jus' gittin' ready fer supper. Well, he be drinkin' some, an' he gets hisself all riled up 'cause I's goin' in ta eat an' it's so early. But I tells him I's gots to eat early on a workin' day, so's I kin git ta bed early, counta I gots ta git up early the next day."

"You two have yourself a little spat, did you?" Frenchy asked.

"No, there weren't no yellin' or nothin'," Jenny said. "Mr. Cory, he be puttin' a new shoe on wonna da horses, right out cheer in fronta the barn, so's Royal, he doan be doin' no yellin'."

"Does Mr. Cory get riled when these young men stop by?" I asked.

"No suh. He don't rightly care. Not so long as it ain't when I's supposed ta be workin'."

"What did Royal want, Jenny?" It was Frenchy again.

She lowered her eyes, but not out of shyness. "Same as always when he's liquored up. Royal, he likes it a li'l diff'nt den, like some boys does."

"How so?" Frenchy asked.

Jenny looked down again, then raised one finger to her lips, indicating her mouth. "An' mos' times I doan like it dat way," she added quickly. "'Cause dem boys, de doan always clean theyselves up real good a'fore they comes here."

Frenchy nodded, and fought off a smile. The woman was standing ankle deep in cow dung, talking about the cleanliness of her gentlemen callers. Frenchy shuffled his feet, then gave Jenny a small, regretful shrug. "Jenny, I'm real sorry to be askin' this, but did Royal get what he was lookin' fer that evenin'?"

"Well, no suh, not really. Not ever'thin' leastways. I tol' him I'd do it fer him, an' I did. But den his fren says he be wantin' the same thing, too. An' I tol' dem I ain't gonna be doin' dat fer two boys."

"There was someone with Royal?" I asked.

"Oh, yessuh. Der was 'nother boy, too."

"What did he look like?" Frenchy asked.

"He was big. Had hisself a big beard, too. One dat covered most all his face."

"Did he tell you his name?" I asked.

"No suh," Jenny said. "I axed him, but he din' never answer me. Later on—after I tol' dem I ain't gonna do what de wants—he gots real mad."

"What happened then?" I asked.

"He starts sayin' how's Royal tol' him he was gonna gets what he wanted, an' dat he wasted all da gas in his truck, driven' all dat way, an' how's it costs eighteen cents a gallon, an' Royal's gotsta pay him back fer it."

"An' what did Royal do?" Frenchy asked.

"Well, fer a time I was thinkin' maybe he's gonna make me do what his fren wants, but den he points out ta where Mr. Cory is, an' he tells his fren ta keep hisself quiet."

"An' then?" Frenchy asked.

"Den, after a little bit more, Royal an' his fren up an' leaves."

We turned off the pavement of Highway 22 and onto the dirt surface of Highway 17, which would take us back to Jerusalem's Landing. Frenchy had been quiet throughout the first part of our trip. Now he turned to me with a single word.

"Damn."

"You don't sound like a man who feels he's done a good day's work," I said.

"If I was workin' fer a defense lawyer I'd sure feel that way," Frenchy said.

"How so?" I asked.

"How so? By pokin' one damn big hole in my 'riginal theory. Tha's how so."

"And what was that theory?"

"You know damn well what it was," he said. "And it wasn't that far off from what that boy's daddy said this mornin' in Miz Shepard's store. That the boy got hisself killed when he got caught sparkin' one of them gals up on Nigger Hill."

"So, it's just like you said at breakfast. You really thought Jehiel did it?"

Frenchy shrugged. "Either him or his son or somebody who was real sweet on one of them gals."

He had thrown me a look as he said the last. It confirmed what I had suspected all along: that I, too, had been one of his suspects.

"Hell, I thought fer a while it mighta been that Jeffords boy," Frenchy said. "He's pretty sweet on that Elizabeth gal. Maybe he's sweet on all three of 'em, fer all I know. Hard to tell with a boy like that." He was trying to cover himself now, but it was too late.

"I suppose," I said. "Except now it seems Royal got his sex from someplace else."

Frenchy nodded. "If it was the same day. But I suppose Abel Turner kin tell me that when I interrogate him tonight."

"Unless he's the killer and doesn't tell you the truth," I said.

Frenchy let out a barking laugh. "That has been known to happen," he said.

"I'd like to be there when you talk to him," I said.

"Oh, you would now, would you? Well, I jus' might be able to arrange that, son."

{ 7 }

Abigail Pierce's boarding house had a wide porch that took up the entire front of the building, and it was there, despite the chill of an early October evening, that Frenchy held his interview with Abel Turner. I was not present, at least not on the porch. Frenchy had placed me inside the darkened parlor, next to an open window; far enough back where I could not be seen, but where I could hear everything that was said.

They were seated in two rocking chairs set about four feet apart. I could see Abel nervously perched on the end of his. Frenchy was out of my line of sight, but I could hear his rocker moving rhythmically back and forth against the floorboards of the porch.

"Tell me how you came to find Royal Firman's body," Frenchy began.

"I already tol' ya that t'other day," Abel said.

"I know you did, son. But I need you to tell it again. Fact is, I may need you to tell it a couple more times before all this is over. So whyn't we get started?"

I listened as Abel told the same story he had when he burst into my office. It was simple and clean, with a minimum of details . . . just like a good lie should be, I thought.

Frenchy was silent for a time when Abel had finished. All I heard was the steady rocking, back and forth, back and forth. In my mind, I could see him stroking his chin in thought.

"When was the last time you saw Royal alive?" he asked suddenly.

Abel seemed surprised by the question, or perhaps just the suddenness with which it had come. He stuttered momentarily.

"Well . . . well . . . jus' the day a'fore. We both of us works fer his daddy, so's we . . . sees each other ever' day. Lessen one of us is sick, a'course."

"Was one of you sick that day?" Frenchy asked.

"Uh, no. We was both of us workin' that day."

"How about that night? You see Royal that night? Or maybe right after work was finished up fer the day?"

Abel shrugged his big shoulders. "We had us some shine, back at my cabin. Preserved, he lets me use a cabin tha's right on the wood-lot he's cuttin'."

"You make yer own shine?"

Frenchy's questions were coming from every direction, and each new tack seemed to throw Abel off stride, just as I suspected they were intended to do. I marveled at Frenchy's talent for this sort of work.

"Don't make no shine," Abel said at length. "I buys it."

"Who from?" Frenchy asked.

Abel began to stutter and I could hear Frenchy let out with a low, easy laugh. "I ain't a revenuer, son," he said. "I ain't gonna go arrest the man you been buyin' yer shine from."

"Uh, huh . . ."

"You get yer shine from Preserved, am I right?"

"Uh, uh . . . No, sir. I gets it from this fella comes through town 'bout once'ta week. Don't know his name. He never rightly tol' me it."

"You know a colored gal named Jenny? Lives over Addison way?"

The question stopped Abel cold, and I could almost see the sweat burst forth on his forehead. He seemed to draw back inside himself. "I hear'd tell 'bout her," he said.

"Me, too," Frenchy said. "I hear tell fer a price she'll do a fella a good turn."

Abel shrugged his shoulders again. "That's what I hear'd, too," he said.

"Who'd you hear it from?" Frenchy asked.

Abel's lips began to move, but no sound came out at first. "I ain't . . . sure," he finally said.

"You think maybe it was Royal Firman? He been goin' over there, gettin' his goose drained?"

Abel began shaking his head back and forth. I could tell Frenchy had gotten to him. Abel's cheeks were reddening, and there was suddenly an angry glint in his eye. "I ain't got no notion what Royal done on his own time," he snapped. "An' I ain't gonna go talkin' all disrespectful 'bout him jus' 'cause he's dead."

There was another silence, punctuated by Frenchy's rocking. "Well, that's nice, son. I do admire you fer yer loyalty to a dead friend. An' I sure do wish I could be as respectful as yer bein'. But you see I got this killin' to investigate . . ."

"Don't see where it takes much investigatin'. Leastways not in findin' out who mighta done it. It was wonna them niggers, fer sure. An' if it wasn't wonna them, then it was that bleached nigger of a constable we got in this here town."

Frenchy met the outburst with more silence. Then his rocking chair came to an abrupt halt. "You know, that's the second time you said that about Constable Bradley. And I still don't understand why you think it might be true."

"Well . . ."

Frenchy had somehow cut Abel off. Whether by raising his hand or by some other means I did not know.

"Now I understand why you might think one of the folks up on Nigger Hill done this killing, Royal's body bein' found up on their property an' all. And it sure does make some sense, that bein' the case. Less of course somebody put his body there 'cause that's what they wanted us to think." There was a long pause. "You see what I'm sayin'?" Frenchy finally asked.

Abel began to reply, but Frenchy hurried on. "But this bizness about Samuel, I gotta confess, that sure does puzzle me a tad. I've know'd him since he was a boy, and I sure ain't never seen a killer hidin' in his skin. So I'm curious why you keep sayin' that?"

"Cuz he hated Royal. He hated him ever since they was kids, an' Samuel found out that Royal's great-granddaddy usta own his great-gramma, back when she was nothin' but a nigger slave, brought up here when Royal's great-granddaddy moved up here from Virginia."

"I hear'd that story," Frenchy said. "Fact is, I hear'd it from Samuel's daddy. All that happened eighty years ago. Sure don't seem like no reason to kill nobody today."

"Well, his other reason is that nigger-bitch schoolteacher," Abel snapped. "Tha's all the reason that boy ever had for anythin' he did."

"You talking about Samuel, now."

"I sure am."

"So you're sayin' the same thing Preserved is. That Royal got his-self killed because he was sparkin' the colored schoolteacher."

"Tha's the truth, fer sure."

Frenchy started up his chair again, each rhythmic sound of rocker against floorboard fueling my growing anger. I hoped Frenchy would drop the subject, but he did not.

"Now that's kinda hard on the schoolteacher, son. How you know she was sparkin' with that dead boy?"

"'Cuz Royal tol' me, tha's how." Abel spoke the words with a snarl. His lips were twisted; his eyes glaring.

I could feel my heart beating in my chest, and I had to will my hand to remain away from the pistol in my gunbelt, my rage so thick it blurred my vision.

"Exactly what did he say?" Frenchy asked.

"He said she was a wild woman in bed. He said ever' time he went up there ta get his daddy's joint medicine, that she pulled him inta her bed an' rode him like the wind. He said one time she done bucked so hard, she threw him outta that bed."

"Sounds like braggin' to me," Frenchy said. "Besides, you jus' tol' me you didn't know what Royal done on his own time. 'Course maybe this is different. You ever with him when he was sparkin' with this schoolteacher?"

"I been up there wit' him." Abel paused and looked quickly at his shoes. "Not when they was doin' nothin'." His head snapped up. "She wouldn't do nothin' when there was anybody else aroun', her bein' the schoolteacher an' all." His eyes took on a glare again. "But I seen the way she looked at him, an' I know'd 'bout what they was doin'. Ever' time he come back from there, Royal tol' me all that she done ta him."

"But you was never with him when he was gettin' hisself a little pleasure."

Abel remained silent. Behind the window, in Abigail Pierce's parlor, I struggled to control my breathing. Then Frenchy spoke again, and my heart raced.

"What about this here Jenny gal, one that works on that farm over to Addison? You ever with Royal when he was sparkin' with her?"

The shock on Abel's face was almost audible. What a clap of thunder would look like if it were visible. He sat staring at Frenchy for almost a full minute, his mind working around the question, testing it for hidden dangers.

"Don't recall I ever was," he finally said.

"Not this past week, maybe?"

"I already tol' ya, no." The hint of a snarl had returned to Abel's voice.

"Seems Royal was there this week. Leastways that's what this Jenny says." Frenchy paused, letting his words settle on the man. "Sounds to me like it mighta been the evenin' before you found his body."

Still there was no response, and I could feel my heart beating like a hammer, as Frenchy closed in.

"This Jenny says there was another boy with Royal. Says he wanted the same thing Royal did, but she turned him down. Says he made up a fuss, so she remembers him real good. Big fella, she says. One that's got hisself a full beard."

Abel jumped up from his chair. "I don't care what no nigger whore says!" he shouted. "I'm tellin' ya I ain't never been there. An' ain't nobody in this county gonna believe the word of no colored whore against the word of a white man."

"Oh, I believe you, if you say so, son. And you sure are right about nobody takin' the word of a colored gal that takes money fer her pleasures."

Frenchy's words of capitulation came so quickly they seemed to strike Abel like a physical blow. He stood there dumbly.

"An' you are sure lucky," he added. "'Cause the man who owns that farm, Mr. Joshua Cory, he was workin' right out in the yard where these two boys pulled up their truck. So I'm sure he got hisself a good look, too. So, if this here colored gal makes herself a mistake, or maybe even lies to us, well, we got us Mr. Cory who can tell us the true of it."

Frenchy sat across from me in the parlor, stroking his chin. He had turned Abel loose after his outburst and had entered the boarding house with a large grin spread across his face.

"Boy's lyin' so hard, he's gonna hurt hisself with all the twistin' an' turnin' he's doin'," Frenchy said now.

"So what are you going to do about it?" I asked.

Frenchy glanced toward the window that looked out on the place where he had conducted his interview with Abel. "First off, I'm real glad you didn't come flyin' through that window when that fool was talkin' bad about your granma." He paused and smiled. "Or about Elizabeth Flood. I know there was some truth in what he said about your feelin's fer that gal."

"That's an old tale," I said, feeling I might choke on the lie. "Back from when we were still kids. We're just close friends now." The truth of that final statement caused a touch of pain. From the look in Frenchy's eyes, I knew he didn't believe a word of it. "So what are you going to do about Abel?" I asked again.

"I'm not gonna do nothin'," Frenchy said, then hurried on before I could object. "You are." He grinned at me again. "Tomorra, I want you to go talk to this Joshua Cory an' get his permission to bring this Jenny gal up here to Jerusalem's Landing. If he won't give it, we'll haveta wait until her day off on Sunday, 'cause I want her to get a look at Abel without him knowin' she done it. Then, if we get us a positive identification, we can move ahead and look at Mr. Abel Turner a little more close like."

"So you think it's possible he killed Royal?"

"Oh, I think it's possible. And if he didn't, I think it's possible he knows who did." Frenchy shook his head. "But there's also a big hole in that theory that we gotta plug."

"What's that?" I asked.

"Royal's truck. The one you found up on Nigger Hill."

"What about it?"

"Well, first off, just that it was there. That Jenny gal said Royal and this friend he was with was usin' the other boy's truck. 'Member how she said that other boy was complainin' that he used up all that gas gettin' there?" Frenchy nodded, more to himself than to me. "And that's the other thing. Royal's truck had almost a full tank of gas. I know that, 'cause I checked it myself first day I was here."

"Maybe Jenny was mistaken about whose truck it was?" I suggested.

Frenchy shook his head. "Still couldn't of been Royal's. They was there at that farm in the afternoon. Girl said it wasn't late, but she also said she was gettin' ready fer supper, so it wasn't all that early, neither. And you an' me both knows there ain't many places to buy gas out in the country that late. Gotta get yerself to a good-sized town fer that, and by the time them boy's coulda done that, even them places woulda been closed. So my guess is that Jenny was right, an' Royal wasn't drivin'. So how'd his truck get up there on Nigger Hill that night?"

"Maybe Abel killed him, then put the body in Royal's truck and drove on up there. Just to make it look like Royal went up there himself. Then Abel could of hiked across the ridge to make sure nobody saw him walking back on the road."

Frenchy nodded. "That would be the only way it coulda been done. Leastways if it was Abel who did the killin'."

"So what bothers you about that?" I asked.

"Two things," Frenchy said. "First, I ain't sure that boy, Abel, is that smart a fella—the kind who sits hisself down and thinks things out. He strikes me as a boy who'd kill somebody then run off an' leave 'em where he lay."

"What's the second thing?" I asked.

Frenchy scratched his chin. "That's the big one," he said. "There weren't no blood in Royal's truck. I know, 'cause I checked it a couple days ago."

{ 8 }

I found Jehiel Flood's mare, Jasmine, tied to a tree behind my house when I made my way across the road from Mrs. Pierce's boarding house. Inside the kitchen my father and Jehiel were seated at the table, intently listening to the radio.

"War break out or something?" I asked.

"Jus' one of Mr. Roosevelt's fireside chats," my father said. "Jehiel rode his mare alla way down here so's he could get my dander up by makin' smartass remarks at the pres'dent."

"Damn fool Democrat," Jehiel grumbled. He raised a finger in the air, looked up at me, and flashed a broad smile. "The country is on the mend, Samuel. Glory be an' hal-le-lu-jah." He slapped his massive hand on the table. "That great white man, who now be our pres'dent, an' who lives in that great white house down in Washington, D.C., has jus' pro-claimed it so." He raised his solitary finger again, as the smile disappeared. "Now don't you go payin' no attention ta them few mil-lion folks who's only eatin' one meal a day, an' who's gettin' that meal from a soup kitchen. Things is de-finitely lookin' up."

"Ya sure don't look like ya been missin' many a meal yerself," my father snapped.

Jehiel rounded on him. "That's because I got me a boy who kin get hisself out in the woods an' bring home a squirrel or a partridge." He turned an accusing eye on me. "Not like some chillin I kin mention. Spends all their time runnin' around tryin' to find out who kilt some no-account white boy."

I laughed in spite of myself, then joined Jehiel's game. "Well, if you folks would stop leaving bodies all over your property, maybe I could get out in the woods and shoot myself a squirrel, too."

Jehiel slapped his hand down again. "My propity. I'll leave what I damn well please on it." He let out a low, rumbling laugh. "So what's that white deputy doin'? He still tryin' t' tie one of us Negroes to that killin'?"

"Ol' Frenchy's a good man," my father said. "He treat ya fair. I already tol' ya that."

Jehiel let out a disagreeable grunt. Mr. Roosevelt's speech had ended, and the radio was now playing Al Jolson's "Sonny Boy."

"My father's got a bit more faith in the deputy than I do," I said. "Although he is taking a pretty hard look at a white man right now. I'll give him that."

"You ever talk to that Jenny gal I tol' you about?" Jehiel asked.

"We talked to her today. Seems Royal paid her regular visits. The last one likely happened the day he died. We're checking on that now."

I shouldn't have told Jehiel any of this, it being part of the investigation. But with Preserved out spreading lies about Jehiel's daughters, I felt the man needed something to ease his mind.

"That why I seen that deputy sittin' on Miz Pierce's porch with that fat-assed white boy, Abel Turner?"

I tapped the side of my nose, indicating a secret that needed to be kept. "That's a pretty good guess," I said. "But you didn't hear it from me."

Jehiel pushed himself up from the table. "Well, if I ain't gonna get myself no more information 'round here, I might as well git myself ta home." He reached out and grabbed my father's shoulder on his good side. "You take care of yerself, Arriah, you miserable ol' Democrat. I be down to see you again in a couple days."

Jehiel turned to me. "Samuel, walk out with me and give me a leg up on that fool mare. She been a bit frisky lately when you try to mount her."

Outside, Jehiel took my arm. "Don't need no help with that mare," he said. "Just want you to know yer daddy is real worried about you. Thinks maybe you should step away from this here killin' and let the deputy handle it."

"I can't do that," I said.

Jehiel nodded. He knew why, although he would never say it. "Then you watch yer back," he said, instead. "That Preserved's a mean sumbitch. I hear'd what he did at Miz Shepard's store, an' maybe that's just the start of it. Man just as soon stick a knife in you as spit."

"I'll watch him."

"You do that," Jehiel said. "Him and his friends both. I intends to do the same myself."

My father was still at the kitchen table when I went back inside. He had placed a bottle of shine out in front of him, along with two glasses.

"Where'd that come from?" I asked. "Jehiel bring that down to you?"

My father gave me his crooked half smile. It saddened me the way only half his face worked. Now, when he smiled, it was as if the two theatrical masks that symbolized comedy and tragedy had somehow merged together on one face. For years now, I'd have given almost anything to see his real face again, the one I remembered as a boy, bursting into great grinning pleasure over something I had done.

"I ain't tellin' ya," he said. "Yer the law 'roun these parts." He raised his chin toward the bottle. "Pour us a touch from that. In another month or two—when that new amen'ment passes enough states an' becomes law—we'll be drinkin' store-bought liquor agin. Gonna miss this shine, I'm thinkin'."

It took my father two drinks to get to the point. His broad features suddenly became solemn. Then he drew a deep breath and he ran his good hand through his wiry hair. "Ya know, son, I didn't much like what I heard ya say 'bout Frenchy."

"I expect you didn't," I said. "But it's how I feel."

My father gave his head a small shake. "Well, I'm thinkin' ya is wrong feelin' that way, son. I know'd that man a lotta years, an' I never seen him out ta hurt nobody didn't deserve ta git hisself hurt."

"I understand that you trust him, Daddy. And I respect your judgment. I just don't feel the same way. I think Jehiel's right. Your friend Frenchy sees things through a white man's eyes."

"An' how do *you* see things, son?"

"I see them through *my* eyes. And only God knows what those eyes are."

The words seemed to shock my father, and he sat quietly for more than a minute. Then he raised his chin toward the bottle, and I poured him another shot of shine.

"Ya trust anybody, son?" he asked at length.

"I trust you, Daddy. I think I trust Jehiel in most things."

"What's yer reservation in trustin' him?

"I'm not sure there really is any, except that I'm not really sure how he feels about me."

"'Cause yer bleached?"

I nodded.

"An' what 'bout Elizabeth? Ya trust her?"

"I'm not sure."

My father was quiet again.

"But ya love her."

I didn't answer. I knew I didn't have to.

"What 'bout Hannah Shepard? How ya feel 'bout her?"

I looked down at the table. "Hannah's a young woman who is having an adventure," I said. "And she's having the joy of scaring the hell out of her mother."

My father nodded slowly, as if he were thinking that over. "Victorious is a fool," he said.

"And she's a racist."

"Yes, she is. An' what 'bout Hannah? Ya think she's a racist, too."

"I don't know. And I don't guess she knows either, whether if she is or not." I let out a small, unhappy laugh. "I think if I suddenly took a real serious interest in her she'd find out quick enough."

My father shook his head. He seemed genuinely saddened by my words. "Maybe she'd surprise ya," he said.

"Oh, I don't think so. If I moved away tomorrow she'd be sad for a day, then she'd get on with her life."

My father drew a long, weary breath. "Sometimes I wish ya'd do that, Samuel. Jus' up an' move away."

"You'd miss me, Daddy. Now isn't that true?" I smiled at him, knowing where he was going.

"Maybe we should both think 'bout movin'." He stared at me, studying my reaction, then continued. "I could stay with yer Aunt Jesse, up ta her place near Burlington. She's axed me enough times. An' we could see each other reg'lar, ya took a job in the city."

"Why not live together in Burlington?" I was just playing along, knowing he would never leave the town he'd lived in all his life, if for no other reason than my mother was buried here. And I would not leave him here alone. Not to the tender mercies of Jerusalem's Landing.

"Ya know city life would never do me, Samuel," he said. "Jus' couldn't abide all them people, an' all that noise."

"I'm not sure I could either, Daddy."

He leaned forward, intent on his subject now. "Samuel, ya ain't got no friends here. An' ya ain't got 'em 'cause ya doan want no friends here. Ya had yerself friends when ya was at college. Even went ta visit some of their homes on vacations, an' such."

But I didn't bring them here, did I, Daddy? I didn't bring them out here to see how a bleached nigger gets treated by the good white folks of Jerusalem's Landing. I said none of this, of course. It would only hurt my father, perhaps even make him think I had somehow been ashamed of him.

"There's opportunities fer a young man in a city," he said. "'Specially a young man gots hisself a college degree from the University of Vermont. That ain't no small thing, son. Too good a thing fer a man ta end up bein' a constable in a small town like this here one."

My hands were folded in front of me, and I stared at them as I tried to find words that would not hurt him. "Why do you think Elizabeth has stayed here?" I finally asked. "She has a very impressive degree. In fact her academic record was better than mine."

"That's diff'ent." There was an edge to my father's voice, a stubbornness that I had hoped to avoid. "'Lizabeth's a Negro, an' she knows she's done 'bout as good fer herself as she's gonna do, bein' a school teacher, an' all. But ya ain't got that problem. You's white, son. Damn, it says so right on yer birth certificate."

"There are folks here who'd disagree with you, Daddy."

"But only *here*." My father had raised his voice, annoyed with my own stubbornness. "Now you listen ta me. I tol' you this a'fore, but it didn't seem ta register none. Yer great-grandma's birth certificate said she was a Negro. Her son's birth certificate—my daddy's—said he was a Negro. My birth certificate says I'm colored. But not yers, Samuel. Yer birth certificate says you is white. 'Cause that's the rule, Samuel. Ever'place else 'cept these goddamn backwoods towns. You is the third generation, an' accordin' ta the rule, after three generations the mixed blood is gone, an' the children is white again."

I looked at my hands again and smiled. "You think Victorious Shepard knows that?"

"Damn Victorious Shepard. Damn all a them that says it ain't so. Ya gotta go someplace where that birth certificate means somethin', Samuel. Not stay here where some goddamn fools is gonna hol' that over ya yer whole life, then looks t'other way when some stupid, backwoods sumbitch like Preserved Firman sticks a buck knife in yer back."

I turned away from his glaring good eye. There was an answer, of course, but not one my father wished to hear, not that I wanted to speak aloud. They held us in contempt, the good white people of this town. They would never tell us that—except for the few truly ig-

norant ones like Preserved Firman. For the others it remained unspoken. They would never say the words, not to us or to anyone
else. But they despised us all the same. What they did not know is
that I held them in even greater contempt. And that was why I
would never allow them to drive us from their midst.

The pounding on the door awakened me two hours later. It had begun to rain as I slept, and when I pulled the door back I found Elisha Bowles staring up at me like a half-drowned barn cat. Elisha
had obviously been yanked from his own bed. He was still wearing
his nightshirt, over a pair of work trousers and rubber boots, and
his eyes were large, white circles filled with fear.

"You better come, Samuel," he said. "Somebody done shot Jehiel.
His children got him over to Doc Hawley's right now."

I grabbed my hat and coat and gunbelt and headed out the door.
I sent Elisha to get Frenchy at Miss Pierce's boarding house, then I
ran through the rain to Doc Hawley's.

As I pushed through Doc's front door, I heard Jehiel bellow forth
with a string of curses, and the fear I had felt quickly drained away.
If he were well enough to shout, he would live.

Elizabeth rose from a chair in Doc's waiting room and rushed to
me. Prince and Jeffords, who had been seated on either side of her,
remained where they were. Prince, I thought, had a hint of accusation in his eyes, and I felt the amusing sensation that he was view-
ing me as a white man whose trustworthiness was in question.

I held Elizabeth close and gently stroked her back. "What happened?" I asked.

"We found Daddy by the side of the road, all shot up," she said.

"Did you see who shot him?"

"No. Daddy's horse, Jasmine, came home alone," she explained.
"Jeffords came in from the barn and told Prince, and he came for
me. Then we went to Elisha, so we could use his car to trace back
Daddy's route home. We knew he'd gone down to see your father, so
we knew which way the horse would of come from. We found Daddy
unconscious alongside the road, just where it starts up our hill. He

had a bullet wound in his shoulder and another one—a flesh wound, Doc says now—on his head." She pulled back and looked at me, her eyes still horrified by what had happened. "When he regained consciousness, he told us someone had shot him off his horse."

"Did he say who?"

"He kept losing consciousness. The doctor said the bullet creased his skull and may have caused a concussion. We were so frightened that he'd die, we just got him here as quickly as we could." I was holding both her arms between my hands, and I felt a shiver pass through her body. "Oh God, Samuel. There was so much blood. I thought for sure he would die."

A loud curse came from Doc's examining room. "Head wounds bleed a lot, even minor ones," I said. I glanced toward the sound of Jehiel's curses. "He sounds well enough now." I smiled, and Elizabeth began to laugh with relief. Then the laughter mixed with sobs and she fell against my shoulder and allowed me to hold her again.

Frenchy arrived by the time Doc finished his ministrations. We found Jehiel seated on the examining table, his legs so long that his feet touched the floor. There was a heavy bandage on his head, and another on his shoulder, beneath his bloodstained shirt. His left arm was in a sling.

"Guess I din' remember ta keep an eye out like I promised," he said.

"What's he talkin' about?" Frenchy asked.

I explained how Jehiel had visited with my father the previous evening, and how, upon leaving, he had warned me to keep an eye out for Preserved and his friends, saying he would do the same himself.

Frenchy looked back at Jehiel. "You sayin' it was Preserved Firman who done this? You get a look at who it was shot you?"

"Didn't see nothin' but a big flash. Then another. Didn't even hear the shots 'til just before I hit the ground. After that I didn't hear or see nothin'."

"Sounds like two quick shots from a saddlegun. Maybe two guns." Frenchy raised his chin to Doc. "You dig a bullet outta him?"

Doc shook his head. "The bullet went right through his shoulder. Never hit a bone, or anything else that might of stopped it."

Frenchy turned to me. "Let's get Johnny Taft on this. I want him to see if he kin find me a fresh-spent bullet inna tree up there. No hope for any tracks. Not with this goddaman rain an' all."

"Why don't you go an' see if Preserved Firman or Abel Turner got theyself some guns that's been fired," Jehiel snapped. "Abel saw me go inta Samuel's house when he was sittin' on Miz Pierce's porch with you last evenin'. Sure wouldn't a'been hard fer him to tell Preserved I be headed home soon, or to rec'nize it fer himself."

"Don't you worry," Frenchy said. "Samuel an' me, we be on those two like stink on a skunk, we get us a bullet we kin tie to this here shooting."

Jehiel snorted. "Sheee-it. It be easier fer me to just go up to Morgan Holler an' shoot them dumb-assed, backwoods, knuckle-draggin' sumbitches myself."

"I sure hope you won't do that," Frenchy said.

"Why not?" Jehiel snapped. "You all set to arrest me for killin' that no-account white boy. Might as well give you somebody I actually done kilt, so's you don't go makin' a goddamn fool outta yerself."

I saw Frenchy's eye narrow and his jaw tighten. "I was kinda hopin' to avoid any more killin', Mr. Flood. Be it Preserved Firman, or Abel Turner, or you, yerself, sir."

Jehiel threw back his head and laughed. "Well, I thank you, sir, fer includin' me in that there list. That's the whitest damned thing I done ever hear'd." Jehiel's mood and tone changed so quickly it took both Frenchy and me by surprise. Suddenly, his voice became little more than a snarl. "But when you see them sumbitches, you tell 'em that they ain't about to catch Jehiel Flood nappin' no second time. You tell 'em, they come fer me agin', they better be ready fer a fight like they ain't never seen before. You hear that, Deputy Sheriff Frenchy LeMay?"

"I hear you, Mr. Flood."

"It's good that you do, Deputy. It's damn good that you do."

It was still several hours before dawn, too early to drag Johnny Taft from his bed to begin searching for the bullets fired at Jehiel. I used the hiatus to drive Elizabeth home, staying close behind Elisha Bowles's car, as if guarding its four occupants from further attack.

Doc Hawley had asked Jehiel to remain at his office under "observation," but the proposal was dismissed out of hand. Jehiel said he had no intention of "hiding from a pair of no-account white men," as he put it. Instead, he would return home with Elisha and Prince and Jeffords, and once there arm himself and his entire family. He suggested that anybody who came calling at either his or Elizabeth's house "announce hisself first from behind a tree."

Elizabeth shivered beside me as we headed out of town. It was cold and damp, and the heater in my Model A was far from effective. Yet, I knew there was more to the cold chill that coursed through her body.

"Your brother looks angry," I said. "Even more than your father. Prince was even giving me hateful looks back at Doc's office."

"Prince is frightened," Elizabeth said. "He loves Daddy. He maybe even loves him better than the rest of us. And he's afraid they're going to kill him. Right now, I think he's angry at anybody who's white."

I let out a bitter laugh.

"Why are you laughing like that, Samuel?"

"It's my color again. It seems to confuse everyone in this town." I stole a glance at her as I pulled my car onto her road. "To you and Prince, I'm all lily white. To most everybody else in town, I'm colored. Hell, Victorious Shepard is scared witless that I'll run off with her daughter and give her a passel of Negro grandchildren."

"I see," Elizabeth said.

We drove on and were halfway up the hill until I could stand Elizabeth's lack of comment no longer.

"You do think of me as white, don't you?"

Elizabeth looked out her window into the blackness of the woods we were passing through. "Once, when we were children, I remember holding you in my arms while you cried and cried and told me you were as white as a boy could be." She drew a long breath. "How else am I to think of you, Samuel?"

I was stunned; unable to help the words that came out of me. "I just want you to think of me with love."

She stared straight ahead. "Love has never been the problem that sat between us, Samuel." She paused, then turned to look at me. "Are you sleeping with Hannah Shepard?" she asked.

Again, I could not control my words. "No, I'm not." The lie burned in my mouth.

Elizabeth stared out into the trees again. "When I see you together, I sense that you are." She raised her chin as if that simple gesture added dignity to her subject. "Women can sense the feelings of other women, you know. So if what you say is true, it's not because Hannah is unwilling."

"I'm not interested in Hannah," I said.

She remained silent, even though I desperately wished to hear her speak.

"You know where my heart lies," I said. "You've always known that."

Still there was silence.

Elisha Bowles pulled his car into Jehiel's dooryard, as I drove on ahead to the narrow lane that led to Elizabeth's cabin. When I stopped, Maybelle and Ruby rushed out; Elizabeth quickly told them that their father had been wounded, but was now safe at home, and she would explain the rest later. She remained in my car as her sisters hurried off to Jehiel's house.

"This madness has to end, Samuel. All of it. It has to be over and done with before someone else is killed."

I shook my head slowly, perhaps even sadly, although I think I was well past sadness. "There's nothing you can do," I said. "There's very little that I can do. Or Frenchy, either. We can only discover the truth and let it be known. But even if we succeed, it won't change anything."

She stared at me, openly incredulous. "The truth always changes things. I believe that. I always have."

"But this has nothing to do with the truth," I said. "This is about hatred. About lines that were drawn years ago." I turned one hand over and stared at the pale palm. I could feel Elizabeth watching me, perhaps even wondering why I was doing it. "Or, perhaps, it is about truth," I said. "Perhaps it's about telling people a truth they don't want to know. Like understanding that I have no color, no race, because no one will allow me to have one." I looked up. Elizabeth was staring at me, her eyes filled with concern. "Perhaps it's like that," I said. "Like telling people a truth that will only make them hate you more."

Elizabeth closed her eyes and shuddered. "Yes, I can see that. And if it is like that, Samuel . . . then I don't know what to do."

"Right now you must protect yourself. Do you still have your old shotgun?"

"Yes."

"Do you have shells for it?"

"Yes. I keep a box handy in case something gets after the chickens."

"Then you should get it out and keep it close to hand. It's all you can do."

Before I left, Maybelle and Ruby returned with Jeffords Page tagging along behind them, a shotgun loosely cradled in his arm. He eyed me nervously until I nodded, granting him some unspoken approval, then he took up a position on Elizabeth's porch. I left Elizabeth then, and went down the road to her father's house. Elisha Bowles's old touring car was still parked in front when I arrived, and it was he who opened the door to my knock. The fear I had seen in his eyes earlier was even stronger now.

"Praise God, Samuel," he said. "Come in and help me bring some sanity to this house."

I stepped past Elisha and found Jehiel seated at his kitchen table, his head and shoulder still swathed in bandages. His old Winchester lay on the table before him, and Prince stood just behind, his own Winchester propped against a wall, a quick reach away.

"You should be in bed," I said.

Jehiel ignored my concern. "You ever hear tell of a college professor named Harry Perkins?" he asked.

I noticed the patois was gone from his speech. It meant I would not be forced to endure his favorite pastime: playing the ignorant, backwoods Negro to someone's "educated white man," his eyes glittering all the while with a barely concealed self-satisfaction.

I knew Professor Perkins all too well, and I despised him. "I believe he teaches zoology at the university," I said.

Jehiel grunted. "Well, I just found out about that sumbitch. I read up on him, accidental like, in one of Doc's medical journals, while he was makin' me sit around bein' *observed.*"

"So you read about his eugenics theories," I said. Since the Great War Perkins had been studying ways to improve the human species through selective breeding. In recent years he had begun suggesting voluntary sterilization of select groups, who, according to his beliefs, were "damaging the nation's seedbed." While many decried these theories, his proposals had received some surprising support in both the scientific and political communities.

Jehiel glared at me. "You knew all about this then?"

"Yes, sir. I did."

"You even knew that the Vermont legislature, because of this here racist sumbitch of a professor, very quietly passed us a voluntary sterilization law?"

"I knew that, yes," I said.

"Then how come you never tol' me?" Jehiel roared.

I looked down at my shoes and fought to hide my amusement. The subject was old to me. Beyond my anger. "Because I didn't want to listen to you yell at me," I said. I saw the faint hint of a smile break on Prince's lips. Then it blossomed as Jehiel began to laugh.

When he stopped laughing he began to shake his head. "I liked to choke when I read all that stuff 'bout pirates an' gypsies," he said, the patois back now. "Man is the sumbitch of sumbitches."

Among Perkins's theories was one that called for the "breeding of better Vermonters," by ridding its stock of pirates and gypsies. These were euphemisms for, respectively, French Canadians and Abenaki Indians, given because of the former's alleged inclination to live and work near lakes and rivers, and the latter's to follow their forefathers' practice of biannual migration to seasonal hunting and fishing grounds. Both groups were anathema to Perkins, and he strongly urged they be eliminated from the breeding pool, thereby saving Vermont's Anglo-American-Yankee stock from irreversible damage.

"You should concentrate on the racists who are trying to kill you," I said. "Perkins is of no consequence."

Jehiel stared at me as though he was being assaulted by some incredible foolishness. "Of no consequence? This sumbitch is tryin' to kill me. Don't you understand that, boy? This man, this goddamn university professor, he's jus' like that bastard Hitler over in Germany." He waved his hand, taking in everyone in the room. "This sumbitch, Perkins, he wants to kill off all of us. Oh, not with a gun, or any t'other uncivil ways. He wants us to sign papers so's he can sterilize us outta existence. That's what he wants." He jabbed a finger at me. "And you, too, Samuel. Maybe he wants you gone most of all. 'Cause you got more mixed, unnatural, goddamn blood in you than all of us put together. Leastways according to that goddamn, racist sumbitch."

I listened to Jehiel rant on. I did not want to tell him that during college I had once taken a class with Perkins, and had sat one day listening as a fellow student propounded the belief that the Negro race descended from Noah's son Ham. It was an old tale, taken from a misreading of Genesis, claiming that Ham—having seen his father naked and drunk, and having taken pleasure in it—had so offended God that he and all his future progeny were condemned to live and work as servants throughout eternity. What had amazed me was that Perkins had agreed. And to this day, I can still see him standing before the class, quoting from *The Black Gauntlet*, Mary Howard Schoolcraft's novel of the previous century, the words so filled with hate they are still burned into my mind.

Perkins had raised one finger and smiled as he quoted School-craft's words: "I believe a refined Anglo-Saxon lady would sooner be burned at the stake than be married to one of these black descendents of Ham." And it was then that I had instantly known why Perkins had not included Negroes among those who were despoiling the genetic structure of Anglo-American-Yankee Vermont. The thought of anyone seeking such a union was simply beyond his comprehension.

I looked down at Jehiel and offered a smile, thinking of the outrage my recollections would produce. "Are you through yelling for a spell?" I asked.

He narrowed one eye at me. "For a spell. A short one I 'spect."

"Then I'd like to borrow Prince," I said. "I'm about to drag Johnny Taft out of bed, and I want Prince to show us exactly where your kinfolk found you."

(9)

Prince had refused to leave Jehiel's side, so Elisha had come with me to rouse Johnny Taft from his bed. But Johnny was already awake and on his second cup of coffee when we arrived, and he immediately jabbed a finger at the preacher, warning away any missionary efforts.

"Don't you go prayin' at me now," he snapped. "Or tellin' me that I'm goin' ta hell. I ain't gonna be standin' fer that in my own house."

Johnny's house was a small, dirt-floored cabin just outside of town, located on a rock outcropping that hung precariously above the river. It was land no one wanted, and Johnny had simply built his cabin years ago, and lived there as a squatter ever since. The parcel was actually owned by John and Sally Ball, a couple so elderly they had probably forgotten that Johnny was even there. So Johnny had remained, content and unbothered, free to tell anyone who would listen that the land had belonged to his tribe long before any white man had laid claim to it.

There was only one large room in Johnny's cabin, and it was

surprisingly clean, given that it housed a lone bachelor who spent most of his days roaming the woods. There was a small handmade table with bench stools for each side, a cooking hearth that also provided the cabin's only source of heat, a bed, and a wall full of pegs that served as a closet. The river below was Johnny's sink and washtub, and his privy was wherever he found it in the adjoining woods.

Elisha seemed to take Johnny's words to heart, and he was unusually quiet while Johnny finished his coffee, and again as we made our way to the turnoff where Jehiel had been shot.

Johnny spent the first half-hour searching out the place where the shooter or shooters had lain in wait, finally locating it a short distance into the woods, just across the road from where Jehiel had fallen. When I asked him how he was certain that was the spot, he pointed to a concentration of tobacco spittings beneath a large pine.

"Ain't from no poacher," he said. "Lessen he was 'spectin' a buck ta come walkin' down the road." He raised his chin toward the spittings. "An' it weren't long ago. Juice is still wet. Whoever it was sat hisself here no later'n las' night. He was chewin' an' spittin' an' keepin' his mouth from goin' dry." He gave me a mirthless grin. "Prob'ly a touch nervous 'cause he know'd he was waitin' fer a man what might shoot back."

"How many shooters are we talking about?" I asked.

Johnny gave me an exaggerated shrug. "My guess is one, from what I kin see. But it's hard ta tell, Samuel. You sure picked a right poor time ta be checkin' on sign. Right after a heavy rain an' all. This boy hadn't been spittin' where he did, all them juice droppin's prob'ly woulda been washed away, too. That ol' pine tree sheltered 'em jus' enough."

Johnny began checking neighboring trees, finally stopping beside a beech. He pointed to an abrasion on the bark and grinned. "Pressed his rifle agin' the side of this here tree ta steady his shot," he said. He began searching the ground to the right of the tree, carefully moving fresh-fallen leaves. Within the first minute he had uncovered one cartridge casing, the shiny brass catching the sunlight as it filtered through the trees. Within another minute he had a second. He looked up grinning again. "You said two shots?"

I nodded. "Let's not touch those casings until Frenchy gets here," I said. "Might be he'll want to send them to some laboratory for this new fingerprint study the police are using now."

"Can tell right from here they's forty-five caliber," Johnny said.

"And you still think only one shooter and one gun? Jehiel said the shots came very close together, and both shots were hits."

"One shooter," Johnny said. "Jus' somebody who knew his way 'roun a rifle." His smile boadened. "Know fer a fact that Preserved Firman's gots hisself a fine forty-five-caliber Sharps saddlegun. Had it modified ta take five shells. Know fer a fact, too, he's a power'ful good shot with it."

"Two shots, both a little off their mark," I said. I gauged the distance to where Jehiel had fallen. "Looks to be about sixty yards, maybe less. Not a real hard shot for a marksman."

Johnny touched his eye with one finger, then pointed toward the spot where Jehiel had fallen. "You forgettin' a couple things, Samuel. T'was pitch black here las' night. No moon, prob'ly no stars neither wit' that storm a'comin'." He let out a barking laugh. "An' the target was pretty dark, too. Add ta that, the man shot at was sittin' on a movin' horse, an' I'm thinkin' it weren't no easy shot."

I considered Johnny's insight and found nothing to argue. I looked out toward the spot where Jehiel had fallen. "I wonder why the shooter didn't walk up and make sure he'd killed him?"

Johnny laughed again. "Think about it, Samuel. If you done jus' shot yerself Jehiel Flood, would ya go walkin' up on him, lessen ya was sure he was dead?"

Frenchy found us half an hour later and told us we'd only done half the job he wanted.

"Need to find them spent bullets if we can," he said. "We get us the bullet that hit Jehiel—maybe even still has some blood on it— an' we match it up ta a particular rifle, then we got enough to charge somebody with attempted murder." He looked down at the paper bag he held in one hand, which now contained the brass car- tridge casings Johnny had found. "What we got here is good—I sure don't mean ta say you fellas ain't done a fine job—'cause these cas- ings an' that mark on that tree, it tells us what direction to look in to find those spent bullets. And if we find 'em"—he shook the bag for emphasis—"well, then this here brass gets even more valuable in makin' our case." He gave Johnny and Elisha and I a small shrug. "But all alone. . . . well, any good lawyer is just gonna say them cas- ings was left here when his client was out huntin'. And there be no way the state's attorney is gonna prove that's a lie. So we arrest any- body just on this, judge an' jury'll turn him loose fer sure."

"We only answer to o-ne judge. And I say a-men to that," Elisha said.

The preacher's words took us by surprise, he'd been so quiet for so long.

"Oh, damn, don't start him up now," Johnny moaned.

Elisha glowered. "You would do well to listen to the Word, sin- ner." His intonation brought a roll to Johnny's eyes.

"I ain't stayin' if he starts in," he warned. "Ya ain't payin' me enough fer that. I'll walk back iff'n I have ta."

"Elisha, what has stirred you up so suddenly?" I asked. "Up 'til now you've been quiet as one of your church mice."

"I've been fearful," Elisha intoned again, his chin elevating with his voice. "I am ashamed to say it, but it is true. May Sweet Je-sus forgive me."

"Oh, Christ," Johnny groaned.

Elisha's eyes snapped to him. "Do not blaspheme. Not in m-y presence."

I held up a hand, stopping them both. "What caused your fear, Elisha?" I asked.

A great sadness seemed to drop across the preacher's face, and I was surprised by the depth of emotion I could see in his eyes. I must confess, I have always considered Elisha somewhat of a fool, despite his education. And possibly a bit of a scalawag, if the rumors about him being forced to leave other towns have any truth to them.

"It shames me to say it now, but I felt certain there would be no serious investigation into the attack on Jehiel," he said.

I felt my blood rise with the words, and I could tell he saw the anger in my face. He raised a hand, as if ready to ward off a blow. "It was not you I was concerned about, Samuel," he said. "But the Lord surely knows that your abilities in this type of investigation are limited." His eyes moved to Frenchy. "It was this man I feared. And I see now that I have wronged him in both my heart and my mind."

Elisha had spoken the words with great flourish, almost as though delivering them from his pulpit. A smile came to Frenchy's lips, and to this day I do not know if it was from the words themselves, or the delivery.

"Well, I'm glad yer mind's at ease, sir." Frenchy spoke through a chuckle. "And I tell ya true. If we find the man who fired them shots at yer friend, I promise you he's gonna find hisself sittin' in my jail." He hitched up his pants and eyed us each in turn. "Now let me show you boys how you can help me find them bullets, so's I kin keep the promise I just made this man."

Over the next hour I watched Frenchy work with increasing admiration, as he improvised a forensic investigation of the crime scene. First, he found a relatively straight tree branch, which he cut down until it was reduced to a four-foot stick. Then he aligned the stick with the mark on the beech tree, and directed it to the approximate height of Jehiel's head and shoulders, were he still moving down the road on horseback.

"Now I want each of you to bend down an' give a long look down the length of this stick. First off, I want you to see how the angle rises as it moves off inta the woods across that there road. Then I want you to pick yerself out the first line of trees that hits yer eye, an' figure how high up that angle crosses 'em. Then pick another line of trees behind the first, an' do the same. Then another, an' then one more. Woods are pretty thick here, so I don't guess them bullets could of gone too far before they hit somethin'. So we shouldn't havta go too far back."

When each of us had done as Frenchy directed, he removed the stick and hitched his pants again. "Now I'm gonna stay here and hold this here stick up so's you boys can look back an' git yer bearings if you need to. But I want you to keep one more thing in mind. Mr. Flood was hit in the left shoulder and the left side of his head. Now, as you look at them woods from here, keep in mind that head crease mighta deflected that bullet a touch to the right. Far as the other shot goes, that shoulder wound went clear through without hittin' any bone, so's the bullet likely lost a little speed by plowin' through a man. My guess is it started to tumble an' drop pretty quick. So you might look a bit lower fer that one as you move on back in them woods." He paused and looked at each of us in turn. "Now you all understan' what I want?"

We spread out and began our inspection of the trees across the road. Not surprisingly, it proved quite a maddening activity. I have lived in Vermont all my life, and have spent much of that time in its woods, and with all the hunting we enjoy one would expect the trees to resemble those of a battlefield. Yet there is something about a tree that seems to reject the intrusion of man. No matter what cruelty we inflict on them, trees seem to literally absorb it and go on as if nothing had occurred. Farmers string barbed wire, using trees as posts, and over time the tree simply grows around the wire, swallowing it up, so to speak. The same is true with bullets. In all the years I've spent wandering our forests and woodlots, I cannot recall any bullet damage drawing my eye. Unless a bullet strikes the edge of a tree and tears away a chunk, the porous nature of wood, and the crevasses and crannies of bark, seem to conspire to hide any entry from the human eye.

Pine trees are the exception, given as they are to oozing a thick gooey sap after being damaged. And it was here that we found the one bullet that would end up in our hands.

Johnny Taft found it, of course. His woodsman's eye readjusted to the unusual task as soon as we began. He seemed to cover each tree like a nuthatch searching out a tasty bug. He closed in on each one he targeted, surveying it, studying it, bringing his eye within inches at times, even climbing a few so he could inspect some anomaly he had spotted from the ground. And then he had it, about ten feet up in a thick pine, sap dripping from the newly inflicted wound.

Johnny climbed the tree and dug it out with his buck knife, and presented the gnarled and twisted bit of metal to Frenchy with a broad, beaming smile. He was like a small boy, pleased with the "treasure" he had found, unfazed even when Frenchy declared the bullet possibly worthless for our purposes, because of its mangled condition.

We never did find the second bullet. It was absorbed forever by the forest. Frenchy speculated it was the bullet that had passed through Jehiel's shoulder; that it had lost so much speed its trajectory had dropped quickly of its own weight, and it had plowed into the ground.

"Some wild turkey'll dig her out some day, while it's scratchin' fer acorns. But I don't reckon we will, lessen we come in here with shovels and strain the dirt through a sieve. I don't 'spect you boys are up fer that. I know I sure ain't."

"What do we do now?" I asked. I was expecting some new forensic sleight of hand, but apparently all of Frenchy's magic had been used up.

He smiled at me. I'm certain he had read my thoughts. "Well, me, I'm gonna take this here bullet inta the university, an' have 'em tell me if there's still enough clear markin's on it to match 'er up with a specific weapon. If there is, I'm gonna ask a judge fer a warrant to seize me a certain forty-five-caliber Sharps rifle I'm partial to havin' a look at."

"Praise b-ee to Sweet Jesus. May your wi-ll be done, Lord." Elisha sang out the words with such conviction, it even made Johnny Taft smile.

"Amen to that, Reverend," Frenchy said. He turned to Johnny. "As of now yer deputized if you want it. I need me a man who's good with a rifle, who kin watch the road an' the woods up on Nigger Hill. You up fer that?"

"It pay hard money?" Johnny asked.

"Dollar an' a half a day," Frenchy said.

"You got yerself a man," Johnny said.

Frenchy turned to Elisha. "I don't know how you feel 'bout guns and shootin', Reverend. But I was you, I'd keep to inside as much as possible, an' keep a weapon close to hand. If you don't think you kin be doin' that, I'd feel better if you bunked in with Mr. Flood, or Miz Elizabeth." Frenchy thought about the implication of what he had said, and quickly added: "Maybe you could use that little cottage she's got." He paused and put a hand on Elisha's shoulder. "I don't think nobody's out to hurt you, Reverend. I'm just afeared they might shoot at color before they even know who that person is."

It was like an actor's cue to old Elisha. His body seemed to inflate slightly; his head tilted back; the words seemed to flow from deep in his chest.

"The Lo-rd is my shepherd. I shall no-t want."

Frenchy patted his shoulder again, hoping to ebb the flow.

"He re-stores my soul. I fear nooo evil, for Thou art with me . . ."

Frenchy took Elisha's shoulders in both his hands. "Jus' so you don't end up dwellin' in the house of the Lord, Reverend. That's all I'm worried about." He turned quickly to me, before Elisha could get started again. "I got a couple of things I need from you, Samuel. First off, I need you to get that gal, Jenny, up here, like we planned, so's she can get a look at that fella we're interested in. Then I need you to set up a little town meetin'." He shook his head. "Thing's are gettin' outta hand here, Samuel. And we need to settle folks down, before they start choosin' up sides." He glanced at Elisha. "I'd sure like to use yer church, Reverend. Churches have a kinda peaceable effect on folks."

Elisha agreed, although I thought I detected a touch of concern in his eyes. I asked Frenchy when he wanted the meeting set.

"Sooner the better," he said. "What say we do'er tomorrow night, right after supper. It'll be Saturday, a night most country folk is lookin' for somethin' to do. What say seven o'clock? That'll give the farm folk enough time fer chores an' chow, an' still get themselves in here to church."

"I'll stop by the store and the barbershop tomorrow," I said. "Saturday is a busy day at both. And I'll put up some notices around town today."

"Be good to take a ride out to some of the farms, too," Frenchy said. "An' while yer there, ask them folks to spread the word to their neighbors. Farmers are good at doin' that." Frenchy gave me a long look I couldn't quite read. "Idea is to get the word to as many folks as possible. Even the ones might give us some trouble." He broke the mood with a smile, then added: "By the time you finish up with all that, you'll prob'ly be ready fer some more police work. I get back an' don't find you to home, I'll look fer you up on Nigger Hill. I 'spect you have time, you'll be up there givin' Johnny here a hand."

I went home and got out some old polling-place posters, turned them over, and printed up a notice of the meeting on the back side. Then I drove around and posted them at the junctions of all roads intersecting the main road.

That done, I drove back to Shepard's Store and its adjoining barbershop. I knew word of the meeting would spread quickly, as any news does in small country towns, and it would spread even more quickly once Victorious Shepard began proclaiming her views from behind her postmistress' window.

It was only eight-thirty in the morning when I arrived at Shepard's Store. Hannah was behind the counter when I entered, and she favored me with a smile that made me think immediately of my bed. I gave her a poster and asked her to display it where everyone who came into the store was sure to see it. Then I went into the empty barbershop and asked her father to do the same.

When I came out Victorious was standing at the counter. The post office at the rear of the store was not yet open for business. Victorious strictly followed the federal government's hours, and refused to open the window before nine A.M. It also closed promptly at four in the afternoon, and although residents were allowed to go to their lockboxes whenever the store was open, Victorious made a point of not filling any with mail until the "official" hour had arrived.

"What's this meetin' about?" Victorious was using her most demanding tone of voice, and it caught me up short. "Does it mean that somebody's finally been arrested?"

"Someone tried to kill Jehiel Flood last night—"

"I'm aware of that," she said, before I could finish.

I paused deliberately, the silence intended to let her know that more reticence would follow if she did not let me finish my sentences. The effort was wasted.

"Well?" she demanded.

"Deputy LeMay is afraid things are getting out of hand. That some people might even be jumping to conclusions that have no merit. He wants to let everyone know what's being done, what we've found so far and what we intend to do." She started to speak, but I raised my hand, stopping her. "Now, he can't tell things that might jeopardize the investigation, but he can set people straight about some facts they may not know, and maybe keep some fool from taking things into his own hands."

"So he's gonna give us a loada cow flop, is he?" She shook her head. "Far as I know . . ." She paused, stared me down, and allowed me to understand that what she knew was considerable. "Far as I know, the only people who's gonna take things in their own hands is the kinfolk of that poor dead boy."

I looked up at the ceiling and took a deep breath. "Damn, Victorious. I am so weary of hearing about this poor dead boy. I can't count the number of complaints that first my daddy, and then that I have got, over all these years. All of them about Royal Firman being everything from a pain in the backside to a bully to an out-and-out thief. Why you, yourself, once had me talk to him about stealing snuff from your store."

Hannah, who had been standing by listening, let out a half-stifled giggle. Victorious drew an offended breath and threw her a withering look.

"But you know it's true, Mama," Hannah said. "You told me I had to keep my eyes sharp whenever Royal came in the store."

"Just 'cause he was a no-account, didn't give those nigs the right ta kill him," she snapped.

"That's the whole point, Victorious," I countered. "We don't know that they did."

"And that's what you intend to tell folks at this here meetin'?" She raised her chin toward the notices I still held and let out a derisive snort.

"I won't be telling folks anything. Deputy LeMay will do the talking. I hope you'll be there to hear him," I said.

"Oh, I'll be there," she snapped. "You can be sure of that, Samuel Bradley."

On my way to pick up Jenny I stopped at some outlying farms to tell as many as I could about the meeting. There seemed little question in most minds about what had happened, even among those who did not know exactly who had been killed. The nigs—probably Jehiel Flood himself—had killed a white man, pure and simple. I tried to explain that folks were rushing to judgement, but had little success in changing any minds. So I urged everyone to come and hear what Deputy LeMay had to say, and to get word of the meeting out to as many neighbors as possible.

I arrived at Joshua Cory's farm shortly after one, and caught him as he was heading back to the fields. At first he was reluctant to let Jenny go on a workday, and pointed out that Sunday was her regular day off. I convinced him to make an exception this once, arguing that in these hard times it stood a man well to have the sheriff's office in his debt.

It took Jenny a half-hour to wash and change, as she refused to go anywhere off the farm in her work clothes. She came out of her cabin wearing a homespun dress with pale pink and green flowers set on a field of yellow, all of it accenting the soft chocolate color of her skin. She was not a pretty woman, as I have said before, being neither slender nor comely, but there was a definite aura of sexuality about the way she moved and held her head and smiled, and all of it stirred my baser nature.

"Tell me about Royal," I said, as we headed to the cutoff that would take us back through Addison Hollow. "Tell me what he was like the last day you saw him, and anything you can remember him saying."

"Well, I tol' you, he wan-sted me ta do him pleasure in t'at spec'l way he likes it."

"And you said you did that for him, right?"

"Yes, suh, I did."

"You're sure?"

Jenny nodded, then turned coy. She lowered her eyes slightly and smiled at me. "It ain't somethin' you forgets."

I felt foolish, and fought against the color creeping into my cheeks.

"But I din' do it fer t'other boy, even when he kep' axin' me. I tol' him he could give me a poke, iff'n he wants, but he jus' keep sayin' he wants the same as his fren gots, an' I wooden do that." A small smile played along her lips. "I doan mind doin' it fer one, you un-nerstan', but I doan like havin' more'n one at the same time."

Jenny kept glancing at my lap as I drove, and I felt certain she was trying to determine if her words were arousing me. I must admit that they were, although I did my best to conceal it.

"Did Royal often bring friends with him when he came to visit you?" I asked.

"No, suh. This was the firs' time he done t'at. He knowed Mr. Joshua din' like havin' a buncha mens show up all together, 'cause I tol' him that a'fore. But like I tol' you, him an' his fren, de was a might liquored up t'at day."

"So this friend, the boy with the beard, he didn't do . . . anything with you?"

"No, suh. He says he ain't gonna pay no fi'ty cents, lessen he gets what he wants. An' I already tol' him I ain'ts gonna do it."

"What about Royal himself? What can you tell me about him?"

"He likes colored gals, tha's all I really knows 'bout him. Says he has hisself one over ta home alla time."

I could feel my stomach knot. "Did he say what that colored gal's name was?"

She shook her head. "I axed him, jus' in case it was somebody I knowed, but he never did say. Coulda been jus' talkin' big. I kinda wondered 'bout t'at, wondered iff'n he gots him a colored gal ta home, like he said, why's he be drivin' alla ways over cheer? An' I 'members the firs' time he come roun', he was jus' lookin' at me neckid, like he done never seen a brown-skin gal a'fore. Tol' me then his daddy would skin him fer sure, he ever even thought he was layin' wit' a colored gal."

I was grateful for her words, although I said nothing. In fact I let the subject drop completely, lest she say something I couldn't bear to hear.

"Do you have many men coming by every week?" I asked.

Jenny gave me a curious look, and I felt I had to explain. "I'm only asking because I'm worried you might be confusing Royal Firman with someone else, or perhaps getting mixed up about when you last saw him."

Jenny shook her head, more vigorously than before. "I ain't confused, mister." She struggled over the word. "He be visitin' me this pas' week, an his fren be with him. I's sure 'bout t'at. It be the dead boy in that pitcher you shows me, fer sure." She glanced out the side window as if she didn't want to look at me when she said the rest. "I gets me maybe three, four boys droppin' by ever' week. Sometimes a little mo', but not so manys as I cain't 'member them."

She looked at me imploringly, and I felt a sudden guilt for the way I had questioned her.

"I's jus' tryin' ta save some money so's I kin have somthin' someday," she said. "I don't wanna grow up an' be some old colored woman what ain't gots nothin'."

I drove Jenny to the river landing where I knew Preserved would be dropping off a load of lumber late that afternoon. We went up onto a high bank on the opposite shore and took a position where Jenny could see the men unloading the horse-drawn wagons.

When Preserved's logging team arrived, I gave her a pair of binoculars I had brought with me, and she spotted Abel on the first try.

"Are you certain?" I asked.

"Yes, suh. Tha's the boy done come wit Royal, the one t'at gots mad at me when I won't do what he wants."

"And you're sure it was this week? You're positive?"

"Yes, suh. They was the only mens I had t'all week. Like I says, it's usual fer more ta come by. But this week t'was jus' them two boys." She handed me back my binoculars and smiled. "Lessen you wants ta be one, yersef," she added.

{ 10 }

The woods are lovely in the deepest dark of night; quiet, except for the sound of wind moving through the trees, or the cautious prowl of animals, some in search of food, others trying to escape predation. It is a time I yearn for, a time that fills me with a peace I seldom know . . . and drives away the endless sense of loneliness.

Elizabeth passed by her window and stopped to glance out into the yard. I made no attempt to hide my presence, as I had so many times in the past. She stared at me, although I am certain she could see nothing more than a silhouette.

Jeffords was in his place on the front porch, so Elizabeth knew the figure in her yard presented no threat. She opened the front door, stood quietly for a moment, then descended the stairs.

"When did you get here, Samuel?" she asked when she reached me.

"An hour ago, perhaps a bit more." She was so close now I could smell her scent, feel the warmth that radiated from her body, and I continued speaking as if through a deep fog. "Frenchy asked me to help Johnny Taft keep watch on the hill. Later tonight he'll come here to spell me."

She smiled. "I like seeing you out here, Samuel. I've always liked seeing you out here."

I did not know what to say. Should I tell her that watching over her cabin had become a part of my life, a part of me? Could I afford to give her knowledge of this power she held over me? But what did it matter? Had she not just told me that she knew?

She was still smiling at me, then she cocked her head to one side and her look became more serious. "Samuel, have you ever noticed how you try so hard to be alone?"

"No, I don't think I have noticed that," I said.

"I think it's because when you are—when there's no chance of anyone being with you—that it's then you feel the safest. Safe because no one can reject you and make you lonely." She paused to think about what she had said, then went on. "Isn't that odd, Samuel? That you seek to be alone to escape loneliness."

I stared at her and said nothing, and she reached out and softly stroked my cheek.

"Would you like some coffee?" she asked, sparing me the need of any words.

"Yes. It would help me stay awake," I said.

"Come inside. Keep me company while I make some."

"I don't want to wake Ruby or Maybelle."

"They're at Daddy's house. They didn't trust Prince to care for him proper. Come inside."

"I should stay here and keep watch."

"Jeffords is here. Nothing will move through these woods without him knowing. He'll call out if he needs you." She wrapped her arms about herself and shivered, the evening chill suddenly upon her. I took her arm and led her back to the cabin.

As we stepped inside I could smell the fresh coffee that Elizabeth had already brewed. I looked at her, curious about her request that I keep her company while she made some. She closed the door and came against me, her arms encircling my neck.

Her lips pressed against mine, her body soft and yielding, as her tongue danced inside my mouth with an urgency that soon made my breath come in quick gasps.

"I saw you driving through town today . . ." Her words were spoken between kisses. "I looked out . . . the school window . . . and there you were . . . driving past . . . There was a Negro woman . . . in your car . . ."

"She was . . . the whore . . . Royal visited . . . the day he died." I struggled with the words, as her mouth absorbed every part of me, mind and body. "Abel Turner was with him . . . and I needed her . . . to see him . . . and say it was . . . positively him." She continued to kiss me, as her fingers unbuttoned my coat, then my shirt beneath it.

"Did you . . . make love to her?"

"No . . . never . . . I would never." I moved my hands along her back, then down to her buttocks and along her thighs. The suppleness of her body as it yielded to my touch was intoxicating, mesmerizing; my heart pounded so I could hear it inside my chest, feel it throbbing so steadily I was certain Elizabeth could hear it and feel it, too. Her hand slid down my body and went to the erection that pressed against my trousers, her fingers struggling to encircle it through the cloth.

"Yes. Yes, Samuel. Yes." She breathed the words into my mouth, as she began to softly bite my lips with her own. "It's . . . been . . . so . . . long."

We were seventeen again; our bodies nestled in the high grass at the edge of the meadow, the overhanging branch of a sycamore shading us from the afternoon sun. Elizabeth lay naked beside me, the sun filtering through the branches dappling her skin with light and shadow. She took my hand and brought it to her breast, smooth and round, the pale brown flesh seeming even lighter next to the darker brown of her areola. Her hand cupped the back of my head and gently brought my mouth down to her, and I heard her gasp as my lips surrounded her nipple.

* * *

The pounding on the door jarred me, the wood moving in the frame and hitting my back with a light, steady rhythm.

"What . . . ?" It was all I could manage.

Elizabeth pressed her face against mine and let out a groan. "It's Jeffords," she whispered. "He says . . . Deputy LeMay's car . . . just pulled into the dooryard." Her breath came in quick gasps, and I could feel a film of perspiration on her face.

"No, no, no, no." I spoke the words like a chant that might somehow change what she had just said. I looked into her eyes as she stepped away from me. There was disappointment there, but also laughter.

"You must go out to him," she said. "Invite him in for coffee. Just keep him outside long enough for me to wash the flush from my face."

"What about the flush on mine?"

"I can't help that," she said. "Let's hope the darkness hides it."

Her words hit at me. It was what we were doing. We were hiding, as if what we felt for each other was something that would so shock people it could never be seen.

"We don't have to hide the way we feel," I said.

Elizabeth stared at me, as if confused I had even spoken those words, perhaps even that I could harbor such a thought. "Of course we do, Samuel," she said. "You know that we must."

Frenchy was stretching his back as I came down the stairs, as if forcing away the stiffness caused by the long drive from Burlington over rough dirt roads.

"There's fresh coffee inside," I said. "Elizabeth just brewed it a minute ago. I was about to have a cup when you drove up."

He continued stretching as if he hadn't heard me. The brim of his hat was pulled down, leaving all of his face in shadow, except his mouth. I saw a small smile from there.

"Yer still pretty sweet on that gal, ain't ya?" he said.

"You want coffee, or not?" I said, ignoring his question. I turned toward the house, and he came forward quickly and took my arm.

"You interested in what they said at the university about the bullet you boys found?"

I turned back to him. "Of course I am."

Frenchy glanced up at where Jeffords sat in a far corner of the porch. He lowered his voice.

"T'was a forty-five-caliber, jus' like Johnny Taft thought."

"What about the markings? Are they good enough for a match?"

"Good enough to have a try." He patted the breast pocket of his red-and-black-checked hunting jacket. "Leastways ol' Judge Hathaway thought it was good enough to give me a warrant."

I couldn't keep the smile from my face. "When are you planning on serving it?"

"Well, that's a question," Frenchy said. "I can't rightly decide if we should get it done before tomorrow night's meetin', or if we should wait 'til after."

I stared at him, incredulous. "Why wait?" I demanded. "Why not let folks see there's more to this killing than they think?"

Frenchy slowly shook his head. "This ain't got nothin' to do with the killin'," he said. "This was attempted murder on somebody else. Keep that straight in yer head, son."

He was right, of course, and my verbal blunder only made me look foolish—perhaps even anxious to place blame far away from where the body was found.

"What about that colored gal?" Frenchy asked, saving me. "You able to get her out here to have a look at that Turner boy?"

"Yes sir, I did." I shook my head. "That's what confused me before." I added the last to try to save face from my earlier blunder. "She says it was him, and that they were both out to her place the day before we found Royal's body. She also reconfirmed that she had sex with Royal then. With her mouth." I added the last quickly, hoping to cut down another bit of physical evidence that pointed to the people on the hill.

Frenchy ignored me. "She say whether Abel Turner had sex with her? I know when we was out there she told us she didn't give him what he wanted. But she never did say if he got hisself anythin' at all."

"She said she offered. Said Abel turned her down. Wanted only that one thing Royal got, or nothing at all." I cocked my head to one side. "Fussy fellow," I said. "Considering he drove all that way out to Addison."

Frenchy nodded as a small smile formed on his lips. "Curious, ain't it?" he said. "Lessen, of course, Abel knew they was goin' someplace else, later, where maybe he'd get hisself what he wanted."

I stared at Frenchy, outraged by the veiled suggestion. "If that's what they had in mind, then why in hell's name would they drive all the way out to Addison in the first place?"

Frenchy shrugged. I could not make out his expression. The way his head was turned, the shadow caused by his hat now covered his entire face. "Maybe you got a point, but maybe they went somewhere's else later so's Abel could get what he wanted," he said.

"That doesn't make sense," I snapped.

Frenchy looked up at me, and I could see his face fully. His eyes were hard, the line of his mouth unwavering. "Why not, Samuel?" he asked.

The door to the cabin opened and Elizabeth stepped out on the porch. "Now, Deputy, Samuel, please come in out of the chill and have yourself some coffee." As we started up the stairs, she turned and looked down the porch. "Jeffords, dear, I'll bring you some if you like."

"I surely would. Yes, ma'am, I surely would," Jeffords said.

Frenchy and I looked into the darkness where Jeffords Page sat, and I wondered if he had heard and understood any of our heated words. I am sure Frenchy was wondering the same thing, although we did not speak of it, or of anything else that night.

{ 11 }

"What I'm concerned about is stirrin' folks up before we have us our meetin'. I don't want everybody in town choosin' up sides, so's we get there tonight and finds out we's refereein' a bare-knuckles brawl." Frenchy swirled a spoon in his coffee as he spoke, trying to dissolve two teaspoons of preciously expensive sugar.

We were seated at my kitchen table, Frenchy having arrived at seven-thirty, filled with the breakfast Mrs. Pierce had served, but greatly in need of more coffee "with some damned sugar in it," as he put it.

"I don't think you'll find that a problem," I said. "Just about everybody I spoke to yesterday had pretty well made up their mind that Jehiel Flood or one of the other Negroes did the killing."

"That so?" Frenchy scratched his chin, making a show of thinking that over. "Not surprisin', I guess. Body was found there. Victim was a young fella, known to like the sportin' life. Three pretty young gals livin' up there. 'Long with a daddy known not to like the young fella. Guess I kin kinda see how they might come to that conclusion."

I sipped my coffee and stared over the rim of the cup. "Sounds right now like you might have come back to that idea, yourself," I said.

Frenchy scratched his chin again. "Suppose it might," he said.

I waited for more, but nothing came. "Have you?" I finally asked.

"Made up my mind?" Frenchy asked. His face was blank and innocent, and I was certain he was playing with me.

"Yes. Have you?"

He shook his head slowly, eyes staring into his cup as if the answer might be there. "Oh, I ain't give up on the idea it could be somebody else. Abel Turner. Whoever. But the idea that it was one of them Negroes sure does look pretty solid, leastways as far as motive an' opportunity is concerned. Iff'n, of course, we kin prove that was the motive." He raised his eyes to mine. "But there's somethin' naggin' at me, Samuel. Goin' at me jus' like a wife who needs somethin' done. I can't put my finger on it, but I got this feelin' that there's somethin' here that we just ain't found out yet." He scratched his chin again. "You ever get that feelin'?" he asked.

His question caught me cold. Elizabeth, and what she still refused to tell me, rushed to mind. But that was something I could never speak about. Not to Frenchy, nor to anyone else.

"But I reckon you're more interested in provin' it wasn't them folks on the hill. Ain't that right, Samuel?"

Frenchy stared at me. The words had shocked me. He allowed the silence to lengthen between us until I finally spoke.

"You think I'm trying to cover up something?" I asked. "Because, if you do, I can step away from your investigation."

Frenchy laughed and shook his head. "Now if I thought that, I'd say it straight out, Samuel." He winked at me, and I was surprised at how much it annoyed me. "An' I sure don't see no point in you steppin' away," he continued. "Ya'd only conduct your own investigation. And I couldn't stop you, could I? And then we'd just get in each other's way. It's better how we're doin' it. Besides, I know why yer tryin' to make things come out that there way."

I felt my jaw harden. "Some more theories about my feelings for Elizabeth?" I asked.

Frenchy smiled at the snarl hidden in my words. "Oh, that's only part of it," he said, his smile widening.

"And what's the other part?" I demanded.

Frenchy made a point of scratching his chin again. "The other part? Why that's easy, Samuel. The other part's the fact that you hate these white folks so much."

I did not see Frenchy for the rest of the day. We had agreed to serve Judge Hathaway's warrant on Preserved Firman after our meeting. It meant a long night ahead, with perhaps some trouble mixed in, and Frenchy said he planned to sleep most of the afternoon. He suggested I do the same.

Of course I did not sleep. Nor did I do what I truly wanted and return to Elizabeth's cabin. She would be at home, hard at work in her "dispensary" as was her custom most Saturdays. Yet I doubted there would be many visitors seeking her herbal remedies and potions. The hill was now a place where a killing had been done. It was the home of murderous Negroes. Reason enough for good white folk to stay away.

And I remained away as well, Frenchy's words having had their effect. My presence, if observed by other people of the town, would only fuel the belief that I was trying to shield Elizabeth and her family from legal jeopardy, even if such harm was truly deserved. And that was something I could not risk. Not if I hoped to help them in any way at all.

Instead I started on the rounds I had promised Frenchy—a Saturday visit to Shepard's Store, and another to the adjoining barbershop run by Simeon Shepard, Victorious's much-beleaguered husband.

Hannah was behind the counter when I entered, her mother's slender, shrewish countenance nowhere in sight. But then the post office was not due to open for another half-hour.

Hannah was waiting on Abigail Pierce's daughter, Mary, the only woman in town who rivaled Abigail in size. Though only thirty, half her mother's age, Mary Pierce was easily fifty pounds heavier, a victim of the same dining table that made the Jerusalem Hotel a favorite yearly stop for timber buyers, drummers and feed salesman.

Hannah and Mary had been chattering eagerly as I entered, but abruptly fell silent. Mary Pierce gave me a guilty look, then lowered her eyes to her purchases.

"I do declare these prices will give my mother a seizure," she said, as if that had been the subject of their earlier conversation. "Bacon, lamb and chicken, all twenty-two cents a pound, same as a rib roast." She let out an exaggerated breath. "Thank God fer pork chops at twenty cents." Mary's eyes suddenly widened in her round, chubby face. "But look'it here. Coffee is twenty-six cents a pound now. Lord almighty. We can't hardly afford ta feed our guests no more."

I waited for the blather to end, then tipped my Stetson to each of them in turn, signaling my need to interrupt. "Hannah, I hope you're talking up that meeting tonight," I said. "Deputy LeMay is counting on a big crowd."

Mary piped in before Hannah could answer. "You don't have ta worry 'bout that, Samuel. My mama called the newspaper in Burlington, an' they's sendin' out a reporter. Word 'bout that gets aroun', an' that ol' church'll be filled ta overflowin'."

I tried not to seem surprised or concerned about that bit of news, but it did, in fact, concern me greatly. So far the Burlington paper had only reported that the body of a young man had been found in our town, and that local and county police were investigating the possibility of foul play. Now, with tonight's meeting, racial finger-pointing could become a matter of public debate, fanned by newspaper accounts that might make it seem like open warfare. It was something I feared greatly, and it seemed unavoidable unless those reports could be directed along different lines.

"Are you having to work all day and all night today, Samuel?"

Hannah's words brought me back from my musings. "This morning and all night, for sure," I said. I caught Hannah's eye, and tried to let her know my feelings. "I'll be trying to catch some rest this afternoon. Deputy LeMay and Johnny Taft and I spent most of the night keeping watch around Jehiel Flood's homestead."

"Seems funny how's you is all protectin' the man ever'body says done the killin'." Mary placed her hands on her broad hips with such force it made the flesh on her upper arms quiver.

I heard the edge in her voice and fought down an urge to respond in kind. "Well, we know for sure that somebody tried to kill Jehiel. Whether Jehiel or any of his kin killed anybody is still a question we don't have an answer to."

Mary screwed her face in displeasure, and together with her lank, brown hair it made her features take on the look of a large, withered vegetable. "Well, you ask me, it was that no-account dummy, Jeffords Page," she snapped. "I seen the way he looks at white folks. 'Specially women."

"You think Jeffords has it in mind to kill white women?" I asked.

My words had held more than a little sarcasm, and it caused Mary's mouth to tighten.

"It ain't killin' he's got in mind," she snapped. "You can sure enough see that in that boy's heathen eyes."

I gave Mary a false smile. "Well, we have us any sexual assaults, Jeffords'll be the first one I go to see," I said. I touched the brim of my hat again, and caught Hannah holding down laughter. I turned away quickly and beat a speedy retreat to the barbershop before Mary saw it as well.

Simeon Shepard's shop was about the size of a small bedroom, with a solitary barber's chair plunked down in its middle. There was also a small sink and a counter filled with various hair-cutting utensils, hair tonics, talcs and a bottle of bay rum. A large mirror took up much of one wall.

An old church bench lined another wall. That morning it held three men, all waiting their turn in the barber chair occupied by a dairy farmer named Cletus Martin. The men all fell silent when I passed through the barbershop door.

"Good morning, Simeon," I began. "Just wanted to remind you to talk up tonight's meeting with all your customers."

Simeon was a short, plump man, with a fast-receding hairline of gray fuzz and a nervous tic in the corner of his left eye, no doubt a gift of his wife, Victorious. Otherwise, he had a round, pleasant face that matched his disposition, and was among the most popular men in town. It was said he'd be running for the selectboard come Town Meeting next March, and if true he was certain to win election.

"You don't have ta worry 'bout that, Samuel." Simeon waved his scissors in a wide circle. "It's all folks kin find ta talk about."

"You hear there's a reporter comin' out from Burlington?" Cletus Martin asked from his place in the barber chair.

"I just did hear that," I said.

"Can't 'member the last time we had us a story writ up 'bout this here town," Cletus said.

"Prob'ly was somethin' back in the big flood in '27," Simeon offered.

"Wouldn't know," Cletus said, deadpan. "Never saw no newspaper. Roads was flooded."

All the men in the room chuckled, and I tipped my hat to them all as I prepared to leave.

"You think Jehiel Flood done killed that boy of Preserved's?" Cletus asked.

I turned back and kept my expression serious. "If he did it'll surprise me greatly," I said.

"Why's that, Samuel?" Simeon asked. "Man has a temper on him would scare a catamount up a tree. An' that boy of Preserved's was known nasty. Ol' Jehiel caught that boy doin' somethin' he shouldn't, he just mighta—"

"Kicked his tail right down that hill," I said, not allowing him to finish. I shook my head for emphasis. "No question in my mind there'd be a good thumping handed out to anybody who hurt a member of Jehiel's family. But I've known that man all my life, and I sure can't imagine him taking a pitchfork to anybody." I paused a beat. "Or being dumb enough to leave a body on his property if for some reason he did."

The statement was met with dead silence, broken only by the steady snipping of Simeon's scissors. No question that judge and jury had rendered their verdict here.

* * *

Hannah slipped into my bed shortly after one o'clock. It was a full half-hour after I had settled my father for his afternoon nap, but I couldn't help considering him awake in his room, aware of my visitor.

I put those thoughts aside and made love to Hannah with a passion that seemed to both surprise and please her. It was unfair and it was selfish, and I wondered how she would feel if she knew my lust was fueled by the interrupted passion of the previous evening. I consoled myself with the knowledge that I had also lied to Elizabeth when she had asked me about Hannah.

Such consolation, I thought, derisively, as the portrait of Elizabeth stared down at me from the wall facing my bed.

Hannah had once asked me about that picture, and I had lied then as well, claiming it was a portrait of Elizabeth's long-dead mother that had been drawn from an old photograph. I even told her the picture had belonged to my own mother and had been cherished by her until her death, and that I had taken it from the wall of her bedroom as a keepsake.

"Elizabeth surely favored her mother," Hannah had said then.

"Yes," I had replied, marveling at her gullibility. "Jehiel says it's like looking at his wife, alive again, every time he sees her." Oh, the lies I could tell.

Lies upon lies, compounded with more lies, I thought now. Sooner or later it would become a whirlpool and suck me under. But lies were so easy for me, so much a part of me. They rolled off my tongue without the slightest concern.

Hannah brought me back from my reverie with a question I had not heard. "What was that you said?" I asked.

"I asked you what you thought when Mary Pierce tol' you that Jeffords Page is out to rape her?" She giggled. "And all the other white women in town."

I smiled at the vision. "I'm not sure Jeffords would know what to do. Unless he's been watching Jehiel's rooster. You tell Mary, he starts flapping his arms, she should run like the devil."

Hannah giggled again. "She does talk about it all the time."

"About Jeffords Page raping her?" I asked.

"About Jeffords an' a whole bunch of other men," Hannah said. "I never hear'd a woman thought more men was after her than Mary does. And her with a backside that's three ax handles wide."

I smiled at the image. "She surely is a woman with a lot to offer a man," I said.

Hannah slapped my shoulder. "Now don't you let her hear you say that, or she'll be reportin' on you all over town."

And what would that matter. It would be just one more lie, I thought. I stared up at the picture of Elizabeth, the first face I saw each morning, the last I saw every night. And why do I not have you here? I asked myself. Why have I never had the courage to bring you into my own bed?

Because that would be a lie, too, I answered. Perhaps the biggest lie of all.

The sign read: "Chicken Pie Supper. November 7, 6:00 P.M. Proceeds to the Church Fund." I smiled as I walked past it, wondering if on that not-too-distant day, I'd still be welcome to attend.

The Free Will Baptist Church stood opposite Doc Hawley's house in a large open field that was equidistant from Shepard's Store and the schoolhouse on the town's main road. It was a white clapboard building with an aborted steeple that had been ended after five feet, fitted with a rounded top and weathervane and presented to its parishioners with broad assurances that it would one day rise into the clouds. Like so much else in Jerusalem's Landing, it was a promise that had not been kept.

It was seven o'clock, and the church was filled to capacity when I entered. Frenchy was already seated behind a small table that had been placed before the pulpit, and I could see an extra chair had been placed beside him, presumably for me. Elisha Bowles, dressed in his Sunday frockcoat and white, winged collar, sat in a high-backed chair behind the pulpit. He was staring out at the audience, the size of which he could only wish for each Sunday, and I could

not help amusing myself with the thought of the preacher asking if
he might pass the offertory plate before the meeting ended.

I dropped my Stetson on the table and placed my jacket on the
back of the chair, then scanned the crowd as I slid into the seat beside Frenchy. I was surprised to find Jehiel, steadfast and scowling,
in the front to my right. His head was bandaged, and his arm in a
sling. Elizabeth sat beside him, staring straight ahead like a beautiful but aloof attending nurse. Prince sat on the other side, much like
a bodyguard, and a glowering Ruby and a frightened-looking Maybelle sat to the right of their brother. Only Jeffords Page was missing, I noted, presumably left at home to guard against attack. I
knew Johnny Taft was there as well, earning his "deputized" pay.

Earlier in the day I had considered calling on Jehiel to suggest he
remain away, but had immediately recognized the senselessness of
such a journey. Jehiel would see it as hiding from his white antago-
nists, which was something he'd be loath to do. And perhaps he'd be
right, I thought now, as I scanned the audience for some sign of the
newspaper reporter from Burlington. I was searching, of course, for
some ink-stained wretch, but found that the only person present
whom I did not know was a slender, bookish young man, who had
stationed himself in the far left corner of the back pew—where he
could see and hear everyone.

Studying him, I thought now that Jehiel's presence was a proper
decision. Had he absented himself, as I would have urged, the racial
tone of the meeting might well have intensified. And that was not
the direction I wanted our reporter to follow.

Now, with Jehiel sitting steadfast and wounded, there would be a
lessened chance of racial slurs, I thought, since few in town would
risk the wrath of his reply, or the appearance of being insensitive to
his injuries. And without that infectious tone of racial hatred and
suspicion, I might more easily direct the reporter to consider the attack on Jehiel as an additional crime, and not merely an act of jus-
tified white retribution.

I let my eyes roam the gathering once more. Victorious Shepard
sat surrounded by Hannah and Simeon, her face a withered prune

of dissatisfaction and suspicion. Hannah smiled up at me, as if we shared a secret, which of course we did, and Simeon simply looked tic-ridden and nervous, seated next to his wife and away from the safety of his scissors and his talc. A few rows behind Victorious, Abigail and Mary Pierce took up much of a pew by themselves, and I couldn't help wondering if Mary was taking comfort in the absence of the libidinous Jeffords Page.

To my right, the well-barbered head of Cletus Martin grinned up at me, and I noticed that he was seated with the same men who had filled the barbershop that morning. It was as though they had moved as a group of newly shorn sheep, I thought.

Frenchy slid a paper across to me, drawing my attention away from the gathering. It held a list of topics he hoped to cover, all dealing with the progress of the investigation.

"You got any suggestions, I'd 'preciate it," he said. "You know these folks better'n I do."

I looked at the list again, and could find nothing with which to agree or disagree. I took a fountain pen from my shirt pocket, removed the cap, and scratched four words on the paper. *"Urge tolerance and patience."*

Frenchy read it and nodded. "That's a mighty high order fer folks that's riled," he whispered.

I looked back at the audience and noticed Doc Hawley for the first time. I turned back to Frenchy, struck by a sudden concern. "I noticed you had the autopsy on your list. You gonna ask Doc to explain what was found?"

Frenchy shook his head. "Wasn't plannin' to. But that don't mean other folks might not ask him." He gave me a curious look. "Whatcha worried he might say, Samuel?"

I stared at the table, absently readjusting the position of my Stetson. "I don't want him going into the theory that Royal was stabbed in the stomach first, and then laid on the ground, suffering, until the death blow to his chest was struck. I don't want him talking about the remains of candles and such found near the body. All that's just going to stir folks up."

"Can't stop him from sayin' it," Frenchy said.

I turned on him sharply. "You can, indeed," I whispered urgently. "You can stop any comment that might jeopardize the investigation."

"An' I will, Samuel." Frenchy's eyes were hard on me now. "But I want folks to help us with this investigation. It's why we're havin' this meetin'. Just in case somebody here knows somethin' we should know. And I ain't gonna get that if I pick an' choose the direction of their thinkin'."

I sat in stunned silence. All along I had believed the purpose of this meeting was to calm people down; to keep them from jumping to conclusions that might result in even greater tragedy. I now realized that those concerns had only been peripheral to Frenchy. His main interest centered on gathering more evidence. He was here to give information, in order to get more in return.

A stir in the crowd drew my eyes to the rear of the church. Preserved Firman and Abel Turner had just entered, and stood scowling just inside the door. I watched, as Preserved seemed to inflate slightly with the attention he garnered. Then he stepped forward and started down the center aisle, followed by Abel.

Halfway down, Preserved fixed his eyes on me, and I watched them fill with a simmering hatred that I knew was reciprocal. He continued to glare at me, until he reached the front row of pews. Looking to his left, he saw Jehiel and his family, and he immediately snapped around to his right, turning his hate-filled stare on a farmer and wife who occupied the aisle seats of that first pew. Preserved continued to stare the couple down until they moved to their right, making those places available for himself and Abel.

Now Preserved glared up at me again, his eyes filled with the satisfaction of victory. And it struck me for the first time that I had seen no sorrow in the man. I had seen only hatred and a need for vengeance. It was then that Jenny's words came back to me, the words she had spoken with such whorish innocence as we drove to Jerusalem's Landing to steal a look at Abel Turner.

We had been talking about Royal's boasting that he had himself "a colored gal" at home. And then Jenny, to my gratitude, had told me she had doubted the truth of his claim. She had talked about the way he had stared the first time he'd been with her—as though he'd never seen a naked Negro woman before. And then she spoke the other words, which in my overpowering gratitude, I had ignored until now.

"Tol' me then his daddy would skin him fer sure, he ever even thinked he was layin' wit' a colored gal."

I sat breathing deeply as the significance of those words connected in my mind. Then I leaned in close to Frenchy, shielding my lips with one hand. "There's something I forget to tell you," I said.

"Go ahead," Frenchy said.

"The other day, when I was with Jenny, she told me that Royal claimed he was laying with a colored woman close to home. She said Royal told her he was afraid his father would find out. Said Preserved would skin him for sure if that happened."

Frenchy nodded, then shielded his own lips. "And yer thinkin' that's why he went alla way to Addison to have him some fun? That he wanted him a colored gal, but one that was far enough away from Preserved bein' able to find out?"

"Something like that." I hesitated, wanting to form the words just so. "But what if he *was* seeing a local Negro woman? What if he was paying visits to Maybelle or Ruby, say? And what if Preserved found out and followed him? Maybe hid in the woods, waiting on him to come out?"

Frenchy glanced at me sharply, then hid his lips again. "Yer sayin' maybe his own daddy kilt him, over him havin' a colored gal?"

The incredulity came through even though his words were whispered, and I felt an urgent need to defend my premise. "It just came to me. Just now. I hadn't paid much attention to what Jenny had said. I thought she was only repeating the bravado of a man who didn't want to admit his inexperience with Negro women.

"But then I looked at Preserved's face tonight, and the rest of it came to me. Except for that first time I saw him—when he'd just taken his boy out of those woods—there's been no sorrow, Frenchy, no sense of loss. There has only been one abiding emotion that has fully consumed the man. Just one thing: hatred."

Frenchy nodded slowly. "We'll have us a look, Samuel. We'll have us a real close look."

Elisha began the meeting with a prayer. He seemed nervous, almost twitchy, I thought, as he asked the Lord to bring reconciliation to Jerusalem's Landing, and peace to the heart of family members who had recently lost a son so tragically. He did not mention Preserved Firman by name, or Royal, either, which I found odd, and ended his prayer quickly by asking for a moment of silence.

Frenchy began his part of the meeting with a folksy recapitulation of what our investigation had found to date. To my surprise he started with Royal and Abel traveling to Addison the day of the murder. And although he spared the audience the purpose of their journey, I watched Abel's face as Frenchy spoke, and I detected clear worry in his eyes. Perhaps he, too, feared the wrath of Preserved Firman for the sin of visiting a colored whore.

Frenchy quickly left that subject and went on to explain that we knew little of Royal's activities after he returned to Jerusalem's Landing that day. The next thing we knew for certain, he said, was Abel Turner coming across Royal's body while hunting on Nigger Hill the next morning, a discovery he reported directly to the town constable.

"Now how that body got there, we really don't know," Frenchy said. "We ain't even sure if that boy was alive, or if he was already dead, when he got to Nigger Hill. So if anybody seen Royal that day, we'd 'preciate it if ya'd pass that information on to us. I kin promise you it'll be kept as confidential as you want it to be."

"But he was killed up there. You know he was." Victorious Shepard blurted out the words, her narrow, pinched face radiating indignation.

Frenchy smiled down at her from our elevated platform. "If you know that to be true, ma'am, then you know more'n we do." He paused a beat while Victorious huffed and shifted in her seat. "We know he weren't killed where he was found," he continued. "The evidence we found at the scene made that real clear. We also know he was carried to that place, an' that he was carried by somebody who put on his boots, so's we would think he walked there hisself. And we know the person what carried him walked right along the same streambed that crosses the road, right where we found that murdered boy's truck parked."

"Are you saying someone might have brought the victim there in the truck, and then tried to make it look like he was killed on Nigger Hill, when he was actually killed somewhere else?" The question came from the back of the church, and when I looked I found the speaker standing. It was the young stranger I had earlier identified as the suspected newspaper reporter.

Frenchy grinned, then made it clear he knew the man. "Now Jake, that sure is a good question. Right there on the money, as always. And I'd expect nothin' less from an employee of our one major newspaper." His grin widened. "You'll notice I didn't say 'esteemed major newspaper.'"

Others in the church laughed, and the reporter gave Frenchy a nod of acknowledgment.

"But yer dead right," Frenchy went on. "It coulda happened that way. It depends how you read the evidence. Fact is, we just don't know fer sure. Our other problem is, somebody else thinks he does know, on account of where that body was found, and it seems he's decided to take the law inta his own hands." Frenchy gave the audience an elaborate shrug. "But, you see, Royal Firman just mighta been killed someplace else an' drug in there by his killer." Frenchy paused a beat, then offered another, smaller shrug. "And he maybe went in them woods hisself, an' got hunted down by his killer. Fact is, we don't know, an' we ain't got a solid motive that would point us in one direction, or a'tother."

Preserved Firman roared to his feet, one arm waving wildly. "Ya know damn good an' well what that there motive was." His waving arm straightened like a spear and jabbed at the heart of the Flood family. "That there motive was a goddamn nigger killin' a white man who was sparkin' with his black, bitch, whore of a daughter."

"No, we do not know that, sir!" Frenchy's voice bellowed out, and

echoed through the church, but all attention had drawn away
om him. All eyes were now pointed to the far right, where Jehiel
lood had risen slowly from his seat.

He turned to face Preserved, moving with obvious pain, eyes glis-
ening with a rage so intense it seemed to leap from his massive
rown face. His resonating voice came from deep within his chest,
nd seemed to reach out for Preserved as if to shake him like a rag
oll.

"Preserved Firman . . . you are a lyin' . . . no-account . . . racist
umbitch. . . . Now, I don't like to see . . . nobody's . . . boy dead. So
m truly sorry . . . yer boy is dead. But yer boy . . . as ever'body in
his town knows . . . was a . . . no-account . . . jus' like his daddy . . .
cowardly . . . bullyboy . . . who'd run . . . from any man . . . what
tood up to him. My daughters wouldn't lay themselfs down . . .
ith a piece . . . of white trash . . . like that. An' he surely weren't
orth killin'. A good . . . kick in the ass . . . woulda been enough for
. . . useless . . . no-account . . . cowardly white boy . . . the likes a
im."

Ruby Flood jumped from her seat, eyes glowing. "Amen to that,"
he shouted, as she stepped next to her father and clutched his good
rm. Suddenly Prince stood beside his father as well. Only Eliza-
eth and Maybelle remained seated.

The sanctuary was washed in a deathly silence. All eyes went to
reserved Firman, who stood quaking with his own rage. His lips
egan to move, but no words emerged. Seated below his shaking
ody, Abel Turner looked back and forth between Jehiel and Pre-
erved, as though wishing someone would tell him what to do.

I watched Preserved's hands, fearful he would reach beneath his
oat for a weapon. My own hand had gone to the revolver holstered
t my waist. Frenchy looked at me and gave an almost impercepti-
le nod of his head. His eyes led mine to his own revolver, already
leared of its holster and lying in his lap.

Preserved's eyes had turned to coals that seemed to burn across
he sanctuary. "I'll kill . . . yer murderin' . . . black ass," he finally
rowled.

Jehiel snapped back. "You already tried that by hidin' yer cowardly self behind a tree in the dead a night, jus' like the trash you always been."

Before I even knew it had happened, Frenchy's pistol came up and was leveled at Preserved, just as the man's hand started toward his coat. Abel had risen to his feet, and I brought my weapon up and centered it on his chest. A gasp went up from those assembled, and several jumped from their seats and scurried out of the line of fire.

Frenchy's voice called out calmly, almost soothingly. "Mr. Firman! Your hand comes outta that coat with anythin' but yer fingers, an' I'm gonna blow yer ass straight to hell, sir. You hearin' me good, Mr. Firman?"

"Same goes for you, Abel," I said.

Abel looked up quickly and saw my pistol leveled at his chest. His eyes darted nervously. "I ain't got nothin' in my coat," he said, the open plea in his words making his voice come close to a whine.

Preserved turned on me, his head snapping with the speed of a snake. "You nigger-lovin' bastard. You bleached nigger . . . son of a nigger-fuckin' whore . . ."

I swung my pistol, until the front sight was set directly between his eyes. The three distinct clicks of the weapon cocking, as I slowly pulled back the hammer, cut Preserved's words in half and brought an audible gasp from those gathered behind him.

"Not another word," I said. "Not one."

Frenchy reached out and laid his free hand on the top of my pistol, his little finger sliding between the hammer and the frame. He gently pushed my weapon down toward the table, and lowered his own. "No need fer shootin', long as Mr. Firman and Mr. Turner keep their hands where we can see 'em," he said. "You got that message, boys?"

Abel nodded dumbly, but Preserved continued to glare up at me. "Tha's the second time ya pulled that gun on me, ya bleached nigger bastard," he snarled. "Next time ya do it, ya better pull that trigger fer sure, or folks'll be layin' flowers on yer sorry nigger's grave."

I stared down at him, allowing the silence to draw out. When I spoke, I struggled to make my voice soft and steady and calm, just as Frenchy's had been. But it still shook with anger. "I've given you a lot of room, Preserved. Out of respect for your grief. But you have run out of room. Do not cross that line again."

Preserved leveled a finger at me. "I'll see yer bleached ass in hell."

I nodded slowly. "That's more'n likely, Preserved. That's more'n likely." I watched him turn and stomp out of the church, Abel Turner trailing behind like a faithful hound. The rest of the gathering watched as well. All except Elizabeth and Maybelle, who, when I turned to look at them, were still seated and staring straight ahead. The only change I noted was that Elizabeth had taken Maybelle's hand in hers.

Frenchy tried to keep the meeting going, but an aura of unspoken hostility had descended, and no matter how folksy his recitation of the facts, or how heartfelt his pleas for information, any hope of co-operation—at least for that evening—was gone. I understood it all too well. The reason was simple enough. An outsider had moved against one of their own, and even if they might find that man wanting, themselves, it was enough to get their backs up. I allowed that thought to play out in my mind as Frenchy gave up and closed the meeting. My eyes roamed the audience, moving from face to face, studying the eyes that met mine, and I realized the anger was greater than I first thought. I had been considering the townsfolk's reaction to Frenchy, and his threat of violence against Preserved Firman. But Frenchy was not the only stranger who had offended them. It was not just he. There were two strangers who had done so. Two, not one.

We stood outside the church, hoping some member of the audience would come up to us. There were a few smiles from elderly women showing their spirit of Christian friendliness, but otherwise we were given wide berth, whether out of genuine dislike or because of some feared disapproval of neighbors, I do not know. The only one to approach was the newspaper reporter, whom Frenchy introduced as Jake Phelps.

"Doesn't seem to be a rush to help the constabulary," he said, as he shook my hand.

Phelps was taller than I had thought, and even more angular, with wrists no thicker than those of the average woman. The brim of his porkpie hat was low over his eyes and followed the slight curve of his longish nose, and curly, brown hair pushed out in tufts above his ears. His suit hung on him as if draped over a bag of bones, all of it giving him a cadaverous look that did not inspire confidence. He looked like a man that dogs would happily chase.

"It is a difficult case, in all aspects," I said.

"Thought I'd have to dive for cover when you boys pulled your guns," Phelps said. There was a hint of pleasure in his voice, at having been part of some adventure.

Frenchy swung a friendly arm around Phelps's bony shoulder and began walking him away from the church. "We had us a situation that could a been a touch dangerous," he said. "Colored fella who was spoutin' off, well, somebody up an tried to bushwack him t'other night. One bullet nicked his head, t'other one went right through his shoulder. And, based on our investigation . . ." Frenchy paused to pat his chest. "Well, I got me in this here pocket a search warrant fer the gun I think mighta been used."

"Belonging to . . . ?" Phelps drew out the question as if he already suspected the answer.

"Belongin' to the white fella who was spoutin' off. He's got hisself a forty-five-caliber rifle that we wanna run some tests on." Frenchy stopped and turned a smile on Phelps. "You behave yourself, yer welcome to come along whilst we serve it."

"Now that white fella, if I'm right, he's the father of the man who was found murdered?" Phelps asked.

"That's true enough," Frenchy said. "T'was Royal Firman's body was found on Nigger Hill, and it's Preserved Firman—his daddy—whose house and outbuildin's that we got us a search warrant fer."

"So you got yourself a blood feud here." Phelps was grinning now, excited by the story onto which he had stumbled. "Damn. The hellish drive out to this Godforsaken town just might have been worthwhile after all." He threw me a quick glance, as if concerned he might have insulted me. "No offense intended," he said.

"None taken," I answered. I smiled to myself. *Godforsaken*, I thought. It was a very apt description of Jerusalem's Landing.

Frenchy and I each drove our own cars out to Morgan Hollow in fear our efforts that night might end in a need to transport a prisoner or two, should either Preserved Firman or Abel Turner take issue with our search. Jake Phelps followed in his own car, a '29 Chevy Imperial that had a running board rusting off its frame, and that looked as road-weary and battered as my own Model A. In contrast, Frenchy's spanking new Ford V8, which was provided by the county, made us both look like poor country cousins, and I quickly concluded that the glamour of being a newspaper reporter was not matched by its level of financial reward.

Morgan Hollow is bisected by a rough dirt road that bears its name. It rises steadily for the first quarter mile, then flattens out into a narrow plain with sharply ascending ridges on both sides that were once covered with some of the best hardwood timber the area had to offer. Most of that old-growth timber is gone now, having been logged off by the Firman family over past generations.

The logging, and the sawmill operated on their homestead, should have made the Firmans financially comfortable. But they were far from that, through either generations of poor business practices or simple waste. I did not know which. I did know our Great Depression had not helped their cause. Timber prices had fallen drastically, since few could afford to build; so much so that the barges carrying lumber along our river to Lake Champlain had decreased from one a day to one or two barges each week.

This impoverishment, and his perception of the unfairness of it, had only made Preserved Firman more bitter toward those who had more than he. Chief among them was Jehiel Flood, although Preserved's racism also played a large part in that particular resentment. As I knew too well myself, the original Firmans had come to Vermont before the Civil War as transplanted slaveholders, and the family appeared to have passed down its southern beliefs that Negroes were an inferior race, worthy of being owned. It was therefore not surprising that Jehiel especially riled Preserved, since he had the basic financial stability that the Firman clan had never achieved. Jehiel lived frugally off his land, raising enough food to feed his extended family and earning an adequate income from the maple syrup he boiled up each spring from his sizable sugarbush. He also earned that money through a keen business sense, traveling his product to wherever prices were best, moving to different county fairs and farmer's markets throughout the summer, some as far away as New York State and Canada. Preserved, meanwhile, was trapped in a single market that exploited him at will.

Yet, all that meant nothing. Certainly not to me. It was merely a striking incidental, a tableau vivant, part of a whole that I had lived with all my life. Racism in Jerusalem's Landing was not limited to Preserved Firman and his arcane reasons and beliefs. It was like the idiot son kept in the hayloft above the livestock. It was seldom openly acknowledged, but it was always there.

The wagon track that led to Preserved's cabin rose an eighth of a mile up from Morgan Hollow Road, climbing between two thick stands of pine that had been left uncut to provide a winter deer yard that could be poached. We followed the track in tandem, first Frenchy, then me, and finally the newspaper reporter, Jake Phelps.

There was little question Preserved would know we were on our way. It was a moonless night, further darkened by heavy cloud cover, and we were forced to use our headlights to keep from veering off the track and into the surrounding trees.

When we broke into the small clearing on which Preserved's cabin sat, the sign was not good. Preserved's flatbed GMC truck was parked next to Abel's old army surplus Nash. They were the only vehicles either man owned, and the only ones that now belonged on the property, since Royal's pickup truck had been impounded by the sheriff's office. Yet the cabin was dark as a grave, despite the early hour of nine o'clock, and I thought it unlikely that both Preserved and Abel would have taken to their beds so soon after our heated town meeting.

Frenchy seemed to think so as well. He pulled his car behind a small stand of pine, killed the lights, and quickly scurried back to us, motioning that we do the same.

Drawing us behind a nearby boulder, Frenchy knelt beside us and shook his head. "I smell me a hornet's nest," he said. He gave Phelps a steady gaze. "You might wanna take yerself down to the road. Sheriff wouldn't be pleased if I got me a newspaper reporter all shot up."

Phelps shook his head vigorously. "I'd rather take my chances," he said. "Makes a better story if I can report being there when it all happened."

The bravado momentarily surprised me, coming from a man who seemed so frail and unathletic. But then I recognized my folly. Had I not learned early on that courage came in all sizes? Country life demanded it be so. Why, then, should it be different for those who lived in cities?

"Yer choice," Frenchy said. He inclined his head toward me. "Now that I got me a witness that you was warned, the sheriff can only take one or two bites outta my ass if you end up fulla holes. And long as yer stayin', you might do somethin' useful fer us."

"And what would that be?" Phelps asked, suddenly suspicious.

"Well . . ." Frenchy drew the moment out. "Me, I'm gonna call out to ol' Mr. Firman that me and Samuel is comin' in to talk. Then we're gonna start workin' our way up to his cabin, each of us goin' in from way off on opposite sides. Now, before we do any of that, we gonna line our cars up so's they's facin' his cabin. And if he starts shootin' while we're walkin up on him, I'm gonna want you to go to each of our cars here and turn on the lights when I call out fer you to do it."

"But won't that backlight you for him?" Phelps asked.

"Tha's why we'll be goin' in from way off to each side," Frenchy said. "We'll be way out of them beams. So them headlamps—leastways 'til he starts to shoot 'em out—are gonna light up that cabin like a Christmas tree on Christmas mornin'." He patted his holster. "And I figure maybe I can discourage his shootin', before he gets all six headlamps."

Phelps thought about it, then drew a long breath and nodded. "If that's what you want," he said.

"Well, what I want is fer him to invite us in fer coffee and let us search his damned house," Frenchy said. "I just ain't sure he'll be that obligin'."

Frenchy and I moved apart, so each of us were on opposite sides of the cabin, and still forty yards out from the porch that ran along its entire front. When we were set he called out to Preserved. He identified himself and said that I was with him, explaining we had a court paper to serve as part of our investigation. His calls were met with silence.

We moved up slowly, as planned. I had my Winchester .30-30, which I had taken from under the front seat of my car, and Frenchy had the double-barreled shotgun he kept in the trunk of his Ford. The shotgun had a killing range of fifty yards and was loaded with two double O buck shells. Each shell held nine lead pellets that each hit with the individual impact of a 30.06 rifle slug. At close range, each shell was capable of blowing a hole through the cabin door the size of a man's fist.

Preserved's cabin was not large, perhaps four or five rooms at best. There were only two windows and one door facing our approach, but I had no idea how many other points of egress existed on the three remaining sides. The one flaw in our plan, I now realized, was the possibility of someone leaving the cabin and circling our position. We would then find ourselves pinned against the cabin wall when Frenchy called for the headlamps to be turned on.

Frenchy waited until we had reached the cabin and had each flattened ourselves against the front wall before he called out again. Each word seemed to bring a new burst of sweat from my pores.

"Mr. Firman! This here is Deputy Sheriff Frenchy LeMay. Constable Bradley and me got us a court paper we need to give you. So don't get riled up when I push open yer door."

Frenchy held up a hand indicating I should wait, then called up to Phelps for the headlamps. They went on one car at a time, and I felt my muscles tense and cringe as each burst of light reached us. I crouched, making myself as small a target as possible, but nothing happened; no projectile smashed into or around my body. I wiped my sweaty palms against the knees of my pants and felt foolish.

Frenchy motioned me forward as he moved in himself, again holding up his hand when we each reached opposite sides of the door. He called out again, then rapped against the doorframe with his shotgun. He called once more, then stretched out a hand, turned the doorknob, and gently pushed the door back.

Light from the headlamps filtered into the darkened room, entering through the open door and two windows, each separate beam spreading a widening glow across the floor and washing the interior walls with a mix of illumination and shadow. With the light, the shadows seemed deeper, the dark corners more ominous, and I found I had no desire to move through the door and confront whatever awaited me inside.

I watched Frenchy bob his head inside the doorframe, once, twice. When he pulled back the final time, he uttered a solitary oath: "Shit."

"What is it?" I asked.

"Preserved is sittin' in there, to the right of the door, far back near the woodstove. He's just starin' out at us, and there's a damned revolver in his lap."

I repeated Frenchy's oath.

"You betcha," Frenchy said. He stood flat against the outside wall and called out once again. "Mr. Firman! This is Deputy Sheriff LeMay again. I'm comin' through yer front door, and I want you to know I'll have me a shotgun loaded up with buckshot." He paused a beat, drew a deep breath, then continued. "Just so we understan' each other, I'm tellin' you now, if I see that pistol in yer lap even twitch, I'm gonna blow a hole in you the size of a barn door. So's it might be best you put that there revolver on the floor, so's neither one of us makes a mistake we's gonna regret."

I watched Frenchy draw another breath, then pull back the twin hammers on his shotgun. I responded by setting my .30-30 on full cock, freeing it to fire. The sound of each hammer locking into place had the snap of distant lightning in the still night air. From inside the cabin I heard the heavy thud of metal on wood, as Preserved's pistol dropped to the floor.

Frenchy went through the door first, his shotgun held out at his hip. I came in behind and to his right, my .30-30 tight to my shoulder, my index finger a hairsbreadth from the trigger. Frenchy moved forward slowly, the barrel of his shotgun never wavering from its target.

Preserved Firman sat in a straightback chair, chin dropped down near his chest, his eyes rolled up and riveted directly on me. His revolver lay on the floor to one side, and I watched as Frenchy reached down and retrieved it, then dumped the cartridges from the cylinder. Preserved never looked at him, even as Frenchy laid the pistol back on the floor and placed the cartridges in his shirt pocket.

A low growl came from the other side of the woodstove, and when I looked I saw a large hound lying there, its back swathed in a heavy bandage. It was resting on a filthy old blanket; food and water set in bowls beside it. The dog struggled to raise itself, its growl deepening, and I saw that its hind legs dragged uselessly behind it. Its back had been broken.

"That dog comes any closer, I'm gonna put it outta its misery," Frenchy warned. "Looks to me like you already shoulda done it fer the poor critter anyways."

"You don't hurt that dog," Preserved snapped. "He's gonna be jus' fine. I'm tendin' to 'im." He turned his eyes from me for an instant and snapped out a command to the dog. "You lie down, Bo. It's all right."

Preserved's eyes returned to me, still filled with hate, and I marveled at the care this man was giving to this poor, sorry beast—this

same man who would shoot a human being from his horse just because of his color.

Frenchy shook his head and let out a long breath, and I guessed
he was having the same thought. "Anybody here with you?" he
asked.

Preserved ignored him, his eyes staying fixed on me.

Frenchy turned and gestured with his shotgun. "Samuel, there's
a kerosene lantern on the table. I'd be grateful if ya'd light it."

I did as I was asked, laying my .30-30 on the table as I lit and adjusted the wick.

Light bursts from a kerosene lantern, as it is wont to do, first
faintly, then with a gradually increasing glow until it reaches a
steady brightness. Now, as the level of light approached its apex,
Abel Turner's face suddenly materialized from the shadows of
a distant corner, making me gasp with surprise and grab up my rifle.

"I ain't armed," Abel called out. "I ain't got no weapon t'other
than my buck knife."

"Stand up," I snapped. "And raise your arms high."

Abel complied without a word, and I moved to him quickly and
searched him for weapons. There was nothing other than his buck
knife, and I pulled it from its sheath and tossed it into a distant
corner.

"What's this 'bout?" Preserved growled, suddenly reanimated.

"We got a court paper fer you," Frenchy said. "Just like I tol' you
from outside."

"An tha's why ya comes in here an' starts taken a man's gun away
in his own house." He was glaring at me, even as he spoke to
Frenchy, his scruffy features looking meaner than normal in the
deep shadow that hid part of his face. "I hear'd ya comin' a long
way off. I wanted ta hurt yer sorry asses, I woulda been out in the
trees layin' fer ya."

Frenchy nodded, his features taking on a solemnity that almost
made me smile, and I knew he was thinking about the shooter who
had lain in the trees waiting for Jehiel to ride up. "I do believe that's
true, Mr. Firman," Frenchy said. "I surely do. But since you

wouldn't answer when I called out, I had to figger there was some hard feelin's in yer heart. And when I saw that there pistol in yer lap, it made me take that concern just a might more serious."

Preserved continued to glare at me. "An' ya was so concerned ya hadda bring this here bleached nig inta my house? Time was a nig knew his place." He raised his chin, as if using it to point me out. "This boy's great-granny knew her place. 'Course she was *owned* by my great-uncle, Amos, so she got taught real good."

Off to my left, Abel let out a snort.

I stiffened with the words, and Abel's reaction, though neither one surprised me. I had come to expect it from each of them. To expect even worse. Frenchy remained silent, then reached into his jacket pocket and withdrew the search warrant. He laid it on Preserved's lap.

"That there's a search warrant issued by a judge in Burlington." He spoke softly, and I found the gentleness of his tone both surprising and disturbing. "Constable Bradley, bein' a duly sworn officer of the law, is here to help me serve and execute it. Now I'd like you to read it, if ya can . . ."

"I kin read," Preserved snapped, as he grabbed up the warrant.

"Well, good," Frenchy said. "And when you read it you'll see that it gives me and Constable Bradley the right to search yer house and property fer a certain forty-five-caliber rifle that we intend to confiscate and run some tests on."

"What kinda tests?" Preserved demanded.

"Tests to see if it fired the bullets that wounded Jehiel Flood t'other night," Frenchy answered.

Preserved snorted. "An' whose gonna run them tests?" He raised his chin toward me again. "This here bleached nig, with the fancy college paper hangin' on his wall?"

Frenchy leaned down until his face was only inches from Preserved. "I ignored you the first time you called the constable that there name, Mr. Firman." Again, his voice was soft, almost silky. "Now I'm gonna tell you this but one time." He allowed a small smile to form. "When I next hear them words come outta yer mouth, I'm gonna rap you upside the head with the barrel of this here shotgun. And I'm gonna keep on doin' it, 'til you can't say them words no more." Frenchy inclined his head toward Abel. "And that goes fer yer lard-assed friend, too. You understand that, Mr. Firman?"

Preserved never looked away from my face, his eyes holding enough hate for a dozen. Frenchy stepped back and waited. It was as though he was daring either man to offer up one more racial slur, so he could make good his promise.

"Rifle yer lookin' fer is in the corner back by the table," Preserved said.

I motioned Abel to stand aside, then picked up the lantern to throw more light into the corner. When I stepped forward I saw the forty-five-caliber Sharps carbine leaning against the wall. It was directly behind the spot where Abel had been standing. Abel, I realized, hadn't had a weapon when I drew a bead on his chest, but he'd had one close to hand all along.

I gave the rifle to Frenchy, after jacking out the five shells it held. After examining it in the light, Frenchy raised the barrel to his nose and sniffed. He gave me a small smile and a nod, then turned back to Preserved.

"You got any other rifles?" he asked.

"Got me a double-barreled bird gun, like your'n, an' a twenty-two fer varmints an' coon. An' I got me my pistol." He inclined his head toward the weapon on the floor by his feet.

It was unlikely there was another heavy-caliber rifle, and if there was, certainly not another .45. Few could afford more than one high-powered rifle, and most country men settled for one large-bore weapon that could be used equally well for deer or bear or moose. Then, like Preserved, they'd have a shotgun for gamebirds, and maybe a pistol, or a light-caliber varmint weapon, or both.

I could tell Frenchy was thinking the same thing, and that he wanted to avoid any further confrontation that might end in violence.

"Well, we'll be takin' this rifle with us, Mr. Firman," he said. "Court order gives us that right. But we'll be returnin' it in a day or so with no harm done."

Preserved continued to stare at me, his mouth drawn in a tight, angry line. He had not moved since we entered his home. Not an arm, or leg; not even a complete turn of his head, until I had moved off to the table, and then to deal with Abel. Each time his head had followed me, his eyes staring at my face.

"Yer gonna set me up, ain't ya?" he said now. "Yer gonna give that there rifle to this . . ." He hesitated, as if considering Frenchy's earlier warning, then continued. "This here . . . constable . . . so's he kin say I done somethin' I never did. Ain't that right?"

Frenchy shook his head as he cradled the rifle in the crook of one arm. "This rifle is in my custody, Mr. Firman. Not because I don't trust Constable Bradley, but because that's the way the judge wrote up this here warrant. So I'll be takin' it to Burlington, and I'll be turnin' it over fer the tests that'll be done. Ain't no way nobody else is gonna handle it. Just me and the technician in Burlington who does the tests. It's what we call a chain of evidence. And Constable Bradley ain't part of that chain, Mr. Firman. So if you got any complaints with the results, you gotta point 'em straight back at me."

We turned and started for the door. I felt an overwhelming relief that we were finally getting out of there, that we had accomplished our objective without giving or receiving gunfire.

I was one step from the door when I heard the sound of a hammer drawing back, the three distinctive clicks followed immediately by the sound of metal striking metal as the hammer fell.

Frenchy and I spun around together, weapons leveled. Preserved Firman sat in his chair, the revolver he had collected from the floor now held steadily in both hands, as he continued to pull the trigger on one empty chamber after another, a look of utter amazement spread across his face as the weapon repeatedly failed to fire.

I stood frozen, my eyes fixed on the barrel of Preserved's gun, its gaping black hole settled on my chest.

Frenchy strode past me in three rapid steps and brought the butt of his shotgun down on Preserved's head. The blow sent Preserved sprawling on the floor and set his dog to barking and snarling. Frenchy stood over Preserved, eyes blazing. "Yer under arrest," he hissed. "Ya stupid, goddamn sumbitch." Frenchy turned on Abel, his shotgun dead on him. "And yer fat ass is under arrest, too." He spoke the words with a snarl.

"But I din' do nothin'," Abel protested.

"Damn if I care," Frenchy snapped. He threw two sets of handcuffs on the table, then turned to me. "Cuff these boys up, Samuel. We gonna drive they sorry asses inta jail."

"Who's gonna take care of my dog?" Preserved said from the floor.

"Damn you and yer dog," Frenchy snarled. Then he looked to me.

"I'll see to it," I said. "I'll ask the folks down the road to look in."

Jake Phelps was overjoyed when we brought both men out in handcuffs.

"What happened? Tell me every scrap of it," he pleaded.

Frenchy told him, and even though I had been there, none of it, not one word, seemed real to me.

{ 12 }

Frenchy joined my father and me for a late breakfast at eleven the next morning, along with a retelling of the adventure that had kept us from our beds until well after three o'clock. The blazing woodstove had the kitchen as warm as a mother's womb.

"I have to admit, I was scared to death," I said, when Frenchy had relived the tale.

"Well, you wasn't the only one." Frenchy slapped his palm on the table. "Thought I'd shit myself when I heard the hammer of that pistol fall."

My father looked down into his coffee and laughed. "I 'member once't, years ago, Frenchy an' me, we went ta arrest this crazy Abenaki who'd kilt his wife an' her two brothers with a hatchet." My father paused and shook his head. "Lord, that boy scared us. He come runnin' at us, out his house, that hatchet raised over his head, an' the blood still drippin' off'n it. Sure 'nuff, we both near wet ourselves that time."

"Whatta you mean, *near?*" Frenchy said, laughing. "My pants, they was drippin'."

"What happened to the Abenaki?" I asked.

Frenchy scratched his chin with one finger. "Oh, yer daddy near took his leg off with a shotgun." He shook his head. "Only thing that ever saved us that day. Then, later, after that poor, sick sumbitch got outta the hospital, the State of Vermont tried and convicted him, and then they sat the poor bastid in the 'lectric chair an' finished him off. Always made me wish yer daddy had kilt him with that shotgun, 'steada just woundin' him like he did."

My father nodded agreement. "Felt the same way myself fer a lotta years after."

Frenchy took a sip of his coffee, and slowly returned the cup to its saucer. "You know, I still can't figger how in hell's name Preserved didn't know his damn pistol was empty. I unloaded the damned thing right in front of his face." He scratched his head. "Damn, I know the light was poor before you lit that lantern, but it weren't that poor."

"He never looked at you," I said. "He never once took his eyes from me." I tried to smile away the next words. "I think the fact that someone he considered a nig had just walked through his front door, uninvited, so to speak, enraged him to the point he couldn't see anything else."

"Man's a fool," my father snapped.

I put my hand out and covered his, grateful for his paternal support.

"Well, that fool's in jail now," Frenchy said. "Even though I ain't promisin' how long we gonna be able to keep him there."

"Why's that?" my father asked. "Sumbitch tried ta kill both of ya."

"Sure enough did. Only it's gonna be a hard thing to prove," Frenchy said. "'Specially when I gotta testify that I unloaded the crazy bastid's pistol right there in fronta his eyes." He shook his head. "We go to that preliminary hearin' tomorrow, the defense lawyer's gonna say the fool was only jokin' us, and that we got all carried away." Frenchy offered up a shrug. "Leastways, they's locked up fer now, the both of 'em. So we gets us a day or two of rest. And maybe it'll be a good thing if the court cuts 'em loose. I 'spect we gonna feel some heat from the townsfolk, hereabouts, they find out we arrested them two sumbitches." He let out a soft chuckle. "I kin just hear that storekeeper of yers goin' on 'bout us protectin' the nigs and lockin' up white folks. Lord, that woman is a mouthy fool. Leastways, we caught us a piece of luck. She won't know about it 'til tomorrow. Jake Phelps never did get back to his newspaper in time to write it up fer today."

"It's best he didn't," my father said. "I'm thinkin' we ain't got us many quiet days left."

"Yes, we'll gather at the ri-ver, the beau-ti-ful, the beau-ti-ful . . . riv-er, Gather with the saints at the riv-er, That flows by the thro-ne of . . . God."

I could hear Elisha's voice rumbling up through the trees as I turned into Jehiel's dooryard. Frenchy had sent me on up to tell everyone on the hill that Preserved and Abel were in jail, so they might rest easy, at least until after the preliminary hearing on Monday. Frenchy, meanwhile, planned to use this Sunday afternoon to canvass as many townsfolk as possible, in hopes of finding someone who had seen Royal Firman on the day of his murder.

As I climbed from my car I found Jehiel, together with Prince and Elisha, busy building a stone wall in the shape of a large "L." The wall ran along the rear of Jehiel's house, then down one side.

Elisha puffed himself up and leveled a finger at me as I approached. His forbidding stance made him look like a sweaty, bald prophet of doom.

"I did not see . . . you at services this mornin'," he intoned.

"That's because I was still to bed," I said.

Before he could launch into a tirade about sin and sinners, I told them all about the arrests Frenchy and I made the previous night, and how locking up Preserved and Abel had gone on well into the morning hours.

"Right now, I'm looking for Johnny Taft," I explained. "I got to tell him to stand down in his guard duty, at least until we see what happens at the preliminary hearing tomorrow morning."

"What time's that hearin'?" Jehiel asked.

"Ten o'clock, at the courthouse in Burlington," I said.

"Johnny's over to 'Lizabeth's house, standin' guard with Jeffords," Jehiel said. "Figured we had us 'nuff menfolk here to take care of ourselves." He turned to his son. "Prince, you run on over there an' tell Johnny he's needed over here. An' tell Jeffords he kin come work on this wall."

Jehiel's shoulder was still bandaged, but he no longer wore the sling. He had also done away with the bandage on his head, and I could see the stitches Doc Hawley had put there.

"You don't look like you're ready to be building yourself a wall," I said, glancing at the large pile of heavy stones off to my right.

"Ain't doin' much liftin' myself." Jehiel waved his hand in a wide circle. "I'm mostly doin' the directin'."

"Amen to that. And praise . . . the Lord." Elisha rolled his eyes for effect.

Jehiel snorted. "Don't you worry yourself. I'm gonna work right along beside ya 'til Prince gets back. An' I'm plannin' on puttin' Samuel, here, to work, too." He jabbed a finger at Elisha. "Man's the laziest Bible thumper I done ever seen. Moans an' groans over every damn stone."

"Don't you go cursing around me, you heathen. Weren't for your girls, I'd never see you in church either."

"That's fer damn sure," Jehiel said. "I'm thinkin' 'bout movin' all three a them gals away, so's I kin get some sleep on Sunday mornin's."

"You sleep a lo-ng time in hell, you do that, brother-man," Elisha snapped.

Jehiel waved the words away with his good arm. "Let's get back to work. I hear'd all the preachin' from you I wants at services this mornin'. Samuel, you lend us a hand here."

Building a dry stone wall is one part physical labor and nine parts art. The laying of stones of all shapes and sizes so they interlock into a solid, unmovable whole is a talent of eye that few possess.

Jehiel was a master at it, instinctively knowing which side of a stone would fit, and exactly where that stone should be placed to make the whole stronger and more enduring. To me, it seemed he "felt" the stones into place, talking to each one as he worked, both his own and the ones Elisha and I carried to the wall.

"Oooooh, that's a good'un you got there, Samuel. 'Cept flip 'er over an place her right there. . . . Oooooh, not bad. Not bad a'-tall. . . . Oh, baby, baby, baby. Slip that'un there, right in that there spot, Elisha. . . . Oh, yes . . . oh, yes. . . . Now, I don't rightly know what we'll do with this'un . . . Oh, yes I do, yes I do. Put her in right there. Now put a few little'uns in behind her. That's right. That's right. . . . Oh, I like that. Look at that one Samuel's got. I like that sumbitch. Give me that one right over there, next to that big flat stone. . . . Oh, yes . . . now we're cookin'. . . . Now give me a little shim. . . . Oh, good'un, that's a good'un."

We continued that way, Jehiel keeping at it, despite his ailing shoulder, even after Prince returned. I broke away from my own labor only long enough to send Johnny on home, the work was that infectious. I listened to Jehiel ramble on, talking the stones into place, defying them not to follow his will, then bellowing pleasure as each one fit snugly against the next, shoring each other up just as he had demanded.

When we broke for rest and water I sat next to him on a section of completed wall, pleased by the solid feel of it beneath me. Then I looked about and came back to the same question that had crossed my mind when I first arrived.

"Why a wall?" I asked. "It's pretty enough. But there doesn't seem to be a need."

"Maybe I just like walls," Jehiel said. "Maybe erectin' walls is my natural callin'."

It struck me then, and I wondered why I had not seen it straight off. "I suppose it is better to fight out in the open than to be trapped inside a house."

He stared off into the trees that began where his dooryard ended. "You ever read any of the writin' about Negroes in the South? Especially the writin' of Miz Ida B. Wells?" he asked.

I shook my head.

"Well, she was pretty famous fer a time. She wrote about what happened down South. The lynchin's an' all the ugly, murderin' stuff that's still goin' on." He shook his great brown head. "Anyways, I read about how them KKK boys likes to set fire to a Negro's house, then gun down the family when they come runnin' out. Ain't gonna let that happen at this house. We gotta leave this here house, we gonna have us a wall to drop in behind. Maybe we even be in behind that wall when they shows up."

"That's not going to happen here. None of it," I said.

Jehiel let out a rumbling laugh. "You guarantee me that, Samuel? You got a piece of paper you kin write it all down on, so's I kin hang it up on my wall?" He slapped a hand on my knee, and laughed again. "Trouble with you, Samuel, is you wants to believe that you is white, and that them other white folks is just like you." He stood up and stretched, then turned back to face me, his massive body looming above me like some great human wall. "But they ain't like you, Samuel. Not more'n one in a hun'red. And you be careful dealin' with 'em. 'Cause you ain't white to them, and they'll turn on you fast as a snake."

"You're wrong," I said, my voice harsh and angry.

"Am I?" Jehiel smiled down at me.

"You're wrong that I think I'm one of them."

"You are such a pretty boy, Samuel. So pretty an' so good. You are the best little white boy in this town." My mother's face beamed with pleasure as she ran the comb through my hair. "Oh, yer hair is so straight an' so silky. It's jus' so lovely, Samuel. An' I can't believe it. Here it is, yer first day of school. Samuel Bradley startin' in at first grade. Seems impossible ya got yerself so old, so quick."

She knelt and straightened my Buster Brown collar, then handed me my lunch pail, took me by the hand, and led me on out our front door. My father was just outside in the road, hitching our horse to the buggy, and he waved to us as we passed by, his tan face smiling and happy beneath the pulled-down brim of his hat.

We strolled off, leaving my father behind, walking side by side down the road to the school, my mother softly singing a verse of her favorite hymn.

"When love is found . . . and hope comes home, Sing and be glad . . . that two are one, When love explodes . . . an' fills the sky, Praise God an' share . . . our Mak-er's joy."

When we arrived at the school, she stopped and knelt beside me, fussing again with my collar. Then she reached into her apron and withdrew an envelope.

"Now in here is yer birth certificate, Samuel. You is supposed ta give it ta yer teacher, so's they kin be sure you's the right age. Now, when you give it ta her, you show her what it says. How it marks down right cheer that you is white. I don't want her markin' down on her school sheet that you is a colored child. Yer daddy may still have that colored mark on his birth certificate, an' tha's all right, 'cause he's a good man, but you is third-generation, you tell her that fer sure. You is as white as a boy kin be. An' it says so right cheer on yer birth certificate."

The courtroom that Monday morning was a bustle of activity, with two rows of the spectators' gallery filled with those who had been arrested over the weekend. The judge, a slender, pinch-faced man with shockingly white hair, did not seemed pleased with the number of miscreants he had to dispatch, and he dealt with the lesser crimes of drunkenness and disorderly conduct with a degree of severity that surprised me.

I looked about the courtroom as I waited for our case to be called. It seemed far too elegant and stately for our troubled times, with its gleaming mahogany walls, freshly shined under a heavy coat of new wax. Behind the judge's bench was a lighter patch of wall where a picture had been removed. Normally, a framed photograph of the president hung there, but the Republicans who controlled the county courthouse, upon removing Mr. Hoover's picture, had not seen fit to replace it with one of Mr. Roosevelt. I glanced at Jehiel Flood, seated in a middle row, knowing that he would approve.

Jehiel had arrived promptly at ten o'clock, accompanied by Elizabeth and Elisha Bowles. When I had gone to greet them, she had told me she had taken the day off from school—the first time she had ever done so—and had sent her sister, Ruby, as substitute.

"I am afraid the children are in for a very strict day," she said, smiling.

It was eleven o'clock when the judge called the case against Preserved and Abel, and the prosecutor promptly sent Frenchy out to fetch them. Since Preserved was charged with attempted murder on a police officer, and Abel as an accomplice, both had been kept in a cell outside the courtroom, and they were now brought before the judge wearing handcuffs and leg irons.

I watched them shuffle in, their movements restricted by the chains securing their legs. Preserved glared at me as he entered, then looked about the courtroom as if seeking out some sign of support, that search coming to an abrupt stop at Jehiel and Elisha and Elizabeth. When he turned back his eyes were filled with a degree of madness I had not seen before.

Seymour Caswell was the defense attorney. He was a Burlington lawyer with a reputation for belligerent cross-examinations, a short, square, bearded man of about fifty, who represented many of the area's loggers. I had seen him work before, and I disliked both his tactics and his manner.

Caswell immediately moved for dismissal of all charges on the grounds that they were frivolous. The judge denied the motion, and the prosecution called Frenchy to the stand to set out its prima facie case.

Charles Brewster was the prosecutor, a young attorney, only two or three years out of law school. He was a tall, slender, stoop-shouldered man, who looked like a question mark as he paced back and forth before the witness stand.

Under Brewster's questioning, Frenchy told the court about the attempt on Jehiel Flood's life, how the defendant, Preserved Firman, had previously threatened the victim, how an investigation of the scene had produced a forty-five-caliber rifle slug, and how it was later learned that the defendant owned such a weapon. He then explained how he had presented those facts to another county judge and had obtained a search warrant for Preserved's home.

Frenchy then told of our efforts to serve that warrant, and I was surprised by the degree to which he recalled even the smallest detail, many of which I, myself, had already forgotten. He took special care to explain that he had unloaded Preserved's pistol before any lantern was lit inside the cabin, the only illumination at the time coming from the headlamps of three automobiles some forty yards distant.

Under cross-examination, Caswell attacked the notion that Preserved was unaware that his pistol had been rendered harmless. He took great pains to load and unload the weapon several times, pointing out to the court every click and snap the pistol made.

He then asked a final question that seemed to take Frenchy by surprise.

"How long have you known Samuel Bradley, the constable of Jerusalem's Landing?" he asked.

"Most all his life," Frenchy said.

"And do you know his father, Arriah Bradley?" he asked.

"I do," Frenchy said.

"And do you consider him a friend?" Caswell asked.

"I do," Frenchy said.

"So would it be correct to describe you as a friend of the Bradley family?" the defense attorney asked.

"I like to think so," Frenchy said.

Caswell smiled, then spun on his heel and walked back to the defense table. "Thank you," he said over his shoulder. "I have no further questions of this witness, Your Honor."

With that, the prosecution rested. Caswell then surprised everyone by calling me as his lone rebuttal witness.

After I was sworn in, the defense attorney sallied forth like a wolf descending on a lamb. He was dressed in a three-piece, pinstriped suit, and his fingers were hooked into his vest, as though preparing to use those points of leverage to propel himself forward, presumably toward my throat. Instead, he came to an abrupt stop two

steps before the witness stand and gave me a wide, fictitious smile
that did not carry to his eyes.

We stared at each other for almost a minute. Caswell was like
other short men I had known. Men who were sometimes aggressive
and combative, often to the point of belligerence. For some, I think,
it is a means of compensating for their size. For Caswell it was
merely a part of his nature.

Caswell began by pacing back and forth, then opened with a series of preliminary questions: my name, my place of residence and
the position I currently occupied. When I had answered he brought
himself to an abrupt halt and squared himself to face me.

"And when was the last time the citizens of your community
elected you to serve as constable of Jerusalem's Landing?" he asked.

"I have never been elected," I said.

Caswell stared at me with false surprise. "How so?" he asked.
"Please tell the court how this came to be?" He allowed his voice to
gradually rise as he spoke, so it added to his implausible sense of
puzzlement.

I shifted in my chair, nervous about what was yet to come. "My
father served as town constable for twenty years," I said, "and had
just been elected to a fifth four-year term, when he suffered a debil-
itating stroke. I was appointed to fill that unexpired term."

Caswell began pacing again, as if using the motion to digest that
information.

"Do you intend to run for re-election when this term expires?" he
asked.

"Objection, Your Honor. Immaterial." Brewster was on his feet,
his body now straight as an exclamation point, his face serious.

"I shall allow it," the judge replied. "This is a preliminary hearing, and I am inclined to give the defense some latitude."

Brewster's body curved in defeat, and he brushed back a boyish
strand of hair that had fallen across his forehead, then reclaimed
his chair with an audible sigh.

Caswell nodded his thanks to the bench, then smirked at me as
he awaited my reply.

"I have not decided," I said.

"Do you fear a referendum on your performance?" he asked.

"Objection!" Brewster shouted again.

Caswell waved his hand. "I'll withdraw the question, Your Honor." He turned away and began pacing again. "So . . ." he said, drawing the word out, "it was the town selectboard, not the electorate, who gave you your post . . ." He paused, and I began to answer, only to be stopped when he hurried on. "And in doing so gave you your long . . . sought after . . . opportunity . . . to persecute . . . Preserved Firman." Caswell stopped directly in front of me, his glare fixed on my face. "Isn't that true?" he demanded, shouting over the equally loud objection now being voiced by Brewster.

The judge gaveled them both into silence, then turned a severe eye on Caswell. "This is a serious matter you are raising, Counselor. If I allow it to continue, it best not prove specious."

Caswell puffed himself up, already sensing victory in this skirmish. "I assure Your Honor, the evidence will show it is far from that. It is, in fact, highly relevant, and clearly supports the innocence of my clients."

The judge nodded, then turned to me, his gaze now slightly jaundiced. "You may answer the question," he said.

"I have never persecuted Preserved Firman, or any member of his family," I said.

Caswell put his hand to his mouth and coughed, as though fighting off laughter. "Are you telling this court that you like and admire Mr. Firman?" he asked.

"No, I am not," I said.

"In fact you dislike him, isn't that true?"

"Yes, it is true."

Caswell smiled again, this time like a man who has just had a sumptuous meal set before him. "Constable Bradley, can you tell the court who Isabel Stewart is?"

I shifted in my chair again. I could feel the sweat gush forth in my palms. "She was my great-grandmother," I said. "She is now deceased."

Caswell hooked his thumbs into his vest again. "And, Constable, can you tell the court if this Isabel Stewart was a woman of color?"

My voice broke slightly as I spoke, and I instantly hated myself for that display of weakness. "Yes . . . she was."

"A Negro?"

I raised my chin slightly, I hoped defiantly. "Yes, a Negro."

"So you, yourself, are colored." Before I could respond, Caswell raised his hand and waved the statement away. "Oh, I beg your pardon, Constable. I believe the term used for persons such as yourself is *bleached*, is it not? You are third-generation, with no other Negro blood in the two subsequent generations, is that not the case?"

His voice was solicitous and contemptible, and I fought to restrain myself. "That is true," I said.

He nodded, turned away and began pacing again. "And tell us, Constable, was your great-grandmother, Isabel Stewart, ever a slave?"

"Yes, she was."

Caswell stopped, turned back to face me, and raised his eyebrows. "Here in Vermont? How is that possible?"

There was a stirring in the courtroom, a buzz of conversation, then a snicker. The judge banged his gavel and called for order.

I stared at Caswell, no longer able to keep the hatred from my eyes. "My grandmother was brought to Vermont as a child, when the slaveholder who owned her moved his family here. Under Vermont law she did not have to be freed until she was sixteen. She was not set free until she reached that age."

Caswell had the look of a man who could not wait to leap into the breach. "And who was her owner?" he demanded.

I drew a breath to steady my voice, but I could not control the hatred that I felt brimming in my eyes. "I am told my great-grandmother was the property of a farmer in Hinesburg, a man named Amos Firman."

Caswell puffed up so he seemed to grow several inches. "Amos *Firman*," he said, allowing the name to sit a moment, before he continued. "And what was the relationship of this Amos Firman to our defendant, Preserved *Firman?*" His voice was silky now, assured.

"Preserved has told me that Amos was his great-uncle. I have made no separate inquiry to discover whether or not that is true."

"But you do know the truth about something else, don't you, Constable? You know that Preserved Firman, and other members of his family, have on occasion taunted you about your Negro heritage, is that not true?" Caswell was almost beside himself with pleasure.

"It is true," I said.

"And you hated them for those remarks, did you not?"

"I hated their ignorance."

Caswell threw back his head as if struck. "Ho, ho," he said. "Only their ignorance?" He stepped forward, glaring at me. "I think not, sir. I think you hated Preserved Firman. I think you hated the ownership his family had over your great-grandmother. I think you despised the way he used it to bait and harangue you. And on Saturday night, when he further baited you by pulling the trigger of an unloaded revolver, you used that opportunity to get your long-awaited revenge, and together with your dear . . . family . . . friend, Deputy Sheriff Frenchy LeMay, you used that foolish act to charge this innocent man with attempted murder. And then, for good measure, and to cover up this improper and illegal arrest, you also charged an innocent bystander, one Abel Turner."

Caswell faded from view as he walked back to the defense table. I was numb, and suddenly tired, and I felt myself slump in the chair. My mother's voice floated back to me. "Now sit up straight, dear. There ain't nothin' more attractive than a boy with good posture." I straightened in my chair and looked out into the spectator's gallery. Elizabeth's was the only face that came back to me, and from the witness stand I could see a solitary tear course down her cheek, and I felt her sadness and her humiliation. And I could feel all of it cut straight into my heart.

{ 13 }

I stare at my ceiling, studying the fine web of cracks I have watched grow ever since childhood. It has been an incalculable spread, the tiniest of hairline fractures in the white plaster, almost invisible to the eye, until the formation suddenly erupts, and is one day found to have crept across the ceiling. Not unlike the nocturnal work of spiders, I think, miraculously appearing the next morning, covered in dew and shimmering in the light of a new day. Very much like my life, or rather, what my life has become.

I let my eyes drop to the picture of Elizabeth that faces my bed, but find I cannot look at it. I roll on my side and face the wall. Now there is only the monotonous pattern of wallpaper that my mother selected all those many years ago. But it offers no comfort, no escape; it only empties me of all my defenses, bringing back visions of this wretched day.

Preserved Firman smiled triumphantly as the leg irons were removed from his ankles. He stared at me as he extended his wrists so the bailiff could do the same with the handcuffs. Throughout the hearing, his eyes were filled with the same mad hatred that had seized him when he first looked out into the spectators' gallery and realized that the only people who had come from Jerusalem's Landing were Jehiel and Elizabeth and Elisha. Then his eyes had begun to blaze with a seemingly unquenchable fire. Now victory mingled with the madness, and I realized for the first time that he sincerely believed the Negroes were persecuting him, if not by their overt acts, then certainly by their denial of his power over them, a power he had just now—to his mind—reasserted.

And, if he truly believed that, how great was his need to defeat someone like me? A hidden Negro, bleached back to whiteness, the great-grandson of a slave his family had once owned, who had now helped bring about this terrible humiliation of having him chained in public. And surely he believed it, just as his lawyer had spoken the words . . . such sweet words; every bit as sweet as those reversing "the injustice."

The court had not quite put it that way. No "injustice" had been cited. The judge had been far more temperate in his ruling. In the convoluted language of the court, our gray-haired, pinch-faced magistrate had found "sufficient reason to believe that Preserved Firman did indeed know his weapon had been unloaded." His Honor reached this conclusion simply by citing the prosecution's failure to present any evidence to the contrary—some "credible proof that Deputy LeMay's unloading of the weapon in question had somehow gone unnoticed by the defendant." He further found that this being the case, and "since no attempt was made to reload the weapon, the defendant's actions, though foolish, could not be viewed as a serious attempt on the lives of the police officers present."

As to Abel, the judge simply ruled that "lacking any true assault by Preserved Firman, there could be no act of aiding that assault by Abel Turner." And with that, both men were freed.

I turned back to my finely cracked ceiling and laughed. While these were the words that set him free, they were, in Preserved's view, only a small part of the whole. True victory had come with his lawyer's triumph in identifying my heritage and my race, in establishing the servitude of Isabel Stewart, from whose body my more immediate ancestors had sprung.

Brewster's ineffectual cross-examination, his vain attempt to redeem me before the court, clearly failed, and Frenchy placed an arm about my shoulder and gave it a squeeze as I returned to my chair. When the ruling was handed down, the young attorney was bitter in defeat. As Preserved and Abel were led away to reclaim their possessions, he turned his anger on Frenchy and me, warning us to never again bring him a case "so lacking in evidence."

Had he looked particularly hard at me? Struggling to see how I had duped Frenchy to my cause? Somehow believing Caswell's arguments? Or just wondering what trickery had allowed someone of such low birth to gain so lofty a position in the law?

I laughed again and turned back toward the wall, my body trembling so that I hugged myself to make it stop, and I must have finally given in to my misery and fallen asleep, for when I awoke it was to the gentle touch of her hand gliding along my chest.

I turned in my bed and stared in disbelief, as she cradled my face in her hands and softly kissed my forehead.

"I've never been to your room before," Elizabeth said. "Has my picture been on your wall all these years?"

"Ever since you gave it to me." I paused, as if trying to remember when that had been, but of course I knew. "It was seven years ago, I think."

Elizabeth smiled. "Yes. It was summer, and we were home from college. Have so many years gone by? It doesn't seem possible."

"It does to me," I said. The words came so quickly I could not stop them. I struggled to recover. "I took the picture back to the university that fall, and it hung in my room there, all through my senior year."

"And my picture came home with you? Home to Jerusalem's Landing?"

"Yes."

She squeezed my face between her hands and kissed me again. Her kisses were not passionate, they were more, and I felt the tension slowly begin to drain away.

"I'm sorry you were hurt today." She whispered the words, as if somehow knowing I could not bear to hear them any louder.

"I saw you crying," I said.

"It was cruel of him to taunt you so. The law should not be cruel."

"He was trying to win. He needed a villain to create doubt. What better villain than a Negro?" I laughed bitterly, and she slid her arms about me and held me close.

"You listen too much to their words."

"To whose words?" I asked.

"White people." She pressed my head against her breast. "Their words are meaningless. It's something you've never understood."

We lay quietly for a long time, as the world about us turned black with night. My eyes adjusted to the dark, but Elizabeth remained little more than a shadow that might disappear if she moved farther away. But she remained, and I felt her smooth, soft breast rise and fall, and finally I reached out to hold the life that filled it.

She inhaled deeply at my touch and pressed herself against my hand. "Make love to me, Samuel," she whispered. "I want you to love me as much as you are able."

"It's more than you could ever imagine," I said.

She didn't respond to my words, she only held me closer. And in her silence I could feel her doubt.

{ 14 }

I drove Elizabeth home before dawn, and as we passed her father's house I saw Johnny Taft's car parked in the dooryard, and I knew he'd be hidden back in the woods, standing guard again now that Preserved was free.

"It's only just beginning, isn't it, Samuel? I thought it was almost finished, but it's not."

Her voice sounded wistful, and I reached across the car and laid my hand on hers. "I want to tell you that it won't be dangerous. But I can't do that."

I pulled my car to a stop in front of her cabin, and she turned to me and smiled. "It's always dangerous for a Negro, Samuel." She turned away again, looking first at her darkened windows, then off into the woods. "Do you remember when we were in school together, how Miss Phillips, our sixth-grade teacher, taught us about the underground railroad?"

"I remember," I said.

She laughed. It was a warm, throaty laugh. "I thought it was so romantic," she said. "White people, just like the people in our town, all of them trying to save runaway Negro slaves. Hiding them in cellars, and in attics and in secret rooms; saving them from the slave catchers who were searching everywhere for them. And the Negroes finally getting across the border and into Canada, where they were safe at last, free at last." She smiled—more at herself than me. "I used to daydream that I was a slave who had been saved that way.

"Then, when I was in college, I learned it was all a lie." She turned her smile on me and tried to brighten her voice. "Or at least an exaggeration. Oh, there were some good people, Quakers mostly, who helped with food and work and transportation. They wrote letters to the slave owners in the South, and tried to negotiate a price by which a particular slave could buy his freedom. I read many of those letters. It was very aboveboard. The Quakers would even tell the slave owners that a certain slave was living and working on their farm. It was never clandestine, and the Negroes were never hidden." She inclined her head to one side as if regretting the absence of romance in what she was about to say. "There wasn't any need. The slave catchers never came this far north. Vermont was simply too distant, too expensive a journey for what they would be paid."

"I didn't know that," I said.

She looked away again. "I wonder why I never told you. Perhaps it was because I remembered how happy you were, all the way back when Miss Phillips told us all those stories, with both of us believing that the white people had saved so many Negroes." She turned back, her eyes holding me sharply. "But we knew, Samuel. Even if we refused to admit it, we knew. We had to. We had lived it all our lives.

"So I ask you, Samuel, what do you think would have happened if some adventurous slave catcher had taken a chance and come this far north? Do you think some white farmer might have gone to him and said: 'You come with me, friend. I'll show you where that nig is hiding'?" She turned back and drew a deep breath. "And what do you think those white people will do now?"

* * *

Frenchy was waiting for me when I returned home.

"Bad news," he said. "Technician couldn't get a positive result on Preserved's rifle."

"It was the wrong gun?" The idea that Preserved hadn't shot Jehiel was incredible to me.

"Didn't say that." Frenchy gave me a shrug. "Technician just couldn't find enough land an' groove marks to say the slug we found definitely came from Preserved's rifle. Judge'd just throw it out, we went to court with it, and young Mr. Caswell, he'd be pissin' his drawers and gettin' all snarly with us all over again."

"Dammit. I'd hoped we'd get him on that. Get him out of the way, so we could finish this thing without him stirring up trouble at every turn."

"You ain't the only one, partner," Frenchy said. "And it's only gonna get worse now."

"How?" I could not see how that was possible.

"Well, you know the story about Preserved's arrest finally got inta yesterday's newspaper. And the story about the judge cuttin' him loose is gonna be in today's newspaper." Frenchy tapped his nose with one finger. "Now, those stories are sure gonna create a stir hereabouts. So whaddya think's gonna happen if that there newspaper runs a story tomorrow sayin' how Preserved's rifle didn't match up with the bullet fired at Jehiel?"

"Has the reporter been asking about it?" I tried to envision the man. He was so eager, so excited when we made our ill-fated arrests. Certainly that excitement had not faded. Especially after our disaster in court. Now he would simply redirect it—with Frenchy and me as the new target.

Frenchy scratched his chin and smiled. "You might say he's been showin' some interest," he said. "I been dodgin' him, but I can't promise what the technician might say if Jake latches hold of him."

"What do you think the chances are he will?"

Frenchy wiggled his eyebrows. "I had me a year's salary, and some fool to take the bet, I'd have a fistful of money before the week was out." He held his hands out and let them fall to his side, indicating the futility of hoping for anything else. "That old Lawyer Caswell, he's a fella likes to see his name in the newspaper. Can't imagine he'd let a chance pass him by where he could point Jake in the right direction, then jabber away about how his client was mistreated by the law, and how one of them new-fangled ballistics tests just done proved it."

Frenchy was right, of course. Only three years ago, newspapers across the country had written glowingly about modern advances in ballistics testing. At the time, forensic technicians, using the new comparison microscope, had been able to match test bullets fired from the machinegun of Fred "Killer" Burke to bullets taken from victims of Chicago's St. Valentine's Day Massacre. The story had made forensic science the new darling of newspapers. Now there would be an equally tantalizing story about a local logger "proved innocent" by this modern crime-fighting science. Without question, it would have our Burlington newsmen salivating on their typewriters.

My father entered the kitchen and I busied myself getting him coffee. "What's the matter with Samuel?" he asked Frenchy. "Looks like a boy whose dog jus' up an' died. He still frettin' 'bout court yesterday?"

"Just this lousy case," Frenchy said. "Gets worse with every sunrise."

My father had been eyeing me all the time he spoke to Frenchy, waiting to see how I would respond. I had come home from court yesterday hardly able to speak. I had struggled through an account of Lawyer Caswell's questioning as I fixed him dinner, and had seen the pain come hard to his eyes. It was more than I could bear just then, and I had beaten a quick retreat to my room. I am sure my father had remained awake long after our conversation. Stress and concern usually kept him from sleep. I am equally certain he heard Elizabeth enter our home and go upstairs, though I doubt he knew it was she.

"Well, hell's bells, ain't nobody gonna tell me what's new with this lousy case?" My father was talking to Frenchy, but his eyes were still on me, still curious.

Frenchy told him about Preserved's rifle, and my father shook his head in disgust. "What's happenin' with that looksee you was takin' at Abel Turner?" he asked.

"Got problems there, too," Frenchy said.

"How so?" my father asked.

Frenchy scratched his chin, as if using the gesture to think things through. "Well, the big problem is our damned theory. We been lookin' at the possibility that Royal an' Abel got inta an argument somewheres else, an' that Abel kilt Royal with a pitchfork. Then, accordin' to our theory, he moves the body on up to Nigger Hill in Royal's own truck, so's we'd think the coloreds did it. Only problem is, we didn't find us any blood in Royal's truck."

"So maybe he brought the body up in his own truck, then realized he hadta have Royal's truck there to hide that fact." My father stabbed his finger against the table as if that gesture gave credibility to his theory. "So then he brung Royal's truck up later."

"Possible," Frenchy said, scratching his chin again. "'Cept we ain't ever gonna prove it."

"Why's that?" my father asked.

He was getting argumentative now, and I set the coffee in front of him and rested a hand on his shoulder.

"You wanna tell him?" Frenchy asked.

I nodded. "We can't prove it because of what happened at the crime scene that I was supposed to safeguard." I gave my father's shoulder a squeeze. "Preserved and Abel put Royal's body into Abel's truck before I could stop them. And that simple fact gives Abel an easy way to explain any blood or clothing or hair fibers we might find there."

"Damn, that's bad luck," my father said, putting the best possible shine on it. He raised a cautioning finger. "'Course if Abel was only helpin' Preserved, after that bastid kilt his own boy, then they might notta used Abel's truck a'tall. Mighta used Preserved's."

Frenchy leaned forward, holding my father's eye. "You thinkin' the man mighta kilt his own boy?" He shook his head. "That's hard, Arriah, real hard." He inclined his head toward me. "Seems like you and yer boy is thinkin' the same thoughts. Samuel, here, was wonderin' the same thing at our church meetin' t'other night. I told him then we'd look inta it." Again, he shook his head. "But I gotta tell you, that's a hard one fer me to swaller."

"Would be fer me, too," my father replied. "Lessen I thought Preserved done caught his boy layin' wit' a colored gal."

"Damn," Frenchy said. "That's a mean 'un." He looked up at me and grinned. "What do you think yer townsfolk are gonna say, they find out we got us Preserved as a suspect?" He threw back his head and laughed. "Oooheee, Samuel. And what do you think Jehiel Flood's gonna say, we tell him we think one of his gals was sparkin' with that boy?" He shook his head and pushed himself up from the table. "Oh, that'll be a hot 'un, fer sure. That'll be hot as hell."

We checked on Johnny Taft and made sure everyone on the hill was taking proper precautions, then began a door-to-door canvass of every house on Addison Hollow Road. It was the only road that connected with Nigger Hill, the very route Royal, or his killer, had to take to reach the place where the body was found.

We started from the hill and worked our way toward town. There were only a dozen or so homesteads, and at each one we were met with a level of suspicion that surprised me.

There was no way to soften our questions. We needed to know what people had seen on the day of the murder. Had they seen Royal Firman driving his truck up toward Nigger Hill? Had they seen Abel Turner headed that way? Or Preserved Firman?

It was the final question that always drew the most curious look, then gradual comprehension, then a hint of anger, perhaps even subdued outrage.

When we reached town at noon, we had talked to every householder, except for old Mrs. Winifred Peabody, who'd not been at home. Otherwise, the results had been the same at each stop. No one had seen any of the men in question driving in the direction of Nigger Hill.

"Puzzles me," Frenchy said, as we stopped at his hotel to pick up the box lunch Mrs. Pierce made for all her guests.

"What does?" I asked.

"Fact that nobody seen Royal or Abel or Preserved drive on up there." Frenchy wagged a finger at no one in particular. "Now if this was a city like Burlington, or even one of the bigger towns, I'd figure it was just the way things was. But there ain't that many cars and trucks in a town this size. And one movin' down a road is somethin' folks notice." He shook his head. "And we sure as hell know that Royal, or his damn dead body, was drove on up there. Damn if it ain't makin' me think it was after dark when that all happened."

Frenchy spread his lunchbox on his lap and offered me half a sandwich overstuffed with ham and cheese. "Can't eat me a whole one of these," he said. "I surely don't think Miz Pierce realizes we got us a Depression goin' on. Every time I sit at her table, there's more food than there was the time before." Frenchy let out a little chuckle. "I dropped in to see my wife after court t'other day, and she said I was gettin' a might porky. Said folks'd think I was taken graft from the bootleggers, I keep puttin' on weight in these hard times were havin'."

"You can tell them the Negroes in Jerusalem's Landing are paying you off," I said.

Frenchy chuckled again, but this time there was no mirth in it. Finally, he turned in his chair and gave me a steady look. "Samuel, I'm a might worried about you."

"How so?" I asked.

"Well, you seem ta have yer mind set on how this here case should turn out." Frenchy held my eyes as he spoke the words, and I had to struggle against looking away.

"Sometimes I feel the same about you," I said. "Sometimes I feel as though you only want to look in one place—the folks on that hill."

"Could be you just don't like me lookin' at that place a'tall."

Frenchy spoke the words as softly as he could. He put his sandwich down and stared at me a long moment. "Samuel, what are you gonna do if it turns out one of them folks up an' murdered that boy?"

I took a large bite of my half sandwich and spoke around it as I chewed. "I'm not sure," I said. I continued chewing, knowing I had not told Frenchy the truth.

We drove back along Addison Hollow Road to see if Mrs. Winifred Peabody was now at home, and found her in her side yard, tending some pumpkins she had growing there.

I have known Mrs. Peabody all my life. She is second-generation colored, like my father, though her complexion is as pale as mine, and she lacks even a hint of Negro features. Still, I have heard her called "nig" behind her back on more than one occasion, and I am certain that our quiet brand of bigotry has caused her much suffering over her seventy-some years.

Mrs. Peabody rose from her pumpkin patch with a large smile, as Frenchy and I approached.

"Why, Samuel, it has been such a pow'rful long time since you stopped by my home," she began. "Now tell me, how is yer daddy doin'?"

Mrs. Peabody was a wisp of a woman, no more than five feet tall and reed thin. She had pure white hair that she kept short to her head, a longish nose that gave her a birdlike look, and deep brown eyes that were as warm as any eyes could be. I quickly told her my father was well, then introduced Frenchy, and explained the business we were on.

"Lordy," Mrs. Peabody said, shaking her head. "I hear'd 'bout that poor Firman boy, but I couldn't believe none of what I hear'd folks sayin', how it was Jehiel or one a his kin done the killin'." She waved her hand, as if dismissing what she'd just said, and continued: "Now a'fore I tell you boys anythin', you gotta let me get you a nice drink of cold, fresh spring water."

Frenchy began to say no, but I interrupted him and said we'd both be grateful for a drink. When Mrs. Peabody toddled off to her house, I turned to Frenchy and explained.

"We don't let her get us a drink, it'll worry her the whole time we're here," I said. "And if she's worried about that, she won't pay attention to anything we ask her. Trust me on this. I've known the lady a long, long time."

Mrs. Peabody returned with our drinks, and Frenchy picked up on what I had said and thanked her profusely, claiming there was nothing like good, country spring water to quench one's thirst. It brought a wide, happy smile to her face, and he quickly launched into his series of questions. I was surprised to see the old woman's eyes light up immediately.

"Why I seen all three of them men," she said. "It was late afternoon, already gettin' dark. Nigh on ta five o'clock, I'd venture. That's when I saw young Royal Firman drivin' his truck all hell bent, with Abel Turner right behind him, goin' jus' as fast. I knowed they turned up on ta Nigger Hill 'cause I watched 'em a spell, jus' 'cause I figgered they was gonna end up in a ditch, fer sure."

Frenchy asked her what day it was, and she cocked her head at a sharp angle, making herself look even more birdlike. "Don't rightly know," she said. "But it was only in the las' week, fer sure. An', a' course, it hadda be a'fore the poor boy was kilt, didn't it?"

Frenchy fought off a smile. Then he slowly worked the old woman back, taking her step by step through each day, getting her to remember what she had done on every one, until he was certain the day in question was the day the murder had been committed.

"Now was it that same day that ya saw Preserved drive by, too?" he asked.

Mrs. Peabody wrinkled up her face, trying to remember. Finally, she gave up and shook her head. "I jus' can't be sure iff'n it was that same afternoon or the next mornin' that I seen Preserved. I jus' remember he looked pow'rful upset, an' he was drivin' jus' as fast as his son and that t'other boy. Maybe tha's why I thought it was the same afternoon, 'cause he was drivin' so fast, and lookin' so growly. But, then, that man always looks growly 'bout somethin'. He's jus' as mean as a snake. An' he always drives like the devil hisself was a chasin' him."

Frenchy slapped his hand against the steering wheel as we climbed back into his Ford. "Damn, that's good," he said. 'That's the first solid piece of eyewitness information we got. Now we know, fer sure, that Royal and Abel drove up on Nigger Hill late on the afternoon of the killin'."

"But what can we do with it?" I asked. "It's not enough for an arrest."

"No, it ain't," Frenchy said. "But it sure is enough fer another search warrant. So I'll go git it, and then tonight you and me is gonna tear that boy's cabin apart." He raised a finger. "And maybe, if we're real lucky, that boy'll be livin' like a good ol' backwoods woodchuck, and we'll find us a passel of dirty clothes." He paused to grin at me. "Maybe even some that's got Royal Firman's blood on 'em."

{ 15 }

Hannah came to my back door shortly after supper. Her face was pale, her eyes jittery, and she kept glancing back as though afraid someone had followed her.

I brought her quickly inside. "What's wrong?" I asked. "You look like somebody who's being chased."

She hugged herself and shivered. "I dunno if I am or not. I'm just afraid somebody might of followed me." She glanced back at the door. "There's a meetin' goin' on." Her voice had dropped until it was almost a whisper. It was as if she feared eavesdroppers might be listening at my door or windows.

I put my hands on her arms, and she fell against me. "I shouldn't be here," she said against my chest. "But when I heard what they were saying, I hadta come."

I gently pushed her back and looked into her face. "Hannah, calm down. Just tell me what you're talking about."

She drew a breath, closed her eyes momentarily, then began. "There's about a dozen of 'em, and more coming. Could be two dozen by now. I just don't know for sure. But they're meetin' in the barn, back of the store. My ma and pa are there, and so's Preserved Firman, and a couple of his friends. They're all talkin' mean about your investigation, and how you and that deputy are trying to protect the folks that lives on Nigger Hill. And how you don't care that a white man's been killed."

It was dangerous news, but I tried not to show too great a concern. "I can't stop them from meeting. I wish I could, but I can't." I gave her a smile and stroked her cheek. "Not unless they're planning something violent. They're not talking about taking matters into their own hands, are they?"

Hannah shook her head, then looked at me, confused. "I don't know what they're plannin', Samuel. I left, soon as I heard their tone. Preserved, he was rantin' on about how the coloreds was takin' over the town. How Jehiel Flood has the best logging land in the county, but just sits on it, and won't let nobody make a living off'n it. And how his daughter was the teacher at the school, and how she was teaching them little kids all kinds of nigger stuff, and was even practicing some kinda witchcraft up at her cabin with all them brews and potions she makes. Then he started talking about you. How you was in charge of the law, and how you tried to get him and Abel Turner throwed in jail so you could protect all them other nigs." Hannah stepped into me again and pressed her face against my chest. "That's when I got myself outta there, Samuel. When they started talkin' like you was a nig, too." She tightened her arms around my waist, as if trying to protect me from the words. "Oh, Samuel, I wanted to tell them to stop talkin' crazy. I wanted to tell them how you was third-generation bleached, and how that made you white just like us. But I was afraid, Samuel. I was afraid what they might do if I said it."

I stroked her back. "You did right not to say anything. It was better you just got out of there and came to me." I continued to stroke her back as I asked the one thing I needed to know. "Hannah, can you tell me who exactly is there?"

She rattled off seven or eight names, and some of them came as a surprise. There were two who were Preserved's woodchuck friends, and who'd go anywhere they thought a fight might be brewing. But the others were more sensible folk. At least I had always thought so.

My father came into the kitchen, and I told him what was happening. Then I explained that I planned to go over to the meeting to try to hear what I could without being seen. I asked him to wait on Frenchy, who was due back any time with a warrant for Abel Turner's cabin. "Just tell him where I've gone," I said. I tried to smile away my nervousness. "And tell him I'd appreciate it if he'd drop by. Just in case I need him."

The barn was directly behind Shepard's Store, and when I slipped back there, using the side of the store and then the barn, itself, for cover, I found more than a dozen cars and trucks, together with again as many horse-drawn buggies and wagons, all parked in a field, well out of sight of the road.

There was a door at the rear of the barn that opened onto the field, and I could hear a deep murmur of voices inside. I moved next to it and put my ear to a small space in the barnboard. Then all hope of clandestine observation disappeared.

"You here ta join us, or just ta spy on us, Samuel?"

I turned to find Victorious Shepard glaring at me. She had come from her home at the rear of the store just in time to catch me listening at the rear door.

I smiled at her out of spite. "Whenever folks talk about Jerusalem's Landing, I always consider myself part of the 'us.'" I made little quotation marks around the final word, and kept the smile fixed on my face. "So the idea of spying never enters my mind, Victorious."

A sneer creased her lips, and I turned to look at the vehicles parked behind her barn. "'Course I've never known folks to hide their cars and buggies in a field this way. Something secret going on?"

Her mouth hardened, the sneer turning into an angry line. "Why don't you come inside and see fer yourself," she snapped.

"I'd like that, Victorious. I surely would." I kept smiling at her, although my stomach was twisting now.

I followed Victorious into the barn, and the gathering suddenly quieted as I passed among them.

Preserved Firman was standing on some hay bales that had been set up at one end of the barn. He was unshaven, and his hands and forearms were stained with pine sap from the day's work, and all of it gave him the look of an itinerant backwoods preacher holding an impromptu revival meeting. He stared down at me with undiluted hate as I approached, and the glare was promptly mimicked by two woodchuck friends who stood to his left. They were fellow loggers whom I knew only as Big Jim and Andy, and each had a level of brainpower matched by the number of teeth in his head, which were few.

"We don't need us any nig constables," Preserved snarled. "This is a meetin' fer white folks."

"Yeah, no niggers been invited," Big Jim added.

"Tha's right," Andy chimed in. "Get yer bleached ass outta here, a'fore we throw it out."

I stared at each of the three in turn, struggling for as much contempt as I could bring to my eyes. Then I turned away slowly and took in Preserved's audience, as if memorizing each face. It was pure bravado. My mind burned with rage at the words that had been thrown at me, but I could also feel my stomach churning with fear. There were far too many people there, and each face I met, each set of wary, or nervous or angry eyes, belonged to someone I had known most of my life. Abigail Pierce and her daughter, Mary. Cletus Martin and his fellow farmers from the barbershop. Simeon Shepard. Victorious. Old David Daniels, nearing seventy, and a longtime deacon in Elisha's church. And others. So many others I would never have picked to be there. And I felt a sudden certitude that none would step to my side if I needed help.

I let my eyes fall on Jacob Fargo, who since I was a child had fished for trout with my father. He was a dairy farmer, closing in on sixty, with a grizzled outdoor face and close-cropped gray hair, now covered by a battered workman's cap.

"Is that how you see it, Jacob?" I asked. "Is it the way Preserved and his friends say it is?"

Jacob stared at his battered boots. I could see his jaw tightening. "We're all listenin' ta what the man has ta say," he answered at length. "Leastways, it's what I'm doin'."

I nodded and looked around the barn again, and now found other eyes avoiding mine. I also realized that there was one person missing whom I would have expected to be there. Abel Turner was nowhere in sight. I stored that bit of information away.

"So, you're all here to listen," I said. I paused and nodded, as if thinking that over. "Is that why you all hid your cars and wagons out back? Just so you could hear what Preserved's got to say?"

"Maybe folks put 'em back there so they wouldn't be spied on." It was Victorious again, her words dripping sarcasm.

I held her gaze, drawing it out longer than necessary, then finally smiled."Well, I'll tell you, Victorious. When I see a few dozen cars and trucks and wagons parked out behind a barn, I start to suspect that something serious is going on, and that maybe it's got folks a bit stirred up. And if that's so, I figure I should find out about it, because that's what keeping the peace is all about, wouldn't you say? And last time I looked, keeping the peace was what the town was paying me to do." I smiled at her again. "Of course some might consider that spying, I suppose. Is that what you think, Victorious?"

"I think ya weren't asked to come here," she snapped back. "An' since it's my barn—"

I cut her off before she could finish. "Oh, I'm sorry, Victorious. I thought you asked me inside." I turned quickly to her husband, putting him on the spot before his neighbors and customers. "Of course if you and Simeon don't want me here . . ."

Simeon glanced nervously from me to his wife. His mouth began to move wordlessly.

"Stay if ya want," Victorious snapped, before he could speak. "Might be good fer you to hear what folks is thinkin' in this here town."

There was a low muttering of approval. I looked slowly around the room again, and found there were now fewer eyes unwilling to meet my gaze. Anger had replaced the initial sense of embarrassment. The realization sent a chill through me.

A crackling voice came at me from the crowd. "Preserved's been tellin' us 'bout some new-fangled test the sheriff's office done on his rifle, an' how it proved he din't try ta gun down Jehiel Flood. Says that'll mor'n likely be in tomorra's newspaper." It was old David Daniels, his bony face and long nose jutting out like an accusation. "He says you and that deputy is still tryin' ta prove he did that shootin' anyways," he continued, "jus' so's you kin keep folks from thinkin' about who done kilt his boy. Says Jehiel prob'ly set up that shootin' hisself ta help hide what he done ta young Royal. An' he says you's in it with him, 'cause you wants ta protect all them coloreds up on Nigger Hill." Old David paused and stared at me. "What you say 'bout all that, Samuel?"

I held Daniel's eyes and let the moment draw out. "I could answer all of it with one word," I said, pausing again for effect. "If there weren't ladies present, that is."

The murmuring started again, but this time it did not sound overwhelmingly negative.

"Yer bleached constable jus' says whatever them nigs wants him ta say."

"Tha's right. An' it don't matter he claims he ain't. He's jus' a damned nigger hisself."

The voices came from behind me. Preserved and one of his woodchuck friends. Either Big Jim or Andy. I decided to ignore them.

"Tell us yer side of this here story," a voice called out. It was Cletus Martin, I thought, and I looked at him as I answered.

"I'd be pleased to," I said, raising my voice to give it authority. "First off, that test the sheriff's office had done didn't prove anything, not one way or another. And that's the truth of it, no matter what Preserved or his lawyer tell the newspapers." I paused and pointed in the general direction of Nigger Hill. "We found a forty-five-caliber bullet in a tree, up there where Jehiel was ambushed.

And the trajectory matched up to where we found some forty-five-caliber shell casings that the shooter left behind. But the people who did the test said the bullet was too chewed up for them to positively match it up with the forty-five-caliber Sharps rifle that Deputy LeMay and I took from Preserved's cabin. And that's all that test found. It did not say it wasn't Preserved's rifle. It said it couldn't tell if it was or not."

"Tha's a damn lie!" Preserved shouted.

Again, I ignored him. "Now as far as Jehiel setting up this attempt on his own life—well, that's a real interesting idea Preserved's come up with. I don't think Deputy LeMay and I ever thought about that." I paused, looked down at the hard-packed dirt floor and shook my head. "But far as I know—and I'm sure some of the deer hunters here know it, too—Jehiel and his boy, Prince, are both partial to Winchester thirty-thirties. And I don't believe Jeffords Page owns a rifle at all. I think he just uses one of Jehiel's shotguns when he needs one. And I know that Reverend Bowles only has a little four-ten for squirrels." I glanced at David Daniels. "You're a deacon in Elisha's church, David. You think the preacher might of borrowed somebody's forty-five caliber and shot Jehiel?"

I didn't wait for an answer. I looked quickly around the crowd as I continued. "Or maybe somebody here thinks one of Jehiel's daughters got themselves a forty-five-caliber rifle and used it on their daddy. That the idea?"

"Maybe you did it, you black-assed, bleached sumbitch."

I spun around with the words and found Big Jim glaring at me. He was a broad bull of a man, with a scraggly black beard and putrid breath you could smell from three feet away. He had me by a good three inches and was an easy 230 pounds, maybe more, all of it rock hard from years of logging. There was no question where a fight between us would lead. I'd have to shoot the man to keep him from killing me with his bare hands. His friend, Andy, was a few inches and twenty pounds smaller, but still a load to handle. He stood next to Jim, grinning and eager for trouble.

"Hell, ever'body knows you'd do anythin' to protect that nigger schoolteacher," Andy said. He had a round, red face with a four-day growth of beard and ginger-colored hair that hadn't been washed in a year or more. He grinned at me with tobacco-stained teeth. "Can't say's I blame ya much. She's a pow'rful good-lookin' woman." The grin broadened into a sneer. "An' I unnerstan' she's willin'."

It took every once of strength I had to keep from leaping at his throat, which is exactly what that cretinous woodchuck wanted. Instead, I let out a dismissive snort and looked back at the crowd. "Is this who you folks plan to follow?" I asked. I let my eyes come to rest on David Daniels, then move on to Jacob Fargo and Cletus Martin. "You want to listen to the rantings of some backwoods buffoons you wouldn't even invite home to supper and take it all as gospel truth? Don't tell me that. Don't do it. Don't say you are gonna believe these three . . . ignorant . . . fools . . . just because they're white."

"Seems like yer willin' to believe anybody who ain't white."

The voice shot back at me from the crowd, but I couldn't tell who had spoken the words.

"I'm sure not ready to believe this trash," I snapped back. "I'd believe almost anybody, no matter what their damned color, before I'd believe these three."

The buck knife came around under my chin and pressed up against my throat. At the same instant, a viselike hand grabbed my right wrist to keep it from my pistol.

"You got a mean mouth on ya, nigger man," Big Jim's voice hissed in my ear, and his foul breath washed over me.

"Cut that bleached nigger's throat," I heard Preserved Firman growl. "Then we'll go get us them other niggers."

I heard gasps from the crowd and was certain I was about to die. Then a voice I had known all my life boomed out.

"Ya do that, mister, an' all three of you be dead a'fore his body hits the ground."

My father's words filled the barn, free of the slurring that plagued his usual speech, and people seemed to part before it, as if pulled aside by its force. I looked down the length of the opening and saw him limping toward me. Hannah was at his side, supporting him by his left elbow. His twelve-gauge was propped on his right hip, his finger resting lightly on the trigger guard.

My father looked at me, and I cannot ever remember his eyes as hard. "I ain't sure I can save ya, son," he said. "I want ta, but I can't promise it. I do promise ya these three bastards'll be dead a'fore ya draw yer las' breath. I swear that to ya on yer mother's grave." His eyes shifted to Preserved. "An' you'll the be first, Preserved Firman, ya no-account, back-shootin' sumbitch."

There was a silence that I can only describe as "deathly," and I could feel my legs tremble as my entire body suddenly filled with more fear than I had ever known. Then Preserved Firman's voice assaulted my brain, driving away everything else.

"Let the nigger bastard go," he hissed.

The knife disappeared from my throat, and the viselike grip left my wrist. I spun around on still-shaky legs and found Big Jim standing before me, the knife still in his hand. His other hand raised up, as if warning me to stay back. I started to reach for my pistol so I could arrest him for assault, but my hand was still too numb from his steely grip. He seemed to realize it, too, and he leaped into the crowd, making any shot by myself, or my father, impossible. Before we could stop him, he had fled through the door and out into the night.

Hannah helped me get my father home, despite vehement protests from her mother. The crowd had already begun to disperse by then, but not before many had received individual tongue-lashings from their longtime constable. My father had called out to them by name, reminding each of times they had come to him for help over the past twenty years. "An' now I find ya all part of a mob that'd spill my boy's blood," he concluded.

Frenchy was seated comfortably in the kitchen when we got home, Stetson still perched on his head, both legs propped up on an empty chair, and the search warrant for Abel Turner's cabin set out on the table next to a bottle of Moxie he had taken from our icebox. His face filled with bemused puzzlement as we entered, I carrying my father's shotgun, Hannah and I supporting the man, himself, between us.

"I miss somethin' here?" he asked.

"Only something my father was supposed to wait here to tell you," I said.

"You best be glad I din't wait," my father snapped. "Or Hannah here, neither. Young gal saved the bacon tonight, an' tha's fer sure."

I squeezed his arm, and held Hannah's eyes, hoping the look conveyed my gratitude. Then I told Frenchy what had taken place.

"Bas-tid," he said. "Sounds like yer daddy's right. Also sounds like we better haul ass on up to Nigger Hill, before Preserved and them woodchuck friends of his gets there and starts shootin' up the place."

A knock on the kitchen door interrupted us before I could answer. When I pulled it back Jacob Fargo filled the frame.

"Came by 'cause I'm 'shamed 'bout tonight," he said. He shuffled his feet, then looked past me to my father and began nodding his head. "You was right in what ya said, Arriah. I jus' never thought about it that way a'fore this whole meetin' business started."

Frenchy stepped forward, taking charge. "Before you get too sorrowful, maybe you kin tell us where them boys is headed now," he said.

Jacob shook his head. "Don't think nobody's goin' no place tonight. I hear'd Preserved tell Andy they was goin' back to his cabin ta wait on Big Jim, so's they could hide him out from you folks. But I think they'll be goin' ta Nigger Hill soon. Maybe tomorrow, or the next day, lessen you arrest one of them folks fer Royal's murder." He studied his shoes, as if regretting his next words, then looked up at my father. "They won't be alone when they goes, I'm thinkin'. There's folks who believe what Preserved says, Arriah. They's sayin' Jehiel and them other nigs up there went too far this time, an' sumthin's gotta be done."

Frenchy raised a finger and slowly pointed it at Jacob's face. "You care about them folks, you best talk to them, friend. You tell 'em fer me, they go up on that hill with anythin' but a neighborly pie in their hands, they likely to do some dyin' up on Nigger Hill, themselves. And there ain't no two ways about that."

Frenchy decided we had no choice but to stay up on the hill that night, and hold back on our plan to search Abel Turner's cabin until dawn. It was a question of playing it safe, he said, and of not leaving Johnny Taft and the folks he was guarding sitting there like squirrels in a tree. Frenchy took some time to question Jacob Fargo more thoroughly, as he tried to get a feel for folks who might fall in with Preserved, and I left him to it, deciding instead to walk Hannah home, just in case she ran into any neighbors still angry about what she had done.

Victorious was waiting like a sentinel when we arrived at the store, standing just inside the open front door, eyes staring out into the night with the same blind hatred that Preserved Firman had washed me with earlier. I was holding Hannah's arm as we approached, and I felt her begin to tremble when she saw her mother standing there. I stopped and turned her toward me, holding her at arm's length.

"What you did was right, Hannah," I said. "And it doesn't matter what anybody else tells you. Not your mother. Not anyone. You probably saved my life, is what you did."

"I couldn't do anythin' else," Hannah replied. "I love you, Samuel."

I continued to hold Hannah's arms between my hands, feeling my stomach twist. I was struggling against what she had said, trying to push it away; ignore it.

"Hannah!" Victorious's voice echoed out into the road. "You get on in here. Now!"

"And it was brave," I said, struggling to ignore Victorious's shout as well. "Not many would have had the courage to help my father like you did. You put yourself in harm's way. And if anyone bothers you about what you did, you come to me. I'll see to them personally."

I heard Victorious's footsteps and turned to face her.

"You stay away from my daughter," she hissed. "You . . . you . . ."

"Say it, Victorious," I shot back. I felt my anger rise and fought it down. "Might as well. You've been saying it behind my back most of my life. And behind my father's back before me, I'd venture." I had softened my voice, and now extended my hands at my sides. "So why not say it to my face this once?"

She stared at me, eyes blazing. Then she reached out and seized her daughter's arm and pulled her away. "Get on inside," she snapped.

Hannah pulled herself free. "Keep your hands off me, Mama. Just leave me be, and stop treatin' me like a child." She turned and marched toward the door, as Victorious staggered back, stunned.

I reached out and took Victorious's arm, just as she had taken Hannah's, and I watched her wince under the firmness of my grip. Then I leaned in close to her, and put a broad Negro patois to my words. "You betta be careful, Miz Shepard, ma'am. Or you be bouncin' some jiggaboo granchillin' on yo knee."

Victorious's eyes widened, and her mouth dropped open, and for the briefest of moments I thought she might fall over dead.

{ 16 }

An early morning ground fog hung above the small clearing in which Abel Turner's one-room cabin stood. The top edge of the fog swirled in the faint, pink glow of morning, and partially obscured the old Nash flatbed pulled up before the front door. There was no sign of life, not a solitary light inside the darkened cabin.

"Looks like we mighta caught him still to bed," Frenchy said. "But stay low movin' in. Use the fog fer cover, just in case he's playin' us a game of possum."

We reached Abel's front door without incident, stood to either side, then waited while Frenchy rapped on the wood and called out our presence.

It took a second knock before Abel pulled back the door, still blinking away sleep. He was dressed in filthy longjohns that fit him like a second sweaty skin, and the stench that came off him, and out the cabin door, seemed to swallow up the cold, fresh morning air.

"Got us a warrant to look aroun' yer cabin," Frenchy said with a broad smile.

"Look fer what?" He sounded truly perplexed by Frenchy's announcement.

"Evidence," Frenchy said. "And fer whatever else we kin find."

"Ev'dence of what?" Abel paused a minute. "What all the hell you talkin' about?"

"Evidence of Royal Firman's murder, son. Now step aside and don't give us no trouble."

Over Abel's objections, Frenchy threw open the windows to air out the solitary room. Scattered about us were food-encrusted pots and plates and a good month's worth of dirty clothing, which, after watching Abel dress himself from the pile, I gathered were worn again and again without benefit of soap or water.

"You got any clean clothes?" Frenchy asked.

Abel stared at him, apparently immune to the sarcasm. "These is clean enough," he said.

"Which ones was you wearin' when you an' Royal went to see that colored whore over to Addison?"

Abel's head snapped around, eyes wary. "I already tol' you. I ain't been to no colored whore. Not in Addison, or anyplace else."

Frenchy pointed a finger at his nose. "Don't waste my time with yer lies, son. We got us a positive identification of you bein' there. We also got us a positive identification of you bein' up on Nigger Hill the evenin' Royal was killed. Fact is, we got somebody saw you follow him up there in yer truck. So right now, I'm interested in any clothes you got what might have blood on 'em."

Abel looked around the room as if trying to decide what to do. He was sweating, despite the cool air filtering in through the open door and windows. Then he did something that surprised me. He did the only smart thing he could do for himself at that moment.

"I ain't sayin' nothin' more," he said. "Them folks that's tellin' ya stuff is tellin' ya lies, an' I ain't gotta prove it's so. It's you gotta prove what they's sayin' is true."

Frenchy reached out and gave Abel's arm a squeeze. "That's exactly what I plan to do, son," he said. "And if I find what I think I will, then I'll be comin' fer you, fer sure."

* * *

After we searched the cabin, Frenchy gathered an armful of suspiciously stained clothing. He wrote out a receipt, listing each item, and handed it to Abel. The clothes were so filthy, so layered with intermingled stains, it was impossible to tell if any might be blood, but I could see that Abel didn't know that. His eyes kept moving from the clothing to Frenchy's face, and he had begun to sweat even more heavily than before.

Outside, as we headed back to Frenchy's Ford, I asked him what he thought we had.

He glanced down at the clothing tucked under one arm. "Here?" he asked. "Prob'ly a big bunch of nothin'." He inclined his head back toward the cabin. "But back there we got us one scared rabbit." He grinned and gave me a wink. "And if you ever hunted rabbits, son, you know they always makes that one big mistake when they gets scared."

"He wasn't so scared he didn't know to keep his mouth shut," I said.

"That's ol' Lawyer Caswell talkin'. He musta tol' Abel what to do if we came around again. But give 'im some time and his scare is gonna grow. Then he'll be talkin' to beat the band."

I glanced back at the cabin and thought about what Frenchy had said. And I decided I would return and have a talk with Abel. But when I did, I would do it alone.

Two deputies were waiting at the Jerusalem Hotel when we got back. "Well, it's 'bout time you boys got here," Frenchy said. He shook each of their hands, then noted the surprise on my face and gave me a big grin. "After that trouble in the barn last night, I had me a brainstorm about how to keep Preserved Firman and his woodchuck buddies off'n Nigger Hill. Or leastways to control how they gets there, which is pretty much the same thing." He inclined his head toward the deputies. "So I called the sheriff fer a little help before we went up on Nigger Hill last night, and he sent these fellas in fer a little crowd control." Frenchy introduced me to the deputies, who were named Bill Stanton and Mike Morse, then explained what he had in mind.

"You know that ol' covered bridge about a quarter-mile before the turnoff to Nigger Hill?" he asked.

I said I did.

"Well, seems to me that if we sets us a roadblock thereabouts, we can turn back any folks we don't want to give even a chance to get up in there. Am I right?"

"They could go around by way of Hinesburg and Starksboro," I said. "But it would take them an hour and a half to get to the turnoff that way."

"That's right," Frenchy replied. "And if I know my woodchucks, they'll pick an easier way, and go on up through the woods." He tapped his nose with one finger. "Well, I had me a little talk with Johnny Taft last night, and he tells me there's but two notches that cut up through the ridge that lays between Nigger Hill and Morgan Holler, and that anybody comin' through the woods would fer sure come one of them ways."

I smiled at his perception. "So your men here will be stopping people from going through the bridge."

"That's right. And the car they come in has a radio, just like the one in mine. So if we catch them woodchucks comin' through the woods, I can get to my car and have these boys shoot on up Nigger Hill in no mor'n five minutes. Lessen of course they hear real shootin' first," Frenchy added. "Then they won't wait fer no radio call."

{ 17 }

"Be quiet, there's a wagon coming." I leaned down, peering out beneath the rafter as much as I dared.

"Who is it? Is it them? Tell me who it is." Elizabeth's voice was filled with urgency and expectation.

I swung back up and put my finger to my lips. "It's them. Wreatha Johns and Joe Carpenter. Be quiet now, they's almost here."

Elizabeth's nine-year-old eyes lit up like candles. We'd been spying on Wreatha Johns and Joe Carpenter for more than six months, ever since we had first climbed up in the rafters of the old covered bridge and had caught them stopping their wagon inside for a little Sunday afternoon spooning. After that we had been there every Sunday, and more often than not, we had got ourselves another show without once getting caught.

Wreatha, who had been given her name because she was born on Christmas Day, was an exceptionally big woman. And when she and Joe Carpenter got to kissing and hugging, the buckboard seat let out some horrible squeaks under their combined weight, which was all right with Elizabeth and me, because the noise hid our barely suppressed giggles.

"Shh," I hissed, holding up my hand again.

The buckboard pulled inside, and Elizabeth and I crouched on the rafters, holding our breath as we tried to blend into the wood that held us up. Below, Joe Carpenter wrapped his arms around Wreatha's stout waist and pulled her to him for a lengthy embrace.

Elizabeth, who was on the beam across from me, looked at me and puckered her lips, and I covered my mouth with one hand to keep from laughing out loud. Then a low, long moan rose up to my ears, and I looked back down and saw Joe Carpenter's hand moving up the length of Wreatha's body, until it stopped at the buttons that ran up the front to just below her neck.

They were still kissing, and now they started grunting at the same time, and Joe frantically began to unbutton Wreatha's dress, until one enormous breast suddenly flopped out into the dim shadows of the bridge. I stared at it, unable to fully comprehend what I was seeing. It was like some giant white watermelon, the likes of which I had never even imagined.

"Holy Jesus Christ," I said, unable to control myself.

The pair below pulled apart and stared up at us, Wreatha struggling to force her enormous mammary back inside her dress.

"Goddamn li'l shits," Joe Carpenter bellowed.

"Run," I yelled to Elizabeth.

We got up and began moving down the rafters, grabbing the struts with our hands, jumping from one crossbeam to the next. When we were twenty feet behind the buckboard, we swung down to the floor of the bridge and began to run.

I heard Wreatha shout behind me. "Get them goddamn nigs and whip they ass, Joe." Then I heard Joe's heavy boots beating a tattoo on the wooden floor of the bridge. But by that time we had already started up the bank that led into woods that would take us back to Nigger Hill and safety.

"Ya goddamn nigs, I'll get ya, an' I'll beat on ya good. Ya wait an' see if I doan," Joe shouted after us.

I stopped and turned to shout back. "I ain't no nig. An' yer too fat to catch us anyways. An' if you try to beat on us later, I'll tell every- body what I saw you doin'."

Of course Joe never did catch us, and he never did beat on us either. Instead, he went to my father and complained. And my father went to Jehiel and told him what we were up to. Then the two of them sat us down and forbade us to go up into the rafters of the bridge again. We obeyed for the rest of that autumn, and throughout the winter, which was far too cold to be climbing up into bridges, anyway. But the fol- lowing spring we were back there again, only to no avail. By that time Wreatha and Joe had gotten themselves married, and their days of spooning in covered bridges had come to an end.

"So exactly what bridge are the deputies stopping people at?" Eliz- abeth asked. A look of relief had come to her face, which had been the sole purpose of this early morning visit.

We were sitting at her dining table, a pot of freshly brewed morn- ing coffee set between us. I smiled across the table. "Same bridge we used to climb up into to spy on Wreatha and Joe Carpenter."

Elizabeth brought her fingers to her lips. "Oh Lord, I had forgot- ten all about that." Her eyes suddenly became sad. "Those poor peo- ple," she said. "Joe killed in that accident with the thresher only a few years later, and Wreatha having to sell their new farm and move away."

"Did that truly make you sad?" I asked.

"Why, of course it did." Elizabeth looked at me curiously.

I recalled how the entire town had mourned Joe's death, and how everyone, in whatever small way they could, had tried to aid Wreatha in her bereavement and subsequent financial difficulties. Everyone, that is, but me.

"All I ever remembered was how they chased us and called us nigs," I said now.

Elizabeth drew a deep breath and looked down into her coffee. "You are a worrisome man, Samuel," she said at length. "Forgive- ness does not come easily to you."

"Should it?" I asked.

She stared at me with some surprise. "Doesn't that thought ever occur to you?" she finally asked.

"At times, I suppose. But it doesn't change the way I feel. I'm afraid it's beyond my control. Its source is forced on me."

"No, it's not, Samuel. If it were, it would be beyond my control as well. Because, you see, I suffer from the same source."

She watched me, seemed to recognize the confusion that flickered through my eyes, then drew another long breath. "You don't understand what I mean, do you?"

"I'm not certain I do."

"That's because you believe, with all your heart, that you should be considered white. And I . . . well, that I am a *real* Negro."

I found myself unable to speak.

"And, perhaps, you should feel that way. Perhaps it's necessary for your own survival." She paused, as if she needed time to look at me more closely. "You see, I truly don't know if you're right in your thinking, or not." She paused again. "And I truly don't care."

"I don't understand. Are you saying it doesn't matter to you?"

"I'm saying more than that. I'm saying it shouldn't matter to you."

A bitter laugh escaped my lips. "How can it not?" I demanded.

She looked down at the table again. "That you don't see it . . . well, that is your tragedy, Samuel."

"Dammit, stop talking in riddles and tell me what you mean."

"I am." She stared at me for a long time, all the while stroking my hand with both of hers. "We'll talk about it again, one time," she finally said. "Perhaps when things are calmer."

{ 18 }

My stomach trembled and turned and shook, and I have no idea if it came from rage or fear or simple uncertainty about all that I believed. I found myself sitting in my car, parked outside the Woodmen of America Lodge. I had driven there after leaving Elizabeth's cabin, and I remember pulling off the road and stopping. I recall turning the key to kill the engine. Yet I have no recollection of any conscious decision to do any of it.

The lodge is a large white building, about the size and shape of a fair to middling church. There is quite a fine stage on the second floor, with elaborately painted scenery that has drawn much praise, all of it owing to the building's history as having once served as the town's "opera house." To this day occasional performances are still held there. This, of course, is through the "generosity" of the lodge's members. The Woodsmen, as it is more commonly known, is the only lodge in Jerusalem's Landing, and, as such, is considered elite by its membership, although I have never understood the reason why.

Yet, with all its trappings, the lodge has always been a mysterious curiosity to the children of the town. It was so in my childhood and it remains so today. This is no doubt caused by the secrecy that surrounds it, together with the bits and pieces of its rituals that have leaked out over time, only to be then embellished by children's minds.

One such mystery was "Riding the Goat."

Throughout my childhood I had heard tales about initiations into the Woodsmen Lodge, in which the riding of a goat supposedly played a large part. Children's stories varied about what the ritual actually involved. Some said the goat was sacrificed with knives and fire and much blood. Others claimed that would-be members raced goats, and that only the winners of those races were then allowed to join. Among older boys there were even whispered stories claiming that members were required to have carnal knowledge of a goat as part of their initiation.

Elizabeth and I were determined to know the truth. We were eleven at the time, and our decision to learn the secrets of the Woodsmen—like most of our resolutions during those years—was made on the spur of the moment.

Our plan evolved when we learned that Willie "Shortneck" Sherman was about to be inducted into the lodge. The ceremony was set for ten o'clock in the evening, which was the customary hour for initiations. Elizabeth and I each slipped from our beds and met outside her window at nine, I having made the trek up Nigger Hill so she would not have to find her way through the dark night alone.

We reached the lodge some twenty minutes later, before anyone had yet arrived, and entered through an open side window. From there, we made our way up to the second floor, where all the lodge's rituals supposedly took place, and hid ourselves behind the stage curtain.

We lay on the stage floor, raising the curtain the barest fraction so we could see beneath it. Before us was an empty room, the chairs normally used by an audience having been moved up against the side walls.

Members began arriving almost immediately, and Elizabeth and I lay there barely breathing. Then she reached out and grabbed my hand, squeezing it so hard that I almost cried out.

"That one in the middle. I think that's Mr. Sherman," she whispered, pointing her finger toward the center of the room.

My eyes followed her finger. All of the second floor was heavily shadowed, illuminated only by candles set in wall sconces, and I could barely make out the faces of the twenty or so men who were present. Finally, as my eyes adjusted, I saw the person she had pointed at. It was, indeed, "Shortneck" Sherman, a short, square, bull-like man, whose head seemed to grow directly from his blocky shoulders. He was our town shoemaker, and I was used to seeing him covered in a leather apron. Now the apron was gone, replaced by his Sunday suit, and he was wearing a strange hat, fixed with what seemed to be goat horns, and he was standing before a committee of men, one of whom was reading from a leather-bound book.

Other men were gathered behind the committee, all dressed in their Sunday best, and when the incantations were completed they separated en masse, forming parallel lines that faced each other.

Shortneck Sherman walked stiff-legged between them, almost as if on parade, obviously cognizant of the solemnity of the moment. Beyond him, at the end of the hall, a door opened and another member wheeled a wooden goat into the room.

Elizabeth and I stared at it with unbelieving eyes. It was like a hobbyhorse on wheels, only with the wooden head of a goat. When it reached Shortneck Sherman, he turned and mounted it, then, using his feet, began to propel it back between the lines of lodge members.

Elizabeth looked at me, bewildered. "Is that it?" she whispered. "That's all they do when they ride the goat?"

I shrugged helplessly and she began to giggle and quickly covered her mouth so she wouldn't be heard. "White men are sure enough silly," she said between her fingers.

It was two years later that my father was put up for membership by his trout-fishing friend, Jacob Fargo. He was very proud, as I recall, although he never said a word about the vanity he undoubtedly felt. But that was something he would never allow another soul to see. Still, I knew he wished my mother were still alive to share that pride with him. So I tried to do it in her stead, and happily spread the news to all my friends.

Lodge membership, at that time, was limited to the most prominent men in town. The town doctor was always a member, as were the town clerk, all elected members of the governing selectboard, and the town's most prominent businessmen and farmers. Simeon Shepard, the town storekeeper and barber, was the newly elected grand ruler of the lodge that year. He had just replaced Luther Pierce, Abigail Pierce's husband and founder of the Jerusalem Hotel, who had recently died of a massive coronary.

I desperately wanted to tell my father about the silliness he would endure when his time came to "ride the goat," but I knew he would not approve of Elizabeth's and my stealth. Instead, we two children decided to be present when his membership was voted on.

Unlike the initiation ceremony, the vote took place in daytime. As before we hid ourselves behind the curtains. Unlike that first time, sunlight streamed through the windows, driving away the dark, forbidding atmosphere, and baring the stark simplicity of the room, and those who had gathered to vote a new member.

My father sat in a chair behind a long table, flanked on either side by Simeon Shepard, as exalted ruler of the lodge, and Jacob Fargo, as his proposer. A black felt-top hat was placed before them. One by one the members left the room and walked solemnly through the door where two years ago we had seen the wooden goat emerge. This time they simply returned, clutching something in one hand, walked to the table and, while keeping their eyes averted, emptied that hand into the top hat.

When all the members had finished, Jacob Fargo and finally Simeon Shepard took their turns. Simeon then placed his hands on the brim of the hat and slowly emptied its contents onto the table.

Elizabeth and I watched from behind the stage curtain as small balls rolled out of the hat and onto the table. The majority of the balls were white. Three were black.

I studied my father's face as he stared at the three black balls, my child's mind not understanding their significance. Slowly, my father rose from his chair. There was no discernible expression on his face, and he did not speak to anyone present. He simply thanked Jacob Fargo, then turned and walked out the door.

Later that night, when I asked him what had happened, he had simply said: "They didn't want me in their club."

I had already fixed my father's lunch and settled him in for his afternoon nap. Frenchy and I were seated at the kitchen table, discussing how we would protect Nigger Hill, when Hannah arrived unexpectedly at my back door. Two suitcases sat on the doorstep behind her, and she stared at me with a mixture of defiance and fear.

"I left home," she said. "An' I'd be grateful if you'd give me a ride to Burlington."

Frenchy told us to take his car, since it was equipped with a police radio that he could use to reach me, if necessary. He seemed amused by the situation, and on this particular afternoon some levity was definitely needed. That morning's newspaper had arrived only moments before, and a front-page headline read: *"Logger Cleared in Shooting. Ballistics Tests Prove Innocence."*

The headline, of course, was both inaccurate and untrue. But it was also certain to fuel our growing racial fires and provide support for Preserved's claim that he was a victim of local and county police, both of whom were trying to protect murderous Negroes.

Hannah sat stiffly in her seat as we passed Shepard's Store. I stared at the open front door as we drove by, expecting to see Victorious glaring out with all the hate her heart held for me. The door was empty, and as I drove on I now tried to gauge the depth of her horror as she watched her only daughter walk out of the store that afternoon, suitcases in each hand, her legs propelling her down the road to my home.

I had not yet asked Hannah the whys or wheres or hows of it, not wishing to risk embarrassing her in front of Frenchy. Now I did.

"I couldn't take it no more, Samuel," she said. "Ever since the other night, she's been callin' me all kinds of stuff." She turned to me, her eyes injured and pleading. "She even called me a nigger's whore." She waited, as if worried that might have some effect on me. "She's been raging about how I turned my back on my own race, and how I disgraced her and my daddy, so's they can't hold up their heads in town any more."

"Where are you going to stay?" I asked. I wanted to end that particular dialogue, and so far I knew only that Burlington was her destination.

"There's a rooming house advertised in the paper," she said. She handed me a torn-out piece of newsprint. "The address is on there. I telephoned it up, and the lady that runs it says it's real respectable, and not too far from the university in case I decide to take me some classes, or such."

I fought off a smile, struggling against the shallowness that would allow me to laugh at Hannah's ambitions.

"Will you come and visit me?" she asked.

"Of course I will," I said.

"Maybe we could go to a moving picture show," she said. "I almost never get to see a moving picture. It's such a long drive to Burlington that Momma and Daddy never want to go. And the theater in Richmond only has movies that are two and three years old, and they say when they're that old, they ain't worth the price. Oh, I sure would like to see that new one that just came out. The scary one about the big gorilla."

"*King Kong,*" I said. "I read about it in the newspaper."

"Oh yes, that's it. Will you take me, Samuel?"

"Of course I will. We'll go to any motion picture you choose as soon as all this trouble on the hill gets settled."

Hannah hugged herself with pleasure, then continued jabbering. "And *The Torch Singer* with Claudette Colbert. I just gotta see that. An' that French movie, *Moulin Rouge,* with Constance Bennett. But it just came out. We prob'ly won't get it for a few months. But oh, I just love the theme song of that picture. 'Boulevard of Broken Dreams.' It just makes me cry every time I hear it on the radio."

What she said seemed to spark a thought, and she began searching the dashboard of Frenchy's new car for a radio.

"Oh, it's got one. It's got one," she exclaimed. "I just hate Daddy's car because it's a '28 and it don't have one. If he had only waited one more year, he could of had a radio in his, too."

I turned on the radio and struggled with it until I finally found a station strong enough to reach Jerusalem's Landing. It was KDKA in Pittsburgh, which ironically was strong enough to make it through our mountains, something none of the Vermont stations were capable of doing. The sound of Rudy Vallee singing "Three Little Words" filled the car. Hannah looked at me and smiled.

"I do love you. You know that, don't you, Samuel?"

I reached out and took her hand and felt her squeeze tightly, almost desperately, I thought, as she awaited my reply. "It matters to me that you do," I said. "Being with you has made my life bearable in that town, and I love you for giving me that; for everything you've given me." I paused, feeling her squeeze my hand again. Then I added what I knew had to be said. "Hannah, there's something else you should do," I began. "I think here, in this new life you're starting, you should see other men, too. It's only being fair to yourself."

"Oh, Samuel, I don't want to see anyone else."

I swallowed hard. "Just promise me you will. Just so you're sure of how you feel; sure of what you need in your life."

"Oh, Samuel, I am sure. I truly am."

"Just promise me," I said. "Please."

"All right, Samuel. If it's what you want." She paused and I removed my hand from hers.

She looked at me and smiled again. "I can't wait 'til the first time you come in to see me," she said.

And I wondered if she had heard anything I had said.

It took us two hours to reach Burlington, most of that time on the unpaved road that ran from Jerusalem's Landing to Route 2, the latter being the main highway that went all the way from Burlington to the state capital in Montpelier. Most of that highway had been washed away in the great flood of '27, and it had taken years to rebuild, effectively cutting us rural folks off from the nearest cities of any size. I had never thought I would miss Burlington, where I had spent four long and lonely years at the university. But I quickly found that I did. Or perhaps it was just being denied the opportunity to go there.

As we entered Burlington and neared the university, large posters began to appear on roadside poles and trees, announcing the University of Vermont's upcoming Kake Walk, the glorious yearly event when the students put on their much-vaunted minstrel show, faces covered in black greasepaint as they went "walkin' for de kake."

"Oh, Samuel," Hannah said, twisting in her seat so she could read the signs. "It's Kake Walk time. I heard about that ever since I was little. Have you ever been?"

"Once," I said. My hands clenched the steering wheel.

"All that time you was here at school, and you just went one time?" she said.

"I was too busy studying," I replied.

"Oh, I sure would like to go," she said. "You think we could? I hear it's wunnerful fun."

I thought about the one time I had gone. Each year, Kake Walk was quietly boycotted by the university's few Negro students. It was done without fanfare, but it was a boycott all the same. I had attended for my own purposes, an equally quiet reinforcement of my "whiteness." It was the same reason I had never invited any classmates to my home on weekends or holidays, a fear that my compromised racial standing might be discovered. I still carried the shame of both actions within me.

"I'm not sure I'll be free in time," I said now. "But you can go," I added. "It's quite safe to go alone, or with another young woman."

"Oh, I just couldn't," Hannah said. "I'd be afraid to go there all by myself, without a man along."

The rooming house Hannah had picked from the newspaper was a large clapboard home on North Prospect Street, only a few doors down from the massive brick building that housed the university's medical school. The mistress of the house was a large, gray-haired woman, about fifty years old, with the hard, blue eyes of someone used to having her own way. Her name was Rebecca Snyder, and she turned those eyes on me with a full measure of suspicion as I carried Hannah's bags into the hall.

"Let's go talk in my kitchen," she said. "I got the iceman filling up my icebox right now, and I gotta make sure he doesn't drip water all over my floor."

Hannah tugged at my sleeve, indicating I should come along. I had hoped to leave quickly, but after meeting Rebecca Snyder new concerns arose about Hannah's possible rejection as a tenant, a scenario that might then require me to drive her elsewhere.

We waited as the woman barked orders at the iceman, and when she finally returned her attention to us, I found it was I, not Hannah, who was the subject of her concern.

"And who are you?" she asked bluntly.

I explained that I was a neighbor whom Hannah had asked for a ride to town.

"And will you be visiting her?" she demanded.

I offered her a pleasant smile. "From time to time, I expect. When my business brings me to Burlington."

"And what is that business, sir?" she again demanded. There was no tone of query in her voice, only insistence upon a forthright reply.

"I'm the constable in Jerusalem's Landing," I said. "From time to time, it requires me to visit the sheriff's office, or the courts."

The woman's eyes widened with both surprise and satisfaction, I thought. "Oh, so you're a lawman," she said. "Well, that's different then." She turned to Hannah now and smiled warmly. "You have to understand, dear, that I am quite particular about the young ladies who live here. We don't allow any hootchie girls, you know. This here's a respectable house. Why only last year one of my girls got herself engaged to one of the young men at the medical school."

Hannah nodded, openly trying to please the woman. "Oh, that's just the kinda place I want," she said. "And Samuel here, he graduated from the university, too."

Mrs. Snyder's eyes fell on me again, even more pleased now. "Well, now, that's wonderful," she said. "And you can be sure you'll be welcome here any time you choose to visit." She added a coy smile. "Providing you keep to the rules of the house, of course."

It was nearly five o'clock when I returned to Jerusalem's Landing, and I found Frenchy sitting with my father, both of them hunched over the radio in my kitchen.

"Big news?" I asked.

"Just that . . . Hitler . . . feller," my father said. He struggled with the words, his effort at speech proving more difficult this day. Then he waved his hand, dismissing the man and the subject as unworthy of further comment.

I turned to Frenchy. "What's the reaction been to the newspaper report about Preserved and that ballistics test?" I asked.

"'Bout what you'd expect," Frenchy said. "Miz Pierce grabbed me at lunchtime and bent my ear for near twenty minutes. She claims folks is pretty riled we're treatin' a white man so poorly." He grinned at me. "I got us a plan for later tonight, might rile some of them backwoods boys up a bit more."

"What's that?" I asked.

Frenchy tipped back in his chair. "Well, I hear there's still a little speakeasy action over to the ol' Mountain Tavern and Hotel, and that Preserved's been over there most nights shootin' off his mouth. I'm kinda bettin' we go there late, say around ten o'clock, we'll find him, and maybe that Big Jim fella that run off on you and your daddy t'other night. I'm also thinkin' its about time we put the fear of God in them boys, if we're gonna keep 'em away from Nigger Hill."

"Wouldn't really call it . . . no speakeasy," my father said. "Jus' a couple jugsa . . . home brew . . . finds their way there . . . 'bout every night."

"Good enough fer breakin' the law," Frenchy said, grinning. "Not that I care much, 'ceptin' now when it serves our purpose."

"Might rile up more'n jus' . . . a few backwoods boys," my father said.

He sounded a bit defensive, and Frenchy picked up on it.

"Now, don't get all turned around, Arriah. I ain't criticizin' the way things are done around here. I just want to use it to my advantage." He gave me a wink. "You get yerself some rest, son, and I'll be back to get you before ten. Okay?"

I wasn't pleased with Frenchy's plan. I thought my father was probably right. But for now it suited my own purpose. And my own plan. One I knew Frenchy would never agree to. I nodded. "I'll be here waiting for you, about ten," I said.

I was waiting for Abel Turner when he returned to his cabin shortly after seven o'clock that evening. I had parked my car behind a stand of trees, well out of eyesight, and I was seated in Abel's stench-filled cabin when he pushed his way through the door.

"About time you aired this place out, isn't it?" I said.

Abel jumped in place, startled by my voice coming from a shadowed corner. "What the hell you doin' here?" he demanded.

"You and I have to talk, Abel," I said. I let the moment draw out. "And I want it to be a real talk this time. Not the lies you've been giving me."

Abel seemed to settle himself, and his eyes became hard and mean. "I ain't gotta talk ta you. My lawyer says so. An' I ain't gonna talk. Not ta no bleached nigger constable. Not ever."

I stood slowly and saw a glimmer of doubt enter his eyes. Then I drew my pistol and leveled it at him. "Get your oversized ass in that chair," I snapped. "We'll see if you've got some talking to do, or not."

He backed up, watching the gun in my hand. "What the hell you think we got ta talk 'bout? I tol' you I ain't talkin'." There was a tremor in his voice now. "I ain't got nothin' ta say, not ta you, or nobody. That's what my lawyer says. An' that's the way it's gonna be."

I smiled at him and raised my pistol so it was leveled at his face, knowing the combined actions would shake him. That and the softness I now put in my voice. "A lawyer's not what you're going to need, Abel. You're going to need a doctor, maybe, or an undertaker. That I promise you. Unless, of course, you sit your *fat . . . ass . . . down . . .* and answer my questions."

Abel's jaw began to tremble as he backed into a chair and sat. The fight was gone out of him now, and he stared up and me, nervous and uncertain about what I might do next. "Look, Samuel. I din't have nothin' ta do with Royal's gettin' kilt. I swear on my mother, I din't."

"You're a liar. And we both know you're a liar. You followed Royal up on that hill, just like our witness said you did. And you were there when he died. And now you're gonna tell me about it."

"No, I weren't there. I weren't," he flared, more out of fear than anger. "Damn, Samuel, you jus' wanna protect them blackasses up on that hill. You know you do. You don't care 'bout nothin' else, 'cause you one of them, an' you always been one of them."

I took a step toward him, then swung my pistol backhand, smashing it into his cheek. He tumbled off the chair and onto the floor.

"You watch your filthy, lying mouth," I snarled. "Now I don't have time to play with you. Preserved and his goddamn friends are stirring up this whole town, and they're going to move against those folks unless I can stop them. And I damn well intend to stop them. And the only way I can do that is to let everybody know what really happened up there. I don't know if it was you or Preserved that killed Royal. But I sure as hell know it was one of you."

Abel lay on the floor, his jaw trembling again, one hand pawing at the blood that trickled down his cheek. "No, it weren't. It weren't," he pleaded. "Leastways it weren't me."

I pointed the revolver at his nose. "Then who was it? You are fast running out of time with me."

"I don't know, I don't. I ran off a'fore it happened." He was whining now, but I hardly noticed, his words had so shocked me.

"What were you two doing up there?" I snapped.

"I can't tell you. I can't, Samuel." His jaw began to tremble again. "Oh God, don't shoot me. I ain't done nothin' worth bein' kilt over."

I glared down at him. "Damn your soul to hell. I will kill you right where you lie, you don't tell me everything you know."

He stared at me, the trembling having moved now to his arms and legs. Then he started to speak. And as he spilled out his tale, my heart sank lower than I had ever known it to be.

{ 19 }

The hooded figure moved down the narrow drive that led to Elizabeth's cabin. It was early evening, and the light was fast fading. In the distance, through the trees, a man could be seen. He was moving away from the barn, his strides stomping and erratic, as if each step away was taken with still-simmering anger. The man stopped and looked back, saw the hooded figure for the first time, then turned and began to run through the trees. After a few yards he paused to look back to see what was happening.

Jeffords Page lay on the ground twenty feet from the barn door. He stirred with the first return of consciousness, reached up to gingerly touch his head and began to moan. Then his body stiffened, as he saw the hooded figure moving down the drive. Jeffords grasped his head in both hands and tried to sit up, but the effort was too much, and he fell back to the ground and lost consciousness again.

As the figure moved forward, Royal Firman backed out of the barn. He seemed to be speaking to someone inside, but his words were inaudible. Then he turned, and his handsome face twisted into a sneer. Again, his lips moved as if he was speaking, but no sounds emerged. Behind him, a pitchfork leaned against the wall of the barn, its tines glinting in the last rays of sunlight.

The hooded figure turned and looked back into the woods. The fleeing man had stopped, as if waiting to see what would take place in Elizabeth's dooryard. Now, as the figure stared toward him, he spun away and began to run again like someone hoping to escape a terrible vision.

I sat in stony silence as Frenchy drove the two-mile stretch of Main Road that led to the Mountain Hotel and Tavern, my mind still reeling with Abel's tale about the hooded figure who had appeared outside Elizabeth's barn, still uncertain if it was truth or a convenient fiction. It was just after ten o'clock when we arrived at the old hotel, a rambling two-story structure, located only a hundred yards south of the Woodmen's Lodge, where my father had been humiliated years before. The hotel was a battered, neglected building, badly in need of paint, with a wide porch that ran along its face and down each side. Preserved's truck was parked out front, along with a handful of others, the motorized vehicles mixed in with a half dozen horse-drawn wagons. I recognized one wagon immediately. It belonged to Levi Kneeb, the town blacksmith. Levi was a frightening sight to first behold, big and burly with a flaming red beard that went halfway down his barrel chest. Yet, despite his size and fierce appearance, he was uncommonly gentle and soft-spoken, a fair-minded man, always willing to offer a hand, someone who unselfishly used his horse and wagon to pull cars and trucks out of the mud bogs that our roads became each spring. I had used him myself for that purpose on more than one occasion, and each time he had refused any payment, owing to some unexplained favor my father had done him years before. Now I wondered what his reaction would be. The Levi Kneebs of the town were few, and if they, too, had turned against us there would be little hope of beating back the more extreme element.

I started to open the door as we pulled to a stop, but Frenchy reached out and took my arm, stopping me.

"You're mighty quiet tonight," he said. "You worried about what we're gonna do, or you just frettin' about yer daddy?"

The question surprised me. "Why would I be worried about my father?" I asked.

Frenchy gave me a long look. "You ain't noticed he's lookin' a bit worse fer wear?" he asked. "I think the other night in Shepard's barn took its toll on him. Seems to me he's havin' more trouble formin' his words than usual."

"I think he's just worn out from all of this. All the worry and uncertainty about what's going to happen." I paused, thinking it through. "And about me, and what will happen when it's finally finished."

Frenchy nodded. "It's somethin' to think on," he said. "What yer gonna do with yerself when we finish up here, I mean."

I let out a short, bitter laugh. "You don't think I'll be welcome any longer?" I asked.

Frenchy gave me a shrug. "Who knows, Samuel. You just might not be. You kin never tell about these things. Not when there's been a bad killin' like this'un."

I looked at him, marveling at the man's lack of understanding. "Frenchy, it's not the killing," I said. "I was never welcome here. Not in all my twenty-seven years."

Frenchy squeezed my arm again, and gave me a sad look. "Part of that's you, too, son," he said. "I hope before this is over you come to understan' that."

I raged inside, but held it all back. I wanted to tell Frenchy about my interrogation of Abel Turner and what I had learned. I wanted to tell him about these people of Jerusalem's Landing. Just what they believed, just what they were capable of. But I couldn't do it. Not yet. There was someone else I had to speak to first if I had any hope of holding any sanity in my life.

And all the while I knew it was unfair. Frenchy was owed that much. He had a right to what I knew, the truth I had discovered, and to withhold it from him was wrong—perhaps even dangerous.

He continued to stare at me with those sad eyes. "You look like there's more you wanna say, son. Is there?"

I shook my head. "No, there's nothing." I inclined my head toward the building. "Let's get in there and get this thing over with."

As I exited the car, Abel Turner's final words raged in my ears: "It ain't gonna do ya no good. No good a'tall. 'Cause if we ever goes ta court, I ain't gonna admit none of it. Not one damn word. Not ever."

The main room of the Mountain Tavern and Hotel had once been a thriving saloon that provided the one thing Mrs. Pierce's rooming house lacked—a place where traveling drummers and timber buyers could meet and mingle with locals over strong drink. Prohibition changed that, and with it the establishment fell into a steady decline. To compensate and hang on to what was left of his clientele, the proprietor, a parsimonious septuagenarian named Timothy Farr, allowed his customers to bring in jars of home brew. He then "rented" glasses at ten cents a drink and sold food to go along with it. Farr would never sell the drink himself and risk losing all he had. Instead, like most rural Vermonters, he applied his own ethic to laws that seemed to infringe on individual rights. Prohibition, therefore, became just another government edict to be ignored or circumvented.

When we entered the dimly lighted main room, the gathering of men fell silent. There were slightly more than a dozen, each one with a glass in his hand, and I quickly spotted Preserved Firman's rage-filled face glaring at me from the end of a long table where most of the men were seated. His backwoods friend Andy sat to his right, offering his own glare, and I quickly scanned the room for Preserved's other sidekick, Big Jim, who a day earlier had held a knife to my throat. There was no sign of him tonight.

"Help you gentlemen?" The call came from Timothy Farr, who stood behind what had always served as a makeshift bar, a wide maple plank set on three barrels. He was a small, wiry, gray-haired man with muttonchop sideburns that seemed to swallow his narrow, hawk-nosed face. He wore a dirty white shirt, buttoned to the throat, and his voice was high-pitched and nervous, almost as if the shirt collar were strangling him.

"Pow'rful smell in this here place," Frenchy intoned, adding a long sniff to accentuate that discovery. "Didn't know it was still against the law, I'd swear I'm smellin' moonshine."

Frenchy had pinned his deputy's badge to his checkered hunting coat, purely for intimidative value, and he softened it now with a smile.

I continued to study the gathering, finally coming to Levi Kneeb, who returned my gaze with hard, disapproving eyes. It was a bad sign.

"Ya here on liquor business, Deputy? Or ya got sumthin' else on yer mind?"

I turned my attention back to Preserved, who now added a sneer to his questions. He felt safe in this element, surrounded by men who believed in his persecution, I decided.

"Law's always my business, Mr. Firman," Frenchy said, adding another smile. This time it failed to carry to his eyes, and I realized for the first time how much he disliked the man.

Frenchy turned slowly to face Timothy Farr. "I seem to be readin' some sign here that I hope ain't true," he said. "I sure wouldn't wanna close nobody down fer selling liquor."

"We don't sell nothin' here but beds and food," Farr shot back nervously. "Fer drinks we sell Moxie an' Sasperilla. Can't help what else folks brings inta the establishment."

Frenchy nodded sagely. "That's sure enough right, I guess." He turned back to face the group. "An' I ain't really here to find out where you boys come up with yer liquor. 'Course I could. And I should. But that ain't my purpose tonight." He paused for effect. "Don't seem like arrestin' folks fer their pleasurable sins makes much sense. Not with all the trouble I'm already tryin' to sort out." Another pause. "'Course if I found any of you boys headin' on up to Nigger Hill in the next few days, I'd be doin' some arrestin' that would make possession of moonshine seem like a picnic with yer best gal." His eyes hardened to coals. "And I promise alla you, that's just what I'll be doin'."

"An' youse gonna have that bleached nig ta help you, I reckon."

Preserved was grinning from one side of his mouth, glaring at the same time, his eyes moving between us, first to me then to Frenchy, his face little more than a twisted, malevolent mask. He seemed swelled with power, and even Frenchy's stare didn't deter him.

"You tryin' to say somethin', Mr. Firman?" Frenchy asked.

Preserved let out a cold laugh. "Oh, I was jus' thinkin' how folks hereabouts might have somethin' ta say 'bout who ya arres'. Ya jus' might find yersef needin' more help'n jus' some nig constable ta make good on yer word."

Frenchy's stare hung on Preserved like a silent threat before he finally spoke. "Well, I'll tell you how it's gonna go, Mr. Firman. You take yer sorry ass up on that hill, and I'm gonna have Samuel here do the honors of arrestin' you. He's gonna put cuffs on yer wrists, and chains on yer legs, and then he's gonna drive you to Burlington and throw yer sorry self in *my* jail." Preserved started to speak, but Frenchy held up a hand, stopping him. "And if you go up on that hill with a gun in yer hand, then yer gonna have me to deal with. You do *that* . . . and you try to use that gun . . . well then, I promise you, sir, I'm gonna personally send you straight to hell."

Levi Kneeb shifted his bulk, almost as though he required body movement to force the words from his mouth. "Seems ta some of us that you fellas is determined ta bring grief ta this man," he said.

I turned to Levi and held his gaze. "Levi, I've known you most of my life. And since I was a boy, my father taught me to respect your thoughts on most things. But the truth of this matter is different from what you're thinking. We're just trying to do our job, and keep everybody safe while we're doing it. And right now, any grief Preserved's getting is grief he's bringing on himself."

"That's jus' a bunch of goddamn, fancy nigger talk," Preserved snapped. "But ain't all them words, or yer fancy college diploma nether, gonna change what it is. 'Cause it's jus' nigger talk, an' t'allways will be."

Before either Frenchy or I could speak, Levi Kneeb turned his massive body toward Preserved, his face as dark as a thundercloud.

"Ya know, I'm jus' about worn down with all that nigger talk. Now, if any of them folks on that hill up an' kilt yer boy, well, then I wanna see 'em sittin' in that 'lectric chair up at the state prison. But right now you talkin' like them folks"—he paused and inclined his head toward me—"an' Samuel here, too, ain't as good as you, somehow. An' I'm here ta tell ya, mister, if that's what yer sayin', well there ain't a lick of truth ta any of it."

Preserved glared at him, allowing the moment to draw out. "Never know'd *you* was a nigger lover, Levi," he finally said.

Levi inhaled a massive breath of air. He shifted his feet like a bull pawing at the ground. "I'll be leavin' now, Preserved. An' I marked down what ya said. But if ya ever decides ta call me that agin', I'm tellin' ya now, ya better be doin' some strong thinkin' 'bout it a'fore ya do."

Levi picked up his jar of moonshine and turned to the door. He looked at me, then at Frenchy. "You fellas feels like ya needs some help, ya know where ta find me."

As Levi left, Frenchy turned to me so his back was to the others, and threw me a quick wink. Then he gave an exaggerated stretch and turned back to face the other men. "Well, seems to me that big fella said all that has to be said." He stared down at Preserved. "And like he said, Mr. Firman, you best be doin' some strong thinkin'. Some *real* strong thinkin'."

When we were back outside, Frenchy clapped me on the shoulder. "You done good in there, son. Real good. You found yerself just the fella we needed."

"You think what Levi said will make any difference?" I asked.

"Can't tell," Frenchy said. "We just gotta hope them other boys in there was listenin'. 'Cause if they was, they just might start usin' they heads on this here thing." He paused as if thinking over what he had said. "The thing that worries me is who wasn't there. That Turner boy was missin', and so was that Big Jim fella t'was ready to slice you up the other night. You add in that Andy fella and Preserved, and we got us four we know is lookin' fer trouble. How many others they can bring with 'em, well that's the big question, ain't it?"

{ 20 }

Frenchy and I drove up to Nigger Hill, stopping first at the covered bridge to see what the other deputies had encountered at the makeshift roadblock. They reported that all seemed quiet and un-eventful.

We found Johnny Taft in the woods that ran along Jehiel's door-yard, told him about the gathering at the Mountain Hotel and Tavern and warned him to keep alert, then went on to Jehiel's house to give him the same message.

The stone wall outside Jehiel's house was now completed and stood as a three-foot-high barrier to anyone approaching from road or woods. Jehiel's son, Prince, was crouched behind it, his rifle propped against the stones.

Jehiel came out the front door as we approached. Frenchy and I told him what had just taken place and expressed our uncertainty about what would happen next.

"That Preserved's a hard one," Frenchy said. "Man's as mean as two roosters in a chicken coop, and stubborn to boot. There ain't no figurin' what he'll do, even if them other boys turns their backs on 'im."

Jehiel let out a grunt. His eyes were hard as stone; his jaw set firmly in his large chocolate face.

"Ain't about to let no backwoods bigots sneak on up here," he said. "And it don't matter much if it's two or three, or a dozen that comes. Anybody come on my propity lookin' fer trouble, they gone find just one thing waitin' on 'em. The goddamn bizness end of my Winchester."

Frenchy blew out a stream of air. "Well, shootin's somethin' we'd sure like to avoid. But you got yerself a right to protect yer family and yer property. Ain't no question about that. You just tell yer people up here to keep a sharp eye. We'll be here if you need us." He let his eyes fall on Prince, still squatting behind the wall. "You got somebody over to Miz 'Lizabeth's cabin?"

"Jeffords be there," Jehiel said. "And them gals of mine, they know their way around a shotgun, they haveta use one."

Frenchy nodded and turned to me. "I gotta spell one of my men so he's fresh in the mornin'. I'd like you to go over and let that Jeffords boy get himself some rest, too. You can let him lay up in Miz 'Lizabeth's barn, so he's close to hand if we need 'im."

"You can let yer deputy lay up in my barn," Jehiel said.

"That'd be good," Frenchy said. "I'll put Johnny Taft in there, too, if yer agreeable, and I'll take his place fer a couple hours, once I get my deputy settled." He paused a minute, as if the next words were hard for him to speak. "You and yer boy get yerself some rest, too. But you hear any shootin' or shoutin', best be you fill yer hands with them Winchesters."

When Frenchy left, I took Jehiel by the arm and walked him away from Prince. I didn't want the boy to hear what I had to say. I stopped next to a towering pine, feeling dwarfed by both the tree and the man beside me.

"You could leave. Just for a spell," I said bluntly. "No one would think less of you if you took your family to a safer place until we get this sorted out."

Jehiel's reaction was not what I had expected. He smiled and took my shoulder in his big hand and gave it an affectionate squeeze.

"I already gave that some thought, Samuel," he said. "I truly have. 'Cause I surely don't want none of them children hurt. But this be my land. And my daddy's before me. I was born here, son. And my children was born here." He squeezed my shoulder again. "So you see, there ain't no way I can let some racist sumbitches chase me off'n this here hill." He gave me a world-weary smile, then drew in a long breath as if sucking in everything that surrounded him. "And that's the sorry truth of it, Samuel. 'Cause it's sure as were standin' here that if I run just one time, them boys'll be back a month from now, or a year from now, and they'll try to run me off again. It's their nature, son, and ain't you or me gonna change 'im."

I looked down at my boots, knowing he was right in everything he had said. "Hell, I can't even help myself against them," I said.

"You can't change ignorance, son. You should know that by now. You been tryin' to change these ignorant sumbitches most all yer life."

"So have you," I said.

Jehiel smiled at the defensive tone in my voice. He shook his head. "Never did try to change one of them fools. You see, boy, they hates me because of what I is, pure and simple. So the only way I could change 'em is if I got 'em to *like* what I is. Or to make believe I's somthin' different. And that ain't ever gonna happen." He stretched his arms out in a "here I am" gesture. "But *I* like what I am, son. And I don't wanna be nothin' else. And that's what they can't unnerstand. They think I oughtta wanna be like them, and it makes 'em feel big that I can't." He let out a deep, rumbling laugh. "And that's when I says to hell with 'em. And I lets 'em know that what they thinks ain't more'n a loada cow flop to me. And that drives 'em crazy. They don't unnerstand that a'tall." He reached out and took my arm. "Yer daddy's done the same thing all his life. He didn't do it all noisy like me, but he done it just the same."

I stared at him, allowing the moment to draw out. "And you're saying it's what I should do."

He shook his head. "Don't tell a man what to do, or what to be," he said. "That's between a man and himself. But I watched you grow up, Samuel. Hell, you was up here on Beulah Hill as much as you was in yer own house. And I seen you grow inta a good man." He let out another laugh. "Hell, I woulda throwed yer ass off'n this here hill if you wasn't. And no matter who says different, that's all anybody got a right to ask of you, Samuel. That you be a good man."

It was hard to argue with the kindness of the man's words, so I didn't try. I had no hope of making him understand. There was one more thing I had to tell him, but wasn't sure how. After a brief pause I just forced the words out.

"Things are going to be said when all this is over," I began. "Things you won't want to hear. I can't talk to you about them yet. I just want you to be ready for it."

Jehiel gave me a long look. "Samuel, I've been hearin' stuff I didn't wanna hear fer a long time, now. I figger I'll be man enough to hear one more thing."

Jeffords was on the front porch when I arrived at Elizabeth's cabin. He argued when I told him to get some rest in Elizabeth's barn but finally went on his way. I knew he would never sleep, never trust anyone else to look after her safety, but at least he'd be rested if we needed him later.

When he had gone I knocked on Elizabeth's door. She answered it, almost as though she had been standing inside waiting for me.

"Samuel," she said, reaching out and running one hand along my chest, "I'm glad you're here."

She looked as beautiful as I'd ever seen her, her hair hanging in loose ringlets along her coffee-colored cheeks, her liquid brown eyes drinking me in, bringing back all the yearning I'd always felt whenever I was with her. She stepped back to make room for me. She was wearing a homemade flowered shift cut low over the top of her breasts, and the lantern light inside the cabin gave her skin a soft golden glow.

"I have to talk to you. And your sisters," I said. I pushed away all the other reasons to be there, all the things a sane world would lay open for us. "It's important," I added. "I'm not sure how much more time we have."

Elizabeth led me to her dining table, then went and got Maybelle and Ruby from their room. Both women were still dressed when they joined us, and I wondered if they had fled to their room when they heard me at the door.

I sat facing the three women. They were clustered together, almost protectively, I thought. The tension emanating from them was palpable.

"I need you to tell me about Royal Firman and Abel Turner," I began. "I need to know what happened when they came up here on the day Royal was killed." I waited in the long silence that followed, then continued. "I need you to tell me what they did to you, and what happened afterward."

Tears began to stream down Maybelle's cheeks, and Elizabeth put an arm around her shoulders and drew the girl to her.

Ruby glared at me, her eyes hard as stones, even though her jaw had begun to tremble.

"They were violated, Samuel. Brutally, unforgivably violated." Elizabeth's voice was so soft I could barely hear the words. She looked up at me, her own eyes moist now with coming tears. "How did you know?" she asked.

"Abel Turner told me," I said.

"Was he braggin' on it?" Ruby snapped, her jaw and lips quivering with a mixture of rage and shame.

"I questioned him," I said. "Then I beat on him until he told it."

"I hope you kilt him," Maybelle said. She began to sob, and Elizabeth drew her head against her shoulder.

"He's alive," I said. "But I have to know if he told me all of it. And I can only get that from each of you."

Elizabeth was stroking her sister's head, her eyes deep with sorrow now. "I came after it was over," she said. "I can't tell you what they did."

There was a long silence, broken only by Maybelle's sobs. Then Ruby jutted her chin forward, her narrow face twisted with anger. "I kin tell you," she said. "I kin tell you all of it."

Ruby took several long breaths, composing herself. Then she began.

"Maybelle an' me was in the barn doin' some chores. We never hear'd them come up. They musta parked down the road an' slipped in through the woods. Jeffords was outside, puttin' some new boards on the outside cow pen. They musta come up behind him and hit him, 'cause later, when I looked outside, he was layin' there like somebody pole-axed him."

She paused again, to get more oxygen in her lungs. "They was in the barn a'fore we knowed it, an' they starts sayin' how they gonna give us some fun." She used the back of her hand to wipe a tear from her cheek. "I thought they was foolin'. They was liquored up some, and that Royal, he was always talkin' dirty like." She lowered her eyes. "But they wasn't foolin'. They said they was each gonna have us, an' there wasn't nothin' we could do 'bout it. An' they was right. There wasn't nothin' we could do. They was too big, an' they both had buck knives, an' they said they'd use 'em iff'n we din' do what they said."

She began to draw deep, ragged breaths, and I waited in silence until she composed herself. She lowered her eyes when she began again, unable to look at anyone now. She seemed frail, and far less fierce than I had always known her to be.

"That Abel," she said, drawing another breath. "He says how he wants ta put his thang in Maybelle's mouth, an' then he puts the tip of his knife up agin' her throat, an' tells her he's gonna cut her, she don' do what he wants. An' then he presses that knife agin' her, until he draws him some blood."

I remembered the small bandage that had been on Maybelle's throat when I had first questioned her, and her claim that she had cut herself while moving a bale of wire. She was still sobbing, as she listened to her sister tell the truth about that wound.

"What happened after they . . . hurt you?" I asked.

Ruby's eyes snapped up, hard again. "Oh, they was fulla they-selves then. They was sayin' how they was gonna wait on 'Lizabeth, an' have her, too. They said they was gonna do it ta alla Jehiel Flood's nigger bitches. Tha's what they said. Jus' like we was all nothin' but no-account whores."

She looked away, leaving her face in profile, and I could see the soft, clean lines of her face. She seemed beautiful that way, and I could see the similarities of her sisterhood with Elizabeth. It was something I had never noticed before.

"Then they started arguin'," Ruby said, her face still turned away. "Royal tol' Abel he could have me, but that 'Lizabeth was jus' gonna be fer him. He says that way each of 'em had theyselfs two of the sisters, an' that was good 'nuff. He says how he been wantin' 'Liza-beth fer a long time now, an' how he weren't 'bout to share her with nobody else." She closed her eyes, still keeping her face averted.

"Then they went outside, an' I could still hear 'em arguin'. Abel doan like it, him sayin' he got a right to have any sister he wants. But Royal tells him it ain't gonna be that way, an' how he should get outta there he doan like doin' like he's tol'." She turned back to me, all the fire gone from her eyes. "Then it gets quiet-like fer a li'l bit, then Royal walks back inside an' tells Maybelle an' me not ta come out, or we gonna get cut up bad. Then he goes back out, an' I hear him talkin' agin' an' laughin', like who he's talkin' to is a no-account."

Ruby swallowed hard and forced herself to continue. "Then there was this scream. Oh God, it was awful. An' I hear'd Royal beggin' an' beggin', but I couldn't unnerstan' what he was sayin'.

"We was afraid to come out, an' we jus' lay there in the barn cryin'. An' then what seemed a long time later, 'Lizabeth come to the door, an' we went out an' saw Royal layin' there dead."

I turned to Elizabeth. "You found him that way?"

"I . . ."

"Do you think it was Jeffords who killed him?"

Elizabeth shook her head vehemently. "Jeffords was still uncon-scious when I got there."

"Did you see anyone wearing a black hooded coat? A long coat?"

Elizabeth hesitated. "I . . . I . . ."

A knock on the door stopped her, and I got up and went to answer it. Frenchy stood outside.

"Got everythin' set. Just checkin' to see if you was here," he said.

I drew a long breath. "I think you better come inside."

The women told their story again. Frenchy listened, asking even fewer questions than I had. When they had finished he turned to me.

"These ladies just up and tell you this?" he asked. "Just this very night?"

"Abel Turner told me first," I said. Frenchy gave me a stern look and I hurried on. "It was just earlier tonight. He also said he'd deny it in court, so I wanted to confirm it with these ladies before I told you. I figured we couldn't arrest him until we had that." Then I related everything Abel Turner had told me.

He looked into his lap and nodded, then raised his eyes to me again. "Do I wanna know what happened that made Abel Turner fess up like he did?"

I studied the tabletop. "No, sir. I don't think you want to know that."

A small smile played at the corners of Frenchy's mouth and then disappeared. He turned back to the women. "Why didn't you tell anybody? Not even yer daddy?"

"We were afraid he'd kill Abel Turner," Elizabeth said. "And that he'd go to prison. Maybe even the electric chair."

"Prob'ly right," he said. "Leastways it woulda happened if I was yer daddy." He looked at each of them in turn, his eyes soft now, as gentle as I'd ever seen them. "I'm sorry fer what happened. I know it don't do no good, but I want you to know it." He took a deep breath. "Now I gotta ask you one more question. It's about this hooded man Abel says he saw. You sure you didn't see nobody like that?"

"The only person I saw was 'Lizabeth, and she was wearin' her school clothes," Ruby said. Maybelle nodded in agreement.

Frenchy gave a small shrug. "Could be that boy was lyin'," he said. "Tryin' to create a straw dog fer us to chase." He turned to Elizabeth.

A shout came from outside and Frenchy and I jumped from our chairs and started for the door. Frenchy's agility surprised me. He moved with a quickness that defied both his age and his bulk and reached the door two full steps ahead of me, his hand already on the butt of his pistol.

Johnny Taft stood at the bottom of the stairs, breathing hard. "They's comin'," he said. "Up through the saddle where we thought they might. I was jus' makin' one las' check a'fore I laid up in Jehiel's barn with yer deputy, an' I spotted 'em climbin' up t'other side."

"How many?" Frenchy asked.

"I seen at least four," Johnny said. "Preserved and three others trailin' behind. I couldn't wait ta make t'others out, lest they see me."

"Were they armed?" I asked.

"Preserved was fer sure. Had him a rifle. Couldn't tell 'bout t'others."

"Ain't likely they came up through the woods with empty hands," Frenchy said. "Which way was they headed?"

"Last look I got at 'em was jus' when they come up through the saddle. Looked like they was headed straight fer Jehiel's house. They put on a lively step, they oughtta get there any minute. I woke yer deputy in the barn. Jehiel an' his son, too. Then I came over cheer fer you."

Frenchy shook his head. "Don't make sense, only four of 'em. All right, you get on back. Go along the road. It'll be faster, and you kin lay up in the trees outside his dooryard. Samuel and me, we'll cut through the woods, see if we can come up behind and get 'em between us. I'll get my other deputy on the radio and have him come on up the road." He turned to me. "You tell that boy Jeffords to stay here with the women, just in case. They's seven of us to their four. Eight if the reverend kin handle a gun."

Johnny was already headed for the road, and when I turned to the barn I saw Jeffords coming toward us. I told him to stay with the women and to shoot if anybody tried to move on the house. Frenchy was climbing out of his car when I finished.

"Damn," he said. "My deputy down at the bridge ain't answerin'. Don't make any sense, lessen' somebody got to him down there. We better get movin', but watch yer back just in case. They got more men comin' up from the road, they could catch us cold."

Frenchy went to the trunk of his car and took out his shotgun, and I suddenly wished my own car were there, so I could get to the .30-30 hidden under the front seat. Instead, I unholstered my revolver and made certain all six chambers were loaded.

When I turned back to the cabin I saw Elizabeth standing on the porch, her eyes wide, her hands gripping the porch railing as if it were a lifeline. Ruby and Maybelle were just inside the door behind her.

"Get inside," I called. "And stay away from the windows."

Ruby and Maybelle quickly stepped back, but Elizabeth remained where she was, still gripping the porch rail as she watched Frenchy and me head into the woods.

We moved as quickly as we could, trying to keep down any undue noise. There was a strong breeze whipping through the treetops that covered some of our movement. But it also covered the sound of those moving against us.

I tried to draw steady, even breaths. This was new to me, this stalking of armed men, and I could feel the sweat building in my palms, making my revolver slippery in my hand. Frenchy turned and motioned for me to stop, and stepped in close. He seemed to sense my unease.

"Just stay right on my tail, about ten yards back," he whispered. "Do what I do, and stop if I raise my hand. Move like you was huntin' deer. But just remember these here deer shoot back, so alla time keep yer eye out fer cover."

I could feel sweat building beneath my hat and small, cold beads forming on my forehead. I looked to see if Frenchy was sweating, too, but saw no indication of it. I nodded to let him know I would do as he said, unsure how steady my voice would be if I tried to speak.

We walked in tandem for about two hundred yards, taking care to avoid any sticks that might snap under our weight, stopping every ten yards or so to listen for other movement. We passed behind Elisha's house, keeping well back in the trees and out of sight. The house was dark and still, with no sign of movement inside or out.

Frenchy signaled to slow down as we moved forward again, and we covered the next fifty yards even more cautiously. When we next stopped to listen, I could hear an engine moving up the road. It seemed to grow louder each second until I was certain it was just outside Jehiel's dooryard.

A shout came from the area where I knew Jehiel's house to be, but I could not make out the words. Then there was a second shout, followed by the loud crack of a rifle. Two more shots came in rapid succession, but I couldn't tell if they were being fired toward the house or away from it.

"Shit," Frenchy snapped. Then he started off again at a trot, his body crouched low to the ground, reducing its target area.

I went after him, slipped to one knee, then righted myself and increased my pace to catch up. He was moving quickly, weaving through the trees, the caution he had taken before abandoned now.

Four more shots snapped out ahead of us. They came from our right, toward the road. Two that seemed to come from Jehiel's dooryard quickly answered them. Then a loud booming shot came from our left, followed by a scream of pain.

Frenchy skidded to a halt and pointed to the sound of that last shot. "That'd be Preserved's .45. He got the house inna crossfire. We gotta head up there and draw his fire away."

We cut to our left as Preserved's .45 opened up again with four rapid-fire shots.

"That was five shots," I called out. "He'll have to reload that Sharps rifle now."

It was unnecessary information. Frenchy had also counted the shots and was now moving as fast as he could through the trees.

Forty yards ahead, I could see the small clearing behind Jehiel's house. The woods made an "L" there, and I could see faint movement at the corner where the two legs joined.

Frenchy slid behind a large boulder about twenty yards from the edge of the woods and waved for me to hit the dirt. I dove forward and began to crawl toward another large rock, slightly to his left.

Frenchy leveled his shotgun toward the movement at the "L," using the boulder to brace any shot he might have to make. Then he called out.

"Drop the weapons, boys! This is Deputy LeMay, and I'm only tellin' you once. Drop 'em an' stay alive."

There was only silence as I crawled up behind the rock ten yards to Frenchy's left. He glanced over at me and hissed out a warning. "There's three of 'em I kin see. One right in the corner, and two more about ten yards apart to the first one's left. You gotta watch close. Make sure nobody drops back to sneak around and come up behind us."

He turned back to the three men. Two more shots came from the road to our right, answered by two from the house. Then there was a third shot from farther down the road. I hoped it was Johnny Taft, now drawing a bead on the men to our right. Two more shots came from the same position in rapid succession, and they were followed immediately by a long, sustained wail.

"Sounds like Johnny got hisself one of Preserved's boys," Frenchy called out, offering the information as much to Preserved as to me.

Preserved's voice came back almost immediately.

"We ain't got no fight with ya, Deputy. Jus' move on out an' leave these niggers ta us."

"I already told you. Drop the weapons and step out into the open. This is yer last chance to walk away from this."

Preserved's rifle erupted, the flame jumping three feet from the muzzle, the bullet ricocheting off the boulder that shielded Frenchy. The others opened fire as well, but in the direction of the house to keep down any return fire from that direction.

To my right I could see Prince and Jehiel crouched behind the

wall. Suddenly, Prince rose up and fired three rapid shots back toward the trees. Two shots came back at him and seemed to throw
him back like a kick from a mule. Jehiel jumped up and ran toward
him, and more fire came from both directions. Jehiel's legs crumpled beneath him, and he disappeared from sight.

Another shot from Preserved's .45 slammed into Frenchy's boulder.

Frenchy came up behind his shotgun and fired toward the muzzle flash, and I heard Preserved instantly scream out in agony.
Frenchy didn't wait, he swung the shotgun toward the second set of
muzzle flashes that had been directed toward the house and fired
again. There was another scream.

"Cover me while I reload this thing," Frenchy snapped.

I leveled my pistol toward the "L," ready to return any fire, but
none came. My arm was shaking so badly I brought my other hand
up to steady my aim.

"Okay, we's done here. We's done here," a voice called out. It was
one of the men farther down the tree line from Preserved's position.

"Fuck we is." The words were growled through clenched teeth.

Before Frenchy or I could respond, Preserved staggered out of
the woods. His left pants leg was a bloody rag dragging behind him,
and he reeled wildly from side to side as he stumbled toward our
position. His rifle was still cradled in his hands, and I pointed my
pistol at his chest as he came to a halt ten yards away.

"Drop it now, Preserved!" I shouted. "Right now."

Preserved's eyes snapped to my position as my voice registered in
his hate-ravaged mind.

"Goddamn bleached nigger sumbitch of a whore," he growled.

His rifle swung up, searching me out as a target. I felt my hand
begin to shake as my finger tightened on the trigger, and it caused
the barrel to wave before my eyes. I stared into the muzzle of Preserved's rifle and felt death rushing toward me like a runaway wagon.

Then Preserved's chest seemed to explode, as Frenchy's shotgun
erupted to my right. Preserved flew back like a broken doll and
slammed into the ground, his rifle spinning away behind him into
the night.

Frenchy began shouting to the others, but the words never registered in my mind. The next thing I saw was Big Jim coming out of the woods. He was dragging Andy with one arm, his other arm held high in the air. Neither man carried a weapon.

The shout from Johnny Taft brought me back, lifting the cloud from my battered brain.

"They all done down here. Two with they hands up, an' one hit bad."

I looked toward Frenchy. He had his shotgun leveled at Big Jim and Andy as he walked toward them.

Then I heard it; a sound I know will live with me all my days. It came from behind Jehiel's newly built wall, a long, low, agonizing wail of unspeakable pain. I turned and ran toward the wall as fast as I could and climbed quickly over it.

Prince lay on the ground, what had been his face now only a twisted pulp of flesh and bone. Blood pooled under his head, cradled now in his father's bearlike hands. The stomach area of Jehiel's shirt was soaked in blood as well, and at first I thought it had come from Prince's massive head wound. Then I saw Jehiel's legs, twisted on the ground beneath him, hanging from his hips like huge, lifeless logs. His face turned up to me, his eyes large as saucers, pleading for me to tell him that the body he caressed so tenderly was not gone forever.

I knelt beside Jehiel and eased Prince's head from his hands, then put my arms around his massive shoulders and pulled him against my chest. His shoulders heaved, his body so large it was like holding onto some ancient tree shuddering in the wind.

"Oh God, Samuel. Oh God, please. Please don't let my boy be dead. Oh, please, God, please, please, please . . ."

Frenchy was beside us as the words trailed off. He closed his eyes and drew a long breath, then reached out and touched Jehiel's legs. He lifted one gently, trying to straighten it, but it flopped back uselessly to the ground like a dead piece of meat.

"We gotta get him inta Doc Hawley," he said. "Then to the hospital in Burlington quick as we can. I think that bullet went alla way through his belly and got his spine." He reached down and touched Jehiel's cheek. "He's passed out. Thank God fer that. Leastways he don't hafta look at his dead boy no more."

I turned to a sound behind me and found Elisha Bowles kneeling next to Prince. His hands were clasped in front of him in prayer. His lips moved without sound, and tears ran down his cheeks.

"Elisha, get your old touring car," I said. "We gotta get Jehiel in to Doc Hawley. The backseat of that car is the only thing that'll hold him."

Johnny Taft came up with his two prisoners, explaining that the third was lying back by the road, hit too bad to move. Frenchy's deputy came in from the other direction with Big Jim and Andy in tow. The deputy was limping from a leg wound he had wrapped with a red neckerchief.

I turned back to Johnny. His two prisoners were transient loggers, who moved from town to town. I had seen them a week earlier working at the river loading dock. They didn't even live in the town. Like Big Jim and Andy, they had probably never seen Jehiel or Prince more than once or twice in their miserable lives. I stared at Prince, the lifeless ruin of a young boy I had known since childhood. I closed my eyes and wondered how I would tell Elizabeth and her sisters.

When I looked back up, Johnny was staring at Prince and shaking his head. "Don't make no sense, do it?" he said. "Killin' that boy they din' even know. An' cripplin' his daddy. An' all jus' 'cause they was colored."

"The one who's wounded, the one back by the road, is it Abel Turner?" I asked.

Johnny shook his head. "'Nother logger, I figger. Seen him aroun', but don't even know his name." He shook his head again. "Damn, I jus' thought it out. I done ta him same thing they all did ta Jehiel an' his boy. Hell of a thing, ever'body shootin' men they don't even know."

I turned to Frenchy. He raised his eyebrows. "Don't seem to make sense that Abel weren't with 'em," he said.

The shot echoed through the trees, almost as if punctuating Frenchy's words.

My head snapped back toward the sound. "Elizabeth's cabin!" I shouted, and I was up and running as the second and third shots reverberated in the night.

Frenchy was far behind me as I raced down the road. He was fast over a short distance, but it was a long pull to Elizabeth's cabin, and he quickly fell far behind. I could hear his shouted warnings to be careful, but none of it took hold in my mind. The pistol was in my hand, but I don't remember taking it from my holster, and the sweat that had formed on my body again had now dried to an icy cold.

I reached the narrow lane that led to Elizabeth's cabin and cut through the towering pines that rose on either side. Ahead I could see the back of Frenchy's car still parked in the dooryard. Then the sound—like something heavy slamming against wood.

Rounding the final bend I saw Abel Turner on the porch, as his big-shouldered body drove against the door, making it shudder in its frame.

Jeffords Page lay on the porch floor, one arm hanging over the edge. A steady stream of blood dripped from his fingertips. If I'd had my rifle I could have shot Abel where he stood, before he'd even known I was there, and I knew in my heart I would have done it. But a pistol was another matter, and I wasn't sure I could hit him and kill him with one shot. Abel reared back, ready to strike the door again, his rifle held in both hands at port arms. I shouted his name and saw him turn, the rifle coming around.

I ran forward and dove for the rear of Frenchy's car, as I heard the sharp snap of his saddlegun and saw the bright flash of the muzzle from the corner of my eye. To this day I believe I felt the bullet pass beneath me, and saw it send up a puff of dirt to my right.

I hit the ground hard, just short of the car, then clawed and scrambled in the dirt until I was behind the rear fender. I pulled myself up, then raised my eyes over the top so I could see where he was. A second shot ricocheted off the car, driving my head back.

"Give it up, Abel!" I shouted. "It's finished. The others are coming, and they'll kill you sure if you don't drop that rifle and get your hands up."

I chanced another look and saw Abel standing there. He looked confused and uncertain, and his rifle had dropped to waist level.

"How bad is Jeffords hurt?" I called. "Put your rifle down and let us get him to a doctor."

The question seemed to bring Abel back, and he lowered the rifle another notch and glanced down at Jeffords's unmoving body, as if to assure himself of what he already knew. Then he turned his attention back to me.

"He's dead," he said. "Now I gotta kill me them nig bitches, a'fore they tells ever'body what happened with Royal an' me." He glared at me across the dooryard, his eyes fierce behind his full beard, filled with the same irrational madness I had just heard in his words. "I'll kill you, too, if you try an' stop me. I will, Samuel. I will." He was staring straight at me, his left hand sliding up and down the rifle stock in a nervous gesture.

I cocked my pistol and stood, ready to throw myself back behind the car if the rifle barrel swung my way.

"I can't let you do that, Abel. There's been enough killing. Preserved is dead, and Jehiel is bad wounded. It can't go on any more." I stared at his face, waiting for his eyes to shift, knowing his rifle barrel might follow when they did. I held my pistol along my leg as I watched him, and I could see the bruises and scabbed-over cuts I had inflicted on him earlier that day.

I saw movement to my left, back at the head of the drive, and I knew it was Frenchy. He seemed to hold back, and I guessed he didn't want to spook Abel into shooting while I was standing in the open.

"It's too late, Abel," I said, hoping to stop him with my words. "The women already told Deputy LeMay what happened." I saw Abel's eyes widen, and I hurried on. "Give it up and take your chances in court. You'll have a chance with Lawyer Caswell, you know that it's true."

Abel shook his head. It was a snapping gesture, as though trying to drive away some demon. The cabin door behind him looked badly weakened, and I was afraid he'd turn and throw his bulk against it again. If he did, he might get inside and kill Elizabeth and her sisters before I could reach him.

I stepped out from behind the car. "Let me come and take that rifle, Abel." I tried to keep my voice soft and easy. I was ready to bring my pistol up and fire, if it came to that, but I didn't want Abel to know it. "Then it'll all be over," I said. "All of it."

He didn't respond, but the rifle seemed to drop a few inches lower. I started walking forward as slowly as I could. I was only fifteen or so yards away when his eyes snapped up to me.

"Noooo!" he screamed, the rifle moving up with the sound.

I brought my pistol up, but it was too late. Abel fired from the hip, and the bullet slammed into my left shoulder, spinning me and knocking me back. I hit the ground hard, the bullet, or the fall, or both, driving the breath from me.

Abel was coming down the porch stairs, working the lever of his rifle, jacking another round into the chamber. To my left I could hear Frenchy running down the drive, but I knew he'd be too late. I had moved closer to the house, cutting down his line of fire.

The pistol was still in my right hand. I was flat on my back, but I raised my head and watched him come. He stepped off the porch and raised the rifle to his shoulder, and I brought the pistol up and fired.

The shot caught him square in the chest. It was a miraculous shot, given my position on the ground and my injury, and I doubt I could ever do it again. Abel staggered back but did not fall. He stood there, his face filled with disbelief. He looked at me, at the pistol in my hand, then down at his chest. A second shot, this one from Frenchy's shotgun, ripped into the side of his head, and Abel's face suddenly disappeared in a spray of bright red mist. His body flew back, and as he hit the ground his heels began to hammer the earth, sending up a thick cloud of dirt.

Frenchy was at my side seconds later, and he pulled open my coat and shirt to expose the wound.

"Ain't bad," he said. "Looks like it mighta chewed up the shoulder socket a bit, but it ain't gonna kill ya."

The front door flew open and Elizabeth raced down the porch stairs. She dropped to the ground next to me and immediately cradled my face in her hands.

"He'll be all right," Frenchy said. "Don't you fret none."

"Oh, Samuel, Samuel, Samuel."

I raised my head and touched her cheek with my right hand. Her skin was soft as silk, and a tear left her eye and ran against my fingers.

"Your daddy's hurt," I managed to say. "They're taking him to Doc Hawley's. You've gotta go to him. He's gonna need you bad."

Frenchy took her arm and helped her rise. "Can you drive?" he asked. When Elizabeth said she could, he handed her the keys to his car. "Take yer sisters with you," he said. "I'll follow with Samuel in the other deputy's car."

Elizabeth stared at him, and I'm sure to this day that she sensed something more.

Elizabeth ran back to the house for her sisters, stopping briefly at Jeffords Page's lifeless body. Johnny Taft came down the drive in his truck. The prisoners, including the two wounded, were chained in the back, along with the wounded deputy.

Frenchy helped me up and into the truck's passenger's seat. "We gotta get Samuel down to Doc Hawley's," he said. "I'll climb in the back with the prisoners." He glanced at the five men. "They move an inch, Doc's gonna have hisself more business." He turned back to Johnny. "Who's stayin' with the bodies?"

"Yer other deputy came on up. Seems that second lot pole-axed him with a rifle butt, so's they could get on up and set up a crossfire. But he's okay now. Jus' a sore noggin."

Elizabeth and her sisters came out of the house and hurried to Frenchy's car. Elizabeth and Ruby kept their eyes averted from Abel's body, giving wide berth to where it lay on the blood-soaked ground. But I thought I saw Maybelle's eyes flick down, just for a second. It seemed to me those eyes were filled with hate.

{ 21 }

They waited five days to bury Prince and Jeffords. Jehiel insisted on it. The doctors in Burlington would not let him travel to the funeral by ambulance any sooner.

I visited him in the hospital two days before. He was paralyzed from the waist down and would never walk again without the aid of braces and crutches, and then only after a long spell of therapy.

Frenchy came with me when I went to him. He wanted to tell Jehiel what had happened to his daughters and to Royal Firman, and spare the women the shame of telling it themselves.

Jehiel lay in his bed, still a mountain of a man. But the loss of his son weighed heavily on him, and his eyes had lost all their resolve and strength. My arm was in a cast that held it out from my body. The bullet that struck my shoulder had exited my side, then smashed my upper arm. The doctors weren't certain I'd ever have full use of it again. So I stood beside the bed like some awkward statue half wrapped in plaster.

Frenchy sat on the edge of the bed and took Jehiel's large hand in his own. His voice and manner were as gentle as I'd ever seen in any man. He told Jehiel the case was solved; that it was Abel Turner killed Royal Firman. He told him how they had gone to the whore, Jenny, earlier that day, and how Abel was turned down for what he wanted. He didn't explain what that was, not wanting to hurt the man more than necessary.

He told how the two men then got themselves liquored up and went on up to Elizabeth's cabin. He explained how they knocked poor Jeffords Page unconsious, then attacked Maybelle and Ruby, who were the only ones at home. Again, he avoided any detailed explanation, saying only that the pair then decided to wait for Elizabeth, so they could do harm to her as well.

"But a fight developed over who would have her," Frenchy explained. "It became pretty fierce. So bad that Ruby and Maybelle heard it from inside the barn.

"There was a pitchfork leanin' up against the barn wall," Frenchy said. "And Abel musta worked himself into a rage and picked it up, and murdered that Firman boy there on the spot. Then he run off. 'Lizabeth seen him way off in the woods when she come home from school a short spell after."

Jehiel turned to face Frenchy for the first time. "How'd the body end up in them woods?" he asked.

"'Lizabeth got Jeffords to do it. She and her sisters was afeared you'd up and kill Abel Turner if you found out what him and Royal did to yer children. So they got that boy, Jeffords, to carry the body inta the woods. He was supposed to bury it, never to be found, but instead he musta got all religious-like. He sat up with it all night and prayed and lit candles and done all that stuff we found with the body. We figger Abel came back to see what had happened early next mornin'—just couldn't help hisself, but to do it—and he scared Jeffords off before any buryin' got done. Then, when he saw what Jeffords had done with the body, he decided to go fer Samuel, so it'd be blamed on you folks."

Jehiel turned his head and stared out the window next to his bed. "And that's why my boy is dead?" he said at length. "'Cause some white trash raped my little gals, then got themselves in a fight over who was gonna rape the last one?"

There was nothing Frenchy could say; no words either of us could offer to salve the man's pain. We excused ourselves and left Jehiel Flood with the misery he would carry in his heart for the rest of his days.

We walked down the hall a way, then Frenchy suddenly stopped near a small waiting room and began shaking his head. "Damn," he said. "We failed that man, Samuel. We failed him bad."

"Yes, we did," I replied.

Frenchy folded his arms across his chest and ground his teeth. "Well, it's over, dammit. I don't know if the folks in yer town are gonna accept it, but far as I'm concerned that murder is solved."

I waited, wondering if I should ask the question. I decided I had no choice. "Are you satisfied with that answer?" I finally asked.

"That Abel Turner done it?"

"Yes, that Abel killed Royal."

"You're thinkin' about that phantom in the hooded coat, are you?"

"Yes, the one Jeffords kept calling the 'dark man.'"

"Thought Jehiel explained that the boy believed in the bogeyman."

"Yes, he did."

"Well, that explains that, then."

He took my arm and started back down the hall, then decided there was still more to say and stopped again. "Samuel, there ain't no question in my mind that them two boys, Abel Turner and Royal Firman, needed killin' fer what they done to them gals. Far as I'm concerned they both got what they had comin'. And between you and me, I wouldn't much care who killed either one of them sumbitches, and I sure as hell wouldn't go outta my way ta prove it was somebody else. 'Specially if I thought it was gonna cause that there family one more day of sufferin'."

I stood there stunned by Frenchy's admission.

He let out a short, barking laugh. "You think that makes me a bad lawman, Samuel?"

"Guess I don't know what makes a *good* lawman," I said truthfully. "I guess I'm carrying too much guilt myself in all of this. But I think it makes you a good man, and I think my father would approve."

He took my arm again and started us back down the hall. "Well, it's what I'm gonna say at the inquest tomorrow, and I'll be expectin' Constable Samuel Bradley ta back me on it. Let's you and me just call it Frenchy's law, and be done with it, once and fer good."

They buried Prince and Jeffords together. The funeral was simple and solemn, and a few dozen townsfolk attended. Levi Kneeb was there, as was Cletus Martin. Even some of the men who had gathered that night at the Mountain Tavern found their way to Elisha's Free Will Baptist Church. Victorious Shepard and her husband stayed away, as did many other citizens of Jerusalem's Landing.

Jake Phelps, the newspaper reporter who had covered our town meeting several days ago, came to cover the funeral. It had become a big story now, how townspeople from Jerusalem's Landing had attacked an isolated Negro farm on Nigger Hill. Frenchy made it clear that Phelps was not to intrude on the funeral in any way and threatened him with arrest if he trespassed on the comfort of the mourning family.

The reporter seemed surprised by Frenchy's aggressiveness. "Could you at least tell me where this Nigger Hill is?" he asked. "Just so I can find the cemetery."

Frenchy took a step forward and took the man by the arm. "Ain't no place in this town called that," he said. "The cemetery you be lookin' for is up on Beulah Hill. And you best remember that when you write yer story."

My father and I sat in the row behind Elizabeth and her sisters. Jehiel's stretcher had been placed in the aisle, but the only sound we heard from him was an occasional gasp as his chest rose and fell with his suffering.

Elizabeth cried with deep, racking sobs, as did her sisters, but she kept her head erect, her chin lifted in a display of dignity that I would always carry in my mind, and I wanted to reach out and hold her, comfort her, but somehow I knew that I should not.

Elisha cried as well, tears coursing down his cheeks, as he read the Twenty-third Psalm, and again when the choirmistress sang the ever-mournful "Amazing Grace."

Prince and Jeffords were buried in the small Negro cemetery that sat in a clearing on the hill where they had lived and died. The cemetery had existed for generations, ever since the first Negro who had found his way to Jerusalem's Landing passed on to that better life preachers are always telling us about.

The cemetery was well back from the road, surrounded by a circling copse of hemlock and reached by a narrow path, so it was not visible to anyone passing by. Jehiel had once told me his predecessors had laid it out that way to protect their graves against the threat of vandalism. And he had erected a defiant sign there as well. It hung as an arch over the cemetery entrance, and said simply: "Beulahland."

When the burial was complete I walked from the cemetery with Elizabeth at my side, her hand holding tightly to my good arm. My father walked ahead of us next to Jehiel's stretcher, supported by Frenchy's arm. Ruby and Maybelle walked on the other side, both women taking turns at holding their father's hand.

The path passed by an old cellar hole from one of the first houses built on the hill, and I found myself wondering who had lived there, and whether they had known my great-grandmother, perhaps even been a friend. Elizabeth's voice brought me back from my reverie.

"In a few weeks we'll be taking my father down to Boston," Elizabeth said. "There's a hospital there that specializes in spinal injuries, and we'll all be staying with him while he gets the therapy he needs. I've been offered a job there, teaching at a Negro school."

The news shocked me. Not that they would be going with their father, but that they would all remain there with him. The further news that Elizabeth had accepted a teaching post made it clear she would be gone a long time, perhaps never to return.

"I want you to do a great favor for me, Samuel," she said. "I want you to care for our homes. I don't want them lost to taxes if we're unable to keep up two households."

"How would you want me to do that?" I asked, still stunned by her news.

"I'd like you to live there. Your father, too, of course. You could live in my cabin. It's quite big enough for the two of you, and you could work the land and the sugarbush, or hire someone to do it. You could keep any profit after the taxes were paid, of course.

"I spoke to the town clerk, and she said I could give you a power of attorney so you could do whatever else was necessary." She drew a long, sad breath and looked out into the woods we were passing. "My father is afraid the land will be lost to us, and he's struggled so to keep it all these years. If it had to be sold to some timber company, I think it would kill him. Especially now that Prince is buried here." She looked up at me, her sad eyes asking me to understand. "I need you to protect the land now, Samuel," she said. "Just as you've always protected me."

We met at the town clerk's office six weeks later. Elizabeth had just returned from Boston. She had been gone most of that time to work at her new job. She had been living at a boarding house in the colored area of the city, and now that her father was well enough to travel, she had made more permanent living arrangements for herself and her sisters and had returned to take all of them away.

Elisha drove her down to the clerk's office and waited in the car while we filed the necessary papers. He, too, was leaving, to pastor a church in far-off Bennington, Vermont. The memories, he said, were too painful for him to remain in Jerusalem's Landing.

The newspaper reporter, Jake Phelps, was at the clerk's office when we arrived. There had been another racial incident in the eastern part of the state, less serious, but still newsworthy. He explained that he had learned that all the Negroes were leaving

Jerusalem's Landing, and that he was gathering information so he could blend the two stories together. When he asked Elizabeth if she would submit to an interview, she told him she would not, and he left the office dejectedly.

When our business was complete, I took Elizabeth out to Elisha's old touring car. I seated her in the rear, telling her it befitted her to ride with the dignity of a great lady.

It was snowing lightly. Deer season was now upon us, and behind Elisha's car a group of hunters were gathered around a flatbed truck, waiting to report the large buck that lay in the back. They stared at us with unfriendly eyes, but I denied them the satisfaction of any response.

"How is your arm, Samuel?" Elizabeth asked from the backseat. She was wearing a wide-brimmed hat that shielded part of her face, but what was still visible to me was so beautiful it near broke my heart.

I touched the sling that still held my arm, the cast gone now for several weeks. "It's better," I said. "It's weak, and I still don't have much feeling in it, but it's better than it was."

"And how are your other wounds?" she asked.

"Which are those?"

She smiled sadly. "The one's you've carried all your life."

I returned her smile. "You sound like your father, now," I said.

She looked down into her lap. "I suppose I do." She paused a long moment, then looked up at me again. "Have you ever heard of the Negro poet Paul Laurence Dunbar? He writes truly beautiful verse in which I've always found special meaning."

"I've heard of him," I said. "But I've not read him."

"There's one particular stanza that I've always kept at my desk at school to remind me of how I must never live. It's from 'Lyrics of Lowly Life.' It goes:

We wear the mask that grins and lies,
It hides our cheeks and shades our eyes,
This debt we pay to human guile,
And mouth with myriad subtleties.

The words cut at me, but I forced another smile, not wanting to mar this last moment together. "Is that how you see me?" I asked. "A man in need of that poetic advice?"

She reached out the car window and took my good hand. "It's good advice, Samuel," she said. "All our lives people have been telling us what we can never be. But that very thing they would deny us is only a fabrication in their minds, something that gives them a sense of superiority that has never existed. Don't you see that?"

"I think I'm just beginning to. Finally, after all these years."

"I hope so, my love. I truly hope so."

I looked down at her hand in mine. "Am I your love?" I asked.

"Yes, you are. Always and forever."

"Will you come back?"

"I don't know. I hope one day I will. It's why I want you to keep my house, and my father's house."

There was a tear in her eye and she brushed it away. Then she reached out and picked up a wrapped parcel that lay on the seat next to her and handed it to me through the window.

"What is it?" I asked, as I took the parcel.

"It's your coat," she said. "The long black coat with the hood. The one you lent me months ago, when you saw me walking home in the rain."

I looked down at her and nodded. "I'd forgotten," I said.

She smiled at me. "No, Samuel. I don't think you did."

The Final Writings of Samuel Bradley, Constable of Jerusalem's Landing

November 29, 1933

The children race through the woods, their lithe young bodies dodging the trees. A light snow covers the ground, and their footprints leave a trail marking their travels. They are laughing as they chase each other, the sound of their pleasure filling the day.

There is a clump of snow in the boy's collar, left there by the snowball the girl hurled at him.

"When I catch you you'll be sorry," he shouts, the words filled with not an ounce of threat.

The girl laughs and keeps running. "You'll never catch me," she shouts back. "Never, never, never."

It is dark and the snow is falling, and the woods that I love when they are deep and dark and lonely are even more beautiful now under this fresh, white blanket. I pull the long, black, hooded coat around me against the chill that quietly seeps into my body.

I am standing on the porch, looking out, as the branches of the tall pines grow heavy under the snow's weight. I can see my youth here. I can see Elizabeth's youth as well—running and laughing through the snow-covered woods, and I am content with these memories I treasure.

My father is inside, listening to Elizabeth's gramophone, and the faint sounds of Bessie Smith's mournful voice filter out into the cold night air. He has not been well. Prince's death and Jehiel's crippling have taken their toll on him, and I know that he will not be with me much longer. I try not to think of life without him. It seems quite unimaginable. But I will endure when he passes, just as we all endure realities we do not want to accept before their time.

He is happy here on this hill. The woods charm him, as they always have, and the knowledge that he is keeping this land for his old friend brings him joy.

Jehiel and his family have been gone nine months now. But soon my father will see his friend again. And I will see Elizabeth. Both will return within the week to testify at the murder trial of the men who attacked their home on that terrible night. Perhaps, with our urging, they will decide to remain.

Still, no matter what they choose, Beulah Hill is now my home. Being here, for me, is painful bliss. But that is not unfamiliar territory. So often I stood among these trees watching over Elizabeth that it seems most natural that I be here now, awaiting her return. It is where I belong. That much I have learned. So I will remain, even when my father is gone. And I will wait.

I smile at my own thoughts, in full realization of what they mean. There is no regret, only acceptance, for it is what I now intend—to live out my days as the last remaining Negro on Beulah Hill.

More Crime Fiction from **AKASHIC BOOKS**

ADIOS MUCHACHOS by Daniel Chavarría

Winner of a 2001 Edgar Award

245 pages, a trade paperback original; $13.95, ISBN: 1-888451-16-5

"Daniel Chavarría has long been recognized as one of Latin America's finest writers. Now he again proves why with *Adios Muchachos*, a comic mystery peopled by a delightfully mad band of miscreants, all of them led by a woman you will not soon forget—Alicia, the loveliest bicycle whore in all Havana." —Edgar Award-winning author William Heffernan

THE EYE OF CYBELE by Daniel Chavarría

413 pages, hardcover; $27.00, ISBN: 1-888451-25-4

Equal parts historical epic, whodunnit-style thriller, highbrow erotica and philosophical discourse. Set in fifth-century B.C.—during the reign of Pericles—the novel fictionally recreates the behind-the-scenes scandals and political intrigues that occupied the Athenian home front at the height of the Peloponessian War.

SPY'S FATE by Arnaldo Correa

More Cuban Noir from Akashic.

302 pages, hardcover; $24.95, ISBN: 1-888451-28-9

"A captivating thriller based on the murky U.S.-Cuban spy wars. Correa deftly paints the history of Castro's Cuban intelligence service and the changing face of the Miami exile community . . . The insightful sociopolitical picture, the nasty maneuverings of both services, and the credible spy plot make this a fascinating read." —*Publishers Weekly*

THE WEEPING BUDDHA by Heather Dune Macadam

360 pages, a trade paperback original; $16.95, ISBN: 1-888451-39-4

"Heather Dune Macadam should be included in that rare category of literary mystery masters such as Lawrence Block, Craig Holden, and Giles Blunt, whose lyrical prose and beautifully developed characters have a great deal to say about the troubled world we live in and its legacy of violence." —Kaylie Jones, author of *A Soldier's Daughter Never Cries*